GRAND CENTRAL
PUBLISHING

LARGE
PRINT

CHAOS

IRIS JOHANSEN

GRAND CENTRAL
PUBLISHING

LARGE PRINT

Copyright © 2020 by IJ Development

Cover design by Flag. Cover copyright © 2020 by Hachette Book Group, Inc.

Grand Central Publishing
Hachette Book Group
1290 Avenue of the Americas, New York, NY 10104
grandcentralpublishing.com
twitter.com/grandcentralpub

First Edition: September 2020

Grand Central Publishing is a division of Hachette Book Group, Inc. The Grand Central Publishing name and logo is a trademark of Hachette Book Group, Inc.

The publisher is not responsible for websites (or their content) that are not owned by the publisher.

The Hachette Speakers Bureau provides a wide range of authors for speaking events. To find out more, go to www.hachettespeakersbureau.com or call (866) 376-6591.

Library of Congress Cataloging-in-Publication Data
Names: Johansen, Iris, author.
Title: Chaos / Iris Johansen.
Description: First edition. | New York : Grand Central Publishing, 2020. |
Identifiers: LCCN 2020008881 | ISBN 9781538713136 (hardcover) | ISBN 978-1-5387-1899-5 (large print) | ISBN   9781538713167 (ebook)
Subjects: GSAFD: Suspense fiction.\
Classification: LCC PS3560.O275 C45 2020 | DDC 813/.6--dc23
LC record available at https://lccn.loc.gov/2020008881

ISBNs: 978-1-5387-1313-6 (hardcover), 978-1-5387-1316-7 (ebook), 978-1-5387-1899-5 (large print), 978-1-5387-1995-4 (Canadian)

Printed in the United States of America
LSC-C
10 9 8 7 6 5 4 3 2 1

CHAOS

CHAPTER

1

ST. ELDON'S ACADEMY
MOROCCO, AFRICA

S creams!
   Shots!

And Sasha had seen the two bloody bodies of the security guards outside in the paddock when she'd released the horses a few minutes ago.

Her heart was beating hard as she ran back into the stable and down the long aisle toward the back stall. She dived into the shadowy dimness and pressed back against the wood, trying to catch her breath.

The *screaming*. She closed her eyes as terror and bewilderment washed over her. They must be hurting those girls, or they wouldn't be screaming like that.

What else could she do to help? Sasha thought

frantically. She'd tried to call the police but there was no signal. She'd even tried to reach Alisa on her satellite phone, hoping that even if a tower was down the satellite might somehow be working. Nothing. The attack had come out of nowhere and the school seemed to be entirely cut off.

And there was no telling when those men who had killed the security guards would decide to come into the stable.

Sasha crouched lower in the back stall where Thor had been quartered before she'd released him. A weapon. She should find some kind of weapon...

"Sasha?" Paul Boujois, the school's head trainer, was ducking into the shadows of the stall beside her. His face was pale, and his voice was shaking. "I'd hoped you'd managed to get away yourself when you released the horses. It might be too late now."

"I had to make sure the horses were heading toward the hills away from the all the gunfire. I'm responsible for them. But I need a weapon, Mr. Boujois. Do you have a weapon?"

He shook his head. "And what are you going to do with a weapon? We're better off giving up as soon as they start pouring into this stable. They might let us live."

"They killed the security guards. And those girls

are still screaming outside." She swallowed. "They're all my friends and classmates. They might be killing them, too."

He flinched. "I know."

Then why wasn't he doing something, she thought in frustration. She'd been working for the past four years as a volunteer at the school's riding stable, and she respected Boujois's expertise with the horses. She even liked him most of the time. But it was clear she was not going get any help from him in this situation. He was even more afraid than she was, and his solution was for her to bury her head and hide?

"I need a weapon," she repeated, looking desperately around the stall. She saw a horseshoe in the far corner, grabbed it, and tore off her neck scarf. She twisted the horseshoe into the scarf, forming a makeshift sling. "Who are they? Do you know why they're doing this?"

He shook his head. "I saw three trucks with machine guns mounted on them. The men are all wearing military camouflage fatigues. I'd guess it's a raid on the school by some military guerrilla group who've heard there are fat pickings to be had here at St. Eldon's with all you rich girls as students."

"Ransom? Then maybe they're not killing them. Maybe there's some way we can save them."

More shots. Someone was yelling outside the stable.

"Sasha. Let it go. Don't fight them." Boujois's hands were shaking as he grabbed her shoulders. "You've done all you can. You've got to live through this."

"You said she ran in here?" Cursing. A man's strident voice as he strode into the stable and started down the aisle. "Find her, you asshole. If she got away, I'll cut your throat, Baldwin."

"I swear I caught a glimpse of her. She's here somewhere."

Run for the stable door. Take their attention away from this stall and give the trainer a chance. If Boujois was right about the ransom, she might be safe, but there was no way he would be.

She *ran*.

She heard a shout as she dived past the two men walking toward her down the aisle. A tall, fair-haired man reached wildly out to grab her arm, but she swung her scarf at his head and heard him grunt with pain as the horseshoe struck his temple.

Just a few more feet and she'd reach the stable door—

Pain.

She stumbled to her knees as the butt of the other man's gun crashed against her temple. Then his hand was tangled painfully in her hair as he jerked her head up so that he could look into her eyes. Through the dizziness, she was only aware of brown, close-cut hair, dark skin, and savage anger. "You're the one who released those horses?" he hissed. "Do you know how long it's going to take my men to round them up and put them in horse trailers?"

"Too long," she said hoarsely. "The police will be here by then and they'll be safe. You won't be able to hurt them."

"The police won't be here for more than an hour. I'll be long gone by then." He gave her a brutal backhand blow to her cheek. "I've taken down the cell tower."

"I've found someone else, Masenak." The fair-haired man she'd struck with the horseshoe was dragging Boujois out of the stall. "He's wearing those same fancy English boots you wear sometimes. It's probably that horse trainer you told me to look for. What do you want me to do with him?" Then he forgot about Boujois as he saw Sasha. "Can I have that bitch in my tent tonight?" His glare was venomous. "She needs to learn a few lessons from me before you give her to someone else."

"We'll talk about it later. She may be of use," Masenak said absently as he looked down at Sasha. "We wouldn't want to damage such a pretty little girl if she can help us get those horses back." He let go of her hair, and his hand touched the nameplate on Sasha's suede jacket. "I believe I've heard a few stories about you, Sasha Lawrence." He turned to Boujois. "Is she really as good at training horses as the rumors have it?"

"She's very good."

"Better than good? What I've heard is she's something of a horse whisperer. She can coax a horse to do almost anything for her?"

"I wouldn't say that good. She's only a student volunteer." Sasha could tell he was searching desperately for what to say that would be safest for her. "I've always found her...efficient."

"Let's see how efficient." He jerked Sasha to her feet. His face was suddenly only inches from her own, his eyes glittering. "I've no intention of hurting those horses. They all have excellent pedigrees. Which means they have enormous value for me. But there are dozens of young girls like you being put on those trucks out there who have very little value for me in comparison. So you will go with my friend Baldwin into the hills and you'll capture every one of those horses you freed and place them into the horse trailers I brought. You'll do it quickly and accurately because I will start killing those girls after the next thirty minutes. There were twelve horses. If you miss retrieving even one of those thoroughbreds, one of those sweet friends of yours will die because you weren't efficient enough. Do you understand?"

He meant it. His lips were pulled back in a feral grimace, and she could see that he was enjoying every nuance of the terror she was feeling. "I might not be able to get all the horses back right away. I deliberately spooked them."

"Then you'd best be better than Boujois was telling me. Because I don't take excuses." He looked at his watch. "Your thirty minutes starts now. Get her up in those hills, Baldwin." He pushed Sasha toward the door. "You'd better hope the police don't show up too soon or the carnage might have to start early. I'm looking forward to seeing you later, Sasha."

"Don't do this." She was running toward the door in panic. "I'll do whatever you say. Just don't kill them. Give me time to get those horses back."

"I'll think about it." Masenak chuckled. "But you should look on this as a challenge to prove your worth in case I decide not to be generous." He paused. "On second thought, I really think you should be punished for causing me this much trouble."

Kaboom.

She stopped. She whirled to see Paul Boujois falling to the floor, his head blown off. Sickness. Shock. Horror.

"I do hope he was a good friend," Masenak said

softly. "Punishment should always be as thorough as possible." He turned away. "Better hurry, Sasha. The clock is ticking."

———◆———

ZAWAR PALACE
MOROCCO

The dogs were barking!

Alisa Flynn froze on the top of the wall as the howls of the Doberman guard dogs broke the silence.

Shit!

This wasn't supposed to happen. She'd planned it all down to the last detail, even to keeping those dogs silent for the time she'd needed to break into the palace and reach Gabe Korgan's study. She'd been told that the dogs had to be given just the right amount of sedation so that they'd be quiet but not appear to be sluggish or drugged. She couldn't believe she'd screwed up that dosage.

The dogs had stopped barking. Their handlers had probably gone to check on them and found nothing suspicious. She might be okay.

Or she might not.

No sign of the sentries who usually patrolled the veranda area of the palace grounds at this time of night. But then they weren't due to make their rounds for another fifteen minutes. She'd *counted* on that fifteen minutes to get in and out of Korgan's study and back over the wall. But now she was sitting here trying to decide if that damn barking would cause those sentries to change their schedule.

And she couldn't hesitate much longer or that brief window would disappear. Go for it? Or cancel and try again tomorrow night? She knew what she should do, what she'd been taught to do.

But that twenty-four hours could make a difference, and she didn't know if she could live with that difference.

So screw it, she thought recklessly. Go for it anyway. Trust that all the preparations she'd made would hold and luck would be with her. That study was just off the veranda and she could be in and out in less than ten minutes. She was already lowering herself from the wall to the courtyard, her eyes on the veranda. After that, rely on the fact that she was very fast and could make it back here before the sentries reached the courtyard...

She *ran*.

No sign of any guards yet.

The veranda was right ahead, the study dark. She'd waited for two hours after those lights had gone out before she'd climbed over the garden wall.

She ran up the veranda steps to the French doors and waved the RFID chip over the security panel's illuminated face. The screen changed from blue to green.

So far, so good.

She keyed in a six-digit pass code, and after a pause that seemed like an eternity, the door unlocked. She pulled it open. No alarms, no blinking lights.

She was in.

She moved to the side of the door and disarmed the interior alarm with another swipe of the RFID chip.

She drew a deep breath and waited, listening.

No sound.

Then she moved toward the desk where she'd seen Korgan working for the past three nights. She was right on schedule. Just another two minutes and she'd have it...

"Enough," Korgan said impatiently from across the room. "Lights, Vogel."

Lights illuminated the room.

Alisa whirled to the easy chair where Gabe Korgan had been sitting in darkness.

She recognized him at once. Why not? Those silver-blue eyes and intense features were familiar to most people in the world these days. And at the moment the bastard's eyes were lit with interest, and he was smiling with satisfaction.

Busted! she thought, disgusted. Why shouldn't he be smiling?

And the man he'd called Vogel was crossing the room toward her with a gun in his hand and a grim expression on his face. "Don't move," he said crisply. "Reach for a weapon and I'll put you down."

She was trying to smother her frustration and gather herself together. She might be able to get out of this, she just had to figure out how. She immediately lifted her hands. "I have no intention of resisting you, Vogel," she said quietly. "I wouldn't be that stupid. I've done my research and I realize how good you are and how loyal you are to Korgan. And I don't have a weapon. Not that I don't carry one on occasion, but I didn't come here to shoot anyone, and I didn't want Korgan to think I did. Search me."

"I will." His hands were already running over her quickly and thoroughly. He stepped back. "Clean, Korgan. Do you want me to call the local police or do you want to question her yourself?"

"Let's not be in a hurry." Korgan's gaze was searching Alisa's face. "So you didn't want to shoot me, just rob me?" he asked mockingly. "How kind. Who the hell are you? And may I ask what you were after, and how you were able to get past my alarms? You were incredibly fast when you were disabling them. You shouldn't have been able to do that at all, much less with that degree of speed."

"I had a little help." She looked him in the eye.

"But that wouldn't have done me any good if you'd had the new XV-17 alarms installed here at this palace instead of the older XV-10. That comes very close to being totally foolproof. The V-10 has been around long enough to be studied and breached if the technician is clever enough. I'm a very good technician."

"Evidently." His lips tightened. "But that doesn't mean I like the idea of you using my own work against me." He paused. "You would have needed an RFID chip to get past these panels. Did you steal one from one of my staff?"

"No, I didn't need to. I cloned yours."

He raised his eyebrows. "Now, how the hell did you manage to do that?"

"When you went to the airport the other day. I played the part of a maintenance worker in a lumpy, unflattering jumpsuit. I'm sure you didn't even notice me."

"I didn't. Lumpy... I assume to hide an RFID reader?"

She nodded. "It's very effective within six feet or so. I know it's on your key ring, but you should really find a way to sheathe that thing. It's a scary world out there."

"Tell me about it. And how do you know about the XV-17? It's still in beta testing. Are you into corporate espionage?"

"No, I don't give a damn about your alarm systems right now. It's you I'm interested in."

"One of my favorite subjects."

She stepped toward him. "No, it's not. You try to keep everything about yourself out of the spotlight. But it's pretty futile. Everyone knows you're one of the greatest minds of this or any other age. An innovative genius who comes up with a miracle or two every couple years. Your upcoming subspace passenger jets are on the verge of revolutionizing the travel industry. Straight up into the upper stratosphere, then down to almost any place in the world. New York to Tokyo in sixty minutes."

He shrugged. "It's looking closer to seventy."

"We'll suffer through it. You won your Nobel prize with your fleet of solar-powered drones that plant, water, and fertilize crops, maybe solving the world hunger problem."

"A fun side project."

"Uh-huh. Like your virtual reality glasses that started as a toy but are now the industry standard for teleconferencing. Hearing aids that bring people back from almost total deafness. Self-driving cars that communicate with each other, reducing accidents to almost zero. Electro-stimulus techniques on the human nervous system that could someday wipe out Alzheimer's."

"I've had an enormous amount of help with that last one."

"Barely a day goes by that I don't see some article that compares you to da Vinci, Edison, or Einstein. I bet that really annoys you. Your design aesthetic is second to none. You designed your mountain-view headquarters in Colorado with the same care and creativity you bring to every one of your projects. And I saw your art exhibition in San Francisco. Breathtaking stuff. More side projects?"

"Just another creative outlet."

"As if you needed one. But you can see I know enough about you to go after one of your other projects if I was a corporate spy. I'm sure your really important inventions are patented before they're off your drawing board. You probably came up with the XV alarms when you were bored and needed something to amuse yourself."

"Close." He was silent, studying her. "Very perceptive. But I'm not sure I like you being that perceptive about me. It indicates you've been studying me, and that means you may have come up with answers that might prove uncomfortable for me."

"Police?" Vogel asked again. "She's smart and she almost got to you. You need to get rid of her."

"Not yet. She hasn't even told us her name." Korgan smiled and turned to Alisa. "Vogel is always eager to protect me from people who might prove to be detrimental to my health. He's particularly wary of very smart, beautiful women because they have more weapons than most. We've run across a good many scam artists in our time. Are you a scam artist?"

"No. I'm Alisa Flynn, and I'm a special operative with the CIA. I'm very honest for the most part. I was only trying to rob you of information, and I had no intention of using that information against you." She shrugged. "Though I can see why you might be skeptical. You're probably not at all trusting. You were a billionaire before you were twenty-five. Now that you're in your late thirties, you must be close to Bill Gates territory."

"No, but I have hope for next year when I have two new operating systems coming out. One must always strive to improve." He leaned back in his chair. "And information can often be the most valuable commodity of all. I value it far more than I do anything else in this palace. I resent having it stolen." He repeated, "Alisa Flynn...CIA. What do we know about her, Vogel?"

Vogel was already pulling up information on his phone. "Agent with the CIA. Recruited in Caracas when she was only thirteen. Very high IQ. Well respected by her superiors. Has qualified in auxiliary training in a number of fields. No family. Travels extensively. No permanent residence."

"Just the kind of operator the CIA would choose to send here to steal information from me," Korgan said dryly. "What does the CIA want from me, Alisa Flynn? Why did they send you?"

Lie? Or go for it? Either way it could be dangerous for her. But she'd already made the decision which path she'd take if she was forced to change directions. "They didn't send me. They didn't know about this break-in."

He gazed at her skeptically.

"I'm telling you the truth. I don't have a choice. Everything I'm going to say to you from now on will be the truth." She added in exasperation, "This wouldn't have had to happen if I could have gotten to you a few weeks ago to talk to you. I thought perhaps we could help each other. But everyone around you was on high alert, and I couldn't get past that gold wall that people like Vogel have built around you. So I decided I'd just try to do it on my own."

"Do what on your own?"

She paused and then said, "Stop Jorge Masenak."

He didn't change expression, but she'd thought she'd seen a flicker in his eyes in that first instant. She'd definitely noticed the sudden tension in Vogel's demeanor. "Masenak?" Korgan said slowly. "Was that name supposed to arouse a response?"

"Yes, and it did." She shrugged. "I thought I'd just cut to the chase and let you know that what I'm after has nothing to do with that empire you've built, and everything to do with getting rid of that son of a bitch as quickly as possible." She stared him in the eye. "He's an annoyance to you. I don't know why yet. I've been trying to find out. I thought if I could find out what you want, then I could offer you a trade. But all I've been able to learn is that for some reason, Masenak is getting in your way. I'm guessing you're looking for a way to remove him from your path and make sure he doesn't bother you again." She added bluntly, "Or maybe you just want him dead." She leaned toward him, her voice suddenly urgent. "Either way, you've been blocked from touching the bastard, just as I have. But we could help each other. I could make it happen."

"My, my, are you offering to kill him for me?" His eyes were narrowed on her face. "A CIA operative turned rogue? So much for your sterling reputation with your superiors. Not exactly plausible. If you went rogue, you'd lose everything you've worked for in your career. You'd be on the run yourself. Would it be worth it to you?"

"Masenak is a monster," she said flatly. "Yes, I would kill him if I had to. Yes, it would be worth it. It would be better than watching what Masenak will do if we stand and do nothing. And it's true, if you make that call, I would lose everything. Everyone in the agency is under orders to stay away from Masenak until the present tinderbox of a situation is resolved." She paused. "I'm not going to wait. Do what you like. But you might consider how valuable I could be in any plot you're weaving."

His brows rose. "Plot?"

"Don't play games. Shall I lay it out for you? Jorge Masenak is one of the most powerful and ruthless mercenaries in Africa. He's a thief, rapist, and killer. Compared with him, ISIS appears positively angelic. But he has the people in the Szarnar Jungle terrified, and a few of the desert tribes have also started to throw him their support. Partly because of Masenak's threats of reprisal, partly because he's bribing the chiefs with women." Her lips twisted bitterly. "Or should I say girls? He's using some of the young girls he kidnapped from St. Eldon's Academy outside Morocco six weeks ago. The chiefs like the idea of young, healthy girls they can screw now and might be able to ransom to their parents later." She added, "But that means Masenak's influence is growing, and it might be harder for you to get what you need from him if you don't move quickly. He's getting stronger all the time—when he raided that girls' school, he kidnapped fifty-nine girls, most of whom were daughters of wealthy businessmen and influential diplomats. All of them were between the ages of ten and seventeen. Since then every time a move has been made against Masenak, the bastard has chosen one of the girls and filmed her being raped or tortured." She was trying to keep her voice steady. "If the girl was considered by him to be unimportant, he showed her being beheaded. An excellent way to keep both government forces and parents in line, don't you think?"

He nodded. "In keeping with the son of a bitch you called him. I can see why there was a news blackout since the raid. The CIA would be under pressure to keep from getting the blame for causing Masenak to torture or kill even more girls."

"But you knew about it, didn't you?" she asked fiercely. "You had to know about it."

"Why do you say that?" he asked warily.

"Because you'd make certain you knew everything that was happening with Masenak. He was on your radar. You had a meeting with CIA director Joseph Lakewood only a week before that attack on the school and offered to finance manpower and weapons to take out Masenak's forces in that Szarnar area as soon as possible. The director was considering it when Masenak launched his attack on St. Eldon's Academy. That blew your deal with him out of the water."

"Did it?" His expression was suddenly wary. "Now, how would you be privy to information about a meeting that I was assured was top secret? I wonder what other classified data you might have decided to appropriate."

"Whatever I had to have," she said steadily. "I have friends in high as well as low places. I was searching for any way to stop Masenak and then I found you. You have all the power and influence money brings. Naturally, I decided to zero in and see if I could tap it." His expression hadn't changed, and she couldn't decide if she was making any impression on him. "I couldn't let it go on, no matter what the director said." Her voice was suddenly passionate. "Look, I don't care what you're planning on doing to Masenak. It can't be worse than what Masenak is doing to those students. That's all that matters to me. I need to get them away from him. You help me, and I'll get you Masenak."

"It's an interesting offer. I admit Lakewood's freezing of any action in the Szarnar Jungle has slowed down progress. And just how do you intend to help me get Masenak?" He leaned forward. "Do you know where his camp is located in that jungle?"

"No, but I have sources who can help me find it. Give me another day or two and I promise I'll have him for you."

"Really? He's slippery as an eel; no one has been

able to capture him for the last eight years. He'll go on the run the instant he believes he's cornered."

"I have contacts in the Szarnar Jungle who can help me, and also a limited number in the desert country. Besides, I can track him myself. You've probably never seen a better tracker than I am. Check on me. I promise I'll find him. After that, it's up to you."

He leaned back again. "And all you want in return is for me to free those girls without getting them killed?" he asked mockingly. "While more than likely dodging your fellow CIA friends who did *not* turn rogue, as you have. And throw in the possibility of causing an international uproar if even one those students is hurt during the escape. Such a small thing..."

"Don't be sarcastic. I know how hard it's going to be. That's why I was trying to work around you. But you *want* Masenak. It could be worth it to you. And I'm telling you the truth. Do what I ask, and I'll hand Masenak over to you."

He was silent a moment, gazing at her face. "You might be telling the truth. You're certainly sincere about saving those students. It's difficult to fake emotion like that."

"They were *innocent*. It should never have happened. He's hurting them. It's got to stop."

"It will stop," he said quietly. "I'll get Masenak.

I'll find a way to bring him down whether or not I have your help. I've already started. I believe I'll be able to bribe my way into finding the location of his camp."

"But probably not soon enough," she said through set teeth. "Not for those girls. Some of them are mere children." She started to reach into her jacket. "Don't shoot me. I'm only reaching for my phone." She rapidly pulled up a photo and held it out to show them. It was a class photo with rows of dozens of young schoolgirls in plaid skirts and white blouses with matching knee socks. "Look at them. They don't deserve this. You don't know what they're going through."

"No, but I can imagine." He added speculatively, "But I believe you do know. This is very personal for you." He tilted his head. "And I admit I'm intrigued by the possibility of using your sources. You managed to get into my study, disable my alarms, and now I find out you know about my meeting with your director. I doubt if you'd have been sent by him to contact me even if he'd had a change of heart about accepting my generous 'donation.' Which means I'm back to rogue agent again. Just what were you after when you broke in tonight?"

She hesitated. He wasn't going to like this. But it would be worse if she lied when she'd told him she wasn't going to. "Why do you think I'm here? I knew you weren't going to give up even though the director shut you out and tied your hands. You came back here, positioned yourself near Masenak's army in the Szarnar Jungle, and started to work on getting what you wanted from Masenak on your own. For you, that would almost certainly mean bribing Masenak's men. That's what you've been working on since you flew here from Washington." She paused. Oh, well, go for it. "I planted a bug in the computer on your desk when I broke in here a few days ago. I wanted to retrieve and monitor any messages you'd received from anyone you were paying to give you information about Masenak."

Vogel was swearing softly. "This is the *second* time? She's dangerous, Korgan. She tells a good story, but it could all be bullshit. We should make sure her superiors know what she's been up to and let them deal with it."

"But then they'd find out what *I've* been up to." He was smiling with amusement. "I'd really prefer that they don't until I'm ready to use them at some point." His smile faded. "You managed to hack my computer in spite of all the firewalls I set up? That's disturbing."

"It was very difficult," she said quickly. "And I'm exceptionally well trained."

"I'm not finding that comforting. Nothing is

foolproof, but I thought I'd developed a security that came close." He shrugged. "Oh, well, back to the drawing board. Now, you said that you'd tried to contact me before but were prevented by my wall of gold." He grimaced. "A term I dislike very much, by the way. What would you have told me if you'd managed to reach me?"

"That I have much better sources than you do in Masenak's territory. That you need to take me with you and let me help you." She added fiercely, "And the rest is just what I've already told you. I could give you anything you wanted, if you let me help those girls get away from that asshole. Tell me what it is, and I'll do it."

"But I'm afraid that would be a mistake. What's to stop you from getting overenthusiastic and bringing Masenak down on me before I managed to get my hands on him?"

"Because I'm a professional and wouldn't do that. Yes, I'm going to want this very badly, but I wouldn't do it until I was sure I could pull it off. I'd hope that we could come to an agreement. You're a ruthless man and you'd crush me like a bug if I made a deal with you and then violated it."

"Perhaps not like a bug. The comparison offends me when I look at you. As I said, you're very beautiful." His smile vanished, and she was instantly aware how much steel was beneath that smooth facade. "But you would definitely know that I was displeased."

"You wouldn't be displeased, not if you help me get what I want."

He was silent again. "I'll think about it." He glanced at Vogel's frowning face. "Yes, I know you believe I should be more careful. You always do. And I agree that her sudden appearance here is coincidental at best and suspicious at worst. But if it's a scam, she's certainly been well prepared for it." He was suddenly smiling recklessly. "Let's see how well prepared..." He was striding to his desk and opening a drawer. The next moment he had spread out a large map on the desk. He motioned for her to come and stand beside him. "Show me what you know about the Szarnar Jungle and Jorge Masenak."

She frowned. "What are you asking?"

"I want to know both your point of view and the depth of your knowledge of Masenak and the area. You've made a lot of claims and promises. I can't tell what you're basing it on."

"Whatever." She shrugged. "The man first, I guess. Though he's more of a monster. Masenak was born and raised in Lisbon, Portugal. He was the son of a local crime boss who headed the gambling syndicates in Spain as well as Portugal. His mother was a prostitute who disappeared from the picture after a few years, and Jorge was taken care of by servants and his father. He traveled from racetrack to racetrack with his father, who trained him to become the arrogant son of a bitch he is today. He liked the gambling, particularly the winning, and he was on his way to following in his father's footsteps. But he and his father didn't get along all that well and he wanted more power than he could get as the head of a syndicate. He ran away when he was twelve after stealing enough money to start the life he wanted. He surfaced a few years later in Morocco as a mercenary when he was putting together his first guerrilla army to start trying to form his own kingdom. You know what he's been doing for the last twenty-five years. Blood and gore and murder." She met his eyes. "That's all I know. Very general knowledge because I wasn't interested in him until he committed that atrocity at St. Eldon's. I've been too busy trying to find him to dig any deeper. I'd rather catch him and stop him in his tracks than find out how he got that way. That's not my priority." She tilted her head. "But I bet you know more than I just told you?"

"Perhaps. Though you did well for skimming the surface. You hit the highlights. Go on."

Alisa looked down at the map. She pointed at the large green expanse of jungle. "Masenak uses the Szarnar as an escape route after his army raids surrounding villages and cities. The entire area is known as the Szarnar Jungle, but a good portion of it is rain forest. He's always found it particularly useful because the foliage is so thick and impenetrable that even the most sophisticated drones aren't able to detect anything below the tree canopies. There are no real villages present there, because Masenak's soldiers have either killed or run out the natives." She pointed to several spots on the map. "But there are still isolated individual bands hiding out in these areas who refused to leave their homes."

"And became part of the network of 'sources' who supply you with information?" Korgan asked softly.

"Perhaps," she said warily.

"And, if you did locate Masenak, would it be possible to lure him into a trap using those very stubborn villagers?"

"No, he's too smart and well protected. It would just mean those innocent villagers would be butchered, and any sources I might have would vanish."

"Pity." He nodded again at the map. "Go on."

She pointed to an extreme area to the south. "That's the northern border of the nation of Maldara. Masenak used to raid over there, too, but after their bloody civil war he found it healthier to confine his raids to north of the jungle. Morocco,

Marrakech, Tangier..." She pointed to a mountain range. "The Atlas Mountains. He raids villages more in the foothills of that area than any of the others."

"Why?" Korgan asked.

"I think you must know. It's convenient. Everyone says he has a fancy castle up there in the mountains where he hides out when it gets too hot for him down here."

"You don't know?"

"No, I don't know for sure." She gazed challengingly at him. "Do you?"

"I'd heard a few rumors that he has a magnificent place in the mountains where he stables his prize horses. Everyone knows he's fanatic about racing." He smiled faintly. "But you're the one who's supposed to be answering questions. You don't have any valuable contacts or informed sources in that area?"

"No, but I could find them quickly if I had to." She grimaced. "After all, it's not rocket science." She gestured to the map. "Am I done? Did you get what you wanted from me?"

"For the time being. At least you didn't promise something you didn't think you could deliver about a trap for Masenak. It's something to consider." He looked over his shoulder as Vogel grunted in the background. "Consider," he repeated to him. "She can't hurt me at the moment. I can hurt her just by making a telephone call. I'm curious if this ingenious and totally bizarre proposition she's offered me could have any substance. If it does, I have a hunch that she might prove just the element we need. Find her a room and I'll talk to her in the morning."

Vogel muttered a curse. "Those damn hunches. They're always getting in your way."

"Only sometimes. But at times they tend to clear the way of obstacles."

Alisa took a deep breath and then let it out. It had been a tremendous gamble, and she still wasn't sure she'd won. "Am I a prisoner?"

"I don't think so," Korgan said. "*Prison* is such an unpleasant word. But that bedroom will be guarded until we do a little more research about you. Tomorrow we'll decide how to handle each other to best advantage." He smiled. "Though you've already decided how to handle me. Just barge right in and hope for the best?"

"I did my research, too," she said coolly. "But in the end, I knew you'd respond best to honesty and your own judgment about my character. You believe in yourself or you wouldn't have become as successful as you are."

His lips were suddenly twitching. "So my belief in you shows how intelligent I am?"

She smiled. "Exactly. Together with the fact that you had the foresight to ignore that I'd tried to steal that information from you. You usually know how to cut your losses and turn them into victories." She turned to follow Vogel from the room. Then she whirled back to Korgan. "You were expecting me tonight. I was able to get in the study with no problem the last time. How did you know? Was it the dogs? They only barked that one time and it didn't alert the sentries. I thought it would be safe. Did I make a mistake?"

He tilted his head. "Would it bother you?"

"Yes, I can't make mistakes."

"You're very hard on yourself." He added quietly, "No mistake. It wasn't the dogs. There's no way that you could have known about the new experimental drone I was testing by augmenting the house security yesterday. It's the most sensitive one I've ever produced, and it reported a brief glimpse of you on the property. Vogel followed up. Satisfied?"

"No. A mistake is a mistake. But you're right, I didn't know about the new drone. It's hard to keep up with everything you're doing in those mega labs of yours."

"That fills me with immense relief," he said dryly. "I'm glad there's something you don't know about me."

"I'm sure there's much more. I didn't have much

time to research when I chose you as a target."
She turned back toward the stairs. "Thank you for
telling me."

"You're welcome. Though I can't say I like you
referring to me as a target."

"I'd think you'd want me to call a spade a spade.
It's not as if I meant you harm. Good night, Korgan." He didn't answer, and when she looked back,
she saw that he was already punching a number
on his phone. She had another sudden thought.
"Korgan."

He looked up at her.

"If you really want to know who I am, you should
phone Special Operative Daniel Zabron. No one
knows me better than he does. Mention my name.
Then I promise he'll answer questions without you
having to worry that it will be repeated to anyone
else in the CIA. After your discussion with the
director, it might be awkward for you to arouse
additional curiosity."

He nodded. "I appreciate your concern. However, I'm not certain I should trust information
from someone who's obviously your cohort. And
you're not the only one who has sources."

She shrugged. "Suit yourself. I just wanted to
save us both time." She turned and started after
Vogel.

"And our sources are very good," Vogel murmured

as he led her upstairs. "He'll know everything there is to know about you by morning. Though he should have really let me check you out before he let you stay here."

"I know that would have made you feel better," she said quietly. "I realize how loyal you are to him. You've been with him for years, and it's clear you also like him. But I'm no threat, Vogel. I admire loyalty, and there's a chance I can use Korgan. I know how lucky I'd be if I could pull it off. It would be stupid of me to run the risk of ruining that opportunity." She grimaced. "Though I'm sure you don't believe a word I'm saying, and you'll be on guard to make sure I don't creep into his room and cut his throat."

"Yes, I will," he said coolly. "It's not that Korgan isn't aware how many nuts there are out there that would target him if they got a chance. But he's been a risk taker since the moment I met him, when we both served in the army. The recruiters took one look at his IQ and wanted to put him in the computer division or OCS, but he decided he wanted to go for special services. I don't know if it's curiosity or that he's such a genius he just gets bored." He paused. "If you're as well prepared as Korgan suggested, then you might have dug deep and found out that info about him. But don't think you can use it just because Korgan sometimes appears so easygoing. He can be tough and cynical as hell. You'd regret crossing him."

Vogel was piling on warnings she could have done without, she thought impatiently. But he was important to Korgan and so he was important to her. At least, respect the effort he was making. "I'd know that just by looking at him. And I was telling the truth about not doing research as deep as I should have done about him. But I assure you that I haven't underestimated him... or you."

"That's good. He earned all those billions because he's one of the smartest men on the planet. But it's too much money for most people, and they can't absorb it without resentment." His glance meeting her own was icy cold. "So I make sure that resentment doesn't get in his way. You said you want to use him? Everyone wants something from him, he's used to it. But no one is going to hurt him to get it."

"Warning taken and accepted," she said. "I told him what I wanted, and I won't ask anything else."

He was silent for a moment. "No offense. I hope you're telling the truth and you're who you say you are. But you're CIA and that means you're trained to be lethal if it suits you. Korgan knows as well as I do that no matter what you claim to want from him, he'd always be a great bonus prize to use as ransom. I thought you should know that I won't allow that to happen." He stopped at the second door down the hall and threw it open. "Here it is. I guess it's comfortable, but I don't like palaces myself. Neither does Korgan. It was the only place in the area available on short notice where I could arrange the degree of security he needs." He added sourly, "Not that it did much good stopping you until we brought in that drone."

"It will be fine." She glanced around the luxurious suite. "Good night, Vogel."

"Good night." He closed the door, and she heard the lock click. Clearly Vogel was following up on those warnings by trying to make sure that she couldn't leave until Korgan permitted it.

Except that Alisa would have no more trouble with that lock than she'd had with the veranda doors. Less. She'd had to study the XV-10 alarms, but these bedroom locks were standard issue. Vogel probably guessed that and would make sure either he or another guard would be on hand to try to prevent an escape.

It didn't matter, she thought impatiently. She had no intention of trying to escape tonight. She'd think about that tomorrow if she couldn't get what she wanted from Gabe Korgan. And that result was still definitely questionable. He was just as much an enigma as she'd learned from her research on him. It wasn't often she couldn't read an adversary, but she hadn't been able to pierce that cool mockery she'd encountered in Korgan. It had caught her a little off balance. She needed to think, to go over his expressions and what he had said tonight, so that she'd be ready when she had to face him again.

But first she had something else to do before she tried to prepare herself for the next bout with Korgan. She reached into her pocket for her phone. The next moment she was swiftly dialing the number.

Margaret Douglas answered on the first ring. "What the hell happened?" she asked tensely. "You should have called me almost an hour ago."

"I was a little occupied. I was busted. I screwed up. Korgan was expecting me. I'm lucky to have been able to phone you at all. Since he didn't take my phone, you can bet that it was deliberate and he's having this call monitored. So change out your burner phone after you hang up, Margaret."

"Screw the phone. Are you okay?"

"Yes, I told you that I wasn't worried about Korgan doing me any physical damage. Not that he wouldn't be capable of extreme punishment if he became angry, but it would involve completely destroying the rest of my life, not taking it." She added bitterly, "It's Masenak who's into torture."

"You still shouldn't have taken the risk. You don't

screw up. You were just in too much of a hurry. You should have waited."

"No, I shouldn't. We're running out of time. Yes, I knew there was a risk, but even if I didn't get the info, I figured I'd only be faced with switching the plan to a confrontation with Korgan. Either way I'd be moving forward. That's better than standing still. Now all I have to do is convince Korgan I can give him whatever he wants if he goes along with me." She paused. "Is everything all right there?"

"Better than with you. No deaths. But I don't know how long I can keep control."

"You'll manage. Let me know if there's a change." She hoped desperately Margaret was telling the truth. "I have to hang up now. If they let me keep my phone, I'll be in touch. If not, I'll still find a way to get to you. Be careful, Margaret."

"You be careful," she said dryly. "You tend to think you're made of Kevlar. You're flesh and blood, Alisa, and I don't want to be left alone to face this nightmare." She cut the connection.

Alisa's hand was shaking as she stuffed her phone in her pocket and dropped down on the bench beside the bed. She didn't feel in the least like Kevlar at the moment, she thought wearily. She was vulnerable and worried and just trying to hold everything together until she found her way to get those students away from Masenak.

Lord, she hated this sudden feeling of weakness and uncertainty. She'd had occasional bouts of weakness as a child during the bad times, but it was rare that she experienced it these days. She couldn't permit it to attack her now. It was intolerable, and she mustn't accept it. Force it away. Get rid of it.

She curled up on the bed and closed her eyes. Do as Zabron had taught her when he'd first made her his student.

Relax.

Breathe deep.

Let everything go.

Think about who she was, what she could do.

Not what could be taken from her.

Now identify the source of the fear and weakness.

Masenak?

Visualize.

Concentrate.

No, it wasn't that bastard Masenak.

It was Gabe Korgan. Lean, strong features, dark hair with a touch of gray at the temples. She could see him standing beside that map, his gaze narrowed on her face. Power. Intensity. That super intelligence that she'd always found more exciting than mere good looks. Those glittering gray-blue eyes seeming to read her every thought. It was the first time she'd seen him up close and personal, and he'd shaken her.

Of course he had. He was the most important person in her life right now. She'd known he'd be a challenge if it came down to a confrontation. So think about him, ignore the fact that she had respect and admiration for his genius, realize that he was only a dangerous man that she had to use to get what she needed.

She concentrated, going over the way he spoke, the way he moved, the way he'd watched her every move while he'd questioned her.

Extremely dangerous.

Now ignore the danger, forget him and think only of what made facing him or any threat worthwhile...

Think of the child who had been so furious with her on that day five years ago...

Naples, Italy

"Who are you? The little girl's huge brown eyes were glaring fiercely down at Alisa as she rode her white Arabian horse across the circus ring toward her. "You've been here for every performance for the past two weeks. Why?"

Alisa stiffened at the antagonism in the child's tone. "Perhaps I'm just admiring your performance, Catriona. You and your horses are wonderful together. You're as fantastic as that Catriona the Great poster out front says you are. I've never seen some of the tricks you did with Zeus here." She smiled at her. "And you're only ten years old? It's amazing." But the child was still glaring suspiciously at Alisa, so she asked gently, "Why do you think I've kept coming here?"

"I've seen how you watch me," she said jerkily. "You're probably one of those welfare people who want to take me away from here and put me in an orphanage. Do you think I haven't had that happen before?" She slipped off the horse's back. "Or maybe you think I don't take good care of the horses and want to take them away from me. Well, I won't let you do that, either. Mind your own business. I get along fine."

"I'm sure you do," Alisa said quietly. "You remind me of myself at your age, and I always wanted to control my own life. I promise I have no intention of whisking you to an orphanage or stealing those beautiful horses from you." She met her eyes. "And I didn't know quite why I came here two weeks ago, but I believe I'm beginning to get a clue every time I come back and watch you. I thought it was about you, but I'm wondering if it's really about both of us." She smiled. "Because I've been just as nosy and interfering as you thought and found out the owners of this circus don't treat you as well as they could. But it never seems to bother you as long as those horses are kept happy and healthy." She shook her head. "Yet for some reason, I found that it did bother me. Because those wonderful horses could be in even better shape, and so could you . . . if you'd let me help you." She leaned forward, her eyes fixed intently on the girl's face. So much

distrust, so much wariness. It was like looking in a mirror of the child she had been herself. "Suppose I promise to buy those four horses for you and give you a comfortable place to stay and work that would allow you to do whatever you wish to do?"

She frowned. "Why would you want to do that? No one does something for nothing."

"You're right, so maybe I do want something from you. You'll have plenty of time to find out and so will I. Because from now on I'm going to be here for every performance that I can manage to get away from my job." She made a face. "That won't be as many as I'd like because I'm certainly not rich, and I might have to work even harder to save up enough money to buy those horses for you. But I'll be here as much as I can, and maybe after every show we'll talk and learn what's possible for the two of us, Catriona."

She shrugged. "I think you're a crazy woman." She jumped back on the horse and turned him toward the tent exit. "Just know I'll be keeping my eye on you. If you're lying to me about that orphanage, I'll know it. I'll go away and you'll never find me." She got to her feet and balanced on the horse's back with effortless grace. In that blue tutu she looked like the ballerina on a jewelry box. "And I don't need help from you or anyone else."

"Certainly not on the back of a horse," Alisa said ruefully, touching her forehead in mock obeisance. "Truly the Great Catriona."

"Yes, I am." She glanced back over her shoulder and said grudgingly, "But since you say you're going to be around for a while, you might as well get one thing straight. Catriona isn't my name. Alonzo Zeppo, the owner of the circus, changed it because he thought Catriona the Great looked better on the posters." She lifted her chin, her smile both proud and defiant, as she stared at Alisa. "My name is Sasha Nalano . . ."

Alisa could remember that smile as well as everything else about Sasha that day. The grace, the strength, the wariness, as she strove desperately to keep everyone at bay, to keep Alisa at bay . . .

And that memory of Sasha was giving Alisa the reason she needed to ignore everything else around her as unimportant. Just as she had known it would, as it always did.

Then her lids flicked open and she was swinging her legs to the floor. The next instant she was on her feet and heading for the door she assumed led to the bathroom. She would take a quick shower, and after she finished she would spend more time thinking about Korgan. There must be something she could offer him to ensure that he would give her what she had to have from him . . .

CHAPTER

2

I nteresting." Korgan turned off the recorder. "I don't suppose you were able to trace the call?"

Vogel shook his head. "Burner. And the call only lasted a few minutes." He paused. "But the signal was satellite and issued somewhere in the Szarnar Jungle."

"Even more interesting. A confederate in place exactly where I'd wish her to be located. Margaret...Possibly a fellow CIA operative stationed in that area?"

"No last name. I've been combing through the personnel records, but I can't find a Margaret working for the Company except in London."

"Then do you suppose our Alisa Flynn set up the call to make sure I'd fall for the bait?" he mused.

"I'd suppose that she's a very clever woman and capable of almost anything." Vogel scowled. "And I believe you're enjoying this a little too much. I could see that she intrigued you from the moment you saw her. Hell, the entire situation intrigued you. You've been bored lately, and the unusual always makes you curious."

"But you heard what she said on the phone." His eyes were suddenly twinkling. "She's going to give me whatever I want if I just go along with her. How could I resist an offer like that? She's totally gorgeous. I should at least test the limits."

"You're not talking about having sex with her. I'd feel a hell of a lot more comfortable if you were. You're not sure if she's trying to con you or if she might actually be of use to get you Masenak." His lips thinned. "Either way, you don't need her. We were always going to bring in that special forces team to take care of the problem. Enough to wipe out Masenak's entire camp, if necessary. All you have to do is be patient until you get the location. We can handle it ourselves. You can tell just by looking at her that she's trouble."

"True." Korgan shrugged. "But that doesn't mean that she might not be worth the trouble. Every invention I've ever created caused me a hell of a lot of trouble because it was new and different, and everyone said it couldn't be done." Then all hint

of a smile vanished as his face hardened. "And I'm
fresh out of patience. I'm not going to wait until
Masenak manages to slip away again. I'll do whatever I have to do to get him."

Vogel could see the recklessness, that brilliant
mind ticking, that restlessness that was almost pal-
pable. He'd seen Korgan like this before but never
with quite such an explosive depth of feeling. He
supposed he should have expected it when he'd
seen the frustration and anger Korgan had shown
when he'd been told that any hunt for Masenak
was on hold. He'd been working ceaselessly on
all fronts since he'd set up these headquarters in
Morocco after he'd flown here from Washington.
"Think about it. This Flynn woman could be full
of bullshit. And even if she's not, she might be
brimming with altruistic good intentions that could
be dangerous for us. She could get in your way."

"I am thinking about it. If she can get me
Masenak's location, she could also pave the way.
She's very clever. She managed to open that XV-10
lock in less than one minute. Plus, she hacked my
computer, and you know all the experts I pulled in
to test those firewalls."

"Which would appeal to you and scare the piss
out of me."

"There's no more dangerous weapon than a fine
mind. And the fact that weapon is pointed at Jorge

Masenak does encourage me to take a closer look at her."

Vogel sighed. He'd known it was a losing battle. "You're going to call Daniel Zabron."

Korgan was smiling again. "Yes, please. And I'm sure you won't let me talk to him without giving me a complete background dossier on him so that I'll be able to make accurate judgments about his veracity."

"You're damn right, I will," Vogel said grimly as he turned away. "I started the minute I came back downstairs. Give me thirty minutes."

———◆———

"Gabe Korgan?" Daniel Zabron was silent and then started to laugh. "Since I'm sure not many people get phone calls from you in the middle of the night, you must be phoning me because Alisa Flynn told you to. She's the only person who would feel free to tell anyone to wake me at this hour."

"She did tell me to mention her name."

"Even more interesting. Has she done anything reprehensible?"

"It depends on how you look at it," Korgan said. "Let's just say she made an impact that won't be soon forgotten. I felt the need to explore the facets of that impact, and she gave me your name and told me you know her best."

"She's right, I suppose I do. And if she sent you to me, then she won't want me to lie or con you." He laughed again. "But I'm curious about what she did to get perhaps the finest mind of our century upset enough to come knocking on my door."

"But not curious enough to be worried about her?" he asked dryly. "I thought you might lie because you were her partner. I see that wasn't a problem."

"I'd lie if she asked me. She didn't ask me. So she must want me to tell you the truth. And Alisa doesn't have partners. She knows partners can be a danger and she's always careful. That's why she's such an excellent agent."

"I suppose you should know. I understand you're the one who recruited her when she was only thirteen."

"Ah, of course you'd investigate me." He didn't speak for a moment. "What little nuggets did you find out?"

"That you're a brilliant operative who's been with the CIA for over twenty-five years. You're practically a legend. The fact that you're also totally ruthless, drink too much, and don't stick to the rules in any investigation kept you from climbing higher in the Company." He paused. "And the fact that you did recruit an orphan off the streets of Caracas didn't meet with any degree of enthusiasm."

"No, but after I trained her, they changed their tune." His voice roughened. "Yeah, I heard all the bullshit about putting a little street kid to work with the CIA when she was barely a teenager. They even thought I was some kind of pervert because I wouldn't back down. Why not find some social service agency to give the girl a decent life? Only at that time Caracas was teeming with starving kids just trying to survive, and I didn't want to lose this one. It's not as if I was particularly warmhearted. God knows, no one ever accused me of that. I managed quite well ignoring all those other kids I'd see out there in the gutters." He paused. "Until I ran across Alisa. She wouldn't let me ignore her. She was always there on the street outside the hotel. Skinny. Dirty. Running errands. Selling information. Watching everything. Fierce as a tiger. When I first saw her, she couldn't have been more than nine or ten. I did my best to not pay any attention to her. But I found myself counting the bruises, wondering if she'd had to sleep out in the rain the night before, trying to judge if she'd lost weight again. Finally, I started to talk to her." He was silent a moment. "And that's when I knew she had me. I could have withstood all that schmaltzy sweetness-and-light crap, but she was probably the most intelligent person I'd ever run across. She took my breath away. I couldn't let that go. I knew I could train her into something extraordinary."

"And did you? I notice she's extremely good at picking a lock."

"It was one of the many directions I pointed her in. That's all I ever had to do. Did you know she has a photographic memory? Show her the way and she'd take off and run with it. Failure was never an option. She learned some rough lessons on the street, and she never forgot them." He chuckled. "She regarded your alarms as a challenge. I believe she had a bit of a crush on you after she started delving into your work. She said you were fantastic. She couldn't wait for the XV-17 to come out."

"Wonderful," he said sarcastically. "But I didn't call you to delve into her talent at safe breaking. I was more interested in asking you if I could trust her word." He paused. "And what do you know about Jorge Masenak."

"You can trust her word if she gives it. Otherwise you have to realize that she's into survival." He was silent a moment. "Jorge Masenak? I'm not going to talk about him. I thought that might be why you were calling me. She came to me first and asked me to help her and I turned her down. I told you, I'm neither warm nor sentimental, and I'm also into survival. But I won't try to turn you against going after him. She believes in what she's doing. For some reason, those kids he's holding matter to her. Maybe she identifies with them." He paused. "No, there's no way she could identify with those little princesses in that school. I don't know what's driving her. All I know is that she wants it so bad, she might be able to pull it off."

"She says she has excellent sources in the Szarnar Jungle and southern Maldara—better than mine. Is it true?"

"It could be. I'm always surprised how many contacts she's developed over the years. Alisa knows the value of working every angle, and she's taught herself how to use people to do it."

"Or were you the one who taught her?"

"Maybe. Do I detect a hint of protectiveness in your tone? Be careful, that's how it started with me." Then he said softly, "Our relationship has always been complicated. Let's just say that once we got together, we taught each other a good many things and, bad or good, neither of us regretted learning them." He added, "And I should remind you that it was Alisa who came to me and stood outside that hotel in Caracas until she wore me down. Determination like that is mind-boggling. You should really consider if she's been using me all these years."

"I believe you could take care of yourself," Korgan said dryly.

"Oh, I can. I just didn't want you to underestimate her. That would be an insult to all her hard work and my invaluable guidance. Is there anything else you wish to know?"

"We've discussed her skills in safecracking. What other talents does she possess that could be of use to me?"

"Oh, now this is beginning to read like an employee application. It depends on what you need her to be for the job. She'll do what she has to do to get the mission accomplished. If you want to know what formal training she's acquired since I took her under my wing?" He paused, thinking. "Data science, cryptology, cyber analysis and hacking, tracking, technology, weapons application, EMT training, and she's fluent in nine languages. But those are only the formal training skills the CIA knows about. I taught her much more that she adapted on her own."

"Then why the hell did you turn her down when she asked for help?"

"I told you, it was too dangerous. She's a superb agent, but it could have turned out to be a suicide mission. I wasn't about to risk my neck," he said curtly. "If she'd been able to find a way to get the Company to go after Masenak, I might have agreed. But I always told her she couldn't count on me unless she could prove a project would be a success. She shouldn't have even asked me." He added, "It's interesting she moved on to you. What are you going to get out of this?"

"I don't think I'll answer that question. And if I decide to go forward with the project, I'll ask your old friend Alisa not to confide in you, either. We have a different work philosophy. If I commit to a project, I don't demand absolute proof that it will succeed, only that every single effort will be made. That allows for a change of course that might lead to a different but equally successful outcome. Thank you for answering my questions, Zabron. It's been illuminating."

"I agree." Zabron chuckled. "But remember when I said I knew the moment when Alisa had me? For me it was the time when she actually started to speak to me, and I could gauge what she could become. But I think you've already gone past that point. Good luck, Korgan. I hope you get what you want from her." He cut the connection.

"What do you think?" Vogel asked Korgan from across the room. "No one could say that he wasn't brutally frank about her."

"He also said that she probably has the sources she promised. It could cut down the time I have to wait to go after Masenak. That's important. The longer he's in that damn jungle, the more likely I might lose him." He added, "And he said she'd keep her word."

"If you could get her to swear to do it."

"People swear and make promises to me all the time to get what they want," he said wearily. "I'd just have to make sure she'll be forced to do it."

Vogel was studying him. "He annoyed the hell out of you, didn't he?"

"Perhaps."

"Yet you're already talking as if it's a done deal," he said sourly. "Don't tell me. You have a hunch."

"It's not a done deal. I'll talk to her and see what she can offer me to get those students away from that bastard." He looked down at the photo of Alisa Flynn on the dossier on the desk in front of him. Truly exceptional, he thought absently. Dark hair, high cheekbones, arched brows, and those slightly slanted green eyes. It was those wide, intense, almost fierce eyes staring at him that had caught his attention from the minute he had caught sight of her across the study tonight.

Wariness and ferocity.

And after he'd listened to Zabron's description of the child Alisa, he could imagine she had not changed all that much.

Fierce as a tiger.

Vogel got to his feet. "I'm going to bed. I think

Zabron was right. I think she's got to you. Tell me in the morning if I'm wrong."

Korgan watched him leave the room before his gaze returned to the photo. Decision time. If Vogel was correct, then it had better be for a damn good reason. It wouldn't be because the woman had intrigued him or that he had a hunch that she could work out for them.

He opened the dossier and started to study everything it could tell him about Alisa Flynn.

———◆———

9:05 A.M.

Alisa could see Korgan sitting in the study at his desk drinking a cup of coffee as she paused near the bottom of the staircase. She braced herself and then went down the last three steps. "Have you been there all night?" she asked as she entered the study. "Even Zabron doesn't know enough stories about me to keep you that entertained."

"Actually, my conversation with Zabron was relatively short. I told you I would never trust a single source. But I did find him interesting, as I did all the other information I found about you." He smiled. "But you flatter yourself if you believe I'd sit here all night poring over your résumé."

"I think you spent a good portion of it doing that." Her gaze was narrowed on his face, trying to read him. Dammit, he was as ultra-complicated as one of his inventions. Yet she thought she could see something… "Be honest with me. I think honesty is going to be very important to both of us."

His smile faded. "You're absolutely right. I did my due diligence, but not all night. I took a two-hour nap, showered, and then came down here to wait and see when you'd break out of that bedroom." He gestured to the thermal coffeepot on the desk. "I even ordered coffee for us. Would you like a cup?"

"Not right now," she said absently. "I'd rather you talked to me. I've been waiting all night."

"You shouldn't reveal eagerness. It's bad strategy."

"Not with you. You don't give a damn about strategy. You just gather all the facts and then decide what you're going to do with them. Besides, I think you've already made up your mind."

"Perhaps. Providing I can receive reasonable assurance that I'll get what I want from you." He took a sip of coffee. "What took you so long to get down here if you were so anxious?"

"I was waiting for Vogel to come and get me. I didn't want to strike a wrong note by breaking out of the room if the decision was still up in the air." She added impatiently, "But he didn't come, and I didn't know if it was amusing you to rig some kind of test about the damn lock, so I thought, *What the hell.*"

He chuckled. "Indeed. What the hell?"

"Now stop talking about things that aren't important. I've already given you all the assurances I can. What else can I do?"

"I'm about to tell you." He leaned back in his chair. "You see, the entire problem is that I'm such a cynical bastard. I don't trust you. It takes me a long time to have faith in anyone, and your breaking into my study wasn't destined to inspire me to do it. You need to erase that mistake."

"And how am I supposed to do that?"

"Proof of intent," he said softly. "You keep talking about an exchange of services, but I'm obviously going to have to perform first to avoid having those students slaughtered. Correct?"

She nodded. "I knew you'd have to trust me." She moistened her lips. "I thought you'd want some kind of bond to seal the deal. I told you I'd be willing to do anything."

"So you did," he said ironically. "I believe even Masenak's head was mentioned at one point."

She stiffened. "Is that what you want?"

"Not initially. You've told me that he couldn't be lured into a trap by your people. And even if you could find his camp, he's exceptionally well guarded. If you attacked him, he'd go into automatic, kill those students, and then go on the run himself. Which was exactly what I don't want to happen."

"I told you I'd track him down for you."

"And so you will. My research affirmed that you weren't lying about your tracking skills. Homeland Security gave you expert status after your training in the Arizona desert."

"These days I'm even better than those reports say."

He chuckled. "And so modest, too."

"I don't want you to change your mind," she said. "You can't do that, Korgan. I can't let it happen. What was that you were saying about proof of intent?"

"I sat here for a long time last night thinking about what would make me trust that you'd keep your promise after I gave you what you wanted."

She sat there, tense, staring at him.

He smiled. "Leo Baldwin. I'm sure you've heard of him."

"Of course I have." She frowned as she tried to remember every detail. "One of Masenak's sergeants in his army. Murderer, rapist, scum of the earth." She paused and then added slowly, "And Masenak's lover." Her eyes widened. "You want me to kill him?"

"No, I just want him captured. Though it would

probably be safer for you and those students to kill him. He's as much a monster as Masenak and could be troublesome for me either way. But I've decided he might be useful to me, so I just want him to vanish in a manner that would not interfere with me removing those students you're concerned about. Which would also mean that no one could think the CIA is involved." He met her eyes. "Could you do it? You said your sources would have problems luring Masenak into a trap, but Baldwin is neither as smart nor as well protected. Possible?"

She thought about it. "Possible," she said slowly. "Why do you want it done?"

"I'm not quite sure. I might have several reasons. Baldwin has been with Masenak a long time and has information I can use. Or maybe I want to catch Masenak off guard, and removing Baldwin will be the best way to do it. Their intimacy would be a weapon in itself. I want Masenak wondering whether Baldwin has left him because he thinks he's a lousy lover, or if he's trying to sell him out to one of the wealthy parents or the CIA. Either way, if you do your job right and Baldwin just disappears into the mist, I'll bet Masenak will be going on the hunt for him. Which might eventually let me spring a trap on Masenak after all." He smiled mockingly. "It would be very complicated as well as dangerous. You'd have to want to keep that deal with me very much to risk it. I couldn't ask for a better proof of intent."

"No, you couldn't." She was remembering that it had been Baldwin who had cut off the head of that schoolgirl. "If I take care of this, you'll find a way to go get those students right away?"

He nodded. "Proof of intent." His smile was twisted. "May my soul burn in hell."

"Don't be dramatic. A deal is a deal. I didn't expect anything else. Of course I'll do it."

"How soon? You said you'd be able to locate Masenak's camp in a couple of days. Baldwin will be at that camp. Two days?"

"More than likely." She came forward and poured herself a cup of coffee. "Now that we've settled that, I'll have that coffee. I need it. I should have expected you'd do something unusual to get your pound of flesh, but it wasn't this. From what I heard, you were more cerebral than physical." Now that she was committed, her mind was racing, trying to think how she could pull this off. "You're right, it's going to be complicated. How soon can we leave?"

He didn't answer that question. "I'm very physical," he said softly. "It's just that most people pay more attention to the cerebral because they assume that's where they can benefit the most. How physical are you, Alisa?"

She could feel the sudden tingle of sensuality in the room, the sheer eroticism he was emitting. It startled her to find her body responding to it. She had been so focused on his words and the opportunity he'd presented that she hadn't been aware of the sexuality. Now she was very much aware, and it had to be confronted. "I have to be physical or I wouldn't be able to do what you've asked me to do." She stared him in the eye. "But if you're talking about sex, say it. I don't think you are, because it would get in your way. So tell me if it's part of the deal. Is it another proof of intent?"

He was suddenly still. "And if it was?"

"I'd take my clothes off. I told you I couldn't let you change your mind."

He was silent a moment. Then he smiled and shrugged. "You did, didn't you? But you're right, dealing in that particular proof of intent doesn't appeal to me." He grimaced. "Well, that's not quite true. The appeal is there, but I've made the deal difficult enough for you. You asked how soon we could leave? Probably within the hour. When I came downstairs, I told Vogel I'd be using the helicopter to fly you down to the Szarnar Jungle at the Maldara border to meet with your so-called valuable contacts." He smiled crookedly. "And to convince me that it's worthwhile going forward with you. After the meeting takes place and I'm satisfied, I'll call Vogel and tell him it's a go. He'll instantly set up the arrival of the team to come and meet us, and we'll make plans to take those schoolgirls away from Masenak." His tone was cool and efficient. "I believe you have time to go to the dining room and grab breakfast." He finished his coffee and got to his feet. "As well as call your friend Margaret and tell her that you've completed your recruiting mission. She should be pleased. Anyone can tell you, I'm a real prize."

"Yes, that's what Vogel said." She turned toward the door. "However, I can't tell her that because I haven't recruited you. But Margaret will understand I have a chance now and she'll be relieved."

"Am I allowed to know her full name now?"

"Margaret Douglas."

"CIA?"

"No way." She saw that he was waiting for her to say something else. "She's my friend. She knew I wanted to help those girls and she showed up when she thought I'd have to do it alone."

"A very good friend. Not like Zabron."

She looked at him in surprise. "I never said Zabron was my friend. He never pretended to be. He just saw potential and wanted to play Pygmalion to my Galatea. He regarded me as a challenge. His ego got in the way, but he did a fairly good job."

"If you don't care about little things like humanity or unselfishness," he said.

"And if you did care, you'd go search out a true friend like Margaret," she said simply. "But I didn't have that choice when I was a kid in Caracas. So I took what I could get, and it turned out okay. He taught me a lot."

"An expert CIA guru as compared with a novice like Margaret Douglas?"

She suddenly chuckled. "You don't know what you're talking about. I said she wasn't CIA; I never said she was a novice. She's one of the wisest people I've ever known. You'll understand when you meet her."

"But you're not about to discuss her in depth now?"

"She's hard to explain. It's easier for you to make your own judgment." She shrugged. "And besides, I haven't recruited you yet. I wouldn't want to reveal confidential things about a friend to anyone unless I knew she could trust him." She paused. "I should tell you that Margaret will likely be helping me with Baldwin. It might not be a job I can handle alone."

"I didn't think it would be. I was planning on giving you help."

"But that wouldn't be a true test, would it? You'd have reason to back out." She shook her head. "I'll get my own help." She lifted her hand. "Call me when you're ready to leave." She moved down the hall toward the dining room. She deliberately didn't look back at Korgan, because she was attempting to gather her thoughts and emotions about him in some kind of order. She'd known he was unique before she'd done that first initial research, but she was finding that contact was adding layers and nuances she hadn't dreamed existed. That sudden flash of sexuality had been... erotic. And his ruthless decision to test her by pitting her against Baldwin had also surprised her. Vogel had warned her that he was tough, and that demand had proved it. There was no telling what other facets he would show her as time went on. She would obviously have to be very careful.

But then there was an element of danger to every challenge, and this one was life or death. She had no doubt she could meet it; she was already experiencing a tingle of excitement as she thought about it. It was like the first moments of excitement when she'd been exploring the intricacies of that XV-10 lock he'd created. The power, the sleek beauty, the darkness of the unknown, the beautiful mind that had seen beyond what was there to what it could become.

Fascinating...

———◆———

"They've almost finished gassing up the helicopter," Vogel said as he entered the study. "Since you didn't call me, I assume that it's still okay? I wasn't sure that she'd be prepared to risk her neck going after Baldwin."

"I was sure," Korgan said curtly. "I didn't doubt the determination once I went over those dossiers. Brilliant. Innovative. Absolutely stellar career so far. She's like a bulldog. I could see she was remarkable. But I have to have that final commitment from her." His lips twisted. "Hell, I knew there was no way I could let Masenak butcher those kids. But it meant a delay I didn't need. If I can't have Masenak right away, I'm damn well going to have Baldwin. Alisa Flynn wants a trade. Let her prove herself by showing me she can give me something I do want."

Vogel nodded slowly. "It was a surprise to me. I thought you were being soft on her. I'm glad it was about those students."

"She's interesting." He suddenly smiled. "Soft? The word you're looking for is *weak*, Vogel. You were close to accusing me of it before you took her upstairs last night."

"Not really," he said quickly. "She just makes me uneasy. She's...different. I wasn't sure of anything about her. I'm still not sure." He made a face. "But I'd rather you were being soft about those students than about Alisa Flynn. It makes more sense." He tilted his head. "Are you actually going to let her go into that jungle after Baldwin?"

"Yes. Why not? She's CIA with extraordinary qualifications. She has sources she says can lure him. She'll be able to handle it."

"Alone? You told me to get our crew ready to send down there right away."

He shrugged. "She said she'd get her own help."

"Korgan."

"I wouldn't want to piss the lady off, would I?"

Vogel waited, watching him. "I don't like it. You're too damn restless. You were like this right before you took off to climb the face of K2 without those ropes. I don't want to have you changing your mind and going into that jungle just to relive your old army days. You're too valuable. Now, who do you want me to call and tell to get the hell down there?"

Korgan frowned. "They were damn interesting years and at least I was never bored. I don't see why I shouldn't occasionally revisit them."

"Because you shouldn't take a chance on being shot before you get Masenak. It's still early days. Give me a name."

Shit. It didn't help that Vogel was right, Korgan thought. He *was* restless, and he'd been that way since Alisa Flynn had disarmed that study door.

She'd brought to the forefront not only an interesting possibility, but the actual opportunity to go after the bastard himself.

"Who?" Vogel repeated.

He sighed. "Gilroy," he said reluctantly. "John Gilroy."

———◆———

SZARNAR JUNGLE

MALDARA BORDER

"You said there would be the equivalent of an elite Delta team coming to help us release those students." Alisa was gazing down at the almost impenetrable barrier of jungle trees and foliage as the helicopter slowly descended. As she'd said, this area was more rain forest than jungle. "I don't see any vehicles down there on the Maldara side of the border yet."

"Have a little patience. They should be coming in by tomorrow night. Vogel had them on standby, but it takes time to activate. I'm not trying to cheat you."

"I know you aren't. I'm just anxious. I don't know what Masenak could be doing to those students right now." Her lips twisted. "And I don't have any right to tell you how to handle your men when I still haven't given you any reason to trust me. It will take a little time for me to set up a way to find and take Baldwin anyhow."

He looked away from her. "It might go quicker if you take me up on my offer to lend you a few of my men."

"I want to do it myself." She shrugged. "The way Margaret and I work is rather...different. If I change my mind, I'll let you know. I'll talk to Margaret and see if there's been any change."

"Change?"

"Things change all the time in the jungle."

"I'm aware of that, Alisa," he said dryly. "This isn't my first rodeo. I spent a year in the Congo searching for a stronger metal to use in the batteries that could best fuel the vehicle I created for the next Mars landing."

"I know you did," she said, deadpan. "But since you're surrounded by those gold walls, I thought you might have spent the entire year in a climate-controlled bubble to protect you."

"Ouch. Wicked," he said. "And the first time I've seen a hint of humor in you. Are you becoming a little overconfident?"

"No, but I believe I'm coming very close to getting what I want, and I should be able to react however I wish as long as I give you whatever you want, too." She was grinning. "It's very wearing being the humble prisoner and being threatened with being tossed back to my superiors every few minutes."

"Humble?" he murmured. "I hadn't noticed. You started out with robbery, and then demands, and went on from there." He shrugged. "But you were at least interesting, and I agree that the brutal honesty you've promised will be healthier than the alternative."

"I thought you'd think so." She was looking out the window again. "If you land near that plateau on the Maldara side of the border, you'll find heavy brush and tree coverage where you can hide the helicopter. I told Margaret to meet us there and have a few village people on hand to help get it out of sight as soon as possible. It's safer on that side of the border, but I still don't want to risk one of Masenak's scouts seeing us."

"More demands?" he asked silkily.

"Intelligent suggestions," she said. "I have no intention of losing you now that I've almost got you. I thought we'd take turns later when we've established a relationship. Will you land, please?"

"Whatever you say. I agree that would be an excellent place." He started the descent. "As of ten minutes ago, there were only seven infrared signals indicating that your friend Margaret and her party are down there to greet us. No weaponry except for one handgun, which I assume belongs to Margaret?"

"Yes. I'm sure she didn't want you to believe you were facing a hostile force." Her gaze narrowed on his face. "Vogel whispering in your ear?"

He tapped the tiny plug in his left ear. "He insisted on a few drone runs along the border to make certain that everyone was going to be happy to see me. He didn't approve of this trip and wanted me to be prepared."

"Then why didn't he insist you not go alone?"

"Vogel doesn't run my life." He smiled recklessly. "I let him take any measures of which I approve, but I'd never accomplish anything if I didn't go my own way. I've watched you work around Vogel and all the rest of the entanglements surrounding me since the first instant I saw you. If I'd brought anyone here with me, it might continue, and I'm getting impatient." He shrugged. "I might have been playing a hunch, but now I need to clear the decks. There comes a point where I have to take charge and cast the dice and see where they fall."

She went still. "And if you don't like where they fall?"

He didn't look at her. "Then I assure you that you won't like it, either, Alisa."

"Margaret!" Alisa jumped out of the helicopter and ran toward her as Margaret came out of the trees, closely followed by her retriever, Juno. Alisa hugged her friend tightly before releasing her. Her gaze quickly raked Margaret's face. "You look tired. Is anything wrong? Is Sasha still okay?"

"Don't be crazy. Yes, I'm tired. I've been monitoring Masenak every night this week." Margaret gave her another quick hug before she stepped back. "And everything is just as wrong as it was when you left, but no worse." Suddenly her luminous smile lit her face. "But according to what you told me this morning on the phone, you might have pulled off a coup to make it a hell of a lot better. Where is the great man?"

"At last, someone who recognizes my importance." Korgan was strolling toward them. "Your friend Alisa very rudely left me in the dirt to greet you." He held out his hand. "You're Margaret Douglas? I'm Gabe Korgan. I've been anxious to meet you."

That brilliant smile never left her face as Margaret shook his hand. "Me, too. Though I wasn't sure I'd get to meet you," she added ruefully. "Alisa thought we might have to rely on what she could pull together by stealing that info from you. I'm glad she managed to make you see the light. You won't be sorry."

"I'm not at all sure you're right about that," he murmured. "But I wouldn't be here if I wasn't willing to be convinced."

And in spite of Margaret's brutally frank remarks, he was smiling at her, Alisa realized. But then everyone usually smiled at Margaret. She had realized that when they had met that day years ago in the Arizona desert. She had first mistaken Margaret for a fresh-faced college girl because of that glowing vitality about her: the gold-streaked hair and tan skin, that luminous smile that seemed to be lit from within, and the blue eyes that were usually shining with humor. It was difficult not to return that smile.

"We'll convince you." Margaret's eyes were twinkling. "Between us we can be very persuasive. Alisa says that you're not a selfish monster like Masenak, and that's a good start. If anything, you've just probably had too much money for too long. It's difficult keeping a good sense of values when everyone thinks you're king of the world."

"I'm glad you might think I'm worth saving," he said dryly. "But I'm having trouble being convinced of anything while I feel this much in the dark. I have the distinct feeling all I'm getting is half-truths from either of you. That's usually not my modus operandi."

"We know that," Alisa said quickly. "I'm not

really trying to keep any secrets from you. Well, I was, but that's over. I just didn't want to startle you or give you any wrong ideas. Vogel said you were very cynical, and I didn't want to trigger anything negative."

"Trigger it," he said crisply. "I'm the one to decide if it's negative or not."

"I'm out of here," Margaret said. "I believe that's the cue for me to fade into the sunset." She glanced at Alisa. "I'll go and supervise the villagers moving the helicopter beneath that tarp beside the lake, and then I have to get out of here. It will be dark in the jungle in another hour and I have to get back to Masenak's camp and see if there've been any developments."

Alisa stiffened as she heard Korgan start to swear when he caught that last sentence. She'd known it was coming, but there was no way to prepare for it. He whirled on Alisa. "Masenak's camp?"

Margaret quickly stepped between them. "Yes, we already know exactly where we can find Masenak. You have a right to be pissed off that we lied about not already having found his camp yet."

"You bet I do." His eyes were blazing in his taut face. "Surprise. Surprise."

"Alisa felt it was dangerous for us to tell you that we'd already located him, and I agreed with her." She added to Alisa as she turned away, "Handle it.

I have to get back to Sasha. She's on edge. Make up your mind what you want to tell him. But he'll have to know everything eventually." She looked back over her shoulder at Korgan. "I know this isn't going to be easy for you to understand. We're doing the best we can."

"Should I go with you tonight?" Alisa called after her.

"No, we agreed on a division of duties, and this doesn't change anything. You'd just get upset with seeing Sasha there." She disappeared into the trees.

"What the *hell* was all that supposed to mean?" Korgan asked Alisa through set teeth. "It was kind of her to give you a choice what bits of info to share with me, but I'm not feeling nearly as generous at the moment. Particularly after she just casually mentioned that she's going to drop into Masenak's camp tonight." She could almost feel the waves of fury he was emitting. "That's *not* going to happen. Do you think I'd risk a blunder like that? You didn't even mention you knew where it was located, much less the fact you've been monitoring what's going on there. If that's not a lie, too, it changes everything." He took a step closer to her. "I told you that I won't let you do anything that might put Masenak on the run. I *won't* lose him." The words were low but spraying out like bullets. "If you want to have even a chance of me going after those students, you'll back off now."

"I *can't* back off." She lifted her chin as she stared into his eyes. "And neither can Margaret. She has to keep watch there tonight, just as she does almost every night. No, I didn't mention we already knew where he was located. You held all the weapons, and that was the only one I had. I did tell you I had sources. How did I know you wouldn't go after him yourself if I'd told you any more? I knew how much you wanted to get your hands on him. I was supposed to *trust* you?"

"Only if you wanted me to go through with the deal you proposed."

"I'm *desperate* for you to go through with what you promised. But I'm not a fool. I knew I was going to have trouble with you when I brought you down here. There was no way you were going to understand what's going on here. But I had to take a chance. Time was running out and you were our only hope."

"No, I don't understand," he said coldly. "Except that Vogel might have been right that those kids were only a decoy and you have another agenda. What is it?"

"It's *not* a decoy. You know it. You can see it. You trust your instincts and you know I wasn't lying to you about that. It was one of the only things I had on my side when I screwed up because of that damn drone." She *had* to convince him. "You're not the easiest man for me to read, but we both know that's true. Don't we?"

He didn't speak for a moment. "My instincts aren't always infallible, and you're very believable."

"But in the end, you trusted them enough to come with me when you had no idea if I was leading you into a trap." She gestured impatiently. "Oh, there were probably a hundred other reasons bouncing around in that brain of yours that made you take the chance, but that was the main one."

"Really?" he said with soft sarcasm. "Do tell me more."

His gaze was probing, taking every word she was speaking apart and weighing it, but she could see that he was at least listening. "There's not much more. Just that I knew you were armed and ready to pull that gun out of your jacket any second when you were shaking hands with Margaret. And you told me that Vogel had already sent a drone down here and knew exactly how many people you'd have to face when we landed. So I knew we were being watched. And do you think I don't know that Vogel probably has one of those new super drones of yours keeping an eye on you that you can activate with a blink of an eyelash? He'd never let you go anywhere unprotected. Yet you still came with me, and you didn't do either one even when Margaret told you the truth and you thought she might blow your plans to get Masenak. That means I'm right, and you want Masenak as much as I want to free those students. So you should just give me a chance to explain." Her hands clenched into fists at her sides. "Look, Margaret has to keep surveillance on that camp. You can't imagine how careful she's being. She won't blunder and Masenak won't go on the run. I promise you." She paused and then added stiltedly, "And I'll promise after she leaves here to go to his camp, I'll tell you everything we've been doing since we came here and who we've been doing it with. Total honesty."

"I've heard that before," he said.

"I was honest about everything I chose to say," she said. "I just couldn't take the risk of going all the way. I was taking an enormous chance with you and I know practically nothing about your motives except that you want Masenak dead."

He was silent, gazing at her. "*Anything* I want to know?"

"Anything." Her lips twisted. "Not that you'll believe it."

"I might. You can never tell."

"No, you can never tell," she said quietly. "But I'll start off with telling you I have every intention of getting you Baldwin as soon as possible. That's the prime thing Margaret is checking out tonight. What will it hurt to give us the time until she gets back from his camp before you make up your mind?"

"But do I really need Baldwin? Were you lying about not being able to trap Masenak, too?"

"I wasn't lying. He's too well protected. You'll see that once I show you what we've found out about the camp."

He was silent. "And are you also going to tell me where Masenak's camp is located?"

"Absolutely. I'll make sure you have that information tonight as soon as Margaret gets back." She smiled faintly. "But I should tell you that Masenak moves his camp every other week. That's why we have to keep on top of him. How's that for total honesty?"

"Questionable."

"Quit while you're ahead," she said wearily. "I've told you I'll practically strip my soul to give you every detail I know. Now it's your turn. Tell me you're not going to stop Margaret tonight. After all, I'm still your prisoner. You could pull out that gun at any time and use it on me. If Margaret does anything you don't like at Masenak's camp, you'll be able to punish me for it."

"True." He tilted his head. "What an unusual phrase. I've never had a soul stripped for me before.

And I'm sure your soul would prove more fascinating than most. Though the process does sound uncomfortable. Sort of like milking a cobra."

"Don't play games."

"I'm not, this is no game to me. I just had to decide if I could resist the experience of dealing with you. But now that you've assured me it was entirely my own instincts guiding me, I feel much better. I have infinite trust in myself." He was silent again before he added crisply, "I won't do anything tonight. I'll wait and see if your Margaret brings back anything about Baldwin I consider worthwhile."

She drew a relieved breath. "Good."

But he wasn't paying any attention to her at the moment. He was frowning absently. "Do you really think I could have a drone drop a bomb here by flipping an eyelash or two?"

"What?" She was confused at the change of subject. "No, but I have no real idea what you can do with those drones. It wouldn't surprise me."

"You give me too much credit. That would be enormously difficult. To have that kind of capability it would have to be large, probably noisy, and yet ultra-complicated."

Her gaze was narrowed on his face. "But you do have some other kind of fail-safe device set up?"

"Perhaps." He smiled. "But the lash-blinking idea as an automatic signal has promise. I used something similar in a high-tech bank vault alarm in Paris, but I'm going to have to consider the drone application. With extreme miniaturization, it could be a challenge..."

It appeared the crisis was over. Thank goodness that brilliant mind of Korgan's had spiraled to another "challenge."

"Only a temporary reprieve," he said quietly, his gaze zeroing in on her face. "We're still teetering on the brink. But you're right, I want Masenak bad enough to take almost any chance." He turned away. "Now we're going to get a cup of coffee from that thermos I brought with us. Then we're going to look around this entire area and make certain there aren't going to be any other surprises that drone didn't pick up. And after your friend Margaret leaves, we'll settle down for that long chat. Isn't that a good plan?"

"Good enough. Since I'm limited for choices."

"Excellent answer." He strode back toward the helicopter. "Coffee, first..."

CHAPTER

3

He might have reserved that "chat" for later, but that didn't stop Korgan from firing off a multitude of questions while they were touring the surrounding area that included the plateau and jungle. He even went a mile or so along the bank of the lake before he turned back and strode back toward the plateau where they had landed. He noticed everything; his eyes were arrow sharp, and so were his questions. She'd thought he was finished almost forty minutes later, but it was only a temporary stop as his gaze fell on the dozen or so villagers beneath the canopy who were just finishing tucking foliage around the helicopter to hide it from above. "Those are villagers from northern Maldara. What are they doing this far south?"

"They agreed to come as far as the border as a favor." She asked curiously, "How did you know they were from the north?"

"Those dashiki shirts they're wearing have an identifying stripe common to the northern tribes. I studied Maldara while I was researching the Szarnar Jungle. I thought I might have to use it as an entry point." He glanced at her. "Favor? To whom? You?"

"No, I don't have any clout in Maldara. But I did do a job once for Jed Novak while the civil war was going on. He practically runs everything CIA in Maldara at the moment."

"I know he does."

"Yes, you would. More research. Anyway, the job went well, and Novak believes in payback. So he talked the villagers into coming here and helping me."

"He knows what you're trying to do? He's one of your sources?"

"Source? Novak always knows everything about everyone. But I couldn't compromise him by admitting anything to him about this. Even if he was sympathetic, he can't involve himself with what I'm doing. Maldara might fall apart again if he isn't on-site to monitor the truce. All I can hope is that I'll get a little help when I need it most." She glanced at him. "And don't think you can coax him into your camp with money. He's one of the good guys."

"But then so am I...sometimes. Can you get those villagers to go into the jungle after Masenak in an emergency?"

"I told you we prefer not to involve them. It's not their battle."

"Just a thought. The unit I'm bringing in will be much more efficient anyway." His gaze wandered to the edge of the jungle, where Margaret was apparently giving last-minute instructions to the villagers. "It appears we're going to lose your friend shortly." His glance shifted down to the gleaming cream-colored coat of the retriever at Margaret's feet. "Beautiful dog. Odd to see a purebred retriever like that here in the jungle. She brought it with her?"

She nodded. "Juno goes almost everywhere with Margaret. It would be odd to me not to see them together."

He stiffened. "Tell me she's not taking that dog with her tonight. A white, possibly barking dog, to set off sentries? It would be like shining a searchlight out there in the darkness."

"Juno won't bark. She never does. And they won't see her. She'll mind Margaret." She added soothingly, "It's actually safer if Juno goes with her." She watched Juno following Margaret into the trees. "And unless you intend to go tackle Margaret right now, I believe our conversation about Juno is over."

"Tempting," he said grimly. "But since I promised you I wouldn't interfere with Margaret Douglas tonight, it might as well include that blasted dog."

"Juno is a wonderful dog, and I wouldn't let Margaret hear you malign her if I were you. She's a peace-loving soul but that doesn't extend to friends or animals, and Juno is both."

"I'll keep that in mind. If your Margaret manages to get back here without having one of Masenak's sentries blow her head off." He turned away and said curtly, "In the meantime, if you need to eat, you'd better go to the supply hut I saw beneath the tarp and grab something right away. I was promised information, and I'll give you the time it takes me to build a fire and get myself another cup of coffee for you to keep that promise."

"I'm not hungry," she said quietly. "I realize you're going to be on edge until you're satisfied that you know everything I do. Go get your coffee. I'll make the fire." She smiled faintly. "You'll find I'm very good at everything to do with camping. In fact, my first meeting with Margaret took place in the wilds. If you like, I might even tell you the story."

"Don't bother. First, I want to see a map of Masenak's camp and any weaknesses I can exploit.

I'm not interested in anything else unless it has to do with this rain forest and Masenak."

"It does in a way." She turned and started to gather wood. "Since it has to do with Sasha."

"And who is Sasha?"

"Go get your coffee."

He turned on his heel and headed toward the hut. By the time he returned and handed her a refill on her coffee, she had a brisk fire flickering. He dropped down on the ground beside her. "Masenak's camp," he repeated curtly. "Numbers. Placement of troops. Vehicles."

"Vehicles." She opened the notebook she had laid out in readiness. She pointed to three boxes near the top of a drawing. "He always travels with three trucks when he's here at Szarnar." She pointed at the oblong figure to one side of the tracks. "Helicopter pad about a mile from the main camp. Masenak never takes a chance on not having an escape route. He has troops on patrol at that pad twenty-four hours a day. And the copter's always guarded by a truck with a mounted machine gun."

"We might still be able to reach him before he's able to take off," he muttered.

"Only if you make the choice to go after him while his men are butchering the prisoners," she said. "Because that's what would happen. He already told the CIA that any move on him would lead to the students being massacred. He meant it," she said hoarsely. "That's why you have to get the students out first. Don't you see?"

"I see that there's a problem." His gaze was narrowed on the page. "But there's usually more than one answer."

"Not this time." Her eyes flew to his face. "I know you like to experiment with solutions, but not with those girls' lives. You can't do that, Korgan."

"I didn't say I would." He was still studying the diagram. "Troops?"

"Eighty-four soldiers located at the main camp." She pointed to a square south of the helicopter pad. "They occupy sleeping bags in this area of the clearing when they're not on sentry duty."

"Prisoners?"

She pointed to one of two long tents running the length of the encampment. "This is the main prisoner tent. There's a side entrance that leads out into the main camp and another the guards on duty use at the far south end to prepare their food and make sure the girls are kept away from the soldiers." She added bitterly, "Unless Masenak decides to reward one of his men and lets him have his choice for a night. Otherwise, only Masenak and Baldwin are allowed to rape them." She shook her head to clear it of that horror of ugliness and get back to reporting something that might help. "The tents are wired with explosives, and Masenak always carries the remote detonator to set them off."

"Do you know what kind of explosives?"

"Of course I do. It's a co-crystal of HMX and CL-20. Powerful but stable. I asked Sasha to go into the tent and get the info while she visited the other students. The girls are chained to posts inside the tents. Forty-one in the first one. Only six in the second. There used to be ten more in that second tent, but they killed the one girl to set an example and Sasha said Masenak sent the other girls as gifts to chiefs in Sudan." She frowned. "She said she tried to find out exactly where they were sent, but she's only located four of them."

"Sasha, again. Who the hell is this Sasha?"

"She's one of the students Masenak is holding captive in that camp. She's just fifteen years old, and her name is Sasha Nalano." She tried to keep her voice steady. "And she's probably going to be next on Masenak's kill list if I don't stop him. She's angry, and she won't listen to us all the time. I don't know long she can take what's happening to her friends in that camp. You heard Margaret—she's on the edge."

"I heard it, but I didn't understand it. I still don't understand it. Why would this particular student be singled out?"

"Because she caught the bastard's attention in the

worst possible way." He was right, she realized: She wasn't being coherent. The moment she'd started talking about Sasha, she'd become emotional. And she couldn't expect him to help them unless he did understand. Perhaps not even then. She cleared her throat. "She loves horses, and she volunteered to work in the stables at the academy giving lessons to the students and helping to train the horses. She did such a great job that rumors were suddenly spreading among the wealthy horse communities in Morocco and Marrakech just how good she was. You told me once that you knew what a passion Masenak had for his own horses. Do you think that he wouldn't be aware of what a fine stable St. Eldon possessed? One of the first things he did during the raid was steal all the thoroughbreds and paperwork regarding their pedigrees. Evidently, he didn't think Boujois, the trainer, was worth keeping, so he killed him immediately." She paused. "Not only was Sasha a student who might be able to be ransomed, but there were also those intriguing rumors she might prove valuable to him in another way."

He gave a low whistle. "He wanted to see if she was any better than the trainers in his own stables?"

She nodded. "And now he believes she might be extraordinary. He told her he was going to send her to his stable in the mountains as soon as he finished the negotiations for the other students. But Sasha had already seen what he was doing to those girls and she told him she wouldn't go anywhere or train any of his horses until he let them go."

"You're right, that's living on the edge. I'm surprised she's still alive."

"Do you think I wasn't?" she asked fiercely. "He was furious with her. He beat her every day for almost a week. I couldn't *stand* it. We'd located him by that time, and I knew what he was doing to her. But if I'd tried to attack the camp to free her, he would have killed her. He finally stopped it himself. He apparently didn't want to damage her too badly." She added sarcastically, "After all, he had to think of his horses. If she was as good as he'd heard, she was of value to him. Besides, he had another idea: He started to make her watch him beat another student every day in her place. It worked beautifully." Alina's voice was bitter. "She said she'd do anything he wanted if he'd only stop hurting them. She stopped fighting him and agreed to go wherever he asked whenever he was ready for her. Masenak knew he'd won. Right now he treats her rather like a pet that he's tamed and keeps on a leash. He even allows her the freedom he doesn't permit the other prisoners so that she remains exercised and healthy. It's clear he's regarding her as property, too." She looked away from him. "But I know her. She won't stand for it much longer. I have to get her out of there."

"That's pretty damn clear." He was studying her expression, "I can see you're upset as hell about this girl. Start at the beginning. She's more than just one of the students. She's important to you."

"They're all important to me."

"*Anything* I want to know," he said, repeating her own words softly. "Tell me."

She was silent. "I've been sponsoring Sasha at St. Eldon's Academy for the last five years," she said finally. "I was the one responsible for her being there at the time when Masenak attacked."

"Sponsoring? That's a very exclusive school. She's a relation of some sort?"

"If she'd been a relation of mine, she would never have been accepted. But I needed her to go to that academy because it was a great school and close enough for me to keep an eye on her while I was on assignments." She shrugged. "That meant I had to forge her application under the name of Sasha Lawrence and create an appropriate pedigree and background for both of us before the administration would take my money." She grimaced. "I like to think we're sisters under the skin. But sometimes I wasn't able to decide which one of us was the kid sister and who was taking care of whom. It doesn't seem to matter. We're both orphans, street kids, and survivors. Once we became used to each other, we were just the family neither one of us had ever had. When I found her at that circus in Naples, we were very wary of each other. She worked with the horses; the first time I saw her, she was only ten years old and standing on the back of a white Arabian stallion dressed in a frilly blue tutu. She was wonderful. I went back every day for weeks to let her get used to me." She paused. "And she did get used to me. We were still wary of each other. Yet there was also a kind of... recognition."

"I do believe you're glowing," he said softly, his gaze on her face. "Careful, you're letting your guard down. I'm sure that's dangerous for you."

"If I have to tell you about her, I can't lie about how I feel. And it's not dangerous, because you can't touch that part of me."

"So you ran across a kindred soul, adopted her, and sent her to school. And now you're blaming yourself for putting her in harm's way?"

"It wasn't exactly that uncomplicated. And you have to realize that she was more a kindred soul to Margaret than to me. It was Margaret who sent me to that circus tent in Naples. That's how I came to find Sasha." She lifted her cup to her lips. "You wanted to know the entire story? Listen to it. Lord knows I'd rather lie, but I promised I wouldn't. So I'll be as brief as I can, and hope I have a remote chance of convincing you. Though I probably don't have a chance in hell."

"I'm listening."

"Several years ago, one of the specialties I was studying was tracking. These days most tracking is done on computers, but I was interested in the actual physical tracking process. I researched and found that without doubt the place to get the best training was with the Shadow Wolves unit of Native American trackers in Arizona. Homeland Security offered the course, but the training was done purely by the Indians. I was on my way the next week. I'd been in training almost a month when I ran across Margaret on a trail in the desert. We liked each other right away. Who wouldn't like Margaret? She worked at an animal clinic on an island in the Caribbean, but she told me she came back to the Shadow Wolves every year for a tracking refresher session. I'd never seen anyone as good at tracking as Margaret, not even the Native American instructors." She smiled. "I learned an enormous amount from her in a short time. When she was tracking, she seemed to be part of the earth, part of the forest, part of all the animals around her. Like I said, we became good friends. She was actually the first friend I'd really ever had. I was always too busy working, searching for answers, trying to be the best." She looked down into the fire. "I watched her, she...fascinated me. I couldn't help but try to take everything about her apart to see how it ticked. It's what I do with everything." She moistened her lips. "And before I left, I managed to do that with Margaret. Though I think that she let me do it because she trusted me." She made a face. "Or maybe she was just as lonely as I was." She glanced at Korgan. "I'm not just meandering. I'm getting to what you need to know."

"Surprisingly, I'm not feeling impatient any longer. You're giving me a picture of the way you think and the person you are that may be valuable to me later." He tilted his head. "Plus a tale of Native Americans and trackers and two friends finding each other. I'm actually finding it rather touching. And what else do I have to do tonight?"

"I don't want you to be touched. No one has to feel sorry for me. I'm just going for understanding." She added wryly, "Which I'm probably not going to get from you in the next few minutes."

"Ah, the meandering is done?" His faint smile faded. "Your entire story was revolving about your friend Margaret. I'd guess you're not finished. What else do I need to know about her?"

She looked back down at the fire. *Say it quickly and get it over.* "One of the reasons Margaret is such a good tracker is that she's conscious of everything around her. She's particularly aware of all the animals in her vicinity."

"Yes?"

She braced herself. *Stop hesitating, just say the words.* "She can communicate with them," she burst out. "Margaret told me she's been able to do it all her life. She knows what they're thinking, they know what she's thinking."

He burst out laughing. "Like Tarzan of the jungle? Do you think I'm crazy?"

"No, and I had the same reaction as you when I realized that's what she was doing. It was all very subtle, but I could see the results, if not what was happening. Then when she told me, it all came together."

He shook his head incredulously. "And you think I'll believe this bullshit?"

"Do you know how much easier it would have been for me to lie to you? I hope you will, because it's true. Animals and humans can communicate both by action and telepathically. After I met Margaret, I did research. The info is scanty at best, but it does exist. Koko, a lowland gorilla from the Gorilla Foundation's preserve in California, used sign language and supposedly knew over three thousand words. Animals aren't all that different from us. Primates have cognitive abilities that permit them to assess the qualities of prospective rivals, allies, and mates, just as we do. They recognize individuals, identify kin, keep track of past interactions with group members. They can even compute the value of resources and services." She could see she was losing him. "And millions of pet owners believe they know what their dogs or cats are thinking. Are they all crazy? Though I do believe the telepathic link between people like Margaret and animals must be very, very rare, and that's why we won't accept it when it shows up. Margaret said she went through hell when she was a child until she learned to keep her mouth shut."

He was frowning at her in disbelief. "You're actually sincere about this."

"It's how we found Masenak," she said simply. "That jungle is a complete nightmare. After the kidnapping, I was trying to track him and coming up with nothing. But when Margaret got here, she found his camp in a day and a half." She smiled crookedly. "There are lots of animals in that jungle, and it appears they're not at all averse to gossiping."

He shook his head. "Bullshit," he said harshly. "And madness."

"That's what Margaret's father told her when she was only a toddler. He beat her with his belt because she'd told him she knew the dog next door was sick because he'd told her so. But their neighbors were glad when they managed to save their dog's life." She added, "And I'm sure that every time you come up with another one of those miracle inventions, a lot of people think you have to be a little crazy to create something no one else has even imagined." She met his eyes. "So I'll embrace that madness if it will keep any more of those girls from being killed by Masenak. I swear it's true, Korgan."

"What *you* think is true. I suppose next you're going to tell me that you can communicate with animals, too?"

"No, I told you it was very rare." She hesitated and then said recklessly, "But Sasha Nalano can do it. That was why I went to see that little girl at the circus in Naples. Margaret was always on the lookout for anyone who could do what she could. She knew how alone she'd felt all her life and wanted to reach out to them. She'd heard of a child there in Naples who was almost magical with horses, and she asked me to check her out if I had a chance. She said sometimes that strong affinity for one animal indicates that same rare ability Margaret possesses. The person just tries to protect themselves by hiding it in an acceptable format, as Sasha did with horse training."

"And lo and behold, you found your Margaret was right."

The sarcasm was beginning to hurt, and she had

to end this conversation. "It doesn't matter if you believe me or not. All you have to accept is that when Margaret comes back, she'll have the info we need about Baldwin as I promised. You shouldn't care how she got it." She got to her feet. "And then I'll go after him and turn him over to you. So that means you'd better be ready to find a way to save Sasha and the rest of those students."

"But your Sasha obviously comes first," he said harshly. "Isn't that a bit selfish? Vogel shouldn't have worried about you being too altruistic."

"What do you want me to say?" she asked fiercely. "Every life is important, but I've never had anybody that I cared about in danger before. I'll do everything I can to save all of them, but I *won't* let Sasha die. She's the closest thing to family that I've ever had." She turned and quickly walked away from him toward the path where Margaret had disappeared. She shouldn't care what he thought. She didn't know why his opinion mattered when she usually didn't give a damn what anyone thought. It had been just as difficult as she'd thought it would be, she thought wearily as she dropped to the ground and leaned back against a banyan tree. She couldn't blame Korgan for being skeptical. How could she, when the concept she'd thrown out there was as crazy as he'd said? She'd had to tell him, because she'd made that damn promise, but if there had been any way she could have avoided it, she would have. Now he must think she was some kind of psycho, and she found that thought intensely painful. Ever since she had heard about Gabe Korgan, she had become intrigued and fascinated by his inventions and how he could change the world around him. She respected his mental abilities more than those of any other man she'd met, and the fact that he would never feel a similar respect for her stung bitterly.

Okay, forget it. She had invaded his life and she couldn't expect anything else. It didn't really matter how he felt about her when the common purpose they had would disappear as soon as it was accomplished. She would just stay here until Margaret came back and avoid thinking about him. Just try to make plans and hope that Margaret was accomplishing everything that Alisa had told Korgan she would.

And pray that when Margaret got to that camp, Sasha was still going to be alive.

———◆———

SZARNAR JUNGLE
MASENAK'S CAMP

Third sentry was changed . . .
Juno!

Margaret stopped on the path. Every muscle of her body tensed. *Where?*

Near creek.

Only one?

A moment of uncertainty. Then the answer from Juno. *One. And she knows about it. She's still coming.*

Margaret let out the breath she'd been holding. If Sasha knew about the change of sentries, she'd be able to avoid that one closest to her tent with no problem. Margaret was constantly amazed at how adept and silent Sasha was when moving through the jungle. Amazed and terrified. The last thing she wanted was for Sasha to gain even more confidence than she already had in her ability to escape the notice of those bastards. She was entirely too reckless already.

A flash of white fur in the darkness ahead and Juno was suddenly moving out of the brush. *Here.*

I see you are. Now where is Sasha?

"Behind you," Sasha whispered. "I had to go around the head of the creek to get to you."

Margaret whirled to see the young girl coming out of the trees. And she did look even younger than her fifteen years tonight, Margaret thought. Young and terribly fragile. Before Sasha had been taken, she'd been slim and petite, but now with strain, horror, and loss of weight she appeared almost childlike. Still, there was nothing childlike in the face Margaret was looking into. Sasha's dark hair was pulled back into a ponytail to reveal her high cheekbones, but those huge dark eyes were fierce and her lips tight as she ran toward Margaret. Then Sasha was enveloping her in a hug. "You're late." Her voice was low and muffled against her. "I was beginning to worry until I sensed Juno. Is Alisa all right?"

"Fine. Better than fine, since she arrived back in Maldara this evening with possible help. We're going to get you away from Masenak, Sasha."

"Maybe." She stepped back. "That Korgan man you told me about? Alisa said he was very smart, but she didn't know whether she'd be able to find a way to use him."

"Well, she managed to pull a rabbit out of her hat. Korgan's making her jump through a few hoops, but I believe in the end she'll have him." She gave the girl an affectionate shake. "So don't be so skeptical. We'll make this happen."

She nodded jerkily. "And it might have to be us who does it. No one else wants to help, Margaret. Can't you see that? All those CIA people and U.N. charities and governments and they won't do anything. Everyone is afraid of Masenak."

"This time it's different."

"Don't tell me that!" Sasha's eyes were suddenly glittering with tears. "It keeps happening. He's never going to stop unless *we* stop him. He's *hurting* them." The tears were running down her cheeks. "And I can't watch it again without doing something, no matter what you say. I won't do it."

Margaret went still. "Again?" She should have realized that there had to be a reason why Sasha's bitterness seemed more explosive than usual. "Something happened today?"

"Jeanne Palsan." Sasha's body was starting to shake. "They...raped her. They dragged her out into the center of the camp and tied her down. She was...screaming. Then they pulled the rest of us out of the tents to watch so we'd know what would happen to us if we didn't do whatever they wanted." She was panting. "There were...three of them. They were filming it and laughing and talking to her parents as they did...terrible, terrible things to her. She's only...eleven and they wouldn't stop. I wanted to kill all of them and all I could do was stand there."

Margaret couldn't bear it. She pulled Sasha close and held her tightly. "I know it was terrible," she said hoarsely. She could feel tears sting her own eyes. "And we will punish them. I promise you it will happen soon."

"Masenak didn't think so. He came to stand beside me while they were doing...that...to her and was telling me how lucky I was that I had something of value to barter. He said that as long as I performed well with the horses in his stable, he might not have to have his men do that to me." She took a step back and was wiping her eyes. "And all the while she was *screaming*, and I don't think he even heard her. She was nothing to him."

Margaret had a sudden thought that sent a chill through her. "Why did that happen to her today? Was Masenak punishing her because he thought the CIA or some other organization was starting another offensive against him? Was there any talk in the camp?"

"That's what he told her parents, but he was lying to them. There wasn't any reason for him to hurt Jeanne like that. He told that man Leo Baldwin that it was just time to have another event to remind everyone he was still in control of the negotiations." She was holding her arms tightly across her body to try to stop the shaking. "'Event.' That's what he called what they did to Jeanne. As if it was some kind of sports game or entertainment where he could show how powerful he was. He likes power." She moistened her lips. "I've been thinking he might have even done that hideous thing to Jeanne to try to frighten me. He's done things like that before, you know. Though I don't know why he'd do it now when you won't let me say or do anything to him."

Margaret had been afraid Sasha would go down that path. "It wasn't your fault," she said quickly. "Stop thinking like that. That's not even the reason he gave Baldwin. You're not that important to him."

"But his horses are. They're more important to him than anything. And I probably said something to provoke him. I didn't do it often. You told me that it would only make him angry and not solve anything. But sometimes I couldn't—it was killing me, Margaret."

"It wasn't your fault," she repeated. "And we won't have to face that problem much longer. As I told you, I think we're very close." She wasn't certain she was convincing her. Change the subject. She reached into her jacket for the notebook and pen she'd brought. "I need the exact location of Baldwin's tent. I have the other diagrams we made, but I have to be certain. Will you draw it for me?" She stood and watched as Sasha swiftly sketched the dimensions of the camp and Baldwin's tent in it. "Is everything else exactly as you've told me? No change?"

"No change."

"Well, Korgan definitely has changes in mind. I'm not sure what they are; he was damn vague. He just told Alisa what had to be done and that he might have plans for Baldwin. But it might involve using Baldwin in some way to trap Masenak." She shrugged. "Which might be good for us. If all goes well, we'll be going after Baldwin tomorrow night. Alisa might need you to go to Baldwin's tent and distract him until she can take him down. Can you do that?"

She nodded jerkily. "Distract that bastard? He was *laughing* this afternoon. I can do anything you ask me to do but watch them hurt Jeanne again. I'd *kill* them."

Margaret nodded in sympathy. "I understand. Unless I let you know differently, go to Baldwin's tent at twelve thirty A.M. And don't let anyone see you. Korgan says Baldwin is just supposed to disappear." She took the notebook from Sasha and tucked it in her pocket. "Now get back to camp. I'll tell Alisa that you're doing as well as you can be, and you're looking forward to seeing her again soon."

"She won't believe you. The only thing you got right was how much I want to see her. She always knows exactly how I'm feeling." Sasha smiled crookedly. "Just as I do her. I could sense how upset she was when she was staking out Korgan's palace. I wanted to find a way to bolt out of here and go help her."

"Then smother that impulse. She's just barely holding on now. You don't want her panicking if she knows Masenak is on the hunt for you." She gave her another quick hug and then turned away. "Try to sleep tonight." She snapped her fingers, and Juno ran after her. "Go, Sasha. Juno will be hanging back until she knows you're in your tent, and I want to get back to the border before dawn. I don't want Alisa worrying."

"I'm on my way. I usually have no trouble slipping in and out. The sentries are used to seeing me move around the camp." Her lips twisted. "I think they believe Masenak is saving me for himself." She added bitterly, "In a way, they're right." Sasha moved quickly in the direction of the creek. "But I don't want Alisa worrying, either. Having me here has been almost as bad for her as for me."

"She wouldn't agree." Yet that tie between Sasha and Alisa was incredibly strong, and it always amazed Margaret. When she had brought the two together, she had never thought that the affection would grow to become this warm, unbreakable bond. Two lonely people who had somehow found each other among the tumult. They were both so wary about giving affection that it was a true wonder it had happened. But that bond could also be dangerous for both of them when they were brought to confront the Masenaks of the world. They were too intense; the instinct to dive in and never let go, too powerful.

She's already reached her tent. We're done here, aren't we?

Juno's reminder was polite but pointed, she realized. In other words, stop dragging your feet. She felt a smile tugging at her lips as she picked up the pace to leave the camp behind. *Yes, we're done here...for now. Thank you for calling it to my attention.*

———◆———

MALDARA BORDER

"You've been out here for hours. Shouldn't your Margaret be back by now?"

Alisa looked over her shoulder to see Korgan standing in the shadows a few yards away. "It depends on how far she had to go out of the way to avoid the sentries. It might even be another couple of hours. Margaret knows what she's doing. I told you she wouldn't take chances. Spooking Masenak would ruin everything for us. So go away and take a nap or something."

"I don't want to take a nap. I'm bored, and I thought I'd come over here and have you entertain me." He strolled toward her, and now that he was in stark moonlight, she could see that his expression was intent but no longer antagonistic. "Don't you want to tell me another outrageous story to amuse me?"

"I'm not in the mood. I've reached the end of my repertoire."

"Maybe you need inspiration. You're probably hungry. I notice you didn't eat anything tonight." He was holding out something to her. "I found some bananas in that hut. They're just ripe enough. I thought I'd bring you one."

She stared at him in bewilderment. "A banana? I don't want it. Why would you do that?"

He sat down beside her. "I have no idea. I've been trying to decide. I think it has something to do with the way you looked when you walked away from me earlier tonight. After I got over the idea that you might just be playing me for an idiot, it sank in that you actually thought you were telling the truth." He smiled. "And crazy or not, treating a mentally ill person as savagely as I did was unkind."

"So you brought me a banana?"

"A very good banana," he said solemnly. "I'm sure Koko the gorilla would approve."

She found herself smiling at him. "You *were* unkind." She took the banana. "And wrong. So this is some kind of peace offering?"

"It might be, though you should be properly grateful that I'm being so generous after what you've put me through." His eyes were suddenly twinkling. "Or it might be that I was craving amusement and I just wanted to see you eating that banana. I don't believe there's anyone on earth who doesn't look a little ridiculous with one sticking out of their mouth. Think about it."

She was thinking about it. She threw back her head and laughed. "That's wicked. It better be a peace offering." She started to peel the banana. "Because I was telling you the truth. You didn't have to be that sarcastic."

"I thought it might help me hold on to my sanity, since it appeared I was the only one around here who possessed any. I was having a good deal of trouble believing anything you said after you'd lied to me about that damn camp." He linked his arms around his legs and gazed out into the darkness. "And about the time I cooled down and decided that you might not be completely nuts, I also remembered that you have very high stakes in what's going on at that camp. You wouldn't have tried to string me along by using that kid, Sasha, to make it plausible."

She felt warmth surge through her. "That's very generous of you. I could have been lying about her."

He said lightly, "But I didn't think you were, and we've already discussed that my instincts are almost always right." He made a face. "Or that at least that I tend to think they are. You never told Zabron about Sasha, did you? He had no idea why you were so determined to go after Masenak just because of those kidnappings. Why not?"

She lifted her shoulder in a half shrug. "I'd given him everything he wanted from me. This was something of my own and I wasn't sharing it." Her lips twisted. "Sasha is very special. I didn't want him to find something in her he wanted to mold and develop to suit himself. There are sometimes prices to be paid in situations like that, and I didn't want her to have to pay them. I wanted her to be free."

He nodded slowly. "I was cruel about your feelings for her, too. Sometimes I can be a selfish bastard, but fairness is important to me. I regard it as one of the prime virtues in a corrupt world. I don't think I was fair to you."

"But I only got one banana," she said solemnly. "You committed two mistakes. I think if this is an apology that you should do it right."

"Be satisfied. You still might be nuts. You wouldn't lie about your Sasha, but you haven't been overly truthful about anything else on record since I met you."

"But I promised to change my ways and I've done it. You just haven't seen the proof yet." She was actually enjoying this odd conversation.

He had started off with humor, and the lightness had continued. Very different from the tense, electric atmosphere between them from the beginning. "As long as you're being generous, you might even find a way to believe it wasn't one huge lie."

"Don't count on it. That was a big stretch. Though I did go on the Net and looked up all those references you mentioned." He nodded at the banana. "Including Koko. Interesting story. I had a vague memory of hearing about the gorilla before, but the concept wasn't exactly on my list of subjects I needed to pursue."

"You Googled it?" She couldn't believe it. "Why?"

"I wasn't going to be caught behind the tide of opinion if Margaret Douglas was the real thing. New and wonderful things are happening every day." He grinned. "And I'm supposed to be a forerunner." His smile faded. "I guess maybe I wanted to believe you. I didn't want anyone who had the brains to disarm that XV-10 alarm to be anything less than I thought she should be."

"That only required skill and memory. You have to begin with an element of faith to believe in Margaret." She was trying not to be disappointed, but she knew what was coming next. "And you still couldn't bring yourself to believe me, could you?"

"No," he said gently. "Not sufficient evidence. I had problems with the fact that the human brain is seven times larger than it should be considering body size. In almost all other species, brain and neural track go along with their comparative sizes. There must be a reason that our minds have to be that complicated, and it's not reasonable that communication would be possible with animals who don't have an equal advantage."

"Yet the dolphin's brain is even larger than the human brain on the comparison scale."

"An exception to prove the rule." He smiled. "But maybe when I get the time, I'll do some research to see how such a brilliant woman managed to delude herself."

"Don't bother. You're a busy man and I don't care if you believe me or not." Not true at this strangely intimate moment. It mattered very much to her. "You were demanding reasons and I gave them to you. You didn't like them. That's the end of it." She changed the subject to escape the sharpness of disappointment. "Did you call Vogel and check on that team that's supposed to show up tomorrow? Did you give him the go-ahead?"

"Tentatively. If I don't cancel after Margaret comes back, Vogel and company should be streaming in here about four in the afternoon to set up a base camp. Weapons. Equipment. Tents. You won't be

able to recognize this place by the end of the day.
Relieved?"

"Yes. It's one step closer." She looked back at him.
"Now, if you don't mind, I'd like to sit here and eat
my banana and ignore you until Margaret comes
back. I might not have told you the exact truth.
I'm always a little worried while they're gone."

"I could see that when I walked over here. The
body language was loud and clear. At least that's
not a lie." He paused and then muttered, "Son of a
bitch. And I've managed to hurt you again, haven't
I? I always think you're so damn tough, and then
you close up inside yourself after I say something.
It makes me feel as if I've kicked that dog of
Margaret's."

She stiffened immediately. "Don't be ridiculous.
You couldn't do anything that would hurt me.
You've no idea who I am or what I've gone
through. No one can hurt me unless I let them.
And you actually think something you could say
would bother me?"

He shrugged and held up his hands in surrender.
"Then by all means ignore me." He added recklessly, "Though I don't know why the hell anything
you're feeling matters to me anyway. In fact, I
might enjoy watching you more than listening to
you. You're a beautiful woman when you manage
to keep your mouth shut. When I look at those

superb cheekbones, I can almost forget what a pain in the ass you are."

She went still. "Cerebral versus physical?" Her gaze was searching his face. "And you told me you were very physical. Is that really why you came back to me tonight? Have you changed your mind about the terms of the deal?"

"Hell, no. That's not what I meant. I told you what I wanted to say."

"And you said it." She was suddenly on her knees facing him. "But sometimes things aren't what they seem." She needed to make sure that he wasn't saying one thing but meaning another. She and Margaret were getting so close to bringing him on board to help those students. She wasn't the one who might suffer if she made that error in judgment. "You're angry now, and that always heightens sexual tension. I believe you're thinking about more than my cheekbones. If you want to change those terms, just tell me."

"So you can offer to take your clothes off again?"

"Of course. I told you I couldn't lose you. It's not as if it would matter to me. It's only sex, but I've been very well trained. You'd enjoy me. Should I do it?"

He was glaring at her. "Yes, I am angry with you, and frustrated, and I'd like nothing more than to pull you down on the ground and screw your brains out. You read that right. But I find I don't care for the idea of a mindless jump in the sack with you. I have more sophisticated tastes these days, and I resent the fact that you'd refer to sex with me as 'only.' You might have heard I'm very competitive."

"I haven't heard anything about you sexually except what I've read in the tabloids, and that was probably lies." She drew a deep breath. "But I've obviously made a mistake. I thought you'd changed your mind and decided you wanted me. I didn't mean to make you more angry. Let's forget about it."

"I'm finding that hard to do now," he said grimly. "With emphasis on 'hard.' And I can't promise that I won't decide to take you up on that offer anytime, anywhere, and to hell with any objections to mindless lust. All I can think about at the moment is what you said about how much I'd enjoy you. I keep imagining all the ways—" He suddenly broke off. "No, that's not quite all. You said you'd been well trained. What did you mean by that?"

She hesitated. "What I said."

"Elaborate."

She shrugged. "When I was fourteen, Zabron got it into his head that my agent training should be expanded. One day he drove me to a house in Morocco called the Golden Door. It specialized in training in sexual acts and specialties. Before he let me out in the courtyard, he told me how Russian agents called Sparrows were often sent to that house and became much more valuable agents for the experience. He said that it would help me survive in any situation." She realized Korgan was cursing violently, and she stopped. "You don't want to know any more?"

"The hell I don't. I want to know how far the son of a bitch went to victimize a fourteen-year-old girl."

"You couldn't call me a victim. I wasn't like other girls."

"I'm sure you weren't. How long were you there?"

"He said I had to stay two months." She moistened her lips. "But it disturbed me, so I made sure that I learned everything I had to learn in half that time."

"What disturbed you?"

"I could do everything they told me to do well, but I couldn't stand the confinement or lack of choice. It made me...not myself. It...smothered me." She shivered. "I'd never be able to be one of those Sparrows. I told Zabron I couldn't go back there."

"Did he give you an argument?"

"No, he said I'd learned what he'd wanted me to learn and I could go on to something else."

"How kind of him," Korgan said savagely.

"I told you he had his own agenda. I never expected kindness. I didn't like that place, but it helped me to learn." She looked him in the eye. "And it gave me something to offer you if I needed to."

"Yes, there's always that to consider." His lips twisted. "You're right, I don't have any idea what your life was like."

"Stop treating me like a martyr. It was just something I had to learn and then go on. It's not as if I don't like most sex these days. It's just sometimes the other stuff bothered me."

"I'm not even going there."

"But Zabron was right about it giving me another way to survive. That was important to me."

"And the bastard knew it was important and used it to put you through that." His voice was fierce. "You're so damn smart. Why can't you see what he did to you?"

She could almost feel his rage, and it put her on the defensive. "Yes, I see that I could have walked away. But if I had, he might have gotten bored or discouraged and decided not to teach me anything else. I was *learning*." She added passionately, "Do you know how important that was to me? Every time I learned something new, it was as if I was given another precious gift that no one could ever take away from me. When I was a child, I could see how ignorance robbed everyone around me. If I'd walked away from Zabron, the only thing anyone else would have been willing to teach me was the same thing the Golden Door did. I had to make a choice." She stopped. "I made it, and *then* I walked away. I'm sorry you think it was stupid or lacking in character, but it gave me four more years to get on my feet. If I hadn't had them, I might not have had the opportunity to learn about things like your XV-10, and tracking, and cyber security, and Mandarin, and...so many other things." She forced herself to unclench her fists. "So I'm not at all sorry I made that choice, Korgan."

"Lacking in character," he repeated hoarsely. "You have entirely too much of that commodity. And I have no right to judge anything you decided to do with your life. I wasn't around there to help you. Hell, no one was there to help you."

"Stop it," she said sharply. "I got along fine. I'll always be fine. I'm strong and I'm smart and—"

"A survivor..." Korgan supplied. "That's your mantra."

"And it's not such a bad one," she said. "But if it's upsetting you, go away. This all started because I offered you something I thought you wanted. Again, my choice. I certainly don't need anyone pitying me."

"I wouldn't dare," he said curtly. "I don't know

what the hell I'm feeling for you now, but it's not pity. Yes, there's lust and anger and frustration and half a dozen other emotions. But now I also want to put Zabron on the same death list as Masenak. Maybe at the top of it."

He meant it, she realized in bewilderment. She hadn't expected this extreme reaction. "That's not reasonable. Zabron is just Zabron. Masenak is a monster. And you're always reasonable. It's one of the things I've always admired about you."

"Wrong," he said harshly. "There are times I'm not reasonable at all."

"I can see that. Why?" She was studying him, and then her eyes widened as she finally understood. "It was because I was so young," she murmured. "That's what's bothering you. It shouldn't, it's not as if I couldn't take care of myself."

"Yeah, you weren't like other girls. I heard you."

"But I don't think that would matter to you." She could suddenly feel her face flushing with excitement. "And that means that I've *got* you, Korgan. If you felt like that about what happened to me, you aren't going to let Sasha and the rest of those girls be abused by that son of a bitch. No matter what happens with your damn proof of intent, you'll go after them."

She could feel his withdrawal. His face was now tight, those silver-blue eyes cool. "Don't be too sure of that," he said silkily. "I can't tell you how I hate to be taken for granted."

"Oh, I know you don't. Vogel told me what a badass you could be." Yet she was so relieved, she couldn't stop smiling. "That doesn't make any difference now that I've found the one weak link."

"You're entirely too confident. You don't really know anything about me, and I don't like the idea you think you can manipulate me. I can't tell you how many times it's happened before." He leaned toward her. "The idea of Zabron abusing that young Alisa might have bothered me, but you're not her any longer. You're the same woman who broke into my study and caused this major headache." He deliberately reached out and stroked her cheek. "And who might have told that sad story to touch me or to remind me of all the things you must have learned at the Golden Door. One of them would have been that sex can trump almost anything on the table. You were eager enough to remind me the offer is still in place. Maybe you would have been a better Sparrow than you thought." His thumb was moving lightly, sensuously to the curve of her mouth. She was suddenly breathless. She could feel the pulse in his thumb pounding against the sensitivity of her lips, the warmth of that touch, the tingling that was moving from the flesh of her face, to her throat, to her breasts. "Right now I prefer to forget that dreary story and think of the seductress you were back then. It has many more possibilities." His hand was on her throat, his fingers rubbing, lightly, his fingertips circling down to her nipples. "Either way, I'm the one in control of the situation, and I'll do what I damn well please."

"Of course you will." He must be able to feel her heart beating beneath those fingers. She felt as if she were melting. "I'm not arguing about that. It was never in question, and it doesn't matter now that I know they're all going to be safe. That's what I've been trying to tell you."

He suddenly froze. "Anything you have to do?" His hand dropped away from her. "Son of a bitch." He pushed her away and got to his feet. "Damn, you're good. You spiraled me right back to that fourteen-year-old girl again."

"I didn't mean to do that," she said quietly. "I was never that girl you're imagining. But I can't pretend it doesn't make me happy if it's going to help me save those students."

He asked through clenched teeth, "Because you think you've 'got' me." He turned on his heel. "No way!" The next moment he was striding into the rain forest.

She drew a long, shaky breath. She hadn't handled him at all well. She had just been so exhilarated she had at last been able to read Korgan, and what she had seen had filled her with hope. But it was clear that he was wary and antagonistic at anyone realizing he might be vulnerable to manipulation of any kind. That was why what had happened afterward had escalated so quickly and emotionally. Now he wouldn't believe she'd never intended to manipulate him—that she'd meant only to show him the honesty she'd promised him. Those few moments with him had been searingly erotic. Her body was still taut and ready. She didn't know what she was going to face when she confronted him again, but she would worry about that later.

Right now she was just grateful that she knew Sasha had a much stronger chance to survive than she'd thought when she'd seen Korgan walking toward her earlier tonight.

CHAPTER

4

M argaret!
        An hour later, Alisa stiffened as she saw
the pale gleam of Juno's coat as the retriever moved
out of the darkness of the rain forest. She jumped
to her feet and ran toward Margaret as she followed
the dog into the camp. "Sasha?"

"Not good." Margaret wearily rubbed the back of
her neck. "Masenak staged one of his horror shows
for the parents of an eleven-year-old classmate and
Sasha had to watch it. I don't know how much
more she can take."

"As much as she has to," Alisa said grimly.
"She's strong and she knows the stakes. She won't
do anything that will get those girls hurt. Just
having you there to talk her through it must help

enormously. I wish I could be there." She paused. "Baldwin?"

"Yes, let's hear about Baldwin," Korgan said as he came out of the darkness toward them. "After Alisa assuring me that was your primary goal for the night, I'm interested to know what success you had, Margaret."

"As good as it could be." She shone the beam of her flashlight on his face. "But you'll probably want more than that considering your less-than-pleasant mood. Did he give you a bad time, Alisa?"

"He had a few problems with the way you choose your friends. One thing led to another. Nothing that can't be overcome if we give him what he wants."

"Yes, nothing that can't be overcome if you give me Baldwin," Korgan said. "Can you?"

Margaret reached in her jacket pocket and gave him her notebook. "The location of Baldwin's tent. It's on the far edge of the encampment. It's going to be very convenient for us that Masenak has been distancing himself from Baldwin lately. Since Masenak kidnapped those students, he likes to be close to them in case he wants to bring one or two of them into his tent for fun and games. He evidently thinks Baldwin might either be jealous or get in his way."

"Trouble in paradise," Korgan murmured. "And

all the more reason Masenak might believe Baldwin would have reason to leave him." He was looking at the pages in the notebook. "I'll have a team here by tomorrow evening. How soon can we move on Baldwin?"

"You can't," Alisa said curtly. "I told you we'd handle it. We know everything there is to know about that camp. I won't have you moving in there and getting any of those girls killed. You said that you wanted Baldwin to just disappear, and that's what will happen."

"How?" Korgan bit out.

"Sasha will go into his tent and distract him. I'll give her five minutes, and then I'll crawl under the back of his tent and take him down." She grimaced. "Very quietly. I know the location and schedule of all the sentries and exactly when they make their rounds. I can have him out of the tent and halfway to the border here within an hour. Sasha will take care of cleaning up the interior of the tent to make it seem as if he'd left on his own. Margaret will fake the exterior footprints and make sure that they lead deep into the jungle in the opposite direction before they disappear." She looked at Margaret. "When? Soon?"

Margaret nodded. "I told Sasha to be ready after midnight tomorrow night." She turned away. "And now I'm going to get what sleep I can manage before we have to welcome your team, Korgan. I'm looking forward to the result, but not the interaction. I've heard you can be a bit of a dictator on occasion. I wouldn't advise you to try that with my friend Alisa." She moved toward the hut. "But I'm going to grab something to eat first. Join me, Alisa?"

She shook her head. "I don't think so." She glanced at Korgan, who was still staring down at the diagram of Baldwin's tent. He was frowning and didn't look at all pleased. Too bad. If everything went as it should, the plan could work, and Korgan would have his decoy to lead Masenak away from the camp. She trusted Sasha, Margaret, and herself, and there was no reason why she should be upset if Korgan didn't have a similar faith in them. She headed for her sleeping bag. "I ate earlier." She gave Korgan a cool glance. "It was a banana, and somehow it didn't sit too well..."

"Everything okay?" It was the first thing Vogel asked Korgan as he led the team of twenty or thirty soldiers out of the Maldaran jungle the next afternoon. His glance went immediately to Alisa. "Any unexpected surprises other than the one you mentioned on the phone last night?"

"No, and that one might turn into a plus if we handle it right," Korgan said. "Where's Gilroy?"

Vogel motioned to the path behind him where a stream of other crew members were carefully transporting boxes of ammo, weapons, and some very unusual drones. "He had to sign off on those weapons as they left the helicopter. Now he's taking a look around. You said to land the Chinook 47 deep in the Maldaran jungle so there was no chance it would be visible. He wanted to make sure that we could get out with no trouble. He's used to Black Hawks, and he said this Chinook was going to be one big headache."

"But you can't get over fifty teenage girls on a Black Hawk," Korgan said impatiently. "We'll be lucky to get them on the Chinook. So Gilroy can just suck it up."

"Don't be rude, Korgan." A man dressed in camouflage fatigues with dark curly hair and blue eyes was strolling out of the jungle. He might have been in his thirties, but he looked younger with that puckish grin lighting his face. "I said that it was a headache. I didn't say it couldn't be done." He shook Korgan's hand. "But then you always like to hand me the jobs that are most likely to get me killed. Vogel says this one is high up on that list. Masenak *and* the CIA?" He turned to Alisa and smiled. "John Gilroy. You have to be the rogue agent who's luring Korgan into this disaster, pretty lady. Vogel let me read your dossier. He's a little concerned about you."

"You have a big mouth," Vogel said sourly. "I just said that you should know everything if you took the job."

"And so he should," Alisa said. "No one should go into a job blind. Did I make good reading?"

"Excellent. It was very entertaining." Gilroy beamed at her. "And you don't have my dossier, but I don't want you to go in blind, either. I'm a very good pilot and I can handle a Chinook 47 and get those young girls out of here. It's just going to be a hassle and no fun for me. But then Korgan makes me do a lot of things I don't like. I put up with it because he pays me so well that I'm on my way to becoming a billionaire myself in a decade or two." He tilted his head. "However, Vogel says this time I actually might not mind some of the work connected with the job." His gaze shifted to Korgan and he asked softly, "What about it?"

Korgan smiled faintly. "Possibly."

"That's good enough for me." He grinned. "I can tell you're jealous as hell." He glanced at Alisa. "Did he tell you we were in special forces together when we were young and stupid? Then he decided to become Einstein and I decided to become Indiana Jones. Of course mine was the better choice since everyone knows Indiana is much sexier and more admired."

"Absolutely," Korgan said solemnly. "And you don't even have to think. That was always a plus with you."

"Ouch," Gilroy said. "Masenak had better be very entertaining to make up for this abuse."

"You don't have to deal with Masenak," Alisa said. "Not yet. You just have to be ready to get those students away from Masenak and his men. That comes first."

"I know. I'm not going to rock the boat," he said gently. "I can wait for Masenak, but I'm not sure that Korgan can. He's been tracking him for the past two years."

"That's too bad. He'll have to wait. We have a deal." Alisa turned and was walking quickly away. "I just have to finish up doing this one thing for him with Baldwin, and he'll be ready to go after those students. He promised me." But he hadn't really promised her, she thought. Not until he was sure that she would keep her own word to him. And now this entire clearing was filled with elite, hard-core military types who could probably take down Masenak's entire army in a single lethal raid. Some of the firepower she was seeing unloaded was both unique and positively deadly. There was nothing really to keep Korgan from using it to take over the operation and go after Masenak now that he was sure of Masenak's location.

And all she could really count on was that he had been angry at the thought that she might have been abused as a young girl, and she was sure that anger carried over to the brutality now being shown by Masenak. But how would that stack up in comparison with the fact that Korgan had such a hatred for Masenak, he had been after him for years? Just because he wasn't a monster didn't mean he would give up a vendetta that meant that much to him.

"Wait." Korgan's hand was abruptly on her shoulder, spinning her around to face him. His lips were tight as he stared directly into her eyes. "One. I did promise you. I have no intention of breaking that promise. But I won't have you ordering me or my men around. Two. I've been thinking, and I've decided that you need backup. You appear to know what you're doing, so I'm not going to have Vogel designate a team to go in with you. They might get in your way. I'll send Gilroy."

"Indiana Jones?" she said scornfully. "No. We don't need him. *He'd* get in our way."

"That he won't," Korgan said with precision. "He'll just make sure that you get out of that camp alive. We've fought together. I know what he can do, and that's why I sent for him. I'm not going to lose our tethered goat because you want things all your own way."

And he wasn't going to back down, she realized in frustration. Why should he? Surrounded by all those elite soldiers and equipment, he had all the power; nothing could be more clear. "He'll obey orders," she said through set teeth. "He'll keep up. And if he gets in my way, I'll blow his head off."

Korgan shook his head. "No you won't. That would be entirely too noisy, and you want this to work as much as I do." He smiled crookedly. "Though judging from your dossier, you're very deadly at karate and several other martial skills and you might break his neck. But I'll leave Gilroy to worry about that." He turned away. "And then you can judge whether he'll be of any value for yourself."

"Korgan." She took an impulsive step toward him. "All this firepower. And those weird drones...I've never seen anything like them. I'd guess that this was the experimental model you were using at the palace? And Vogel didn't set this team up overnight. You've been preparing for a long time. Gilroy said two years?"

"A little longer. That's why I know how elusive the son of a bitch can be. This is the closest I've ever gotten." His lips twisted. "Isn't it lucky for you that I was already prepared to go in after Masenak when your director had a crisis of conscience about those students?"

"There's no luck involved in this. All I have to know is that those men you've brought here are the best you have to offer and that they won't make the mistake of killing those students because you've made the wrong choice."

"It won't happen. I'll promise you that, too. You give me Baldwin and I'll get your show on the road. What time are you leaving tonight?"

"Eleven. That will give us time to grab Baldwin and get everything in place before the camp starts rousing at dawn."

He nodded. "I'll tell Gilroy."

"You do that," she said dryly as she turned away. "I don't know how we'd cope without Indiana Jones."

———

SZARNAR JUNGLE
12:05 A.M.

"How close?" Gilroy whispered as he glided suddenly out of the trees beside Alisa. "I'd judge we should be within fifteen minutes of the camp. Am I right?"

"You might be." She shrugged. "If you'd stayed

nearby instead of disappearing every few miles, you might not have to ask."

"But that would have been boring and no challenge at all." His white teeth gleamed in the darkness. "I wanted to keep an eye on Juno, and she's moving very fast. It's even hard for your friend Margaret to keep up with her."

She stiffened. "And why do you want to keep up with Juno?"

"Because she's leading the pack. You and Margaret are wonderful trackers and obviously familiar with where you're going, but you're ignoring me. It's that exceptionally beautiful dog who's going to tell me what I need to know."

"Why do you say that?" she asked warily. She jumped to a conclusion. "Korgan?"

He chuckled. "Korgan didn't tell me anything before we left but to get the job done any way I could. He was a bit bad-tempered because I was going to do something interesting and he was stuck back there talking strategy with Vogel. Sometimes being Einstein bugs the hell out of him. But that's his problem."

"Because he could have been Indiana Jones?"

"Maybe. But I'm much better at it than he'd ever be. He'd get distracted saving the world."

"And you're getting distracted chasing after Juno?"

"I wasn't distracted. I was watching and admiring.

I've worked with service dogs before from the minefields in Afghanistan to the jungles in Brazil, but I don't think I've seen one as good as Margaret's dog, Juno. She knew exactly where she was going and how to lead you past those sentries that started popping up during the last two miles. She's very interesting."

"Particularly since she was also leading *you* safely past those sentries?" she asked dryly.

"Of course, but by that time I assumed she'd be able to do that. I was just paying attention to her body language to see if I could gauge how soon we'd arrive at Masenak's camp. Juno is almost totally silent, but every movement tells a story. It's part of the dog-wolf heritage. Every tensing of muscle, every pause... And there was an eagerness about her in that last five minutes I was on her trail. She's almost reached her target..." His eyes were narrowed on her face. "Hasn't she, Alisa?"

She nodded slowly. "Less than ten minutes now."

"I knew it!" He was still whispering, but it was brimming with triumph. "*Yes.*"

"You're very perceptive." She added, "And extremely savvy about everything connected to jungle warfare." She gazed at him appraisingly. "Trained in the Philippines?"

"For a while. How did you know?"

"Because they're the best at what they do.

They've even been known to send teams to other countries to train their special forces. Their climate is perfect for adjusting to jungle warfare conditions, and they sometimes use service dogs trained to hunt down fugitives to hone their skills. I'd guess you were probably in one of those units while you were there."

"Yes, I was. Excellent."

"Not particularly. Just guesswork," she said. "Besides, Korgan wouldn't have brought you here if you weren't the best. He knew I'd be angry about you coming anyway, and it would have compounded the insult if you didn't know what you were doing."

"I know what I'm doing," he said quietly.

"Right. I've been watching you since we left. Though I didn't find you nearly as interesting as you did Juno." It wasn't entirely true. She had seldom seen anyone move with such speed and dexterity through the jungle. He had faded in and out of those trees, making no sound. She was aware how long it took to gain that degree of proficiency. "But as long as I was stuck with you, I had to be sure that you wouldn't get us killed. Korgan said you wouldn't, but I'm responsible." She shrugged. "You're clearly enough of a professional that I can trust you to watch my back when I go into that tent after Baldwin." She reached out and touched his arm, stopping him on the path. "Which will be very soon. The camp is right ahead. Sasha will be heading for Baldwin's tent in a few minutes. Stay out here and make sure that none of those sentries wander close to camp. And keep an eye on Margaret. Nothing must happen to her. If you believe something's gone wrong, get her out first. I'll call you if I need you for anything else. Be ready to slip on Baldwin's boots after I take him down so that we can show his prints leading away from the camp. And you might be useful helping me get Baldwin out of the tent."

"Since Baldwin is supposed to be almost six feet tall and no lightweight, I'd say that's likely."

"Not necessarily. It's not as if I'm unprepared. I'm very strong, and I'm trained in transporting heavy weights. There's a carrying strap in my backpack." She was gliding forward, her eyes searching the camp in the distance. It was nearly twelve fifteen and everything appeared quiet, no sound from any of the tents. Totally dark except for a low-burning fire near the center of the camp where she knew Masenak had his tent. How she would love to slip into his tent instead of Baldwin's. It would take only seconds to cut the bastard's throat. *Not possible. Don't even think about it.* But it was hard not to think about it when she remembered all the torment he'd caused Sasha and those other young girls. "But I'll definitely keep you in mind if there's a problem."

"I do hope so," he murmured. "Because Korgan gave me one more instruction before I left. On no account was I to let you get killed before I delivered you back to him tonight." He was fading back into the shadows of the trees. "Let's not do that, shall we?"

———

It was time.

Sasha paused outside Baldwin's tent to gather strength to go on. It was going to be okay, she told herself. It wasn't as if Alisa and Margaret didn't have a reason and a plan for having her do this. They would never have sent her here if they'd thought Baldwin would be a threat to her.

Except they didn't realize that Baldwin had never forgiven her for that first encounter when she had nearly smashed his head with a horseshoe. She hadn't told them that Baldwin had insisted on being in her tent every time Masenak had her beaten during that week of punishment.

Well, screw him, she thought recklessly. And don't think about herself. Remember how he'd laughed when Jeanne had been suffering.

She pressed her lips to the tent opening. "Baldwin," she said softly. "I need to speak to you. May I come in? It's important."

She heard a curse and then Baldwin was standing in the doorway, hair tousled, wearing a wrinkled undershirt and smelling of whiskey. He looked beyond her toward Masenak's dark tent. "You want to come in? Where's Masenak? He wouldn't like you showing up here." His voice was bitter. "He won't let me touch you. He has such big plans and he thinks you can be part of them. The son of a bitch never thinks about me or what I want anymore."

"That must be difficult for you." She edged closer to the entrance. She needed to get inside the damn tent before she was seen. "Everyone knows he uses those girls every night now. I really do need to talk to you. Maybe we can help each other."

He turned and went back into the tent. "Maybe we can. Why shouldn't I have what I need, too? What do you want, bitch?"

She quickly followed him. "Masenak scared me yesterday. I couldn't believe he'd hurt Jeanne that badly for no reason." She bit her lower lip. "I think he's crazy and might do the same thing to me. And because of the horses, he won't ever let me get away. You don't want me here. Can't you find a way to help me escape?"

"I could do that." He took a swallow of whiskey. "But Masenak would probably know it was me and he'd cut my balls off." He turned to face her. "I could see that Masenak's little 'event' bothered you. I was enjoying it. Just as I enjoyed how you flinched when that whip stroked your back while Masenak was having you beaten." His lips curled. "But it wasn't enough. He didn't let me do it myself. Everything has to be special with you."

He took a step closer. "I can't even screw you now because it might piss off Masenak. But you'd let me do it, wouldn't you? You're scared and I don't look so bad to you now." He lowered his head and whispered, "But I've learned about the way to handle you from Masenak." She could smell the whiskey on his breath as his tongue touched her cheek. "And that's why I'm going to take you over to that prisoner tent on the other side of the clearing and give myself a treat. That's where they're keeping Jeanne Palsan."

She stiffened. "Jeanne?"

"Masenak told the men she was off limits and to leave her alone until she healed." His tongue touched her upper lip. "But he'll make an exception for me since I'm being so tolerant of his other whores. I'm going to let you watch me give Jeanne another 'event' to match the one she already had."

"No." She inhaled sharply. "You can't do that."

"But I can and I will." He took another swallow of whiskey. "And if you try to stop me, it will only mean the pain will be worse for her. I told you I'd learned how to handle you. Was I right?"

"You were right. I can't imagine anything more horrible." She moved to the left so that to face her, his back would be to the rear tent wall. Her voice was trembling. "Please don't do this. She's gone through too much already."

"Begging me?" His eyes were gleaming with malice. "I like that, Sasha. Remember to do that every time she screams when I—"

He gasped desperately for air. His eyes were suddenly bulging!

"You'll be the one who's begging," Alisa said grimly as she rose swiftly from behind him, her fingers pressing the carotid artery in his throat. His eyes glassed over as she pressed harder. He slumped forward to the floor unconscious. She pushed him aside with her boot and went around him to Sasha. "Are you okay?"

"I am now." Sasha shuddered as she fell into Alisa's arms and clung to her. "But you'll have to teach me how to do that. I couldn't have stopped him, and Jeanne would have been the one to suffer. He was going to—"

"I heard what he was going to do," she interrupted as she held Sasha for a brief moment before she pushed her away. "Bastard." Then she was kneeling, duct-taping Baldwin's mouth, before she handcuffed his wrists. She took out a hypodermic and gave him a shot. "I'll definitely put it on the schedule, but this isn't the time to teach you karate. We've got to get him out of here. That sentry will be doing his rounds in another fifteen minutes. We have to have Baldwin across that creek and this camp quiet as a grave by then."

Sasha was nodding jerkily. "I was just wishing we could put Baldwin in a grave of his own. It would make Jeanne safer. It would make all of them safer." She was picking up the whiskey bottle Baldwin had dropped when Alisa had attacked him. She capped it and then tucked it into Baldwin's backpack. "Margaret said Korgan wanted Masenak to think he'd just disappeared? Nothing more permanent? Too bad." She was swiftly packing up Baldwin's clothes and toiletries in the backpack and strapping it on him. "I'll help you drag him out the back of the tent and into the jungle. Then I'll come back and clean up the rest."

"Not necessary. I'll help her."

Sasha whirled to see a man with dark curly hair sliding underneath the edge of the tent with one lithe movement. "I'm John Gilroy and you must be Sasha." His eyes were fixed warily on the whiskey bottle Sasha had instinctively grabbed to use as a weapon when she'd seen him. "Introduce us, Alisa. Quickly, please."

"Gilroy," Alisa said curtly. "Korgan sent him with us. He has some kind of bizarre notion that he's a second Indiana Jones. I told him to stay outside and keep an eye on Margaret."

He shrugged. "Just being proactive. You're a few minutes behind schedule, and I do take my instructions from Korgan." Gilroy was dragging Baldwin's limp body toward the back of the tent where he'd entered. "How long will he be out?"

"The sedative will last another thirty minutes."

"Then let's get the asshole out of here." He jerked Baldwin's boots off him and threw them outside the tent. "You go ahead and check that sentry. I can handle Baldwin by myself." He glanced at Sasha. "It's risky to leave her. If that sentry is on time, we'll be shaving it pretty close. Are you sure you don't want to bring her with us?"

"Hell, yes, I want to bring her with us," Alisa said harshly. "She just won't come." She looked back at Sasha and said thickly, "Take care. We'll be back for you all as soon as we can."

"I know that, Alisa." Sasha tucked the whiskey bottle back in Baldwin's backpack and fastened the strap. "I'll be fine. Don't stand there looking at me. Get out of here."

She watched Alisa wriggle under the tent before she turned to look at Gilroy and said coldly, "If it turns out to be *really* close, you forget about what Korgan told you to do. You kill Baldwin. I don't care how. Bury him in the jungle or tie

a stone around his neck and toss him in a lake.
Then you get Alisa and Margaret safely back to the
border. If you don't, I'll come after you. Do you
understand?"

"I understand you're a lot like Alisa for such a
youngster." He was smiling faintly as he dragged
Baldwin the last few feet out of the tent. "Don't
worry. She was only a couple of minutes late. We'll
still have time to make it..."

He was gone.

Sasha stood there for a moment. No sound. It
was probably going to be okay. Gilroy had seemed
to be very strong and competent and so confident
she had wanted to hit him. *Don't worry*, he had said.
But she was always worried these days.

Then stop it. Just do her part to keep everyone alive and well. First, she'd finish making the
tent look as if there had been no foul play and
Baldwin had just flown the coop. She'd make certain no one saw her go back to her own tent,
and then she'd lie there and wait for the camp
to rouse.

And listen to make sure there was no gunfire from
any of the sentries who might have caught sight of
Alisa and Margaret. Nothing to worry about...

BORDER BASE CAMP

"They've been sighted two miles south." Vogel hung up from talking on the phone and turned to Korgan. "Gilroy, a prisoner, and Margaret Douglas and that dog. No sign of Alisa Flynn."

"Shit!" Korgan strode out of the shelter and headed into the brush. "Then where the hell did they lose her? I told Gilroy not to screw this up."

"Then you should have sent more men," Vogel said bluntly as he followed him. "You let Alisa Flynn call the shots. You can't blame Gilroy if she wasn't as good as she thought she was."

"You don't know what you're talking about," he said harshly. "She *is* that good. And it could only have worked with a team that small and knowledgeable. Do you think I would have let her go if I hadn't gone over those plans half a dozen times myself to see if there was a better way? This shouldn't have happened. Gilroy screwed up. I should have gone myself."

"Bullshit." Gilroy had appeared around the curve of the path ahead. "I was perfect. I never screw up. Ask Margaret." He shoved Baldwin stumblingly forward. "I whisked this piece of crap out of that tent and through that jungle with the superb skill that you could never hope to equal. Isn't that right, Margaret?"

"He was adequate," Margaret said dryly. "And it was good to have someone strong enough to carry Baldwin until we reached the creek bed where footprints didn't matter. That's why we decided to let him come along."

"Adequate?" Gilroy repeated, outraged. "I was far more than—"

"Where's Alisa?" Korgan asked curtly. "Since Margaret hasn't seen fit to sic her dog on you, I take it you didn't get her killed."

"About a mile behind us," Gilroy said. "You said you wanted Baldwin to disappear. It seems Alisa is taking you at your word. It didn't matter how slim the chances were of anyone seeing those footprints. She's been erasing them and getting rid of all hint of spoor since we left the creek bed."

"She doesn't like to risk making a mistake," Margaret said quietly.

"I know that," Korgan said. "Vogel, get a couple of men out here to pick up Baldwin and take him to the tent for interrogation, then get rid of those damn footprints Alisa is so worried about."

"She'll want to do it herself," Margaret said.

"I know that, too." He started down the path. "I'll take care of it. You go on to camp and get some rest, Margaret. You've done your job."

"And quite 'adequately,'" Gilroy said. "But I was superb."

She smiled. "Maybe. But Alisa won't admit that until you get that prisoner across the border yourself so she can tell Korgan the mission's completed."

"Then by all means let's give her what she wants." He nudged Baldwin forward again. "Let me escort you and Juno to the finish line, asshole."

———◆———

"You're done, Alisa," Korgan said flatly. "Margaret turned over Baldwin to me. Now stop trying to clean up the entire jungle to prove how efficient you are."

She turned around and lifted the beam of her flashlight from the ground to see his face. "You're angry again," she said wearily. "Nothing pleases you, does it? I've done what you wanted. You have Baldwin. Proof of intent. But I'm not quite finished. Go away and I'll get this last bit done."

"You're done," he repeated. "You've done more than I ever had a right to ask you. You've given me what I wanted. Now just get the hell back to camp, will you?"

She went back to carefully brushing all signs of footprints from the path with the branch she was using. "When I've finished."

"You're *done*." He took two strides and was grasping her shoulders. "Just do what I told you to do.

I've spent all night waiting to know if Gilroy was going to bring you back in a body bag and I'm sick of it. I want this over and you back at camp." His grip tightened. "Is that too much to ask?"

"No, but it's not reasonable. I should finish what I started."

"I've already told you sometimes I'm not reasonable. But it's also not reasonable for you to stay out here doing this idiotic cleanup when I can have it done quicker and more efficiently. Why would you do that?"

"Because I *need* to do it." She lifted her eyes to meet his own and blinked back the stinging tears as she said fiercely, "Satisfied? Because if I keep busy enough, it helps me not to remember I had to leave Sasha back there in that tent. I always have to leave her. What if someone saw her last night? I know she's careful, but all it would take would be—"

"Shit." He pulled her into his arms, his hand cradling the back of her head. "Shut up. Nothing happened to her. You know it or you wouldn't have left her. You wouldn't have taken the chance. If she's as smart as you say, she'll do great."

"She's very smart," she said. "But Baldwin frightened her last night. She's just a kid. She said I should teach her karate so that he..." She drew a shaky breath. "And I've got to do that. It's not as if I don't still have time. You're right. Nothing's going

to happen to her tonight. And it will be the last
time. I swore I wouldn't let her run another risk
like this." She pushed him away. "I'm sorry, I told
you that I have a tendency to become emotional
about Sasha. This has gone on too long, and every
time I see her, I can see a change..."

He was silent, gazing at her. Then he shrugged.
"No problem. I'm surprised you apologized." His
face was totally without expression. "When you
also told me that you knew telling me about her
couldn't be a danger to you because I couldn't touch
that part of you—I'm sure that hasn't changed."

"No." She cleared her throat. "I know you're
going to want to talk to Baldwin as soon as possible.
You said you had to see if there was any way you
could use him. Well, I did my part. I brought him to
you. You've wasted enough time here with me."

"Yes, I have." He turned away. "So get moving
and finish what you have to do here. I'll stay with
you and keep the flashlight trained on the path to
hurry it along. I know you'd prefer to do it alone,
but that's tough. You know I like my own way."

"The whole world knows that." But she found
she didn't want to be alone right now. As usual,
she was having trouble reading him, and these last
minutes had been both complicated and bewildering. Yet his words, his touch, had brought comfort
when she had been in pain. She wanted to keep

that comfort for a little while longer. "But I guess I can tolerate giving in on such a small matter." She bent down and used her stick to bend several more blades of grass and brush them back into their original positions. "I suppose there will be bigger battles for us to fight."

He smiled and nodded and then shifted the beam of the flashlight away from her face to the path. "I'm absolutely sure of it."

———

MASENAK'S CAMP
8:15 A.M.

Uproar!

Sasha sat in front of her tent, her arms linked around her knees, trying to keep her face expressionless as she watched Masenak striding around the camp, firing questions at his men.

It had been going on for the last forty minutes. He had sent out a troop to search the jungle, and they had come back with nothing. He had even gone into the prisoner tent and questioned the students. She had heard them crying with fear as he shouted at them. What in hell did he think he was doing, she thought angrily. He might be frustrated and angry about not knowing what had happened to Baldwin, but those girls had been terrified after what had happened to Jeanne yesterday. Did he actually think they'd do anything that would draw attention to themselves?

He had caught sight of Sasha and was striding toward her across the camp. She automatically braced herself and then forced her muscles to relax. She lifted her chin defiantly as he glared down at her. "Lose something, Masenak? I hope he stays lost. Maybe a python ate him."

"And maybe you know something about this," he said harshly. "Python? Perhaps. Are you a snake charmer as well as a horse whisperer?" He bent down, and his fingers tangled in her hair as he yanked her head back. "I don't think so. But Baldwin disappears overnight, and I don't like not knowing where the hell he's gone. I thought you'd learned your lesson but here you are talking back to me again."

"Because you're striding all over the camp shouting at those poor girls. You should know they're too frightened to do anything but hide from him."

"So protective." He gave another tug at her hair. "Always running around trying to help and comfort all your friends. How grateful they must be to you."

"No. If anything, they resent me because you give me special treatment. They don't understand."

"Say the word and I'll punish them for you," he said softly.

"No." He would love doing that, she knew. The guilt she'd feel would be a new way to hurt her. "I don't care."

"I can see how the fact I let you have the run of the camp might make them consider you a traitor." He smiled down at her. "And since I do let you have that much freedom, that would mean if anyone saw Baldwin, it would probably be you. You have keen eyes and you're very sharp. When was the last time you saw Baldwin, Sasha?"

"Before I went to my tent last night, I caught a glimpse of him going into his own tent clutching a whiskey bottle. I remember thinking that I hoped he'd pass out before he sent for one of those poor girls to come and entertain him." Her lips twisted. "You haven't sent for him lately, so they've been taking a lot of punishment from Baldwin." She suddenly lashed out, "If you don't want him any longer, why don't *you* feed him to a python? Everyone would be much better off."

"You think he's jealous?" He shrugged. "It's possible, but he has to learn his place." His eyes narrowed. "But I'm wondering if he might have been upset enough to go after you against my orders. Did he?"

She shook her head. "He's too scared of you.

He wouldn't do that unless he was very drunk, and even then he'd think twice." She paused and added, "Though I'm sure he's wondering why you made me out of bounds. Sometimes I do."

"Because you have to be perfect," he said. "Perfect in body and mind and able to think and concentrate totally on the horses. I've heard about the power of horse whisperers all my life and never run across one. I was beginning to think the concept was only a myth until that day I sent you up in the hills to bring those twelve horses back to me. I couldn't believe it when you managed to get them in those horse trailers in less than forty minutes. Even Baldwin said you were amazing—and he was furious with you at the time." His smile was mocking. "Though I did give you an excellent impetus to make it happen, didn't I? I wish I could have been up there in the hills to see you scrambling desperately to save your friends from the same fate I'd dealt Boujois. I would have found it wonderfully amusing."

She shuddered. "You're a horrible man."

"How unfair you are. And here I've just told you I want to keep you in perfect shape, not shattered or shaken or broken like those other girls in that tent."

"Yet you threatened to treat me like Jeanne."

"Only if you didn't perform properly. Then you

would be of no use to me." He released her hair and took a step back. "Do you know how bored I'm getting sitting here in this jungle when I could be back in the mountains watching the wonders you can do with my horses?"

"I don't care about your horses. What about the horses you stole from me? How are they? You don't seem to have any faith in your own trainers. Are you sure my horses are being treated well?"

"Quite sure. My trainer and stable help are good enough, and they know the penalty for mistreating the horses." He smiled. "And you sound very possessive about those horses I stole from St. Eldon's. You were just an assistant trainer at the school. None of those horses belonged to you, did they?"

"No, of course not." She met his eyes. "But I worked with them every day and they felt like mine."

"How touching. But now they're *my* horses and you should be glad I'm going to let you keep on working with them. You'll be happy to know they all made the trip in good shape and seem to be doing well." He frowned. "With the exception of the black stallion. He tried to kick the stall down and then savage my trainer, Davidow. They had to put him out in the field and are having to keep their eyes on him to prevent him from jumping the fence. What do you know about him?"

She should have known there would be a problem with the stallion. The horse had been trouble from the moment he was born. She kept her face completely without expression. "Not much. Boujois just persuaded the school to buy him from a breeder as an investment last month, but he hadn't been able to do anything toward breaking him yet. He was going to start that same week you raided the school."

"And he didn't ask you to do it for him?"

Think quickly. "I was a student. The horse had already tried to savage one stable boy. The school wouldn't permit it."

"That's reasonable." He tilted his head. "But I'm wondering how you managed to catch that horse and put him in the trailer. Baldwin didn't mention you having trouble catching any of the horses that day of the raid."

"I was wondering that myself. He was probably worn out."

"Well, he seemed to have regained his strength by the time he reached my stables. Bought as an investment? Very valuable?"

"Boujois said he had potential. He made sure he was well taken care of from the minute he bought him."

"Then I'll make sure I follow his example. Does this bad-tempered stallion have a name?"

"Of course he does. Chaos. His name is Chaos."

"How amusing, since he appears to be raining down Chaos on my trainer and all his stablemen. As Davidow doesn't seem to be able to handle him, I think I might have to bring the two of you together sooner than I intended." He reached down and stroked her cheek. "I can't wait."

She forced herself not to move away from that touch. She had to keep him from asking more questions about Chaos. Even a mountain range away, the horse was still causing her problems. "Shouldn't you go look for Baldwin?"

"Yes, but I admit you distracted me when you started asking about the horses. After all, it's the only value you have for me. Unless I decide to go for a fat ransom from your parents." He paused. "Now that I think about it, I remember it was only a few days ago that Baldwin mentioned we should explore that possibility. I'd told him I had other plans for you, but he kept pushing. He said it was peculiar that your parents hadn't tried to establish contact with us to initiate negotiations like all the other parents."

"My parents aren't rich or influential," she said quickly. "Why do you think I was interning in that stable with Boujois to earn my tuition? They're probably waiting for you to offer some kind of package deal with the U.N. or CIA."

"Poor Sasha. You do sound like a destitute little orphan. Though I can see why even your parents would have difficulty putting up with you. You've been a constant headache to me. Yet you'd think they'd make a token gesture." He tilted his head. "Of course, I knew Baldwin probably only wanted me to get rid of you any way he could. But I'm wondering if he might have taken it into his head to do a little negotiating on his own. What do you think?"

"You know him better than I do. But he'll get nothing from my parents. My mother divorced my father ten years ago, and she's always complaining that he cheated her on the settlement."

"We'll see. You seem to be very eager to convince me, and that makes me want to dig a little deeper into exactly who you are and why your loving parents are not so loving. You're such a treasure that I feel I need to know everything about you." He smiled faintly. "But I think I have to find Baldwin first and ask the bastard a few questions about whether he's already talking to your parents and starting negotiations."

"The python," Sasha said flatly. "Or I told you he was probably drunk."

He shook his head. "He walked out into the jungle and took all his gear. No noise. So no helicopter or vehicle. Yes, he could be somewhere in the jungle sleeping off a hangover. Or he might have hiked to a place where he could be met to discuss ransom negotiations. He might be stupid enough to talk to your parents, but there's no way he'd set up a meeting near here and chance revealing the location of the camp. He'd know what I'd do to him." He turned on his heel. "I'll know as soon as I track him down. But don't get your hopes up that you and your friends will get away from me anytime soon. He might just be trying to stage a little protest to show me that I should pay more attention to him." His voice was cold. "Fool. When I find him, he's not going to like the attention I intend to give him before I'm through."

Sasha collapsed back against the tent as she watched him walk away. Those last few sentences had been totally unexpected, and his reaction had been both bad and good. Good, because he seemed to have believed what she'd said about Baldwin's jealousy and that his disappearance had nothing to do with a possible trap. Bad, because he was now interested in Sasha's background—and that might eventually lead him to Alisa. She felt a bolt of panic at the thought. Not only was the fact that Alisa was CIA a threat that Masenak might use to stage another one of his "events," but her connection to Sasha was a weapon he could use against both of them. That was the last thing she'd wanted to happen. It had seemed unlikely, because he'd been interested only in her ability with the horses. But thanks to Baldwin, he had started questioning everything about her, and she was most vulnerable where Alisa was concerned. Masenak had learned he could get anything he wanted from her just by using the people she cared about. She didn't have any doubt that if Masenak found out how close she was to Alisa, she'd be a prime target.

Not only that, but Chaos had suddenly appeared on the scene to cause his usual brand of devilment to pique Masenak's interest. He'd only heard about him so far, yet Sasha could see trouble looming. Once he actually saw the stallion, she knew he'd investigate everything about him. That was another path that could lead him to Alisa.

But Alisa wasn't helpless as Jeanne had been, she told herself frantically. She was stronger and smarter than anyone she had ever met. Masenak wouldn't be able to hurt her.

Unless he used her as a weapon against Alisa.

Because the love they felt for each other would be the weapon he'd choose. A double-edged sword that would render both of them helpless. That was why Masenak had to die before he found out how easy it would be to make her do anything he wanted her to do just by threatening or abusing Alisa.

She closed her eyes, her hands clenched into fists

by her sides. Easy enough to say. She felt terribly helpless at this moment.

It might be all right. Maybe this Korgan would make a difference. It was a little promising that he'd taken that bastard Baldwin out of the equation and away from any harm he could do Jeanne. Maybe whatever he was planning to do next would turn the situation around...

But it had to happen soon.

Please God, let it happen soon.

CHAPTER

5

The duct tape had been ripped off Baldwin's mouth by the time Korgan and Alisa arrived at the tent where Gilroy had taken him. He was spewing curses and venom at Vogel, and when he caught sight of Korgan the venom became even more toxic. "Are you in charge here? Who do you think you are, you son of a bitch? You can't hurt me. I'm important to Masenak. Once he finds out I'm gone, he'll just set up a call to the CIA or U.N. and one of those girls will be tortured until you let me go."

"Only if he's sure that you were taken at all," Korgan said as he moved into the tent. "I'm Gabe Korgan. And my friend Alisa here has made sure there will be doubts about your intentions. After all, what are the odds of anyone walking into Masenak's camp and actually being able to snatch you from under his nose?" He paused. "Even though he didn't really give a damn, he would still find it more likely you'd left under your own steam. And then he'll start to wonder what would make you want to run that risk."

"He knows he can trust me."

"Until he can't," Alisa said softly. "He hasn't shown you lately that he cares one way or the other, has he?"

"You were one of the bitches who took me from camp." His eyes were narrowed on her face. "Maybe you were even the one who put me out." He made another jump. "Sasha was standing in front of me, and the attack came from behind. Sasha set this up." He was cursing again. "I'll kill her."

"You'll do nothing to her." Korgan's voice was cold. "You won't have the opportunity. If you're lucky, you might live through this. But only if you forget that Sasha was involved in any part of it."

"Threats won't get you anywhere." Baldwin's lips curled. "Masenak and I have been together for a few years. He'll believe anything I tell him."

"Then we'll have to make sure you tell him exactly what I want you to tell him." Korgan stared him in the eye. "And you'll also tell me everything I want to know about Masenak, Baldwin.

I'm particularly interested in Jubaldar Castle. Such an interesting place. How many times have you been there?"

There was a sudden wary flicker in Baldwin's face. "I don't know what you're talking about," he said belligerently. "I've never heard of any Jubaldar Castle."

"You have," Korgan said. "You must have just had a lapse of memory. But we'll help you remember every single thing about it. It might take a day, maybe two, but it will all come back to you." He leaned forward, and his voice was lethally soft. "Because you're nothing to me, scum of the earth, and I have men who are very adept at getting what I want from assholes like you. Though I'd prefer to do it myself, and I might allow myself the pleasure if you hold out that long."

"You're bluffing," Baldwin said hoarsely.

"Look closer. Am I bluffing?"

Baldwin finally tore his gaze away. "I'm not afraid of you."

"You will be." He glanced at Gilroy. "By tomorrow I want a radical attitude adjustment."

"You'll get it." Gilroy grimaced. "Maybe before. I really don't like this bastard, and I can tell you don't, either. You might be a little too eager to snatch him away from me."

"I might at that." Korgan turned to leave. "But

you'll have until tomorrow." He walked out of the tent.

Alisa caught up with him a few steps later. "What is this Jubaldar Castle you were asking about?"

"A name that came up when I was investigating Masenak's trips to the Atlas Mountains. I need to know more about it."

She was studying his expression, trying to remember every nuance of the conversation about that mountain stronghold he'd mentioned so briefly. But the reference had been too fleeting; he'd gone immediately on to other questions. She said slowly, "I believe you already know more than you led me to believe that night in the study."

"Perhaps. Why not? We were both on guard, and you were the one being interrogated. I told you I might need to ask Baldwin questions."

"But I didn't think it would be about Jubaldar Castle. I've never heard of it."

"No reason why you should. Not many people have, and I didn't specify. But I'm very interested in Jubaldar. You gave me the opportunity, and I went directly to ask Baldwin that particular question."

"That he's not willing to answer."

"He'll see the error of his ways."

She was searching his expression. It was harder than she'd ever seen it. "Gilroy was right, you were...eager in there. I told Margaret you weren't into torture. Was I wrong?"

"It depends on the subject. Let's say I have to be motivated. I've heard stories about what Baldwin did to villagers when he was on raids with Masenak." He added: "And I have no trouble requiring he be totally compliant when I'm ready to move." He looked at her. "Were you shocked?"

"No, I always knew you were tough. I just wasn't sure how far you'd go. It surprised me."

"I go as far as I have to go to get what I need," he said simply. "As I told you, I believe in fairness. And I believe an eye for an eye is a very fair concept." He smiled. "Plus I never turn the other cheek. There you have my philosophy."

"You're not that uncomplicated." She shrugged. "And I wasn't criticizing. Baldwin beheaded one of Sasha's classmates and he has girls brought to his tent almost every night. He deserves anything anyone does to him." She stopped and turned to face him. "But I have to know what you're going to do. There was an...urgency about you in there. You were intense." Her gaze went to the drones and weapons beneath the munitions enclosure. "You said you *might* be using him to trap Masenak. There's no *might* to it now, is there? You're going to try to do it." She moistened her lips. "And it's going to be right away."

"As soon as possible. I wasn't sure you'd be able to pull off bringing me Baldwin, but you did it." His eyes were glittering. "And that means that I can start planning toward gathering up Masenak."

"Not yet," she said quickly.

"I know. I know," he said impatiently. "Those students first. I didn't forget."

"I know you didn't. I was just reminding you where the priority lies."

"For you, it lies with that fifteen-year-old girl you had to leave behind in the tent last night. That couldn't be more clear. Don't worry, I'll get her out. I'll get them all out. I've already got a plan in the works that was intended for Masenak. All I have to do is adjust it to the situation. You've seen that I have the men, the weapons, and the helicopter to transport those girls to safety." He added grimly, "I'd just like to try to give myself a shot at taking down Masenak at the same time if I can work it out." He held up his hand as she opened her lips. "I said *if* I can work it out. It's going to be difficult as hell. If I can't, I'll just go for rescuing the girls and chase down Masenak later. I won't be any worse off than I was before you showed up at the palace trying to burgle me. And now that I have Baldwin, he could be a storehouse of information." He was frowning thoughtfully. "I tried to line up a few different scenarios last night when I was waiting for you to show. I'll go back to my tent and work on some more today." He glanced at her. "You'd better go get some sleep. I'll discuss it with you later."

She shook her head. "What are you talking about? You've just said it's a go, that you'll do it. I'm too excited and nervous to sleep." She could feel the excitement zinging through her. "I need to go back to your tent with you and help set it up. It's not as if I haven't been trained to do this." She was talking fast, trying to convince him. "I'm not an amateur. If anyone is an amateur, it's you. What if you do something wrong? I need to be around to provide checks and balances."

He swore softly. "You're impossible. Why do I feel as if you're trying to take over the operation? Back off, Alisa."

"I can't. Okay, I was too pushy. Don't shut me out. This is too important to me. I promise I won't get in your way." She whispered: "Please."

He looked at the desperation on her face and slowly shook his head. "I'm not certain I can trust you. You want this too much." Then he shrugged. "But I did have one idea that I thought you might be helpful exploring. You can come to my tent and have coffee with me and we'll discuss it."

She breathed a sigh of relief as she followed him to his tent. "You can trust me. It's just that I'm so close now. I'll do anything you want. But you should listen to me. It would be a mistake not to use me."

"And you do hate mistakes." He smiled sardonically as he knelt before the fire outside his tent and stoked it before reaching for the coffeepot. "You have a few minutes before the coffee will be ready. You can go in my tent and clean up a little if you like. Feel free to use anything I have. I don't mind sharing. Though you'd be better off if you'd go to your own tent and take that nap I suggested."

"No, I wouldn't. This will be fine." She ducked into the tent and paused a moment in the dimness. The air was warm and close, and the spicy, clean scent of him was all around her as if he was still standing next to her. But then she was always aware of him no matter how near he was to her. His backpack with a shirt tossed on top was lying on his cot, which was pushed against the opposite wall. She saw the toothpaste, bucket, and water canteen on a camp table. She moved quickly across the tent and splashed water on her face and neck, brushed her teeth with her forefinger, rinsed out her mouth, and spit in the bucket. Then she grabbed the camp towel and wiped her face. That faint scent of Korgan clung to the towel, too, she realized. She folded it neatly and laid it back on the camp table.

Then she was back outside the tent. "I took you

at your word," she said as she took the coffee he handed her. "I definitely shared. I probably have your scent all over me."

He went still. "What an erotic thought." He met her eyes. "But you weren't in there long enough for it to be *all* over you. And that also requires a certain amount of my participation."

She stiffened. "Yes, it would. I didn't think of that. But you did."

"Yes, I did. Immediately. I'm still thinking about it. I could have resisted the urge to tell you about it, but I'm having enough trouble resisting urges around you." He reached out and touched the curve of her upper lip. "However, I'm not going to act on what I'm thinking because any minute now you'll offer to go to bed with me again because you're excited and happy and you want everything to keep on going that way." He took his finger away from her lip. "Right?"

Her lip felt soft, swollen. She wanted that touch back. "Maybe."

"Probably." He took his own cup of coffee and sat down across the fire. "And the next time it might happen. But not if I can hold out until I don't end up feeling guilty about it."

"You shouldn't feel guilty. I told you that I—"

"Drink your coffee."

She dropped down on the ground and lifted

her cup to her lips. "I *am* excited and happy, and naturally I want everything to go well."

"So do I." He was frowning thoughtfully. "Now hush while I try to forget everything that rushed into my head when you came out of that tent. I need to concentrate on asking you a few questions about your Sasha that I thought about last night."

"Sasha?" She frowned. "Why do you want to know anything more about Sasha?"

"Because ever since our helicopter landed here, it's been all about Sasha Nalano."

"Because I care about her. Because we've got to get her and those other girls away from that monster."

"I get that," he said gently. "But I have to know more about her. Because it's not what she is to you or what we have to do for her." He paused. "It's how far we can go to use her to help us as we go forward."

She stiffened. "Use her? She risked her neck last night to help me get Baldwin for you. I thought that would be the last thing I'd have to ask her to do. That's enough, Korgan."

"It should be, but she's a weapon that we might not be able to do without. At the least, it would make retrieving those students easier and safer."

"How?" she asked fiercely. "You don't know that,

Korgan. You have that elite team and all those fancy weapons. Use them. Dammit, she's fifteen."

"I don't know how yet," he said quietly. "I don't know enough about her, or what I could ask of her without her falling apart and getting caught. All I know is that we have a person in the right place at the right time. That's why I have to know everything about her so that I can make a decision." He met her eyes. "Because I don't want to get her killed if I make the wrong one."

"Using her at all from now on would be a wrong decision," she said curtly. "We can do without her."

"We could, but she'll probably have a better chance of staying alive if she helps us." His gaze held her own. "Admit it. That's what you thought yourself."

"What do you mean?"

"You're scared of me using her, but what were you doing before you decided to pull me into this? You were already planning on how you could get her out. You asked her to find out about the explosives in the prisoner tent. You even asked her to get the exact CL-20 device."

"She said it wouldn't be dangerous. I told her not to do it if it was."

"But you asked it because you're CIA, and experience has told you that you might need that information to save her." He repeated softly, "And she was in the right place at the right time. It was the intelligent thing to do." He took a sip of his coffee. "I called Vogel that same night you told me about it and told him to bring a signal jammer to block the detonator for the CL-20 when he brought the team. It's in that munitions shed over there with the other weaponry along with a few other items that might prove useful."

Her gaze flew to the shed. "It's already here?"

"And ready to use. You and Sasha did it. I only followed through." He added, "But it's only a start. Will you tell me about Sasha so that we can decide if there's anything else she can do to help herself and those friends of hers?"

"Do you think I don't realize you're trying to manipulate me into doing what you want?" she asked through clenched teeth. "You're making it seem as if we're a team working together. You're entirely too used to getting your own way. I don't like this."

"I know you don't, but will you trust me enough to do it anyway?" He smiled coaxingly. "All I'm asking for is information, and that's something we're both committed to searching out wherever we can find it. Then we'll discuss it, and I won't ask anything of Sasha until we agree it's necessary and within her ability to perform." His smile faded.

"Because if we're not a team, then we're in deep trouble, Alisa. You're the one who came to me and asked me to find a way to save those girls."

She stared at him for a moment before her gaze dropped back down to the flames. "I know I did, but I was hoping you'd use me and keep everyone else out of it."

"That might have been possible if Sasha had kept herself out of the line of fire. But she didn't, did she?"

"It wasn't her fault," Alisa said quickly. "All of those girls are victims."

"I don't doubt it. I'm just saying that she seems to attract more than her share of disturbing attention. Do you disagree?"

"No. But it's not because she wants to cause trouble. Sasha knows that the more invisible she appears, the better for her. Things just happen to her because she's—" She stopped.

"Different?" Korgan finished. "And who told her not to draw attention to herself. You?"

"Heavens, no," she said. "She learned it herself. Just as Margaret did. But it was even more difficult for her because she worked at that circus with the spotlight always on her."

"You're still insisting that she can communicate with animals?"

"I'm not insisting anything. I gave it up when

you said you didn't believe me. But Masenak thinks it's true, because Baldwin saw her working with the horses that first day at the school and there wasn't any way for her to just fade into the background after that. So if you want answers, you'll have to accept that they'll be what I know is true and not what you believe or don't believe. I won't cater to your ignorance."

"Ouch." He smiled faintly. "I can't remember when anyone last called me ignorant."

"Too bad. If it happened more often, you might be more willing to accept a few different concepts than the ones you create yourself."

"Admit it. I did not reject the idea out of hand."

She nodded reluctantly. "But it bothered me that you thought I was guileless enough not to recognize hogwash if I saw it." She waved an impatient hand. "Never mind. Perhaps that makes me as arrogant as you to expect you to accept that I was worth believing without cast-iron proof."

"Ignorant and now arrogant?" He wrinkled his nose. "I'd better quit when I'm ahead. I do want answers, and it seems I'm going to get them?"

She nodded. "As you said, it's only information. I'm not committing to anything. Don't expect it."

"I promise I won't. Why did Sasha find it more difficult to remain in the background than Margaret?"

"The spotlight," she repeated. "She was a wonderful performer from the time she was four or five. Probably earlier than that, but her father kept anyone from knowing just how good she was."

"To protect her?"

"No, Sasha said that she thought he was using her as a foil to make himself look good. Dominic Nalano was an equestrian performer himself, but he was never anything but second rate until he brought his baby daughter into the act. Then he took off like a rocket." Her lips tightened. "I don't know when he stumbled on the fact that Sasha was a positive genius with the horses. But she was only four when he started using her full-time in his performances. You can imagine how the sight of that tiny little girl doing tricks and balancing on the back of those beautiful horses with her handsome father would bring the audience to their feet." She looked down into the coffee in her cup. "Particularly since there would have been no fear, but only pure joy in her expression. When I first saw her perform when she was ten, that was my impression. The freedom, the grace, the sheer joy...Later she told me that the only time she could remember being happy was when she was with the horses. She understood them much better than she did anyone else. A mother who deserted her when she was two, a father who was an alcoholic who paid attention to her only when he needed her to do something, the circus folk who thought she was a little touched because she hardly spoke. She didn't even realize how unusual it was that she and the horses understood each other so well. Because she was so bright, she picked up somewhere along the way that she was just different from other people and adjusted to it. So she kept on doing what she loved and ignoring everything else around her until she was six, when her father was killed. He got a little too drunk one night and ran his truck into a telephone pole. Then she couldn't ignore everything any longer because Alonzo Zeppo, the owner of the circus, wouldn't let her. Sasha and her father had become minor headliners in his little circus during the last few years, and Zeppo had invested in a few very expensive horses to use in their act. He was furious that he was going to have to sell them now that her father had been so stupid as to get himself killed. Sasha was terrified at the thought of losing the horses, so she showed Zeppo all the other tricks she knew that her father had never let her put in the performance."

"This is beginning to read like a matinee where the understudy takes over the leading role and becomes a star," Korgan said.

"That just shows you don't know her. She didn't

care anything about being a star. All she wanted was to keep her horses. And she did it."

"Yes, she did," he said thoughtfully. "Only six and she thought out the problem and then found a solution." Suddenly his eyes were twinkling. "Unless one of the horses whispered it to her. What do you think?"

"It's possible." She found herself smiling back at him. "But if he did, he should have spent more time making it easier for her. Zeppo let her keep the horses and take over the act but left her pretty much on her own. She not only had to care for the horses and do the performances, but since she had no living relatives, she was always having to find ways of dodging the school truancy officers. She found the easiest way was to just keep ahead of her current grade and have Zeppo write a letter saying she was constantly on tour and was schooled by a qualified teacher. It worked most of the time."

"And you're proud of her," he said softly.

"Every day. Every way." She lifted her cup to her lips. "Every time she came across an obstacle, she jumped over it." She chuckled. "And I don't mean on one of those wonderful horses. I could tell you stories..."

"You have been. And I like to watch your face while you tell them. All that light..." He tilted his head. "But you said you were wary of each other in the beginning. I bet it took you a long time to get her to tell you some of those stories."

"Of course it did. Anything worth knowing is worth the time it takes to learn. But once you learn, it's there forever." She added, "But you know that, and now you're just probing."

"Perhaps. But humor me. Tell me a little about how the two of you managed to break through a few of those barriers."

"Why? You want me to entertain you again? I'm not your personal court jester." Sasha had always been a very private part of her life that she had never discussed with anyone, yet she found she had enjoyed sharing that intimate connection with Korgan. His intensity as he listened, the way he watched her and responded...She smiled as she had a sudden thought. "I might tell you how I broke through one of those barriers. Probably the most important one. Sasha's horses. I had to find a way to beg, borrow, or steal those horses away from Alonzo Zeppo."

"Now, that's an intriguing way to start a story. How?"

"I wanted to get her away from that circus so that I could take care of her. It took over six months for her to trust me enough to want to be with me, too. But one of the things I'd promised her was that if she agreed to come with me, I'd find a way to buy her horses and give them to her. I knew she'd never leave them behind. The problem was that I worked for the CIA, and there wasn't a chance in hell of my being able to afford to buy them. Not only were they highly trained, pedigreed thoroughbreds, but when I approached Zeppo, he jacked up the price to almost double because he knew he might lose Sasha. I had to think of a way to get the money without resorting to robbing a bank."

"And what did you do?"

"I robbed a bank." She shook her head as he started to chuckle. "Well, it was really the banks of a few casinos. I taught myself to count cards, and I visited three casinos in Macao and managed to get the amount I needed in one night. But they didn't appreciate it and sent a few of their men after me to retrieve it."

"I believe my amusement in your story is beginning to fade. How close did you come to getting your throat cut?"

"Not too bad. I'd already arranged an exit strategy. I was careful to disguise my features to avoid the video cameras. People seem to remember my face."

"I can see how that would happen," he said grimly. "So you got Sasha's horses?"

She nodded. "All four of them. Though I had to apply a little pressure on Zeppo. He got greedy and wanted to keep upping the price. But I wasn't about to hit those casinos again."

"Excellent decision." He finished his coffee with one swallow. "But if you run into the need for a bank again, come to me. I won't ask questions, and I'll give you terms you won't be able to beat. One will be a guarantee I won't try to cut your throat."

She shrugged. "It was a risk worth taking. I was able to give Sasha her horses, a life at St. Eldon's where she could keep them, and a fine education along with it. I could visit her, take her on trips. She was happy." Her lips twisted bitterly. "I had no idea that Masenak would pick that school to raid."

"How could you?"

"I should have found a way to keep her safe. Next time I'll do it." She looked at him. "But I can't even make sure I can keep her safe now, can I? You've listened and probed and you know Sasha now. You've found out all the answers you need, haven't you?" She smiled crookedly. "Tell me. Who is Sasha?"

"An extraordinary human being," he answered quietly. "Clever, resourceful, full of endurance and extreme inner strength, able to think on her feet, kind to animals, able to adjust to new situations. She was also able to command your trust and affection, which is a talent in itself. You'd rarely give

either willingly." He paused. "I noticed considerably more, but that's all I needed. She could do
anything we asked her to do."

"Of course she could. That doesn't mean we have
to ask her. I didn't commit to anything."

"Not yet," he said. "But I'm not letting you walk
away until you do." His eyes were narrowed on her
face. "You agree that the most efficient and safe
way to get those girls out of the camp will be to
let Sasha handle it with whatever help we can give
her. Is that true?"

She was silent before she said reluctantly, "Yes,
that's true."

"And that's how it should be handled? How you
would have handled it yourself if I hadn't become
involved?"

She couldn't deny that, either. "I would have
probably had to handle it that way. But it would
have been difficult to ask that of her."

"But you *will* ask her," he said. "Because she
wouldn't forgive you if you'd kept her from helping
if something happened to one of those students."
He stood up and moved around the fire to pull
her to her feet. "We both knew that, but I had
to make sure I wasn't going to send her on any
suicide mission." He grimaced. "And you had
to admit to yourself that you'd probably have to
do the one thing that you'll hate above all. We

couldn't move forward without coming to terms
with both."

"Move forward." She leaned toward him, her
gaze searching his face. "You already have an idea
of something definite you want Sasha to do, don't
you?"

"She's one of the essential keys," he said simply.
"Right place. Right time."

"I'm beginning to hate those words." She added,
"And I'm not feeling too friendly toward you at the
moment. You're a very dangerous man. I can see
how you manage to manipulate all those directors
in your boardrooms."

"My least favorite thing in the world, but I have
to do it to free myself to get back to my labs. But I
wasn't manipulating you, Alisa. I just had to—"

"Move me forward?" she repeated. "Well, you've
done that, Korgan. But only if you can show me
that we can keep her safe. I want to know what
you're planning for Sasha."

"As soon as I have a firm plan. It's all in stage
one," he said. "So go to your tent and get some
sleep. I promise nothing is going to happen that
can't be reversed after a few hours. I'm going to talk
to Vogel about the drones and give Gilroy a few
orders. You're not going to miss anything of major
importance. You can still try to take over and run
things when you wake up."

She hesitated. She could see he was determined to get rid of her, and she might let him do it. She was exhausted, and that discussion about Sasha had been a troubling mixture of warmth and sheer anxiety. "You'll fill me in on what you did when I wake up?"

"Absolutely. Feel free to grill me."

"I will." She covered a yawn as she turned away. "But I'll try to be polite about it..."

Korgan stood there watching until Alisa disappeared into her tent. It wouldn't have surprised him if she'd changed her mind and turned around and come back. All it would have taken was a sudden question or idea that she decided she needed to share. He'd learned during these last days that she was always questioning, trying to find the answers. She had probably been doing that since childhood, he thought. Well, so had he, and that might be why his emotions toward her had tended toward being convoluted and extreme.

Hell, face it, he could tell himself it was bonding, but the extreme end was definitely sex. Which made everything else he felt for her all the more volatile and frustrating and very—

"I wasn't sure that you'd manage to get rid of

her. I was going to rescue you." Vogel was walking toward him, his gaze on Alisa's tent. "While you were questioning Baldwin, I was watching her expressions. At one point she lit up, and I could tell she was zeroing in."

"No rescue needed," Korgan said quietly. "You might be uneasy about her, but she's no threat. No sinister plots to take me down. She just had her own agenda and felt she had to lie a bit to facilitate it."

"You're making excuses for her, which means the threat could be still present." He held up his hand. "But I'm not uneasy about her intentions any longer. Gilroy said that everything about Masenak's camp and the situation there was just what she said it was. And she brought you Baldwin, an action that speaks louder than words." He smiled. "I'll even admit I'm beginning to have a guarded liking for her. It's hard to dislike anyone willing to risk everything to save those schoolgirls." He paused. "Even though I realize that there's every possibility she's going to get in your way. Those questions to Baldwin about Jubaldar were too pointed not to mean that you might be going in that direction."

"Not if I can help it," he said. "But I have to be prepared. I don't know enough about Jubaldar Castle, but I will before this is over. Has Gilroy started questioning Baldwin yet?"

Vogel shook his head. "Just preparation. He spent

the past hour with Baldwin listing all the information he wanted him to spill, and what he would do to him otherwise. He was very explicit, and Baldwin believed every word. Then he left him alone to think it over and went to take a nap."

"No one can say he's not confident," Korgan said dryly.

"There aren't many people who aren't intimidated by Gilroy when he makes the effort. Baldwin isn't one of them. He'll be sweating blood by the time Gilroy comes back. He can be a wonder on a job like this." He shrugged one shoulder. "But you know that. Why else would you choose him?" His gaze narrowed on Korgan's face. "Do you want me to wake him?"

"No, let him sleep. Just send him to me before he goes back to Baldwin. I might have something else for him to do." He turned and moved toward the munitions shed. "Right now I want to check out those drones and make certain the targeting sensors are adjusted correctly."

"They're correct." Vogel followed him quickly. "I checked them before we loaded them in the helicopter. Give them a path and they'll blow their way through anything around them."

"One more time," Korgan said absently. "I trust you, but it won't hurt to be careful. It might make a difference..."

MASENAK'S CAMP

It was almost midnight before Sasha felt free to leave the girls Masenak had upset so terribly in the prisoner tent and make her way back across the camp to her own tent. Not that she'd been able to do very much to soothe them, she thought wearily. What she'd told Masenak about the wariness and resentment the girls felt toward her had been true. She could only try to intercede if the guards became too brutal, heal what wounds she could, and listen to them when they poured out all their fear and bewilderment. The listening was the most painful, because she was totally helpless to do anything about the ugliness and desperation that surrounded those girls.

Try to sleep and forget that helplessness for a few hours. Think of Chaos and how she felt when she was riding across the hills. How the wind felt in her hair, and that smooth, joyous togetherness she never knew at any other time.

Back in the tent, she stood there letting her eyes become accustomed to the darkness. Masenak had supplied her with this tent but no lantern, and she didn't like to use up the batteries in her flashlight. She didn't mind the darkness when light revealed only—

She wasn't alone in the tent.

She froze.

She could hear someone breathing.

A shadow near the back of the tent!

One of the guards? Masenak?

Her grip tightened on her flashlight, getting ready to swing it when he leaped for her.

A hand clamped down on her mouth from behind!

"Shh. Not a word. I won't hurt—"

Her teeth sank into his palm!

He cursed, but his hand remained on her mouth.

And she recognized his voice. She reached up and tore his hand off her lips. "What the hell are you doing here, Gilroy?" she hissed.

"Bleeding, at the moment," he whispered ruefully as he lit his small pocket flashlight. "I risk my life to see you and you sink your fangs into me."

"Because you're incredibly stupid and shouldn't be here. Masenak has had the camp in an uproar since last night, and I don't know how many search parties he's had out trying to find Baldwin. And you come back and park yourself in my tent? You'll spoil everything Alisa was trying to do."

"No, I won't. Because from what I've been told, Alisa's main objective was to do whatever Korgan wanted her to do with Baldwin. I'd say that's definitely been done. I just came back because Korgan

added a few other things to our list." He was pulling her away from the door to the other side of the
tent. "Now will you sit down and let me tell you
about them so I can get out of here?"

"Go *now*. I don't know how you got in here to
begin with."

"Because I'm very, very good. Though I have to
add that it also helped that no one seems to be
allowed near your tent, which gave me the privacy
I needed to wriggle in myself." He knelt, and she
saw he was reaching into the flap of his backpack.
"And I can't leave now. I haven't given you the
present Korgan sent you."

"Present?"

"A very thoughtful present. But then Korgan is
always thoughtful when it comes to weapons." He
lit a tiny flashlight and shone it down on the small
black control switch in the palm of his hand. "A
little something Korgan whipped up. It can jam
any device that's rigged to wirelessly trigger those
bombs in the prisoner tent."

She inhaled sharply. "Any device?"

He nodded. "It blocks all cell phone frequencies,
Bluetooth, walkie-talkies, you name it. Korgan
developed it for the armed forces in Afghanistan.
Almost every vehicle there now is equipped with
one to lessen the chances of an IED attack."

She couldn't believe it. "So long as it's powered

on, he won't be able to remotely trigger those bombs?"

He shook his head. "Home free for about twenty minutes. After that it will blow. Korgan thought you'd need it to be very small, and he couldn't give you more time than that."

"Give me more time?" She reached out with her index finger and touched the signal jammer. So small, yet she was fascinated by the power it represented. One press and she'd be able to withdraw the threat hanging over all those girls in the prisoner tent. "You're talking about me being able to do this?"

"Korgan said you gave Alisa the information about the explosives. He said if you're as bright as he'd heard, you wouldn't have just obeyed orders blindly. You would have already thought about the possibility of having to do it yourself."

"Yes," she whispered, her gaze still on the jammer. "But that seemed...impossible. That maybe it would be me and Alisa together." Her eyes flew to his face. "But you're telling me that maybe I should think about doing it without Alisa."

"No, that's what Korgan is telling you. It will be difficult finding a way even to get Alisa into the camp at the crucial time. It might be dangerous for both of you. He said no matter what the situation, we'll give you all the help we can to make it happen and get your friends out of this camp. But he wants you to know that if Alisa had her way, she wouldn't want you to have anything to do with any of this if she could help it. You'll have to decide for yourself what's best. If you don't want to do it, then that's the end of it. He only wanted to prepare you for anything and everything."

"Prepare me to do what?"

"Be ready to jam the signal that would blow the CL-20."

"With the hostages still chained to those posts?"

"Not if you can find a way to break the link that binds the chains to the posts at the right moment." He was digging in his backpack again and brought out a bottle. "It's one of Korgan's favorite chemical combos, nitric acid combined with hydrochloric acid. Pour it on the link, give it a minute, and then make sure it's covered with dust and mud. One strong jerk will cause it to break free from the post." He sat back on his heels. "After that, all we have to do is get those girls out of the tent to vehicles and away from the camp."

"All? Am I supposed to do that, too?" Sasha asked shakily. "This Korgan doesn't ask much, does he?"

"He asks a hell of a lot. But he asks a lot from himself, too. I believe he assigned the rest of us the job of removing the students. Unless you want to volunteer?" His smile faded. "Or opt out entirely. Your choice, Sasha."

"I *can't* opt out," she said harshly. "I told Margaret once that I knew it would end up being the three of us who had to get Masenak and his men away from those girls. That no one else would help us."

"Then you were wrong. I promise we'll never let you go through this alone. We have an entire team ready to help." He touched his chest with a flourish. "None more extraordinary than me. Korgan might disagree, but he wouldn't have sent me here if he hadn't believed that I—"

"Hush." She had heard something. She jumped to her feet, straining to listen. "Masenak. He's talking to one of his men, but he's coming this way . . . Keep quiet. I'll go and meet him outside the tent."

"I could take care of him," Gilroy said quietly. "I guarantee I'd get a bonus from Korgan."

"*Shut up!*" She drew a deep, steadying breath and then pushed open the canvas door. She took a couple of quick steps forward and let the door swing shut behind her.

Masenak was standing only a few feet away from her!

Close. It had been so close . . .

She squared her shoulders. "What are you doing here besides bellowing and waking everyone up, Masenak? Still looking for Baldwin?"

"Rude. Very rude." He trained the beam of his flashlight on her face. "I'm not in the mood for listening to your nasty tongue at the moment. I'd be very careful, Sasha."

She hadn't intended to antagonize him. She had been acting instinctively out of sheer panic. "It was only a question. Then why are you honoring me with your presence? You never come here at night."

"Because you have your place in my life and it's not to entertain me." He chuckled. "I rely on your friends in the prisoner tent to do that when I feel the need. Haven't they told you all the things they have to do to please me?"

She felt rage tear through her. Don't let it loose. This wasn't the time. "They don't talk about you. I just wish you'd find Baldwin and leave them alone. No sign of him?"

"Not yet. But the trackers found one of his cigarette butts about four miles west. They'll locate the asshole once they find his trail again, and we'll have a long talk." He took a step closer and said softly, "And maybe one of those subjects will be you, Sasha. As I told you, I was curious why Baldwin was pushing me to arrange ransom for you, so I decided to explore it further. I contacted Larry Hoffman, the lawyer I use as my hostage negotiator, this morning and asked him to delve deeper into your background and find out why no one appeared to be particularly eager to have you returned to their loving arms."

"I told you why."

"Yes, you did. But Hoffman just called me back, and there seems to be a problem. Once he started to dig into Sasha Lawrence's personnel records from the school, he found he kept running into discrepancies. Nothing obvious, but still troubling. For instance, your mother, Hannah Lawrence, was no longer at the address she gave in London and he was having to take more time to discover where she'd moved."

"My mother always moved around a lot."

"But wouldn't she want to be sure to be able to be reached when her daughter was in such danger?"

"She's probably listed with one of the U.N. charity organizations." She lifted her chin and stared him in the eye. "What are you getting at, Masenak?"

"I was wondering if Baldwin was trying to set up a ransom deal of his own and ran across the same stumbling block as Hoffman. But he might have had more time to find answers. Did he? Is your name really Sasha Lawrence? I had an intriguing thought. What if your parents who enrolled you at St. Eldon's are perhaps mafia or some other crime family who might offer me a great deal of money if I realized what a treasure I'd stolen from them?"

"No," she said curtly. "Don't be ridiculous. Why would I be working in the stable if that was true? Not everyone has money. My mother did the best she could."

"So defensive." His gaze was searching her face. "I don't really care if you're lying to me. I'll learn the truth eventually. Regardless, whatever your parents could offer now wouldn't be enough to tempt me away from taking you to the mountains." He paused. "However, it might have a strong influence on Baldwin if he found out that you were a pot of gold he could tap. That might be the reason why he took off when he'd ordinarily be scared shitless."

"Ridiculous," Sasha repeated. "He was just jealous or drunk. Though you're right, he's probably too scared to face you."

"We'll see, when I find him. I'm leaning toward believing my own reason why he took off, and I know him better than you."

She shrugged. "Two of a kind."

"That's an insult. Baldwin would never be my equal. He only serves me, as you will soon." He turned and started across the grounds toward his tent. "Which reminds me, you're beginning to bore me, and I need entertainment. Any recommendations? I've been using the older girls, but I became quite excited at the event the other day. Perhaps I'll go a bit younger..."

She didn't answer. He only wanted to hurt her. She knew no matter what she said, he would do whatever he wished. She stood there, fists clenched, watching until he disappeared into his tent. Then she threw back the canvas door and entered her own tent. She could see Gilroy's shadow on the far end of the wall. "He's gone," she said shakily. "He's just reached his tent. But you can't leave yet. He's going to send for one of the girls, and that means guards moving around. There will be...disturbance."

"I heard him," Gilroy said quietly. "I heard everything the son of a bitch said. Are you sure you don't want me to kill the bastard? There are all kinds of ways to do it that wouldn't leave even a hint of evidence."

She nodded. "And Alisa knows them all, but she couldn't do it, either. Not until we get all those girls out of here. Masenak and Baldwin were the only ones permitted to rape or torture them on a regular basis, but without Masenak in control those soldiers would become savages."

"Pity," Gilroy said. He looked down at the signal jammer and the chemical solvent. "What do I tell Korgan? Yes or no?"

"What do you think? Of course I want to do it. I *have* to do it." Masenak had been gone long enough to give the order, she thought desperately. It should happen anytime now. Don't think about it. Just keep talking. "How long should I wait before I use that solvent on those links?"

"As soon as you can. No longer than two, three days max. I'll check in with you every few days to see if you need me."

"Not you. You may be as good as you say you are, but Juno is a better messenger and Margaret doesn't have to get close to the camp to receive word from me."

"Juno..." he said thoughtfully. "I thought something was going on between them. I knew a few dog handlers when I was in training in the Philippines who had that sort of mystique. Interesting."

"I'm glad you think so." She barely knew what she was saying. She was tensing up. The girl must have been delivered by this time. It would come any minute now.

A scream tore through the night.

And then another one.

Dear God. Let it not be one of the young ones.

Make him stop!

She wanted to reach out and strike and strike and strike and strike!

"Easy. It's me." Gilroy was holding her wrists against his chest. "I don't mind a little punishment, but I won't take Masenak's."

She had been hitting out at him with all her strength, she realized dazedly.

Another scream.

"Or maybe I will." He pulled her closer and covered her ears with his hands so that she couldn't hear. "Take deep breaths. Stay still for a little while and we'll get through this."

"No we won't," she said hoarsely. "We'll never get through it. I hear it even when he stops." She was clutching him desperately, and she could feel the tears running down her cheeks. "And there's nothing I can do about it. I kept telling Alisa I had to do something about it, but she—"

"Shh. And now we'll do what needs to be done." He was rocking her gently back and forth, his hands cupping her ears. "Just ride this one out with me. I'll make sure he pays, I promise. Just listen to my voice and nothing else, okay?"

"I told you, it's not okay. What are you doing? Stop treating me like a kid."

But he was still talking, and she stopped listening to the words and blocked out everything but the comforting rumble of his voice.

And several minutes later he was taking his hands away from her ears and gently pushing her away from him. "I think the worst part is over now. I don't hear her. She seems...better."

"She's not better. She won't be better until I can get her and the rest of them away from Masenak." She pulled away from him and tried to steady her voice. "You should leave now. It would be a good time to slip out of camp before the guards come back to get her. He'll keep her with him for a little while longer and then send her back to the prisoner tent."

He nodded grimly. "You appear to know the schedule. This happens a lot?"

"Of course it does. He knows it hurts me. I think the reason he stopped sending for Baldwin and using him was that he wanted to show me what could happen to me if I didn't cooperate. It's his way of training me." She shook her head. "It works very well. Because I usually don't have anyone covering my ears so that I don't hear the lesson he's trying to drum into me." Her lips curved in a bitter smile. "And I don't even know what you were saying. I was trying to block everything out."

"Good. Because I was just making noise and mumbling bullshit to help you do that. I think I ended up telling you the plot of the first episode of the Indiana Jones movies."

She shook her head in bewilderment. "What? Indiana...I remember Alisa said something..." Then she said flatly, "You must be totally weird."

"There are rumors to that effect drifting around." He was moving quickly toward the back of the tent. "But I prefer the term *unique*. I'll give Korgan your message. And I'll tell Alisa my new friend,

Sasha, is doing well considering all the scum around her. Though again, I might prefer to use a stronger term. I'll be in touch."

He was gone.

Sasha held her breath, listening. No sound. Total silence. But that only meant he might have gotten out of the camp without being caught. He still had the sentries in the jungle to contend with after he'd left the main camp. She would hear a shot or outcry soon if that happened.

She waited.

Nothing.

After fifteen minutes she gradually relaxed. Perhaps Gilroy was as good as he'd told her. At any rate, Korgan must have faith in him if he'd sent him on a mission that could have been deadly. Yet Gilroy had been almost casual about both the mission and any possible ramifications. He was just as weird as she'd called him.

But he'd accepted what she'd told him about Juno, and he'd blocked those agonizing sounds of pain and horror with his hands and his voice. He'd called her his friend in this place where she had no real friends. What difference did it make if he wasn't like anyone else she'd ever met? The whole world seemed turned upside down and weird right now.

And he'd given her the weapons to help stop the monsters. She gazed down at the signal jammer. It was in her hands now. She was responsible to help make the escape happen. But how was she going to do it? There were forty-seven girls in those prisoner tents. She should probably try to get help from one of the other students if she could. Which one? How to recruit someone reliable? She didn't know how to do stuff like that.

Well, she'd better learn. Lie here and think and attempt once more to block out Masenak if he decided not to send out that poor girl right away. She quickly hid the jammer and chemical away beneath her blankets. She'd find a better place later, but this would do for now. She closed her eyes. *Think about the prisoner tents, picture them. Think of the posts and how the chains are fastened . . .*

CHAPTER

6

W ake up," Korgan said the minute Alisa picked up his call. "If you were even asleep. You were so annoyed with me by the time you went to bed, I thought you might be having trouble in that area."

"I had every right to be annoyed," she said tartly. "I was just trying to ask you questions and find out what was happening. And all day you kept closing me out and having meetings with Vogel and your other men."

"Then come over to my tent right now and you might get a few answers." He cut the connection.

She muttered an oath, but the next moment she was out of her sleeping bag and splashing water in her face. Two minutes later, she saw the glow of a campfire before Korgan's tent as she crossed the grounds. He was standing beside John Gilroy, and they both had bottles of beer in their hands. "Join us?" Korgan looked up as she approached them. "Gilroy had a rather busy night and was thirsty when he came back." He smiled crookedly. "And I thought the alcohol might fortify me for what was to come."

"I'm not thirsty," she said impatiently. She looked at Gilroy. "Busy? Doing what? I thought you were questioning Baldwin."

"It didn't turn out quite that way. Korgan found something else he thought was more important for me to do today." He paused. "He sent me back to Masenak's camp to make sure that Sasha was safe. He said you were worried about her." He added gently, "You didn't need to be concerned. Masenak doesn't really suspect her of anything connected to Baldwin's disappearance."

"Thank God." Alisa released the breath she'd been holding. "You're sure?"

"I'm sure. I talked to her. I heard that son of a bitch, Masenak, talk to her. As I told Korgan, the only doubts he has are about who Sasha's parents are, and if Baldwin is trying to screw him out of any ransom."

"You actually talked to her?" she asked

incredulously. "You went into the camp on the night after Baldwin disappeared? Are you crazy?"

"Not crazy. Not weird as your friend Sasha called me. Merely doing the unexpected, which works in the majority of cases." He took a swallow of his beer. "And Korgan insisted on conversation and delivery as well as a report, so I obliged him."

"Thank you," Korgan said dryly.

"You should thank me," Gilroy said. "Though to be honest, she didn't need any urging to accept that delivery. She was already almost there. All it took was the signal jammer."

"Signal jammer?" Alisa repeated. "What are you talking about?"

"Since I was having Gilroy check on her, I thought I'd accomplish two aims at once," Korgan said. "I sent him with a signal jammer to temporarily disarm the CL-20 detonator and a chemical to dissolve the chain links connected to the posts."

"What?"

"But I told her that it was Korgan's idea to give it to her, and it was without your approval," Gilroy said quickly. "And that it had to be her choice."

"'Choice'?" Alisa repeated harshly. "Dammit, the minute you gave her that jammer she had no choice. It was like giving candy to a baby. She can't think of anything but helping those students." She whirled on Korgan. "I thought we'd talk about any action we asked Sasha to take. Yet you sent him to toss that jammer in her lap without even consulting me?"

"I wanted to get the equipment she might need to her right away," he said quietly. "I'm moving fast, and I didn't know how many opportunities I'd have to make certain she had it if she needed it. I was sending Gilroy there anyway, and I took advantage of it."

She was in such a rage she was having trouble keeping her voice steady. "You certainly did."

"Yes, I did. But I didn't coerce her. I just gave her the weapons to help and told her we'd be behind her . . . if she decided to do it. We'd both agreed that to involve her was the best and safest way to handle the extraction. I didn't tell you I was doing it today because I knew you'd agonize over it and delay and worry about how to handle it. I didn't want to put you through that and thought I'd merely present you with a fait accompli."

"Of course I'd agonize over it. Are you an idiot?" She wanted to hit him. "Sasha is *family* to me. You had no right to do anything concerning her without letting me know."

Gilroy chuckled. "I think I'll go finish my beer somewhere else, Korgan. Much as I'd like to stay and watch her take you down, I'm feeling a little sorry for you since I let myself become involved." He turned to Alisa, suddenly no longer smiling.

"But he was right to give her anything he could so that she wouldn't feel that helpless again. I saw a little of what she was going through tonight, and I wanted to blow Masenak and every one of his goons to kingdom come." He glanced back over his shoulder at Korgan as he started down the hill. "And though I hate not to charge you my usual exorbitant fee, anything that I can do to get her out of that hellhole is on me." He added grimly, "So let's get moving." He disappeared into his tent.

Alisa's eyes widened and her gaze flew to Korgan. "Did he tell you what happened with Sasha tonight?"

He shook his head. "Only that she probably has more guts and stamina than anyone he'd ever run across." His lips tightened. "But that last offer he made says it all, doesn't it?"

"Yes." Her teeth sank into her lower lip. "Since the kidnapping Sasha won't talk to me about anything that's happening to her most of the time. She's afraid I'll worry too much and get upset over something I can't change." Her lips twisted. "Isn't that funny? She's worrying about *me*. That's why Margaret usually contacts her. Sasha will talk to her, and we find out more."

"Not funny at all," he said quietly. "She obviously loves you and wants to take care of you. Perfectly natural when you feel the same way about her. She might be a kid, but she evidently doesn't consider herself one."

"No, how could she? All her life she's been used, first by her father, and then the owner of that circus. Now she's struggling not to be used by Masenak. I only bought her a short reprieve when I managed to send her to St. Eldon's."

"Five years isn't that short. Not if she was as happy there as you say." He paused. "Are you going to forgive me for not clueing you in about sending her the jammer?"

"No, you should have told me. You can't just try to run my life as if it was one of your corporations. Not if it concerns Sasha. You will *not* do that again." She added coldly, "I'll accept anything that you do to me because I owe you and have no choice, but even then, I deserve respect. Do you understand?"

"You couldn't be any clearer. But I told you anything I did could be reversed. You're not telling me to do it." He smiled. "And I doubt if anyone in your life has respected you as much as I do, Alisa."

"Then show it," she said crisply. "I gave you Baldwin, and instead of interrogating him, you sent Gilroy to Masenak's camp to do something you knew I'd object to."

"Gilroy and I both knew another night of leaving Baldwin alone to stew would only soften him. He

should be ready for Gilroy after a few more hours."
He paused. "And don't you feel better knowing
that nothing terrible happened to Sasha after we
took Baldwin?"

She frowned. "You know I do."

"Then that made my action at least fifty percent okay. Making certain Sasha had possession of
defensive weapons to save herself and her fellow
students took care of the other fifty percent." He
smiled faintly. "And something Gilroy mentioned
he'd heard Masenak say to Sasha put me way over
the top."

"Of course it did. You wouldn't accept anything
else. The top wouldn't be good enough for you."
After a silence, she asked, "So what did Masenak
say?"

"That he'd been investigating Sasha's parents because he'd suspected she might not be who her
paperwork claimed she was. One of the ideas he
was toying with was that she might be the daughter
of a mafia head or some other underworld figure
who'd wanted to hide her at the school for safe-
keeping."

"Not a bad guess," she murmured. "And it would
make sense to Masenak. That's his world. Sasha was
probably relieved he hadn't connected her to me. I
don't want to think what his take would be about
her being the ward of a CIA operative."

"No, he went the crime family route. And Masenak also mentioned that the reason Baldwin might have left camp was that he found out who her parents were and hoped to cash in by contacting them." He smiled. "If we convince Baldwin to present that same scenario to Masenak, he might swallow it hook, line, and sinker since he's had the same thought himself."

"How would you use it?"

"I have no idea yet. But it's a piece of the puzzle we can work on until it comes together. It might be a way to let me get my hands on Masenak as well as those students. That possibility is fading away fast." He finished his beer and put the bottle on the ground by the fire. "I'm open to suggestions. Feel free to offer any solutions as they come to you."

"Oh, I will," she said dryly. "How kind of you to allow me to step into your world. Now I know you respect me."

"Sarcasm." He sighed. "I can never please you."

"Yes, you can. Save those girls, get Sasha out of there, and you'll never hear another bad word from me." She turned and started toward her tent. "Now I think I'll go back to bed and get some sleep. I have to be on the alert. I can never tell when you might come up with some plan that you 'forget' to tell me about."

"But you'll sleep better now that you know that Sasha is still safe," he called softly after her.

She glanced back and saw him standing there by the fire, his hair touched by the glow and those silver-blue eyes searching, appraising, reading her. She was caught and held as she always was by that intensity. She was tempted to lie to him, but she could never lie about anything connected to Sasha. She shrugged. "Yes, damn you, I'll sleep better."

———◆———

Margaret was standing in the doorway of her tent when Alisa reached it a few minutes later. "All right?" she asked quietly. "Juno heard you leave your tent and told me to check on you. She's becoming very domineering since I've been letting her take over watching Sasha when we're at Masenak's camp. She thinks she should protect everyone in sight."

"Bless her." She reached down and stroked Juno's head. "I'm fine. I just had a summons from King Korgan and had to run to see what he wanted. Heaven forbid he has to wait until morning."

"You sound bitter. He annoyed you again." Margaret was smiling. "As I remember, you were trying to talk to him earlier tonight. Always be careful when you get what you want. I take it this wasn't a satisfying conversation?"

"No, I learned a few things that didn't make me particularly happy." She filled her in on what Gilroy had done at the camp with Sasha in a few terse sentences. "I should have known Korgan would try to take over the world if he got the chance."

"Yes, you should," Margaret said. "I could tell that just from what you told me about him when you had him under surveillance at the palace. You thought it was worth it. Have you changed your mind?"

"No," she said impatiently. "Of course I haven't. Look what he's done in a few days. We're sitting in the middle of a damn armed camp that could rain fire and brimstone down on Masenak. I just wish he wouldn't try to manipulate me and let me—"

"Manipulate him," Margaret finished. "That's not going to happen, and you know it. The best you'll get is a draw." She paused. "And personally I like the idea that he sent that jammer to Sasha tonight. The sooner he finds a way to get those girls out of there, the better. It makes me uneasy that Masenak's looking into Sasha Lawrence's parents. I know you laid out a false trail complete with forged documents to get her into that school. How good was that forged identity?"

"Good enough to fool any school administrator." Her lips twisted. "Not good enough to survive a full-scale CIA or FBI investigation. For Pete's sake, why on earth would I think she'd need an in-depth personnel file like that? She was only a ten-year-old girl entering a snooty private school."

"No reason why you'd dream a Masenak would appear in her life," Margaret agreed. "Only he did. We've just got to hope we can keep him from finding anything about you before we can get Sasha away from him. Korgan seems to be on the right track for doing that."

Alisa nodded wryly. "He's moving at top speed, and that means he's pushing Sasha ahead of him by giving her that damn signal jammer. It scares me to death."

"Do you trust him?"

"Yes, why do you think I went after him? He's the smartest man I know, and if anyone can save Sasha and those other girls, it will be him."

"Then after all you did to get him to commit, may I suggest that you stop all this weeping and wailing and go help him do it?"

She frowned. "I'm not weeping and wailing. I was only telling—" She broke off and started to laugh as she saw Margaret's faint smile. "Well, maybe a little weeping and wailing. But it's only because it's Sasha, and you're the only one in the world I'd show it to. Anyway it's partly your fault, because you're the one who sent me to that circus tent to check her out."

"Only to let me know if I should go see her for myself," Margaret said. "I never told you to take her under your wing, did I? Or snatch her away from that circus, or buy those four horses for her? How did I know that you'd take over her life?"

Alisa shrugged. "It seemed the right thing to do. We were a good fit."

"Yes, you were," Margaret said softly. "I thought the same thing the first time I saw you together. It's friendship that matters, what you saw in each other, not only what you have in common."

"Because I definitely don't have what you and Sasha have in common," she said ruefully. She took a step closer. "But when I met you, that didn't matter, either, did it?" She gave her a warm hug and then stepped back. "Okay, I'll admit to a *little* wailing. It was only a temporary failing and I'm over it now. Korgan just doesn't know Sasha as we do. Tonight Gilroy gave her the means to help those students escape, and she won't wait. I'll make a bet that she'll dive in right away and start working on how to do it."

"Which means you'll start worrying right away," Margaret said. "But when have you ever stopped since all this began?"

"I haven't," Alisa said. "But now I have to stop worrying and force myself to trust Sasha to know what she's doing when I can't be there for her. That's going to be a hell of lot harder than trusting Korgan." She shook her head and gave Juno a final pat. "It will be fine. Go on back to bed. I'm sorry I woke you." She gave her a little push. "Good night, Margaret. See you in the morning."

Margaret gave her a long look and then nodded. "Try to sleep." The next moment she was walking in the direction of her own tent with Juno at her heels.

She *would* sleep, Alisa thought as she lay down on her blankets. She mustn't think of the danger to Sasha right now. She would trust Sasha to be as smart as she knew her to be. She would close her eyes and let herself go back to that time in the circus tent when she'd first spoken to the magical little girl riding her white horse. Then she would sleep, and when she woke, she'd get busy with Korgan on finding a way to do her part to keep those students alive.

Remember the little girl who had been able to shape her world to suit herself. Just don't think of what Sasha might decide to do tomorrow.

———◆———

PRISONER TENT

NEXT DAY

"It's going to be better, Jeanne," Sasha whispered. "I know you don't think it will, but I promise you that we'll get you home and back to your mother and father."

Jeanne Palsan didn't answer. She hadn't spoken to Sasha or anyone else since that first day she'd been brought back to the prisoner tent after the assault. She just stared straight ahead into nothingness except when one of the guards came near, and then the shaking began again. Sasha had tried to stay close and keep between her and the mocking cruelty of those guards, but sometimes it hadn't been possible. Then that shaking could go on for hours.

"It's not going to be better. Why are you lying to her?"

Sasha's gaze left Jeanne's face and went to the girl chained to the post next to Jeanne's who had just spoken to her. Natasia Petrov. She was pretty, older than Sasha, with her pale-blond hair in a single braid down her back. Natasia was one of the most popular girls in the school. Probably because Sasha had heard she was the great-granddaughter of one of the Romanov princes, and also the daughter of some cyber executive who was rumored to be on the road to becoming the next Russian president.

She had never had much to do with her except
for the few times that Boujois had told her to take
Natasia out on the trail for a riding lesson. She had
found her a little arrogant, but that hadn't mattered
as long as she was fairly intelligent and kind to the
horses. "I didn't lie. I'll find a way to keep my
promise." She looked at her coolly. "But you're not
helping her by telling her that this is going to be all
she has to look forward to. She's gone through hell.
We all saw that."

"And she'll go through it again," Natasia said
fiercely. "We all will, whenever one of those pigs
decides to hurt or rape us. Like that asshole,
Baldwin, did me. You shouldn't comfort her, you
should tell her to be strong, to be patient." Her lips
twisted. "And then when she has her chance, she
should cut his heart out. That's what I'll do if Baldwin comes back." Her gaze was suddenly narrowed
on Sasha's face. "And that's what you'd do. Some of
the other girls think that you slept with Masenak
to get him to treat you decently, but I've heard he
took a whip to you."

Sasha stared thoughtfully at her. This might be the
person she'd been looking for when she'd decided
she might need help last night. Since she'd gone
back to the prisoner tent this morning, she'd been
searching, trying to unobtrusively locate someone,
anyone, she might count on. But most of those

poor girls were so frightened and beaten down that they appeared numb. Natasia might not be right, either, but she wasn't beaten down and there was nothing numb about her.

"No, I didn't sleep with Masenak," Sasha said. "But I would have probably been as helpless as you if he'd decided to rape me. Yes, he did take a whip to me." She met her gaze. "And I believe your ideas about how to handle those sons of bitches who did that to you and Jeanne are excellent." She paused. "As far as they go. But the odds are against you, and you'd end up dead. It would be much more efficient to find a way to even those odds and then make a move."

Natasia leaned forward. Her eyes were suddenly bright with eagerness. "How?"

Sasha didn't answer.

"*Tell me.* You know something. You have some plan, don't you?"

"Maybe we'll discuss it." Sasha shrugged. "Or maybe we won't. I don't like the way you spoke to Jeanne. I don't see how I could trust someone that unkind. If I see a change of attitude...for instance, if you distract the guards when they start spitting those taunts at Jeanne, I might change my mind, too."

"Change my attitude?" Natasia was glaring at her. "I just spoke the truth. She'd never survive if she listened to you. I never liked you, you know. You never treated me with the respect everyone else did. I tried to tell myself you were just stupid, and didn't understand that you were only stable help and didn't realize the difference in station." Her lips tightened. "But you're not stupid, you just didn't care."

"No, I didn't care," Sasha said quietly. "All I cared about was that you were kind to the horses. Actually, kinder than you were to the other students in your clique. Definitely kinder than you've been to Jeanne since she was almost torn apart by those animals." She stared her in the eye. "I'm trying to tell myself that it could be that you felt torn apart, too. But it doesn't work for me. If there's ever been a time when we should be kind to each other, it's now." She got to her feet and looked down at Natasia. "I need help, but you're not the person I'd pick if I had a wider choice. Still, you're strong and smart, and that will have to be enough for right now. So you'll be kind and you'll cooperate and you'll do everything I ask without question. Then perhaps you'll end up free of those chains and go home to Moscow to all of those adoring people who appreciate you as they should. Do we understand each other?"

Natasia was silent. Then she said impatiently, "Of course we do. Now tell me how you're going to make this happen."

Sasha shook her head. "You'll have to be content with bits and pieces." She looked back at Jeanne. "Take care of her. Try to talk to her. It's all we can—"

"Taking care of our little Jeanne?" Masenak asked from the door. "You shouldn't waste your time. I hear she's been no trouble at all since I had her properly taught at the event."

"Taught? She did nothing and you almost—"

"Quiet!" His voice was sharp. "Unless you want to see me give a few more of your friends lessons. Come out of that stinking tent." He turned on his heel. "I want to talk to you."

Sasha gave a final glance at Jeanne before she hurried toward the door. "Take care of her," she muttered again to Natasia. "I don't know how much she understood of what he said. He might have scared her again."

Then she was ducking out the tent door to face Masenak. "I'm here," she said curtly. "And if you wanted the tent not to stink, you should tell the guards to clean it and let the girls bathe. I'd be glad to help them."

"Maybe. Though I have the guards make sure the girls they bring to me are clean. That's all that matters." He smiled. "The one last night was very clean...and fresh. I enjoyed her. She screamed with joy. Did you hear her?"

"No, I went right to sleep after you left me."

"I believe you're lying." He tilted his head. "You do it well, but I've discovered you lie to me even more than I first thought. After I finished with that little slut last night, I was still restless, so I decided to call my head trainer, Simon Davidow, and have him go through those files I sent him when I shipped the horses we took from St. Eldon's."

She tried to keep her face expressionless. "Why? You said you were stuck here. It's not as if there's any urgency. You're still negotiating for those students."

"That doesn't mean I'm not curious. My horses are everything to me, and I suddenly acquired several new wonderful ones thanks to St. Eldon's." He added softly, "Or perhaps thanks to Sasha Lawrence. Those files were very interesting."

"I don't know what you mean."

"I mean that you've been playing the poor orphan telling me how you had to intern in the stables so that you could afford to go to that very expensive school. But then I asked myself: What if that was bullshit? What if I was right about your parents sending you to St. Eldon's to keep you safe from their enemies? What if there was another reason why you worked in those stables? So I thought I'd ask Davidow to go over those files and check out all those horses' pedigrees and see what clues he could find."

"Really?" she asked warily. "And what did he find?"

"Nothing." He smiled. "That was what was so interesting. I sent twelve horses to Davidow and seven of them were properly marked and documented. But there were five that had no documentation in the file. Just a photo and a name, nothing else." He held out his hand and counted them off. "Zeus, Diana, Apollo, Vulcan." He lifted his index finger. "Chaos. All very fine specimens, obviously high-end examples, and very well trained except for Chaos. Undoubtedly the best of the twelve horses I took from St. Eldon's. So why no documentation?"

"How should I know? I wasn't the trainer. I didn't handle the paperwork."

"I think perhaps you handled *this* paperwork. As I said, those horses are incredibly well trained. You obviously spent a lot of time and effort with them. My guess is that they had no documentation or details in those files because you didn't want to have problems if your parents decided to remove them from St. Eldon's." He reached out and touched her cheek. "Which they might do if you'd brought those horses with you when you enrolled at the school. The horses were yours, perhaps gifts from your parents to make it more palatable to you when they sent you away to school? That would make it entirely reasonable that the reason you were interning with Boujois was that it was a way to be close to the horses you love."

"You have it all worked out. Except that it's all completely wrong."

"I don't think so. But I'm still curious about Chaos. Chaos must belong to you just like those other four horses, but for some reason I can see he stands alone in your mind. Why?"

"I told you, Boujois bought him. I've had nothing to do with him."

He shook his head. "There's something else. Your reaction when I was talking about him was...different. I didn't put it together until I received Davidow's report today." He added softly, "You're a mystery, Sasha. It's a mystery I could solve in a heartbeat if I chose. All I'd have to do would be to bring out one of those girls in that tent and stage an event and you'd tell me everything. Of course, then I wouldn't know if you were lying. And I'd also be bored out of my mind with nothing to intrigue me here in this jungle. I'd prefer to put the puzzle together myself." He shrugged. "Otherwise, in the end I'd have to break you, and that would be a defeat for me. I want to have you as perfect as those horses you trained so beautifully. So I'll just have Davidow go back to Chaos and give me another report on him. I do hope they don't kill each other."

"You wouldn't let him kill Chaos. He's too valuable," Sasha said quickly. "I don't care what happens to your trainer."

"But I don't know if he's valuable. I have no papers to prove it. All I have is your word. Perhaps Davidow is more valuable." He turned away. "If I grow bored with this mystery, I'll decide for myself which one of you should fade into the sunset."

She watched him walk away and realized her hands were clenched. He had known the threat in that last sentence would have the effect he wanted. He might be playing a game, but he always wanted to twist the knife. He was clever and diabolic, and she never knew which way he might strike. He had already started to figure out the rudiments if not the details about her horses.

Well, he'd only scratched the surface with Chaos. And he knew nothing yet about Alisa. She could only hope that it stayed that way until they could get the hell out of this place.

But she had to be ready when that happened, and she'd need all the help she could get. She turned, entered the tent, and strode back to Natasia. "Listen to me," she whispered as she fell to her knees beside her. "Things are getting very bad and we might not have as much time as I hoped. That means I have to trust you whether I like it or not." She looked over her shoulder at the canvas door leading to the guard room. She could still hear them laughing and talking. "Those guards come through here checking only about every forty-five minutes to an hour and then they're gone again. But I can't be sure that they won't change their routine and I have to have warning. That's *you*. You keep watch, and the minute you see one of them come through that door you make noise and distract them."

"Distract them from what?"

"We have to get everyone out of this tent." She nodded at the CL-20 explosive fixed to the post. "I need to weaken those chains so that we can manage to break them." Sasha took out the solvent she'd placed in her jacket pocket that morning. "I'll apply the chemical to do it. All you have to do is keep watch." She was now pouring the acid on the links connecting Jeanne's chain to the post. "He said to give it a minute to set and then it will turn brittle."

"He?" Natasia's eyes were suddenly glittering. "You *do* have help. You can get me out of here." Her gaze shifted to Jeanne's chain, which Sasha was now covering with dirt. "Why are you bothering with her? She can't help us. If that stuff will loosen those chains, do it to mine."

"I believe I'll wait and coat your chain last," Sasha said dryly. "You're a little too eager. I wouldn't want you to try to slip out of here tonight on your own. They'd undoubtedly catch you, and then they'd check all the other chains and you'd ruin any chance of getting anyone else out. You know what he'd do to them if he thought we had any outside help." She glanced at Jeanne. "You saw it."

"We could go together." Natasia lifted her chin. "They might not know we had help."

"No," Sasha said curtly. "My rules, Natasia."

"I might be able to make my own deal with Masenak."

"I don't believe you're that selfish." She paused. "If you are, then consider who you're dealing with. Masenak would betray any deal in a heartbeat. You'd still be stuck here."

She frowned. "I might still be stuck. Who's helping you? CIA?"

"My friends. You won't be stuck. I trust my friends."

"I want to know *more*."

"When I came in here today, you had no hope at all. And you just threatened to betray your classmates. Do you think I'd trust you with information that might hurt my friends?"

"No." Natasia paused. "That wouldn't be intelligent. And I would have found a way to help my friends once I was safe. I just have to think of myself first."

"Yes, I can see that's a priority," she said caustically.

"And I might even be grateful to you if you manage to get me away from these monsters. They *hurt* me." She looked impatiently around the tent. "I'll do anything I can to help. How long is it going to take for this first step?"

Sasha shrugged. "It's actually forty-seven steps. Forty-seven chains to weaken so they'll snap. I don't know how long. I hope by the end of tomorrow. It depends how often the guards come in to check and how long they stay. It's not a question of how fast I can do it. It only takes a minute or two—you saw how quick I was. But it might have to happen when they're sleeping, or if I can find another reason to be here." She had a sudden thought. "Though I might be able to use that crack Masenak made about this tent stinking. Anyway, I have to follow my usual routine and keep as many girls as I can from knowing what I'm doing." She grimaced. "One of them might give something away. The guards are used to me bandaging and putting ointment on the girls' scratches and wounds, but they might be suspicious if I do too much."

"Then you shouldn't bother doing it," Natasia said flatly. "We can't trust them."

"I didn't think I could trust you. But I am, so

if I run across one of your friends who finds out what I'm doing I'll have to rely on you to use all that charm and influence you ooze to keep her quiet. That shouldn't be a problem for a well-bred, popular girl like you." She stared her in the eye. "Will it, Natasia?"

"Of course it won't," Natasia said sourly. "I just don't see the sense of it, and I want everything to happen *now*."

"Do you think I don't?" Sasha gathered her bandages and ointments, hid the acid blend in her jacket pocket, and started toward the next row. "So watch very close and keep me from getting caught."

CHAPTER

7

Y ou've been sitting there under that tree all day watching me like a hawk." Korgan turned to Alisa with a quizzical glance. "Why? I told you why I didn't tell you about Gilroy's visit to Masenak's camp. Do you actually believe I'd do anything that would upset you again? The effort wouldn't be worthwhile."

"No, it did occur to me, but I agree I'm not important enough for you to waste your time." She looked around the bustling camp that looked vaguely like a SEAL team barracks. "So I decided to watch you and try to pick up anything I could about what was going on." Her gaze shifted to the drones stored in the munitions shed across the way. "You're going to use those drones for the assault on

Masenak's camp? How are they different from the ordinary drones that couldn't pierce that overhead jungle canopy?"

"Faster, smaller, more powerful, absolutely precise. The usual drone is bat-blind in comparison. We won't have to go overhead and through that canopy of trees. Thanks to your map of the camp, we can skim through the jungle and target the exact area where Masenak's soldiers are located. The avoidance capability has tested out at a hundred percent as long as the correct numbers are entered. If the attack is unexpected, they'll be able to take them out with two bombs. The cleanup team will be there to take care of the sentries and stragglers the bombs don't get. We'll have two trucks in the jungle near the prisoner tent with a team designated to grab the students and bring them here to the border camp."

"All very efficient. What if a bomb hits the prisoner tent instead?"

"It won't."

"What if one of those sentries escapes and runs to the tent and opens up fire on the girls?"

"It won't happen," he said quietly. "You can sit there all day and give me what-ifs. But these men are the best, and so is my equipment. Vogel has been getting ready for this for months. What we're doing now is only the final icing on a very lethal cake. I've told them the consequences if they fail, and they won't." He paused. "I notice you don't mention the possibility of Sasha failing to do her part in freeing those girls."

"Because I can't bear to think about it," she said tightly. "You do know I'm going to be on the team going to get those girls from the prisoner tents to the trucks?"

"I never thought anything else. No objections as long as you follow Vogel's orders."

"Vogel?"

"You thought it would be me? I wouldn't trust anyone but myself to launch those drones. As soon as they're on their way, I'll decide whether to head for the camp to help retrieve the students or to Masenak's helicopter if he goes on the run after the explosion. It depends on what move he makes."

"But you're still hoping to trap him?"

"Of course," he said coolly. "But Gilroy has been questioning Baldwin all morning, and the results haven't been promising. He's a lousy liar and pretty stupid, which makes it hard to manipulate him."

"Then why not try to kill Masenak?" she asked bluntly. "You know where he is, and with all the firepower you have now, you might be able to do it."

"Yes, but there are reasons I prefer to keep him alive. A trap would suit me much better."

"That's not what you told me in the beginning."

"But then in the beginning neither of us was tempted to trust or confide in the other. You certainly weren't, Alisa." He got to his feet. "I'm on my way now to ask him a few questions myself. I assume you're going to want to accompany me?"

She nodded as she stood up. "What kind of questions are there that Gilroy couldn't ask him?" She followed him toward the tent. "Or is all this backup in case you can't use him as you'd prefer to do it?"

"You'll see for yourself," he said wryly. "You always do." He opened the tent door. "I'll feel fortunate if you allow me to get in a few words now and then. But in this case, I'd like you to keep your mouth shut so that you can concentrate on any of Baldwin's reactions I might miss. As long as you're in the mood to observe, I might as well profit from it."

"By all means," she said.

Leo Baldwin was chained to a chair in the middle of the tent. He looked terrible, she thought. Stressed, strained, and a little wild-eyed. He was glaring at her from the moment she came into the tent. "What are you doing here, bitch? Are you reporting back to Sasha? You can't get anything from me."

"I imagine we could. Gilroy hasn't really been

trying yet," Korgan said. "And if you're not polite to the lady, I'll tell him to immediately change tactics."

"Delighted," Gilroy murmured. "I have more interesting work to do than softening up this goon. He's really pissed off at that kid, Sasha, and I'm tired of hearing him bad-mouth her. You said you didn't want him damaged yet, but it's hard to wait."

"It won't be long." Korgan took a step closer to Baldwin. "I just want to ask him a few more questions about his home away from home with Masenak." He bent lower and looked him in the eye. "Let's talk about Jubaldar Castle, Baldwin."

Baldwin stiffened. "I don't know anything about it. I told you, I've never been there."

"Yes, that's what you told me. But we both know that's a lie. I want the location. I want the complete plan for Jubaldar Castle and grounds." He paused. "And I want to know what quarters Marcus Reardon occupies when he's at the castle. I particularly wish to know that, Baldwin."

Silence. "I never heard of any Reardon," Baldwin finally said roughly. "You're barking up the wrong tree. No castle. No one named Reardon."

"I'll ask again. Where are Reardon's quarters located? What day is he supposed to arrive at the castle?"

"You can ask me that all night. I can't answer

what I don't know." He glared up at him. "Go
screw yourself, Korgan."

Korgan slowly nodded. "Whatever. Maybe Masenak never took you to the castle. I thought you
were more important to him." He turned away.
"Forget about the castle, Gilroy. Just concentrate
on how to use him to get to Masenak here in the
jungle." He strode out of the tent.

He wheeled to face Alisa as soon as she joined
him. "Well?"

"I don't know what you want from me." She
shrugged. "He was lying. Anyone could see through
him. He knows about the castle. He knows about this
Marcus Reardon." She frowned. "Though he might
not know where Reardon's quarters are located in
the castle. There was something...hesitant." She
glanced at him. "Or it might mean that Reardon's
quarters aren't in the castle? Is that possible?"

"Anything is possible with Reardon. I thought the
same thing. I just thought it likely he'd have quarters
in the castle. And maybe he's just too frightened
of Reardon to talk about him. Don't worry about
it. We'll know soon enough. I just wanted prelim-
inary answers to the questions about the castle and
Reardon so that I could have a base of comparison
after Gilroy administers the zantlatin."

"Zantlatin?" She shook her head. "What the hell
is zantlatin?"

"A form of truth serum that was recently developed in one of my labs in Bolivia."

"Truth serums don't work," she said flatly. "The CIA has been experimenting with them for years, and even sodium pentothal isn't reliable. You might get a little truth, but you're more likely to get fantasy, deception, and garbled speech. You're better off getting the subject drunk."

"Which produces the same effect. That's why I thought I should find a truth serum that did work. Torture can be satisfying on occasion, but it's messy and not always reliable, either. Dr. Gonzalez worked very hard at producing a pharmaceutical that was foolproof and didn't involve fantasy but what the subject believed to be reality." He smiled. "And by combining it with certain other chemicals, it removes the memory of the subject ever receiving the injection; they believe they never divulged anything they didn't wish to reveal. It also can make the subject believe that he's felt and done anything the controller suggests to him."

She gave a low whistle. "Holy shit," she said. "Why didn't the CIA ever find out this stuff existed?"

"Because Dr. Gonzalez isn't a trusting man. He didn't want to work with either the drug cartels or the FBI or CIA. He wanted to pocket his money in a bank in the Caymans and give me the headache of patenting it whenever I chose to. I believe he's currently living on an island near Fiji."

"That you found for him? Evidently he trusted you."

"Sometimes people do," he said mockingly. "Gonzalez knew a discovery like that could be dangerous to his health and thought that I could handle it better. I don't know why. I'm such a peaceful man."

"Are you finished with him?" The tent door was pushed open, and Gilroy came out. "I'm sick of this." His gaze was on the bustle going on down at the munitions shed. "I have to check out that helicopter and do something besides hold the bastard's hand." His gaze shifted back to Korgan. "Zantlatin?"

Korgan nodded. "I want to know everything about that castle and what goes on there. I want to know how Masenak feels about Reardon and the race. Squeeze him. Record it. Everything."

Gilroy made a face. "If I'm going to get you everything, I'm still going to be closeted with Baldwin for most of the day. You don't want him to remember anything about the interrogation?"

He shook his head. "It might not matter, but I don't want to take any chances."

"Okay, at least then I'll be done with the son of a bitch." He ducked back into the tent.

Alisa's gaze went back to Korgan. "Gilroy always knew you were probably going to use that zantlatin?"

"He knows I prefer it. But a show of force is always more intimidating as a lead-in for the drug. And it's better if the subject goes under the drug thinking he's being physically tortured. It helps the illusion when he comes out of it." He tilted his head. "I don't have to tell you that I'm trusting you not to reveal anything about zantlatin to Langley. It would cause me difficulties."

"Trusting me?" Her brows rose. "How unusual. I'm surprised I've at last earned back your trust." She paused. "Since you just said that neither of us have been able to trust each other from the beginning."

"We're getting there," he said quietly. "If you give me your word, I know that no one will hear about zantlatin from you."

"Then I'll give you my word." She smiled recklessly. "But you aren't being fair. I want payback. Stop leaving me in the dark. Tell me what's going on at that castle, and who the hell this Marcus Reardon is. I promised you I'd help you get Masenak when this was over. You never said anything about anyone else."

He nodded. "Reardon wasn't in the deal. I might not even need you for Masenak if Baldwin gives me enough info."

"But I want to know about Reardon, too. And I want to know what Masenak did to you that made you go after him."

"You said it didn't matter."

"It matters. Because you know everything about me."

He chuckled. "And you're curious?"

"You can call it that." It wasn't curiosity. It felt more urgent, yet more intimate. She wasn't sure what it was and didn't want to put a name to it. She certainly didn't want Korgan to take apart what she was feeling. She just knew she had to know what had hurt him... and share it.

His smile faded as he gazed at her expression. Finally he slowly nodded. "Okay. Trust deserves trust." He strode over to the lake and sat down beneath a palm tree. "I wouldn't want to be the one to refuse to break new ground."

"Masenak," she said as she dropped down on the ground beside him. "What did he do to you?"

He lifted his shoulders in a half shrug. "Killed a friend, burned a village, destroyed a way of life. The usual things Masenak does so well."

"That's no answer."

"It's a very good answer. Quite complete. I don't believe I left out anything."

"You left out the beginning, the middle, and the end," she said brusquely. "You cheated."

"And you're not going to let me get away with it?"

"I can't do anything about it if you're going to cheat." She met his eyes. "Except be disappointed in the man I believed you to be. But then what do I really know about Gabe Korgan?"

He tilted his head. "Subtle, and yet a very telling blow. Entirely worthy of you."

She waited.

He picked up a rock and threw it into the lake. "The beginning was a letter I received several years ago from a college student attending classes at Cairo University. His name was Karim Raschid, and it took almost three months to get to me because my secretary thought it just another request for a donation and was just going to send it to the appropriate office for consideration. But Vogel ran across it because the student had also sent a copy to my head engineer in the drone laboratory in California." He smiled. "Karim was nothing if not determined. He'd decided I had what he needed, and he wasn't going to give up until he got it. Rather like you, Alisa."

"What did he want from you?" She snapped her fingers. "Drone lab. He wanted a drone?"

"Not just one drone. He wanted an entire fleet. Karim was a graduate engineering student and he'd been searching for an answer to his problem since he was a boy. He was from Noura, a small country on the west coast of Africa. It was very poor, and the only source of wealth were wonderful forests rich in timber that the villagers could harvest to make their living. Karim loved his country, and the people, and all the traditions that made it his home."

"Past tense?" Her gaze was searching his face. "What happened?"

"Marcus Reardon. A lumber baron who made deals with half the countries on the west coast for lumber rights to their forests. He decimated Noura's forests in a little more than fifteen years and then moved on to devour the next country on his list. No replanting, no fire protection. He followed almost a scorched-earth policy in Noura after he pulled his crews out of the country. The villagers were left without any hope of making a living and preserving their way of life." He threw another stone into the lake. "But they didn't count on Karim. He'd studied, and he'd found a way to take it all back from Reardon. He heard about California and their terrible fires that wiped out acres and acres of forests." He paused. "And somehow he heard about me and the drones I donated to the state to bring those forests back to life." He shook his head. "I don't know how because I'm careful to keep the donations anonymous. There are always factions who think that it's just a tax write-off or publicity gimmick. Either way, I don't like to deal with it. But Karim did his homework, and then sent those letters asking me for the drones."

She frowned, puzzled. "To do what exactly? I told you, I don't have any idea what you did in those drone labs."

"A drone can bomb a hundred thousand seeds into the earth in an hour. We're talking about billions of new trees in a year. And the spraying can help not only with the planting but fertilization and herbicides to keep them healthy."

She nodded slowly. "Not just a weapon to spy or destroy. I can see how it would interest you."

"It's a chance to save a little of the planet we seem determined to destroy. Karim's letter intrigued me. I flew to Noura to take a look for myself. I met him and spent a month with his family while I arranged for the shipment of the drones." He threw another rock. "It was a good month. They were good people. I told Karim that after he got the reforestation started and his village was back on its feet, I wanted him to come and let me work out a position for him on my staff."

"Did he agree?"

"No. I didn't think he would. I saw what he had in that village that he wouldn't have with me no matter how much I paid him. So I left Noura, but I tried to keep in touch in case something went wrong. I wasn't really worried, because Karim was smart and had let me know when he was in trouble before. I moved on to working on a new idea in the commercial space program that I was finding a challenge." He paused. "But I should have kept in touch. Karim was excited and full of triumph as he saw the reforestation taking place in Noura's forests. He saw what a boon it was to his people and wanted to help other countries that had been gutted. But he didn't want to involve me. He wanted to do it on his own." He cleared his throat. "I think he wanted me to be proud of him."

"You were proud of him," she said gently. "And everyone wants to be independent." She paused. "What happened?"

"Reardon. I'd made sure that Noura was safe from any pirating of resources again. But Karim started to contact other countries and show them what Noura was accomplishing. He talked to reporters and showed them how Reardon had almost destroyed the villagers who had lived there all their lives. He started pushing to have laws enacted to prevent it from happening again." He picked up a rock and hurled it full force into the lake. "He made himself a pain in the ass to Reardon, and that wasn't going to be allowed. There were a few warnings by Reardon's underlings to pull back and stop, but Karim ignored them. He felt as if he was getting somewhere and saving—" He stopped. "And he didn't let me know what was going on. I could have told him that—I knew all the weapons and how they could be used against him. No, that's not true. I didn't know *that* weapon, but I might have found out if I'd had the chance."

She wanted to reach out to him. She could *feel* his pain. "What weapon are you talking about?"

"Don't be in a rush," he said bitterly. "We're only a little past the middle. You wanted beginning, middle, and the end. We've reached the point where Reardon had found Karim someone not to be tolerated. He was getting in the way of his business and even causing useful political contacts to draw back a little because of the media stories that Karim was beginning to generate. He had to be stopped quickly and thoroughly and with no hint of blame to Reardon or his corporation." He looked at Alisa. "Are you ready for the end of the story?"

She didn't answer.

"That weapon Reardon found was Jorge Masenak. He hired him to stage raids on Noura and two other countries on the west coast that year. The attacks were savage, particularly in Noura. Villages burned, new forests destroyed, over two hundred deaths. Including Karim, his mother, and his sister, who were beheaded along with thirty-two other victims. Reardon's orders must have been explicit to make sure Karim and his family were singled out. The carnage was massive in all the countries he raided. In one of the raids Reardon even lost a substantial amount of money and personnel to avoid being thought complicit." His lips twisted. "The attacks were over within a matter of a few weeks, and Masenak was gone. It was like a lightning storm, a blitzkrieg. The few forces that the villages could muster were helpless because Masenak seemed particularly well supplied and funded during the raids. It aroused a certain amount of suspicion, which was dissipated when Reardon sent help and money to all the villages under siege. He came out of the fray looking pristine and even a little patriotic."

"Then how did you know he wasn't?"

"I didn't. Like the rest of the world, I was focused on Masenak and all the blood he was spilling. I was in Silicon Valley when I heard about the attacks, and I boarded my jet and headed for Noura when I couldn't get in touch with Karim. Masenak had chosen to invade Zarrit first so that it wouldn't appear Noura was specially targeted. It was a country even smaller than Noura, but it was just eighty-seven miles south of Noura's border. They tore through Zarrit and then crossed the border within less than twenty-four hours." He said hoarsely, "Masenak was very fast, very efficient. By the time I cut through the U.N. and military red tape and reached Noura with a special forces team, it was all over. Noura was a wasteland and Masenak had moved on to the next country on Reardon's list."

"You didn't go after him?"

He shook his head. "I sent the special forces team to see what they could do about locating him. I had other things to do in Noura. I wanted Karim and his family to have burials in accordance with their traditions before the media started pouring into the country." He paused. "And I wanted to say goodbye myself."

"I think I would have gone after Masenak first."

"Perhaps. You're very fierce." He smiled crookedly. "Or maybe not. Think if it had been Margaret or Sasha. I have a problem with not honoring the people I love who have fallen by the wayside." He paused. "Before I cut the heart out of the person who has struck them down." Then he added, "But the delay only adds to the pleasure because I can savor it as it does happen. So maybe we aren't all that different. If I'd gone after Masenak that day, I'd probably never have stopped until I found and butchered him. Which would have meant I might never have known about the Reardon connection. I would have been cheated. As it was, I had time to sit back and think about what had happened at Noura and notice a few discrepancies in logic and continuity. Masenak had displayed savagery in the past, but he was smart and picked ripe, prosperous areas to raid. This had been an all-out attack that yielded very little commercial advantage to him and seemed to aim principally at shock and awe. Then there was the fact that weaponry and funding seemed more than ample. Was it possible Masenak had been paid to make the attacks? I decided to take another look and see who might have benefited from bringing Noura down."

"And you found this Reardon."

"Who seemed to fill the bill. I even arranged to have a few meetings with him to check him out. I had a hunch that I'd hit pay dirt. But when I set Vogel on him to check out any connection with Masenak, he came up with nothing. Reardon was on his way to becoming a very rich man, building corporation after corporation, setting up political contacts in half the countries in Central Africa. Other than deplorable policies on environmental issues and bribery, he appeared squeaky clean. No criminal interaction with any group of any sort, certainly no contact with a monster like Masenak." He shrugged. "But I'm a cynical bastard who never believes anyone is entirely squeaky clean, so I sent Vogel to dig some more."

"It could have been a onetime transaction enacted by a third party."

"It could. But from what I'd learned about Reardon, I didn't believe he'd trust his squeaky-clean image to a third party. He'd handle it himself. If I was right, that would mean there had to have been a meeting. I told Vogel to find out where and when." He nodded. "That time he came up with pay dirt. He looked at everything we knew about Masenak and then cross-referenced it with Reardon info. Completely different individuals in every way but one: They were both gamblers addicted to horse racing, and they both had stables and horses of their own. Reardon's horse farm is located outside Marrakech, which would have been convenient to the Atlas Mountains Masenak frequently raided. It would have been easy enough to arrange a meeting at one of the races in Cairo, where they'd blend in with the crowds. We checked video camera shots at several races but found only one meeting. But it was enough to set us on the right path."

"What path?"

He shook his head and abruptly stood up. "Enough. I've assuaged your curiosity as much as I'm willing to do today. Some memories should stay memories." He pulled her to her feet. "I've got to get back to Vogel about planning something that's much more important to you."

It was, but what he'd told her was important, too. And the fact that he'd revealed those memories to her was even more valuable in her eyes. "You kept asking Baldwin about Jubaldar and Reardon's quarters at the castle. What path?"

The corners of his lips turned up. "You never give up, do you?"

She shook her head. "And the race you mentioned. I want to know about that, too."

"Once we realized that they actually knew each other, Vogel dug very deep and found out a few surprising facts. He paid heavy bribes to all and sundry and traced their relationship back at least eight years. Two very addicted gamblers who were also highly competitive decided they would stage a private race of their own once a year with enormous stakes to make it worth their while. But of course, Reardon couldn't be publicly associated with Masenak, so they arranged for the races to take place at Masenak's castle in the Atlas Mountains."

"Enormous stakes," she murmured as a chilling thought struck her. "Maybe Reardon wouldn't have had to pay Masenak for attacking Noura and those other countries."

"The thought occurred to me." He held up his hand as she opened her lips to speak again. "Later." He grimaced. "Or figure it out for yourself." He turned and was heading back toward the munitions shed.

"I will." She called after him, "And I'll find

Masenak for you. I keep my promises. I'll throw in that scum Reardon, too."

He chuckled. "Two for one? My deepest gratitude. I must have impressed you."

"No, Karim is the one who impressed me."

His smile faded. "Me, too." He disappeared into the munitions shed.

———◆———

"Tired of being Korgan's shadow?" Margaret asked teasingly when Alisa came into her tent fifteen minutes later. "Find out anything interesting today?"

"Half and half." For some reason at the moment she was reluctant to tell Margaret about Karim and the relationship forged between him and Korgan. Ridiculous. Margaret was her friend and ally. Yet it seemed almost like a breach of trust, because Korgan had lowered his defenses and shown her a very personal side of the man he was this morning. *Trust.* It was a word that had been used by both of them today... "Korgan is always interesting, but he did mention a few things I didn't know about Masenak. I'll tell you about them later."

"You're right, he's never dull," Margaret said as she slipped a water bottle into her knapsack. "That could be a very dangerous thing for you. Being boring is a deadly sin as far as you're concerned."

She snapped her fingers for Juno and headed for the door. "And it must be for me, too, or I wouldn't have let him talk me into this hike."

"Hike?" Alisa repeated. "What did he talk you into?"

"Precise measurements for the most direct way through the rain forest to Masenak's encampment from here. Plus, clearing brush from any trees that might interfere with his precious drones' passage." She grimaced. "I suppose I should be complimented that he chose Juno and me to do the job instead of one of those high-tech engineering experts he's had streaming into camp for the last few days. But I'd just as soon bow out of having Korgan looking over my shoulder. He's going to be nitpicking as hell."

"But so will you. Maybe even more than him. Besides, you have Juno, and we won't have to worry about one of those 'experts' blundering into a sentry and setting off alarms."

Margaret nodded. "That's what I told Korgan when he said he wanted to send someone with me to watch my back. I was surprised when he dropped it and didn't insist. He's polite about Juno these days and recognizes her as a valuable asset, but he still doesn't grasp the concept."

"He's stubborn. He'd have to see for himself." She shrugged. "And he probably realized that I'd go along and watch out for you anyway. Give me a couple of minutes to get my backpack." She was frowning as she strode out of the tent. "Why didn't you mention what you were going to do? I might have missed you."

"Because I don't need you. And I got the distinct impression that Korgan wouldn't want you to go. I don't know why. But he's doing a damn good job of putting this operation together and I don't want to do anything to upset the momentum."

Alisa had an idea why he didn't want her to go with Margaret: It probably had something to do with his vision of her as some kind of victim of abuse. When the hell would he get over that bull-shit? "It wouldn't upset anything to have me in that jungle watching your back and taking the notes," she said impatiently. "You're indulging him as much as everyone else does around here."

"Because he puts things together and makes them work," Margaret said quietly. "That's a gift beyond price. You know that as well as I do. He's the one who's going to give Sasha back to you. And I think it's going to be soon." Her gaze wandered over the busy encampment. "Feel the electricity? I can." She smiled. "Even Juno can. She's getting restless. If you're coming, hurry up. I want to give Korgan those figures he needs."

"I'm definitely coming." Alisa's gaze had followed

Margaret's, and hope suddenly surged through her as she felt that same electricity. "I think you're right," she murmured. "It's going to be very soon."

———◆———

MASENAK'S CAMP
PRISONER TENT

Three more posts to go.

Sasha moved down to the next prisoner in the row. Danella Cozarl. Seventeen. She was one of the lucky ones who had been spared being raped or beaten as yet, but she had watched it happen to her friends and was still terrified. Her expression was panicky as she watched Sasha dip the washcloth into the basin. "What are you doing? The guards will be angry."

"No, they won't." She was gently wiping Danella's face with the wet cloth. "I spoke to Masenak yesterday about giving you girls a chance to get clean. I've been doing this all day, and so far, the guards haven't stopped me." She dipped the cloth again and handed it to her. "But you'd probably rather do it yourself. I'll just watch and keep an eye out to make sure there's no interference from the guards."

Danella slowly took the wet cloth.

And Sasha moved a little nearer the post, her gaze on the lower guardroom door through which the guards had disappeared thirty minutes ago. Natasia had done her job and distracted them twice already today when they'd unexpectedly strolled into the tent, but it would be better if she didn't draw too much attention to herself. All Sasha needed was another moment to rub the chemical solvent on the chain linked to the post as she'd done with all the other prisoners today...

"I need a word with you, Sasha." Masenak had thrown open the side door and was striding down the aisle toward her. "Or perhaps several words."

He was angry. His eyes were blazing and his lips tight. Why? Had one of the guards seen her coating those links? Her heart was beating hard as she got to her knees. "What's wrong? You said this place was stinking. It's not these girls' fault. I'm just trying to—

"I don't give a damn about what you're doing with those stupid girls." He was towering above her. "I want to know about Chaos." He added through set teeth, "I want to know everything, and you're going to tell me."

"I told you that I—"

She broke off as his fingers tangled in her hair and he jerked her head back to look into her eyes. "Tell me. This isn't a game for me any longer. Not since

Davidow took Chaos out of the pasture to the track this morning and made him run. He said his time was incredible. He's a bloody miracle horse. But then you probably know how fast he is. None of my horses can touch him. Davidow was comparing him to Secretariat."

"That's ridiculous."

"Where did you get him?"

She didn't answer.

"Tell me." He kicked Danella in the ribs. "Or I'll call the guards to come and play with this little girl until you do. Don't make me do that."

He meant it. Try to tell him as little as possible, just enough to satisfy him. "Boujois bought him from Antonio Rossi, a breeder who ran a horse farm near Naples. It's the same breeder who sold him the other four horses. He's a three-year-old whom Rossi hoped would bring him big bucks when he sold him to a racing stable in Kentucky. But he couldn't be broken, and Rossi didn't want to injure him and destroy his value. Then Chaos bucked Rossi off him and trampled him. His back was broken, and it took him a year to recover. After that Rossi just wanted to get rid of him. He sent word to Boujois that he'd sell him Chaos if he thought he could tame him."

"Or if he thought *you* could tame him?" Masenak asked silkily. "Boujois never had that reputation, but you did, Sasha. Of course he'd buy that horse as long as he knew he had you in that stable. How close have you come to breaking him?"

"No one can break him," she said flatly. "Some horses are like that. Rossi was right: Try to break him, and you'd destroy him."

"Except if it was you. You were able to get him in that trailer after you'd freed him. So you must have gotten very close to doing it. Isn't that true?"

She didn't answer.

He kicked Danella again. She screamed!

"True?" Masenak asked again.

"Yes," Sasha said quickly. "Stop *hurting* her."

"You've actually ridden him?"

"Sometimes. Not often."

"With speed like that, it doesn't have to be often." He released her hair. "I'm going to have Davidow send me a video of him running. I want to see for myself."

"You're making a mistake. Chaos loves his freedom." She added desperately, "If they try to force him to run, he'll kill them. Or they'll kill him. They can't treat him like that."

"Then I believe I might have to take you up to the mountains to keep him company. No matter how profitable and entertaining your friends are proving to be, I may have to put the negotiations on hold for a bit. The race is a hell of a lot more

important to me than those sluts. I've waited a
long time to beat that son of a bitch Reardon, and
you might need to spend a little training time with
Chaos before he's good enough to do it. I'll make a
decision after I see the video, but I think we might
be flying up there very soon."

"Listen to me. You'd be sorry. Chaos is good, but not
that good. Your trainer lied, and you should—"

"I trust Davidow. I'm done listening to you," he
said savagely. "I've always known you were lying.
It even amused me to toy with you and play the
game because I always knew I'd win. But I'm
finished with it now. I know what I need to know
about those horses, which is the most important
thing." He reached in his pocket and pulled out his
phone. "As for who brought you and those horses
to that school, I'll find that out soon enough.
There are security video cameras mounted all over
the grounds at St. Eldon's, and I had my men
pull them during the raid. You can never tell what
might prove valuable when you're dealing with rich
parents and their spoiled chicks. My lawyer's clerk
went through them. Most of them were no help,
but this one was interesting." He handed her his
phone. "It was you sitting on the paddock fence
and smiling down at a woman. A very affectionate
smile. The woman is older than you but not nearly
old enough to be your mother."

It was Alisa on her last visit to the school when Sasha had been so eager to show her Chaos's progress. "She was just a visitor. She liked the horses."

"Another lie. You look eager, almost loving. As I said, not your mother. Sister? She doesn't look like you. Though she's extremely hot. Perhaps she's your father's mistress come to check on his daughter? Possible?"

"She was just a visitor," Sasha repeated.

"No, she wasn't. But I'll find out the truth. Now that we have this photo, we can run a facial recognition program." He turned on his heel. "Not that it matters right now. Chaos is more important than what I might be able to get for you later."

She watched him walk away and then turned back and knelt beside Danella, who was sobbing in terror. She felt as panicky as the girl as she took her in her arms to comfort her. These last minutes had been fraught with terror and confusion for her, too.

Masenak was getting much too close to finding out who Alisa was and what she meant to Sasha.

He'd mentioned a race. What race?

Who was Reardon?

And Masenak knowing about Chaos's potential might bring sudden and complete disaster.

The only thing that was perfectly clear to Sasha was that time was running out.

CHAPTER

8

1:40 A.M.

M asenak's camp is just ahead." Margaret turned to Alisa as she closed her computer and slid it into her backpack. "We've got all the measurements we need. From here, the drones would only have to take a sharp right over the camp clearing before they zero in on Masenak's troops using infrared." She grimaced. "And then if Korgan gets his technical calculations right, we'll have a very satisfying big boom."

"Korgan always gets his technical calculations right," Alisa said as she came to stand beside her. "And if he said those drones will get through this blasted jungle without crashing, they'll do it."

"Such faith," Margaret murmured.

"You said yourself he gets things done. I knew if

I could get him to commit, that would be half the battle. And the other half was you. You get things done, too. I know every one of those measurements you took was correct." She was frowning, her gaze searching the darkness. "Where's Juno? I haven't seen her for the past two miles."

"She's close. She probably ran ahead. You know she's gotten used to checking on Sasha whenever we're near the camp. She seemed particularly anxious tonight."

Her gaze flew to Margaret's face. "Why?"

"I don't know. It might be nothing. Dogs don't always think the same way people do." She paused. "But I think we'll wait for a moment or two before we start back. Juno has become very attuned to Sasha during these last weeks. I don't want to—"

Worried. Should I go to her?

Margaret broke off, her head lifting. *Juno?*

Alisa tensed. "What's happen—"

"Hush." She held up her hand to stop the flow, her expression intent as she concentrated. *Where are you, Juno?*

Sad. Worried. Want to go to her. She says no. I should go to you and tell you. Can I go to her anyway?

Is she hurt?

Not hurt. Worried. Afraid. Needs me.

If she's not hurt, then do what she told you to do. She'll know best.

Needs me.

Stubborn as always. *Come back. You can help her later.* She could sense reluctance that might soon become rebellion. She concentrated firmly: *Come back, Juno.*

Wrong.

But she was coming reluctantly, Margaret sensed with relief. Now reinforce it with what Sasha had told Juno to do. *And while you're on your way, will you tell me what Sasha wanted me to know?*

"Am I allowed to speak now?" Alisa asked as Margaret turned back to her a few minutes later. "Is Juno okay?" She swallowed. "And please tell me nothing's happened to Sasha?"

"Juno will be back any minute. She'd staked herself out in the forest watching Sasha's tent, and she didn't want to leave. I had to persuade her." She looked her in the eye. "I'm not going to lie to you. Something probably did happen to Sasha that wasn't good. But Juno said she wasn't hurt, only worried and afraid and sad. She wanted Juno to give me a message. I think the reason Juno was so on edge coming here is that Sasha managed to reach her."

"She's not hurt?" Alisa's relief was enormous. But

it was immediately followed by another wave of terror and impatience. "Why should I pay attention to Juno? You know she doesn't always understand or interpret the way we do. I need to go see for myself."

"Which is why the message went to me," Margaret said dryly. "Sasha knew that would be your first impulse. But I might mention it was also Juno's, and that should let you know that you're reacting with the same degree of need and response as my dog. I had to talk her out of being unreasonable. Don't make me go through it again."

Alisa frowned. "What was the message?"

"Just a few words, and she probably made it as clear and simple as she could since she was going through Juno." She paused. " 'Everything changed. Mountains. Hurry. Get them out.' "

"That's not enough. We need more. I can go and—" She stopped. "I know. We can't take a chance on me being caught and ruining everything when we're so close to rescuing them." She whispered, "I'll have to leave her again, won't I?"

"She didn't give you details, but she was clear enough about cause and effect," Margaret said. "And I believe the main word she wanted you to grasp was 'hurry.' So don't you think you should go put a little more pressure on Korgan? As if he didn't have enough."

Alisa gave one last look at the path leading to Masenak's camp before she nodded jerkily. "He thrives on pressure. This will only be a little bit more." She turned and started back toward the border. "And he's going to particularly dislike the idea we're applying it because Juno told us to. I might decide to wait and go into that detail later..."

———◆———

But she didn't wait or hedge about anything that had happened on their mission to the camp. She was done with avoiding the truth as she knew it. He could believe what he liked about Juno, but it was beginning to be important to Alisa that he believe in her. Hell, beginning? Be honest, it had started before she had even met him. Everyone needed someone to respect and look up to, and it was natural that she had chosen him. Just as it was natural for him not to feel the same way.

"You believe what Sasha told Margaret?" Korgan leaned back in his camp chair, his gaze on her face. "You think that we might be in trouble if we don't strike hard and fast?"

"I think it might not happen at all. Sasha said there had been a change and to hurry. She was scared, but she doesn't panic. She was trying to tell us that she's afraid everything might fall apart. You have to get those girls out right away before it does."

"Just like that?" He muttered a curse. "Do you know what that entails?"

"No, I don't, but you do. So go ahead and do it."

He looked at her incredulously and then smiled. "Damn you."

"Damn Masenak. He's the one who's caused all this. How quickly can you adjust your plans and go in to attack?"

"You're pushing again."

"Yes, I am." Her hands clenched on her lap. "And Sasha's pushing even harder, and I've got her back. How soon can you do it?"

"What time is it?" He glanced at his watch. "Maybe twenty-four hours? Is that too long? I'm almost ready. I just don't like to be rushed."

Twenty-four hours. She tried not to let him realize how excited those words had made her. "Too bad." She was frowning. "But even that might be too late. We don't know what's happening, but it has to have to something to do with a change in Masenak's plans. Sasha mentioned mountains... You probably know more about that than I do."

"I know a good deal more about them now than I did before Gilroy had his in-depth discussion with Baldwin today. Jubaldar. I can only guess about what else Sasha meant." He shook his head. "Regardless, I can't move before at least midnight or later. I'll send Gilroy up there today to keep an eye on what's going on as far as an unexpected exit from that camp is concerned. But don't expect me to wake him up right now. He's going to be very busy later."

"I could go instead."

"No, you couldn't. You're going to be busy, too. You and Margaret are going to be in that munitions room with me going over those measurements you gave me as I program those drones. Then you've got to brief the teams about every detail of Masenak's camp and the locations of all the sentries, so they won't have any surprises when they go calling. I want you to pay particular attention to the troops protecting Masenak's helicopter pad. He's so arrogant that no one gives orders to his troops but him. We might have to do something to lure him away from the main camp." He frowned. "Or eliminate him entirely. Though I don't want to do that if I can avoid it. I want to use him for bait for Reardon if I can manage it. I'll have to think about it." He got to his feet. "I've got work to do. If you want to grab a nap now, I'll wake you when I need you. Any objections?"

He was moving, planning, already four steps ahead of where anyone else would have been. Heady excitement was suddenly zinging through her. He was going to make it happen. No, *they* were going to make it happen. She shook her head. "I wouldn't dare."

"Bullshit." He grinned at her over his shoulder. "You'd dare anything. We'll just have to make sure you don't get killed doing it."

———◆———

MASENAK'S CAMP
5:40 A.M.

Message sent.

It was all she could do, Sasha thought. Now stop worrying about it.

Easy to say. She drew a deep breath as she tried to relax on her blankets. She had been on edge about whether she was going to be able to get through to Juno, and she was still tense hours after she knew that she'd communicated with Margaret. She realized it was because she felt so powerless, but that didn't help. She hated the idea of leaving the fate of those girls in anyone's hands but her own. She knew Alisa and Margaret would do everything they could to stir Korgan into moving faster, but it might not even be possible.

And what if Masenak decided to jerk her away from the camp later today? He'd been so damn eager...

Think positive. She'd given warning and she had
to trust in them to follow through. She'd done all
she could do for the time being. She'd done what
Gilroy had told her to do about weakening those
chains. She had the signal jammer device tucked
away safely to stop any detonation.

But hell, she had no idea what time she was
supposed to press that button!

Think positive, she told herself again. Gilroy had told
her they wouldn't leave her alone to do this and she
believed him. He'd find a way to give her that information and anything else she needed to know even
though she'd told him she didn't want him here.

It would get done.

All she had to do was to have faith, watch,
and wait.

None of which was easy for her.

Okay, then just be alert and ready for any emergency. She could do that.

She was definitely ready.

———◆———

BORDER BASE CAMP
7:05 P.M.

At last.

Alisa saw Gilroy stride out of the jungle and head

for Korgan's tent. She'd been waiting for him for the last two hours and rushed to intercept him. "Korgan's not there," she said quickly. "He's at the munitions shed with Vogel and a roomful of team leaders discussing strategy. Unless you have something urgent to tell him, you have a few minutes to talk to me."

"And even if I did have something urgent, you'd still make me take the time," Gilroy said impatiently. "I called Korgan when I started back and told him that Masenak was still at the camp and showed no signs of leaving. He must have told you that the attack was still a go."

"Yes, but that's all he told me. He's been too busy to take a breath all day, and he brushed me off like a mosquito buzzing around him. He's been making decisions on all fronts and he doesn't want to deal with me." She added shakily, "And that's okay. I'm not stupid enough to get in his way right now. I've watched him, and he knows exactly what he's doing."

"Yes, he does." Gilroy's voice was no longer impatient. "He's almost as good at this kind of thing as I would be. But he lacks a certain finesse in the details. He'll never be Indiana Jones." He smiled. "For instance, I would never treat you like a buzzing mosquito. I'd realize, if I did, your bite would give me West Nile virus."

"Right. But I have certain priorities, and Korgan

is providing almost all I need. The only thing missing is information. So I waited to get it from you. I'll let you go as soon as you just answer a few questions." She swallowed. "Did you see Sasha?"

"I thought that would be the first question," he said gently. "Only from a distance. It would have been dangerous for both of us for me to make contact with her. I saw her going in and out of the prisoner tent several times, and she seemed in fairly good shape. If you were worried about any mistreatment by Masenak being part of the reason for the SOS she sent out, I believe you can rest easy. Something else must have triggered it."

"Of course I was worried." She grimaced. "Sasha has been the one who's taken all the punishment since this nightmare began. It drives me crazy that I can't seem to stop it. I knew you were doing surveillance today, but I didn't know if you'd get close enough to the camp to catch a glimpse of her."

"I said I couldn't contact her, but there was no way I could keep from going into the camp," he said quietly. "After Korgan decided on the exact time of the drone attack, I had to let Sasha know. I waited until after dark, and then paid another visit to her tent to leave a message."

She inhaled sharply. "You shouldn't have done that. If you'd been caught, you could have ruined everything."

"But I wasn't caught, and I didn't. Korgan and I both agreed it had to be done, and he wasn't going to trust info like that to Margaret's canine friend." He shrugged. "And how else was I to get a message to her? Climb a tree and shoot an arrow into her tent? I'm not Robin Hood, Alisa."

"No, just Indiana Jones." It would have been an incredibly dangerous act at any time, but after Sasha's warning it could have had lethal consequences for Gilroy. "Korgan should never have told you to do it."

"It was a mutual decision." He shook his head. "No, it was really mine. I would have done it no matter what Korgan said. I made Sasha a promise. I had to keep it." He was gazing restlessly at the munitions shed. "Are you finished with me? I need to report in and then do a final check on the helicopter before it's time for us to start out for Masenak's camp. It all may come down to split-second timing."

"I'm done with you." She took a step back and then said haltingly, "Thank you, Gilroy."

"No problem. I may see you later at the trucks. It depends on what Korgan decides about Baldwin. Either I lead the goat that lures Masenak to the slaughter, or I join your team to help get those students out of that tent." He was turning away. "It's all about the timing..."

"You keep saying that," she called after him. "What timing? And what was the time on the message you left for Sasha?"

He only answered the last question before he disappeared into the munitions shed. "One forty-five A.M."

One forty-five A.M.

Sasha took a deep breath as she looked down at the single line of script on the notepaper on her pillow.

One forty-five. And it was now nine fifteen. In a little more than four hours, the attack was going to happen.

She was starting to shake. Lord, she was scared. The responsibility was terrifying. If she did anything wrong, if she gave anything away, someone could die. *She* could die.

But she had known it was coming. She had been the one who had made sure it would come. So stop being a coward and just face it. Try to pretend it was like the first time she'd ridden Chaos, when she knew he still hated her and was going to try to kill her. She had ended up in the dirt, but he hadn't stomped on her. She might end up in the dirt again, but she wouldn't be alone as she had been that day.

Gilroy had kept his promise today, and she would have Alisa and Margaret. That meant she would have someone else to help pick her up and get back on her feet if the going got too rough.

But in the end the responsibility was her own and she had to accept it. She put on her jacket and slipped the signal jammer in the pocket. She left her tent and headed for the prisoner tents. She wanted to be there to rouse the girls quickly when the time came. Perhaps even warn some of them ahead of time if she thought it safe. It was unusual for Sasha to go back at night, but she could always pretend she was concerned about Jeanne. It wasn't really pretense. The child had been hurt physically as well as mentally, and Sasha was afraid of infection.

But if all went well, Jeanne might get the help she needed before the night was over. Only a little longer...

One forty-five A.M.

BORDER BASE CAMP
11:25 P.M.

"It looks like a military staging area for a major invasion," Margaret said dryly to Alisa as she glanced from the teams getting their final orders before they got ready to move into the jungle to the two waiting trucks. "Which it probably will be."

"Which it *has* to be," Alisa said tensely. "We don't have any choice. We won't get a second chance if we screw up." She moistened her lips. "And Sasha and those students won't have a chance in hell to survive."

"Then don't screw it up," Korgan said. Alisa turned to see him coming out of the munitions shed a few feet away from where they were standing. "And stop complaining. I'm giving you the best shot I can, and it should work. It's all a question of timing. All you have to do is keep to the plan."

"I'm not complaining, I'm commenting." She was on edge, and that remark had suddenly sparked her anger. "And you wouldn't be barking at me if you weren't worried that something might go wrong. Yes, you've done a good job, but nothing is ever totally without fault. Neither of us expects it to be." She took a step closer to him and said fiercely, "And I know it's a question of timing. You've drilled it into all of us all day. You're sending Margaret to show the sharpshooters and the team you've designated to take out the sentries their exact locations, but they can't make a move before your drones attack at the camp. Our two trucks with another team will approach from the west, park in the jungle a mile from the main camp, and wait for the big boom. But we'll have to wait, too. Because you're timing the drones to hit Masenak's troops at exactly one forty-five." She threw up her hands. "Boom! Presto. No more army. Fire and death raining down from the sky. Smoke to cover us when we go to the prisoner tent to get those girls and take them to the trucks. Then the sharp-shooters surrounding the camp will hopefully give us cover fire for the few soldiers left in the camp after your bomb does its work."

"Not hopefully," he said sharply. "They know their job and they'll do it." He turned to Margaret. "Any complaints from you?"

She shook her head. "Just about your bad temper. But Alisa's right, you're only on edge because you know you're not perfect, and it bugs the hell out of you." She chuckled. "What a terrible burden when everyone on earth believes you can't be anything but flawless." She shrugged. "Though I imagine you might have come pretty close with this plan. It will be clean and unexpected."

"Thank you," he said dryly. "I can only try to please you, Margaret."

"Then you shouldn't have been an ass to Alisa. She didn't need that bullshit tonight and you know it." She turned to Alisa and gave her a quick hug. "I have to go join my team. It's time for us to start that hike through the jungle. I don't have the luxury of hopping a ride in a truck to Masenak's camp like you. I'll see you and Sasha back here later."

"Yeah, later. Take care."

Margaret smiled over her shoulder. "Always. You, too."

Alisa felt a ripple of trepidation as she watched her friend move toward the forest. Margaret was supposed to be guide, not warrior, but roles and situations changed constantly. Margaret wouldn't hesitate if she thought Sasha needed her.

"She was telling you the truth." Korgan's gaze was on her face. "There's no reason why you shouldn't be able to bring Sasha back here tonight." He paused. "Margaret was right, I'm on edge, but not because I doubt myself. I never said I was perfect, but I've done the best I can down to the last detail. It's a damn good best. Those students are going to be on Gilroy's helicopter out of here by dawn tomorrow. I promise you."

"That's good. That's all I wanted," she said wearily. Then she made a face. "No, I also wanted you not to growl at me when I dared to say there might be problems tonight. You were acting like the ass she called you."

"Yes, I was," he said immediately.

"That was almost too easy." She hesitated. "And I'm worried about Masenak. He could give Sasha trouble after those drones takes out his troops unless you stop him before he can make a move. What about using one of the sharpshooters?"

"Excellent thought, but I prefer to get him away from the camp entirely and not rely on even the finest marksman. It's already arranged."

"How?"

"Thanks to Gilroy, Masenak will get a call from the soldiers guarding his helicopter site. They'll tell him that Baldwin wandered into their camp drunk as a skunk and wanting to talk to him. That should bring him running."

"And then?"

"And then you leave Masenak to me," he said softly. "There might have to be a third drone launched in his direction to make sure he's no longer a problem."

She was silent. "You didn't want to do that. You wanted to use him to trap Reardon."

"I told you I'd make a decision. I've made it. The timing is running too close. I promised you that I'd get those students out. I might not be able to extract them unless I get rid of Masenak at the beginning of the operation. I'll take him down now and find a way to get Reardon later." He turned away as Vogel came out of the munitions shed but then abruptly swung back to her. "You don't have to go in that truck tonight. Vogel's team are experts, and he has plenty of men. He doesn't need you."

She stared at him in bewilderment. "But I need to go," she said quietly. "Sasha..."

"Why did I even try?" He was cursing softly as he turned back toward Vogel. "Then at least stay in the truck, dammit."

———◆———

PRISONER TENT
1:25 A.M.

"Burning the midnight oil?" Masenak asked mockingly as he strolled down the aisle to where Sasha was kneeling beside Jeanne Palsan. "Tell me, are you going to take care of my horses as well as you do these sluts?" He gazed at Jeanne critically. "Frankly, I think she's a lost cause. Does she have a fever?"

"Why do you think I'm here so late? She has a temperature and I'm trying to bathe her and bring it down." She put a cool cloth on Jeanne's forehead. "I asked the guards for more medicine, but they said they'd have to ask you. I'm asking you now. She'll die and you won't be able to get any ransom for her at all if she doesn't get antibiotics."

"I'll think about it." He shrugged. "After I used her in the event, she might not be worth nearly as much as before. Her parents might consider her damaged goods."

Sasha had to grit her teeth to keep from lashing out at him. "You could be surprised. Not everyone regards victims as disposable." The clock was ticking. She had to get him out of this tent in the next few minutes. "I don't believe you came here tonight to tell me to stop treating Jeanne. Particularly if you think she's not worth your while to save. Why are you here?"

"Actually, it was purely selfish. I care nothing about your little friend, but I don't want you to become overtired caring for her. I want you to get a good night's sleep." He smiled. "Because tomorrow morning we're going to go to the mountains, and I'll let you do something of which I do heartily approve." His eyes were glittering with excitement. "I received the video from my trainer. Your Chaos may make my future very profitable. I can just imagine that son of a bitch Reardon choking with rage when I take that race."

That name again. "Reardon? I don't know who you're talking about."

"You will very soon. In fact, the bastard may try to steal you from me if you perform well." He looked down impatiently at Jeanne. "So get out of here and go get some sleep. She's not worth bothering about. After you leave tomorrow, there won't be anyone but the guards to look out for her anyway."

"All the more reason for me to spend a little more time with her. I might be able to break the fever. Let me just spend another hour or so."

"I told you she wasn't worth—" His phone was ringing. He looked down at it impatiently. "It's Sergeant Rosaro at the helicopter pad." He pressed the ACCESS button. "What the hell is wrong, Rosaro?" He listened. Then he began cursing, low and vehemently. "That stupid asshole. I can't believe it. I'm going to break his neck. I'll be right there." He cut the connection and turned to leave. "Baldwin just showed up at the camp helicopter pad stinking drunk and telling everyone he has to see me. After I find out what he's been up to, I'm going make him sorry he ever caused me all this trouble."

"I told you he was either drunk or eaten by a python. I would have preferred the snake." She added quickly, "Can I stay one more hour with Jeanne?"

"I don't give a shit." He was striding out of the prisoner tent; his attention was clearly focused only on Baldwin. "I might feed him to that python myself..."

Sasha gave a profound sigh of relief. That had been incredibly close. It was one thirty-five. Ten minutes to go until—

"That scared me," Natasia whispered. "It's going to be all right, isn't it? It's still going to happen."

"I was scared, too," Sasha said. "Eight minutes. It will happen in eight minutes." She reached over and broke the chain link binding Natasia to the post. Easy, brittle... It was like snapping a pretzel. "Don't do anything until you hear the explosion. Then you can start making sure the girls are loose and ready for the team to get them out of here. I'll go to the back of the tent and start in the last row and work forward." She frowned as she glanced at Jeanne. "You're in charge of getting Jeanne out of here. She's not going to know what's going on. Call me if you need me."

"I won't need you." Natasia's cheeks were flushed. "We're really getting out of here, Sasha?"

"We really are." She felt like crossing her fingers as she said the words. It seemed to be too good to be true after all that had gone before. "Just get those girls in both tents loose and keep them quiet for the next seven minutes."

—◆—

MASENAK'S HELICOPTER PAD
1:43 A.M.

"I'm here." Baldwin's voice was slurred as he saw Masenak stalking toward where he was sitting by the fire. "Are you glad to see me? It was all your fault I left, you know. Everything is always your fault. You treat me with no respect."

"I treat you better than you deserve," Masenak said grimly. His gaze raked Baldwin from head to boots. "You're filthy and you stink, and you've caused me more trouble than you're worth." He turned to Sergeant Rosaro, standing next to him. "He's in good shape? No sign of damage or abuse?"

"No bruises. He seems fine. Except he's so drunk he's having trouble standing up. He came weaving into our camp calling your name and saying he'd made you pay, but now he was ready to forgive you."

And that was humiliating in itself, Masenak thought angrily. Dangling their relationship before his men and making him seem weak. Rosaro wasn't even meeting his eyes now. "Forgive me?" he hissed. "I'll roast that bastard over a fire like a—"

The earth shook and threw Masenak to the ground!

He was stunned for an instant and then he saw the flames billowing from the infantry quarters of the main camp. Before he recovered, another explosion hit the camp!

Attack. He was being attacked! A bomb of some sort. A drone? CIA? It didn't matter. He'd *kill* them all. He'd show them they couldn't do this to him.

He was reaching for his detonator as he jumped to his feet. He pressed the remote explosives switch.

Nothing. He pressed it again.

Nothing.

He didn't understand. This shouldn't have happened. The attack on the main camp had come out of nowhere and been too smooth, too focused.

And someone had known about the remote detonator and taken care of deactivating it. That meant they might know about the helicopter and where he was at this very moment.

Son of a bitch, he could be the next target! He had to get the hell out of here.

He started to run.

1:48 A.M.

Another explosion!

Sasha had thought there were only going to be the two, but she wasn't about to question it. It was only important that by pressing that signal jammer she had kept this prisoner tent from going up in flames.

But the girls were screaming and starting to move around. It might be only a moment before the guards ran in here and saw that she'd managed to free them.

She stiffened as the door to the guardroom flew open.

But it was Alisa who stood in the doorway, her gaze wildly searching the crowd of students. "Sasha!"

"Here!" She was pushing her way through the girls to get to her. "I thought you might be the guards." Now she could see that Alisa was surrounded by a dozen or so men dressed in the same camouflage she wore. They were already streaming forward and starting to shepherd the students out of the tent. "What happened to the guards?"

"What do you think happened to them? We were on the attack at that back entrance sixty seconds after that bomb hit." She was gazing frantically at Sasha's face. "Are you all right?" She didn't wait for an answer. "Yes, I can see you are." She gestured toward the students. "We've got it under control. There are two trucks parked in the jungle a couple minutes west of here that will take you all to the border. Now get out of this tent. It could catch fire any minute from sparks from that blast. Korgan's drones hit his target right on the nose, but there's a wind and it's blowing in this direction."

"I can help."

"You've already done your job. I want you in that first truck out of here." As she saw Sasha open her lips to argue, she said impatiently. "If you want to help, go to the trucks and do a count to make sure we haven't missed anyone. You're the only one who can do that."

Now wasn't the time to argue. Alisa was right: She was familiar with all the students and could identify them. The last thing Sasha wanted was to leave even one of those girls behind. She turned and ran for the trucks.

The air was full of smoke, and she could hear the flames crackling and the screams of the soldiers from the area where the drone had dropped the bomb. Don't think of them, she told herself. Think only of what had been done to those girls.

Then she pushed through the brush and reached the trucks. The enclosed back of the first truck was almost completely occupied, and she brushed aside the soldier who was trying to help her into it. "No." Do what she had been sent here to do, she told herself. She looked carefully at the faces of the girls. Remember every one...

Then she ran to the rear of the second truck. Only half full, but there were still students streaming from the prisoner tent. She could see Alisa and her team moving quickly, efficiently, guiding the last of the students toward the trucks. As they came toward her Sasha's gaze scanned the new arrivals' faces to identify them. Laurel. Kela. Solange. Natasia. Christine—

She suddenly stopped short

Natasia.

Natasia was at the head of the pack coming toward her, her cheeks flushed with excitement.

But where was Jeanne?

Sasha ran toward Natasia and grabbed her arm. "Where's Jeanne? I told you to bring her."

"Let me go. I have to get out of here." She jerked away. "I tried to get her out. She wouldn't come." She ran toward the truck. "I'll tell one of those soldiers to go back for her."

"That might be too late." Sasha knew Natasia wasn't listening; all the girl cared about was that she saw freedom beckoning and she was going to grab it. Sasha whirled and elbowed her way through the crowd of students to run back through the smoke toward the prisoner tent. Her eyes were stinging now, and she could barely make out the figures of several of Masenak's soldiers who had escaped the explosion as they staggered across the camp in confusion.

Shots... She heard shots from the edge of the camp. Sentries?

Don't worry about it. Concentrate on finding Jeanne.

Then she was back in the prisoner tent.

Fire!

Alisa had been right in her prediction; the north corner of the tent was now enveloped in flames.

Screams.

More smoke.

She was coughing, her gaze searching the tent. "Jeanne!"

No answer.

The smoke was growing heavier.

But she heard someone whimpering, coughing.

"Jeanne." She made her way toward the sound. "Jeanne! Answer me. Where are you?"

No answer. But that coughing sounded a little closer.

And then she saw Jeanne Palsan, huddled on the floor near the guardroom door. She was gasping, struggling to breathe. But at least Natasia had broken her chain and dragged her this far before she'd abandoned her, Sasha thought bitterly.

She slipped her arm around her. "Come on, Jeanne. Help me. We're getting out of here." She half pulled, half lifted the young girl to her feet. She wasn't heavy, but she was a deadweight. "Just help me a little. It's going to be fine. We're going to get away from them."

"You bet we are." Alisa had come back into the tent and was slipping her arm around Jeanne from the other side. "Keep walking, Sasha. We only have another few minutes to get out of here before this tent goes up in flames."

"Natasia . . . told you I was . . . here?" Sasha's throat

felt raw, but she managed to get the words out. "She said...she'd tell someone."

"Only after I cornered her. I saw her talking to you and then I didn't see you." She was coughing. "Hurry. Vogel already sent the first truck toward the border. I want you out of this damn country."

"I am hurrying." And Jeanne didn't seem nearly as heavy now that Alisa was with her, Sasha thought. Everything was always easier when Alisa was there. Together they managed to get Jeanne out of the tent in the next few minutes, laying her on the ground to see if she needed resuscitation. She was pale and gasping a little for breath, but she didn't appear to be injured in any other way. "She seems okay, but we have to get her to a doctor. They...did things to her. She was hurt even before this happened."

"This must be Jeanne? I'll have one of the guys bring a stretcher." Alisa was pulling out her phone. "She'll have medical attention as soon as we get her to the border. The director will probably want to whisk all the students away to some secure European facility, but we'll make certain that she—"

She stopped as a whistle of sound broke the silence.

At first, Sasha thought it was the crackling snap of the fire in the tent behind them. Then she saw Alisa jerk and cry out and saw the blood flowing down the front of her jacket!

Sasha screamed as she watched Alisa fall to the ground.

A bullet, she realized in panic. Shot. Alisa had been shot!

"She's not dead yet," Masenak said from where he stood just inside the tent behind Sasha. His gun was now pointed at her. "I was careful to aim for the upper body. But if you don't come back into this tent and go with me out the main door, I'll put another bullet into her that she won't have a chance of surviving." His lips twisted. "I take it that would make a difference to you, since she must have been the person who paid for your tuition all those years. Am I correct?"

Nightmare. Alisa was so still, her eyes closed. "Yes," Sasha said hoarsely. "She's bleeding. You're sure she's not dead now?"

"Very certain."

"Then will you let me stop the bleeding?" She dropped to her knees on the ground beside Alisa. "I'll do anything you say, if you'll let me help her."

"We don't have time. If you're lucky, one of the bitch's friends will find her and stop the bleeding. All you'll get from me is that I won't finish the job this time." His eyes were blazing. "Do what I tell you. You don't realize how much I want to hurt you. I don't know how you managed to do this to me, but you had something to do with it." He spoke through bared teeth. "I want you *dead*. But you're still useful, so I'll let you give me what I need." He motioned with the gun. "Move."

She didn't move. "Let me stop the blood. I'll be quick. Why should I trust that she won't die anyway if I leave her like this?" She added hotly, "And if you shoot Alisa again, I swear that you won't get anything from me."

He muttered an oath. "You have one minute. Do it."

She swiftly ripped off part of her shirt and belt and fashioned a pressure bandage on the wound in Alisa's shoulder. *Be safe*, she prayed. *You're strong. I need you. You've always told me that we were a team no one could separate. Don't you leave me now.* Then she jumped to her feet and moved toward him. "You won't get away, you know. Alisa is much cleverer than you, and she's not alone."

"Yes, I will. I've got a reputation for slipping away from my enemies, and this will be no different. All this smoke and confusion will only help." He pushed her toward the canvas door at the side entrance. "And they'll probably think I'm dead anyway. Your friends took the precaution of blowing up my helicopter after luring me toward it with that fool, Baldwin. By the time they discover that I'm not also a fool and among the dead, we'll be gone. I always have a standby plan. We'll be going upriver and be picked up in one of the northern villages and taken to the mountains."

"It *will* be different," she said fiercely. "You're slipping away with practically nothing. Those girls are free now and every parent and organization you were taunting all these weeks will be on the hunt for you. And I don't have to tell you that you're a laughingstock to the CIA now."

"Only until the next raid." His fingers bit into her arm as he pushed her toward the jungle. "Then I'll show them all I won't be laughed at. And as soon as I get to the mountains, you're going to help me recoup everything I've lost here. You and your Chaos..."

CHAPTER

9

S he was being carried...
  Korgan. Alisa knew that scent...Dark, spicy, clean. The fragrance that had clung to her when she'd left his tent that morning after she'd brought him Baldwin. But Korgan shouldn't be carrying her. Not now. Wrong...

And there was pain, and that was wrong, too.

"Put me...down." She tried to open her eyes. "I think...you're hurting me."

"I'm not hurting you," he said roughly. "You managed to do that for yourself. And I'll put you down as soon as I get you into my tent to wait your turn at boarding. Gilroy wanted to load all the students before they put you on the helicopter so you won't be jarred."

Helicopter? "We're back at base camp? I don't remember..." Why didn't she remember? "And I didn't... hurt myself." Why was he so angry?

She must have asked the question out loud because he answered. "Because you would have been safe if you'd done what I told you." In spite of the harshness of his tone, he was putting her down on the cot with utmost gentleness. But she still tensed as hot pain shot through her upper shoulder. "Why couldn't you have just stayed in the truck with Vogel?"

"Sasha. I told you... We had to get them out." But the thought of Sasha had started alarm bells ringing. Her eyes finally flew open. "Sasha. Where's Sasha? Is she okay?" She was struggling, fighting to sit up. More pain. Ignore it. "She was with me. And that poor child, Jeanne Palsan... She needed a doctor."

"Stop *fighting* me." Korgan's arms tightened around her. "You've been shot, and I'm trying to keep you from doing any more damage to yourself." He added jerkily, "I won't lie. Sasha wasn't with you when we found you. But I believe she must have been there because it had to have been her who rigged this tourniquet to ease the blood flow. If she was well enough to do that, then chances are she wasn't hurt herself. Masenak must have just taken her with him."

"Masenak?" she whispered. She couldn't com-
prehend the horror. "It was Masenak?"

"Jeanne Palsan was hysterical when Vogel found
the two of you, but she kept screaming his name
and begging Vogel to keep Masenak from taking
her, too." His lips tightened. "And there was a
sighting of him at the main camp after that third
drone took out the helicopter pad."

"You said Masenak would be killed. You promised
me." Her voice was shaking. "He'll be in a rage.
He'll be blaming everyone. He'll be blaming *her*."

"I've sent Vogel and a team to find them with orders
to kill Masenak on sight and bring her back."

"If she's still alive." That thought was too agonizing, and she couldn't take it. "She *is* alive." She was
trying to sit up again. "I have to go after her myself.
I'll find her."

"You're not going anywhere." He nodded at
someone out of her range of vision, and she felt a
prick as the hypodermic entered her arm. "Except
to the same hospital we're taking Jeanne Palsan." He
took her hands in his own as she tried desperately
to strike out at him. "Yes, I know you believe no
one can take care of Sasha but you, and that I failed
you by not killing Masenak. You're right, I did fail
you, but I won't do it again. I'll get that son of a
bitch, but I won't risk you dying. It's going to be
my way, Alisa."

The tent was beginning to dim around her. She was only aware of his face and the intensity of those glittering silver eyes gazing down at her. "Everything is always your...way. But you couldn't stop Masenak from taking her. I think I...hate you." Her voice sounded blurred even to her. "If she dies...I'll kill you, Korgan."

"I know that, too." His lips twisted. "Either way there will be punishment in my future. Now let yourself go so that I can get you on that helicopter. The sooner I get you to that hospital, the sooner you'll be able to go after me with knives drawn." He paused. "But while you're planning my demise, it might comfort you to go to sleep remembering how strong your Sasha is and how she's stayed alive all this time. There's no reason why she won't be able to hold on until we take the bastard out."

He was right, she thought dazedly. Sasha would never give up, and Masenak had wanted her alive from the time he'd taken her from that stable. It was only panic that had made Alisa forget that in this moment. But Korgan had not forgotten, and he'd given her this lifeline to hold on to when the darkness came.

And then the darkness was there...

UNIVERSITY HOSPITAL
GENEVA, SWITZERLAND
THREE DAYS LATER

Sasha!

Alisa's eyes flew open and she sat up straight in bed. Pain! Ignore it. She had to get to Sasha.

"Lie still." Korgan's hands were pushing her down. "You can't go anywhere yet. You've been out for three days, and if you don't keep quiet, I'll have to ask those doctors to put you under again. You'll hurt yourself if you—Shit!" He grabbed the fist with which she'd just struck his mouth and pinned it to the bed. "Correction. You'll hurt *me* if you continue to fight," he said grimly. "And that's not going to happen until you're able to do it with a clear head. So just lie there and I'll let you stay awake and you might get some answers. Deal?"

She shook her head dazedly. "Sasha..." Something was terribly wrong... She had to gather her thoughts and try to remember.

Korgan's tent at base camp.

Korgan looking down at her and telling her that even if Sasha was lost, he'd find her.

Masenak!

"You're tensing up," Korgan said. "But I don't think you're ready to sock me again. I believe you might be ready to listen."

"Only if you tell me that you know Sasha is still alive," she said shakily. "That's the only thing that matters."

"I believe there's a very good chance she's still alive," he said. "As I told you, she's tough, and he wants to keep her alive." He paused. "And when Vogel showed up here at the hospital this morning, he gave me a report that he and his team had tracked down Masenak. He escaped upriver and then boarded a helicopter at a village on the Moroccan border." He smiled faintly. "He wasn't alone, Alisa."

"You're sure?" she whispered. "He must have been so angry with her."

"Not angry enough to cheat himself out of something he wanted just to get revenge. I can't give you a guarantee, but it was a young girl who accompanied him on that helicopter, ponytail, boots, riding apparel that was dirty and smoke-stained. Know anyone else who fits that description?"

"No." She closed her eyes for an instant. Alive. Sasha was *alive*. Then her lids flicked open. "But why can't you give me a guarantee? Couldn't Vogel find out where Masenak went in that helicopter? Couldn't he follow him?"

"Never satisfied. Masenak had been gone for over a day when Vogel tracked him down. He called me yesterday and asked me if he should try to keep on tracking him. I told him to come back here. I think we both have an idea where Masenak is heading."

"Jubaldar."

He nodded. "You've said he's been threatening to take her to the mountains since the day of the kidnapping. Now that there are no longer any hostages for him to barter, he has no excuse not to do it."

"But we can't be certain she has any real value to him to balance what he believes she's done," she said fiercely. "He swore that if anyone tried to go rescue those students, he'd kill them all. Now that they're free, he'll feel frustrated and humiliated. He'll be striking out in all directions, and she'll be the only one in reach. He could change his mind at any moment. There's no time to waste. I have to go after her."

"Not before we're ready. You're wrong, there's still time." He looked down at her wrists, still pinned to the bed. "And if you promise not to try to take me down again, we can discuss it."

She'd almost forgotten that he was still holding her down. "It was your fault. You shouldn't have said you were going to have the doctors put me to sleep again."

"Obviously," he said dryly. "May I point out that you weren't behaving reasonably? I was afraid you might hurt yourself. Do I have that promise?"

She nodded. "As long as you don't threaten me again. Three days? There was no way I should have been unconscious for three days. You must have told them to do it. Just like you told them to give me that shot in your tent."

He nodded. "I admit it seemed the simplest way of handling the situation until I got it partially under control. But there were medical reasons for me to do it or the doctors wouldn't have agreed." He released her and dropped down into a chair beside the bed. "You're at the University Hospital in Geneva, Switzerland. I use this hospital whenever I can when I'm in Europe or Africa. It's only a little over two hours from Morocco by air, and the doctors are brilliant. But there's no way they'd interfere with the treatment of a patient just to keep me happy."

She looked at him skeptically. "Everyone wants to keep you happy."

"Some people have ethics. Inconvenient, but refreshing. However, I might have mentioned that once you woke, your condition might deteriorate due to stress. Which it clearly has. Your wound itself wasn't serious, but you'd lost a lot of blood. If Sasha hadn't rigged that pressure bandage, you'd have been in really bad shape. Still, by the time we landed the helicopter at the coast, you were in shock. I put Gilroy in charge of dealing with the

CIA bigwigs who were there to meet us and loaded you, Margaret, and Jeanne Palsan on a medical jet to Geneva."

"Gilroy? I wouldn't think he'd be diplomatic enough to handle a situation that delicate."

"You'd be surprised. Gilroy can handle almost anything that comes his way." He made a face. "Though sometimes that only constitutes holding off the dragons until he can set them loose on me. He's not self-sacrificing by any means."

"He probably regards that as being entirely fair. I've can't fault anything he's done in regard to helping Sasha. He's been wonderful." She jumped to something else he'd mentioned. "Margaret? She's here, too?"

"She wasn't going to trust me to take care of you. Besides, I thought I might need help with Jeanne. You wanted her to have immediate medical treatment, but every time I mentioned her going home to her parents, she got hysterical. Margaret seemed to be able to keep her calm." He paused. "That poor kid wouldn't let anyone near her but Margaret."

"You can hardly blame her after what she's gone through. I'm glad Margaret is here."

"She's already persuaded her to start therapy." He grimaced. "But Margaret left it up to me to call her parents and talk them into leaving her alone until she feels she can face them. That won't be easy."

"But you'll be able to do it. Stop whining. Her parents will be flattered you called and grateful that you were able to get her away from the monsters. You'll know exactly what to say, you always do. You're the golden boy."

"Was that bitterness?"

"No, just the truth," she said wearily. "You have talent and people skills. Use both of them to help Jeanne. That's what Sasha would want you to do. When we get her back, I want to be able to give her good news."

"I'll do my best."

"And I'm sure it will be a superb best." She was silent a moment and then added, "Much better than when you said you'd make certain Mase-nak wouldn't be anywhere around to cause Sasha danger."

"Now, that *was* bitter," he said. "But I deserved it. The drone explosions on the infantry at the main camp were right on schedule. I had to stagger the delivery of the bomb I'd zeroed in to take out Masenak and the crew at the helicopter pad so that it wouldn't interfere with the main strike. There couldn't be any interference with the trajectory because the drones were spearheaded at such a low altitude. But I calculated that the shock and disorientation Masenak would feel after the first strike would still give me the time I needed to do it. Only it didn't work out that way. That bomb at the pad landed only a little less than a minute behind those first drone strikes on the main camp, but evidently that was enough time for Masenak to recover and guess he might also be a target. That helicopter pad and every single person at the site was destroyed. Except Masenak. The bastard must have hit the ground running and bolted immediately."

A little less than a minute, she thought. Such a short time in that instant of fire and screams and exploding bombs. Who would guess that Masenak would be able to realize what was happening and react that fast to save himself? "But he still wanted Sasha enough that he ran toward the main camp to get her."

"And almost killed you," he said harshly. "I can't blame you for being bitter. But you're no more bitter than I am. I'll make this right, Alisa."

She was silent a moment. "I'm not really bitter. Though I want to be." She realized to her surprise that this was true. She was sick with anger and worry, but Korgan's plan should have worked. He'd done what he'd thought would get rid of Masenak and protect Sasha. "You told me how slippery Masenak has proved over the years. You did the best you could. It's partly my fault. I should have kept a better eye on Sasha. And I trusted you too much. I thought you were different. I should know by now I can't trust anyone but myself."

He flinched. "I suppose you're being very generous considering."

"Yes. Only because I'm feeling as guilty about my part in this as I am about yours. Though there's a good chance I would have killed you if that miscalculation had cost Sasha her life. You might still be on the hook if I find out that it did. And yes, you'll definitely make it right."

"That's what I said," he said curtly. He got to his feet. "And now I'll go tell the nurse to bring your breakfast while I pay a visit to Margaret and let her know you're awake. She'll want to see you right away." His lips twisted. "Providing you still trust her."

"Did that sting? Why should you care what I think? Of course I trust her. We've earned each other's trust." She looked down at her bandaged shoulder. "How soon can I get out of this hospital?"

"Before the end of the day. I'll clear it with the staff. You'll still be a little weak, but nothing you can't handle. And that should give you time to rest and for us to get some kind of plan together about Jubaldar."

"I want to leave now."

He shook his head. "Later. I'm expecting a call from Gilroy, and I want info from him before I make a move." He put up his hand as she opened her lips to speak. "No. I'll get you Sasha, but it will be my way. You're not the only one who hates making mistakes. This one hit me damn hard, and I'm not going to risk making another one. I'll let you have input, but you won't be in control."

"The hell I won't."

"Exactly. I'll see you later."

He strode out of the room.

———◆———

"You look better than I thought you would," Margaret said when she walked into Alisa's hospital room an hour later. "I was getting tired of seeing you snoozing for the past few days." She gave Alisa a careful hug. "How do you feel?"

"How do you think I feel? I'm fine. I need to get out of here and Korgan is being Korgan. I should have been out of here two days ago. He said that he didn't influence those doctors, but everyone does what he—"

"They tried to let you regain conscious," Margaret interrupted, "but you were . . . agitated. They decided to give you another day."

"Agitated?"

"Sasha," she said quietly. "You were tossing and turning and calling to her. They were afraid you'd damage your shoulder again." She sat down in the chair. "But Korgan said you'd hate to be kept under for any longer than they had to, or to be restrained. He said if they brought you out of it slowly, he'd stay with you through the night and make sure you didn't hurt yourself."

"He didn't tell me that." But she might have been aware that he was there, she realized suddenly. That presence in the darkness, that hand holding her own had been almost dreamlike. Not that she'd needed him there. She didn't need anyone. "But that doesn't make any difference. It just shows he's still trying to control me...and Sasha. I can't let him do that, Margaret."

"Yes, you can," she said gently. "Not entirely, but you've always been one to take what you need from every situation. And this time, because it's Sasha, you're feeling possessive and don't want to let Korgan have his way. You know damn well you need him, and you should work it out and make it happen. He's feeling so guilty that you only have to give a little and he won't try to trample you."

She shook her head doubtfully. "Maybe."

"He's worth an effort. He persuaded the hospital to let Juno stay with Jeanne in her room. Juno's doing an amazing job with her. She's not a therapy dog, but I think she's doing as much as that therapist Korgan hired with all the letters after her name."

"Of course you'd think that. It's Juno." Her smile faded. "How is Jeanne?"

"They cleared up the infection. Otherwise, not so good. It's going to take a long time. By the way, drop in to see her before you leave. All she remembers is you lying bleeding on the ground beside her. She's still not sure you're alive. She's not certain about anything. But Korgan is sparing no expense, and he won't let her leave this hospital until she's on her way back." She paused. "When he saw how good Juno was with her, he asked me to get a therapy dog for her when she did go home. He's very intuitive. He thought the problem she was having about seeing her parents might be that she was afraid they'd judge her. What she went through was so horrific, she's confused and scared they might blame her. Just telling her that none of it was her fault isn't doing any good right now. But she can see Juno is all love and totally accepting... it's healing."

"I can see how it would be." She found herself smiling. "And I'll bet that you already have a therapy dog picked out for her."

She nodded. "Lili, one of Juno's pups, has the perfect temperament as a therapy dog and will be just right for Jeanne. Korgan is flying Lili in from

Summer Island in the Caribbean where she's been in training. She should be arriving early tomorrow morning."

"I'm a little surprised you're not going to let Juno go home with her for a while."

"Jeanne needs permanence. Juno decided she belonged to me a long time ago. For which I'm duly grateful. Besides, I might need her when we go after Sasha. So I'll pick Lili up and bring her here and let Jeanne become accustomed to her while Juno is still with her. Then we'll fly back to Morocco the next day and join you and Korgan."

"If Korgan decides he's going to let me come along," she said caustically. "He made it clear that he's in charge."

"In which case we'll just go after Sasha ourselves. But that's not the way it's going to turn out. I've watched Korgan during these last days. He's fairly incredible. We were only aware of him as top gun and head military honcho before." She leaned forward. "In between watching over you and making certain Jeanne had everything she needed, he was on the phone with CIA director Lakewood, smoothing down ruffled feathers and persuading them that they should take full credit for the rescue. He said he wouldn't dispute anything they said to that effect." She paused. "But only if they named you as the heroine of the hour, you kept your job, and they didn't press any charges against you for insubordination. He got what he wanted. It wasn't easy. Lakewood was furious with him, and it didn't matter that he'd saved not only those students but Lakewood's own ass. Korgan pulled every string he had, and you came out of it smelling like the proverbial rose."

"But without Sasha."

"That will be next on the agenda. He's cleared the decks. He's ready to support you. He's just scared he's going to get you killed. I don't imagine he's a man who is often scared, and he doesn't know how to handle it." She reached out and pressed Alisa's hand. "Don't mess this up because you want to cling to your independence and not let anyone take care of Sasha but you. You've always closed every-one out of what the two of you have together."

"Not you."

"No, I was allowed to slip in under the wire. But you can't afford to close Korgan out. It would be dangerous for Sasha." She was silent a moment. "And not fair to Korgan. He promised he'd get those students out of that camp, and he did. That was practically a miracle. Yes, he failed to free Sasha, but he was within a heartbeat of taking out Masenak and getting her, too. Now it's only fair to give him another chance to do it with our full cooperation."

Fairness is important to me. I regard it as one of the prime virtues in a corrupt world.

"Maybe you're right," she said slowly. "I know Korgan believes in fairness, too. I'll think about what you've said." Her voice dropped to a whisper. "I'm just so afraid for her, Margaret. I thought I was close to having Sasha back. Then I wake from this nightmare and find her gone again and Korgan telling me what to do. It made me feel helpless, as if he was taking her away from me again."

"Bullshit. You've never been helpless in your life." She got to her feet and bent down to brush her lips against Alisa's cheek. "By all means, get your thinking straight. It's Masenak who took her away. It's Korgan who's going to get her back, along with help from us and any friends he pulls into the mix. If you don't want to trail behind him, jump ahead." She was heading for the door. "I suppose you wouldn't pay any attention if I told you to rest. Do what you like. If you feel like bathing and dressing, I think you'll find a complete wardrobe that Korgan ordered for you in that closet. He had some expert flown in from a Paris department store asking me about preferences. I should really get back to Jeanne. Though she scarcely misses me if Juno is around. I'll see you later."

As usual, Margaret was moving, planning, trying to keep ahead of any problem as she'd just told Alisa to do. Evidently Korgan had been also doing that during these last few days. She was the only one who'd been lying here, wounded, weak, and doing nothing to address the danger to Sasha but worry and complain.

That had to change immediately. Think. Analyze. Take the situation apart and put it back together in the way she wanted to go. When Korgan came through that door, she needed to be ready for him...

———◆———

3:35 P.M.

Alisa was standing at the window, fully dressed, and gazing out at the Alps in the distance when Korgan came into her room. She glanced at him over her shoulder. "It's a beautiful, serene view." She made a face. "But looking at it didn't make me feel serene. It reminded me of those mountains where Jubaldar Castle is supposed to be located."

"The Atlas Mountains are reputed to be beautiful, too," Korgan said. "But I don't think either of us is going to find them serene." He was scanning her expression. "And when I left here, serenity was the last thing you were after. You were in fighting mode. Something's changed."

"I'm still in fighting mode." She turned to face him. "I'm just trying to control it until I find the right person to strike out at. Margaret said I wasn't being reasonable or fair."

"And you always pay attention to Margaret," he said mockingly.

"So do you. You listened to her about Jeanne and then you reached out and tried to solve the problem. And you had big doubts about Margaret and Juno in the beginning, but it didn't stop you learning to respect her in other ways."

"Anything else would've been both foolish and unfair. I hope I'm neither." He was still looking at her speculatively. "And those words were remarkably generous when you're so upset with me. Evidently Margaret has more influence than I thought."

"Because I won't have her believing I'm unfair." She tapped her chest. "And I won't believe I'm unfair, either, just because you did something that hurt me and I couldn't think through the pain." She drew a deep breath. "But I've thought it through and I'm okay now. I won't let it get in the way of us working together."

"I'm glad to hear that."

"It's going to be hard for me," she said stiltedly. "I have to warn you about that. This means too much to me, and I might explode every now and then if things don't go as they should. But I want you to know that I realize you tried to do the right thing."

"I just didn't do it," he said bitterly. "And I could have gotten you killed. So I can take an explosion now and then. But I'll just have to make sure that everything does go as it should from now on." He glanced at the sling she was wearing. "The doctors told me they'd released you, but why don't you sit down instead of standing there staring at the scenery? I know they told you to take it easy for a while."

"I don't really need this sling. The doctors just said it was a precaution. I feel fine. Well, almost fine. A little woozy." She sat down. "I won't pamper myself, but I won't waste strength I might need, either. Now tell me what you've found out about Sasha while you were gone."

"Not much." He held up his hand. "It's too soon for an explosion. As I told you, Masenak had that castle built somewhere in the mountains years ago and made sure that it was carefully hidden away. No one knows where that damn thing is. I've had aerial reconnaissance for the last two days trying to locate Jubaldar, but no sightings." He grimaced. "Those mountains in the Atlas range are so twisty-turvy that you could tuck an entire city in corners of them and never see it from the air. It just means that we'll have to track them on foot. You said that wouldn't be a problem for you, remember?"

"That was when I was trying to persuade you to make a deal about Masenak," she said. "Now it's Sasha, and everything is a problem. You said Gilroy got some information about Jubaldar from Baldwin. Can you give me a starting point? Surely he knew where that helicopter set down?"

Korgan shook his head. "Baldwin wasn't the sharpest tool in the shed. Gilroy said once Baldwin reached the castle, he could give precise directions how to get around inside. But he paid no attention when Masenak was flying them up there. He only knew they were heading for the south range. When they landed, he could only remember that it was a few miles from the landing pad to the castle. They were met by a few guards and several servants, who appeared to be locals, who had been sent to carry their luggage. He thought he might have seen a stream when the helicopter was descending."

"That's all?"

"I guarantee that's all Baldwin remembered. Gilroy doesn't make mistakes when he's interrogating. Everything Baldwin knew, we know." His lips tightened. "And I'm afraid that you won't be able to reexamine him if you're not satisfied. He's no longer with us. I used him to lure Masenak to the helicopter pad. I hope you won't be upset."

After all the ugliness and cruelty that Baldwin had committed? "Only that it did no good." She got to her feet. "The south range. We'll have to start there. And if those servants were locals, then they probably came from villages in those mountains. Can you send someone up there right away to start asking questions?"

"Already done," he said quietly. "Gilroy started up there the minute the aerial reconnaissance report came in. He speaks the language, and he established Berber contacts when I sent him to the Atlas Mountains last year to try to find answers about Masenak. He'll meet us at Akbar, one of the largest villages in the foothills, when we arrive there sometime after midnight tonight." He shrugged. "Who knows? There might even be a chance he might have info for us by that time."

"Gilroy again. He appears to be all over the place."

"What good is it to have an Indiana Jones around if you don't use him? Besides, he's very pissed off and worried about Sasha and is craving blood."

"So am I. Can we please leave now? I have to get *moving*. You can fill me in on anything else I should know on the plane to Morocco. I only have to stop by and talk to Margaret and Jeanne first."

"I'll meet you in the lobby." He grabbed her duffel from the bed. "Tell Margaret I'll arrange for transport for her and Juno as soon as she calls to say she's ready."

"It will probably be day after tomorrow." She wished it was sooner. But she couldn't expect Margaret to leave Jeanne until she had her settled. They didn't have a location for Jubaldar yet. They weren't even positive Sasha had been taken there. Still, it would be a logical move for Masenak to bring her there— that had been his intention since the kidnapping.

If she was still alive. Sasha was in danger every moment she was with Masenak. Even if he hadn't been so enraged that he'd decided to kill her yet, all it would take was for Sasha to say the wrong word and it might be over. Considering that they'd barely been able to keep her in check during these last weeks, Alisa wasn't optimistic.

But she had to be optimistic, she thought desperately. Hadn't Sasha done a fantastic job in helping free those students? Don't think of the possibility of failure. Sasha was clever. She'd live through this. All Alisa had to worry about was finding her.

———◆———

JUBALDAR

"You didn't eat." Masenak was frowning as he stood in the doorway of Sasha's suite. "I told you when

I brought you here that you were not to do anything to damage yourself. I won't let you disobey me, bitch."

She stiffened. She hadn't seen him since he'd virtually thrown her into this room and locked the door after they'd arrived here yesterday. However, it was obvious his mood hadn't changed. It was just as foul and dangerous as the moment he'd forced her from that camp at gunpoint. He'd barely spoken to her on the trip upriver to where they'd boarded the helicopter to bring them to the castle. "Skipping a meal isn't doing damage," she said. "I didn't have an appetite. I've been cooped up in this glorified harem for two days and I was sick of it. I'll eat when I'm hungry."

"You'll eat when I tell you to eat," he said coldly. "Things are different now and it's time you learned it. I'm through with indulging you." He came into the room and slammed the door. "There are always ways to force you to do whatever I like. I taught you that before, Sasha."

"But you lack the means to do it now. Those girls you used to persuade me are safe. You can't touch them any longer." She gazed at him steadily. "Unless you intend to go back to beating me. But didn't that defeat the purpose of keeping me healthy and undamaged?"

"I always manage to get what I want. This time

it might mean I have to reach out and take what I need, but that might only be more satisfying." He dropped down on the gold satin tufted couch and crossed his ankles on the matching hassock. "And you're being very disrespectful of my beautiful castle. I spent two years having it built to my exact specifications. Even Reardon is impressed by it. He once offered to buy it for an enormous amount, but I couldn't bear to let it go. It was worth it to me just to know I had something that he wanted." He glanced around the suite. "But you're right, it does resemble a harem in both appearance and purpose. I intended it to have this exotic Arabic ambience. Using it to keep you locked up and secure is only an additional advantage. I have three suites like this that I use once a year to entertain very important guests who are allowed to sample sexual partners of every description. You can see the locks are necessary. Naturally, one would want to make sure the women and men brought here for that service were confined and available at all times. Of course, the races are the most important entertainment to be provided, but for some people sexual stimulation seems to add to the pleasure."

"I'm sure you're among them," she said jerkily. "I remember Jeanne Palsan."

"And others," he said softly. "I knew you hated knowing what I was doing to those students. It made the pleasure all the more exciting for me. It was a game I enjoyed." His lips thinned. "Until you spoiled it for me. You believe you've not only beaten me but made a fool of me. I have to change that. You have to learn that if I choose, I could let you be used as one of the whores who occupy this suite."

Her heart skipped a beat. "Yes, I suppose you could do that. But you told me it would be counterproductive."

"And it might be. But I might not be able to resist. You've made me very angry. I'll have to see what method of control I should use on you. Let's see..." He tilted his head. "The oldest subjugation known to man?" He paused. "Or bringing in Alisa Flynn to make you come to heel."

She inhaled sharply, her body tensing.

"No answer?" he asked mockingly. "Of course I know her name now. After the humiliation I went through, did you think I wouldn't immediately find out everything connected to the sons of bitches who were responsible? What do you believe I've been doing for the last two days?"

"I have no idea." She must be very careful if she was to get through these next few moments. She could almost feel the rage he was emitting. "I tried not to think of you at all. Something unpleasant, I imagine."

"You'd better start thinking about me." His voice was hoarse, his eyes glittering. "Because everyone connected to what happened to me in that jungle is going to pay. That attack came out of nowhere like those damn drones, but now it's right in front of me and I'm going to find out every detail. I already know a lot about Alisa Flynn. It's all over the news. I had no idea when I shot the bitch that she was spearheading that operation. I only thought she had a connection with you and might be trying to save you." His lips curled. "But now the CIA is saying that she was much more important, that the operation would never have taken place without her invaluable help. How very heroic of her. No mention at all that she had a close connection to a Sasha Lawrence who was enrolled at St. Eldon's Academy. Let's discuss that, Sasha. Who is Alisa Flynn to you?"

There was no sense in lying any longer—and it would probably be dangerous. "My friend," she said simply. "I guess some people would call me her ward. And the reason the CIA probably didn't publicize any connection is that they didn't know about me. Alisa doesn't tell the CIA everything. She has a very dangerous job that might put anyone close to her at risk. Besides, she's a very private person."

"Evidently. She wasn't available to give any

interviews, so I dug deeper and found out that she'd been taken to a hospital in Geneva to treat her wound."

Sasha tensed. "But she's all right? They said she was okay?"

"What do I care? The CIA didn't say anything different. She'll live until I determine how to kill her in the most painful way possible. And you'll be there to see it." His voice harshened. "If I'd had any idea what kind of associations she'd been forming, I'd never have let her live that day I shot her."

She moistened her lips. "You're talking about the CIA?"

"Bullshit. I'm talking about Gabe Korgan. He flew her to Geneva." His teeth were gritted. "And you barely have to read between the lines of that speech the director made about how wonderfully the CIA had performed to free the captives to see Korgan moving behind the scenes. I made phone calls, and his name kept popping up. How long has she known him?"

"I'm not certain. I've never heard her talk about him." That at least must have the ring of truth. "Not long. Why does it matter?"

"Because this isn't the first time Korgan has gotten in my way. A few years ago, he sent a team of special forces after me when I was invading Noura. I was forced to cut the operation short and move on to the next country on the list. I had a silent partner at the time who wasn't pleased with the decision. I need to know if the CIA and Korgan were working together at the time."

"If they were, it didn't involve Alisa. You don't need to sharpen your knives and go after her. Look, Alisa never talks about her job to me, but I'm sure she had no deep plot brewing against you. I wish there had been. The only interest she had in you was that you'd kidnapped me. It was entirely your own fault that you caught her attention." She frowned as a sudden thought occurred to her. "Silent partner? Everyone knows you work alone."

"Do they? Perhaps because I'm the important one in any partnership?"

"That would be your opinion," she said absently. "But you're cautious and you don't seem to want to appear stupid or careless to this partner. So he's more important than you want anyone to know." She was thinking back over their conversations in these last weeks. "You've spoken about some of the people who work for you, and there was Baldwin, but you had no respect for him." She suddenly snapped her fingers. "Reardon. Two or three times you've mentioned a Reardon. The last time was when he offered to buy this castle. You'd definitely have respect for a man who could afford to do that."

"And am I supposed to admire the fact that you've figured that out?" he asked coldly. "I never made any real attempt to hide my association with Reardon from you. You weren't that important. I always knew you were meant to fulfill only one function in my life. That function may be connected to Reardon, but it really has to do with the horses in that stable we passed on the way to the castle. As long as I get what I want from you, you'll stay alive. When I don't, that will be the end." He paused. "And I never intended that you get in the way of my business arrangements with Reardon or anyone else. So I'd advise you not mention it to Reardon during the next week. He might make a demand with which I wouldn't be willing to comply if he gets nervous about your curiosity."

"You mean he'd want you to kill me? I wouldn't think that would bother you." She smiled recklessly. "If it does, just strike another deal with him. You're obviously two of a kind."

"The only reason I'd have problems with it is that I can't afford to have you dead if you can produce the results I need in that race in two weeks." He tilted his head. "So tomorrow you're going to go down to the stables with me and show me you deserve to live another day."

"Two weeks?" she repeated. "I can't believe that

you'd arrange a race to take place in two weeks when you were still in the middle of Szarnar Jungle."

"I didn't, it was set up for two months from now. But the minute I arrived back here, I called and changed it to two weeks." His face was flushed with anger again. "Everyone was laughing at me. I needed a chance to save face." He growled. "And there were financial considerations."

"Why? I've heard nothing but you muttering about this race you want me to win, but I really know nothing about it. How many horses are in this race?"

"Two."

"What?"

"That's all that's necessary." He shrugged. "Reardon and I are very competitive. Seven years ago we decided it would be amusing to have a race to see which one of our horses is the fastest thoroughbred from our respective stables. So I set up a festival of sorts every year and invite thirty or forty guests with very deep pockets to come here to bet on the race and make it more interesting. Of course, the biggest bets are between Reardon and me. They became larger and larger, and the stakes are not always cash."

"And who won?"

"I won the first two years. Reardon won the third and I came back and took the fourth. Then the son of a bitch managed to buy Nightshade, a Triple Crown winner, and he's won the last two races. I couldn't let him do that to me."

"How long is the race?"

"A mile and a half. The same as Belmont, the longest race in the Triple Crown. We had to make it interesting. I wanted to make sure everyone knew I was better than Reardon."

"Until you weren't. How terrible for you," she said sarcastically. "So you decided you'd pick up a few new thoroughbreds yourself by raiding St. Eldon's? You must have been desperate."

He got to his feet. "I'm never desperate. I just look for opportunities." His grasp bit painfully into her shoulders. "You were an opportunity, and I thought I might find a horse fast enough to beat Night-shade." His voice lowered to silken softness. "And I got lucky, didn't I? I found you, and I found Chaos. So you're going to make certain I win this next bet with Reardon. Because I'm going to need to get a new start after Korgan and your friend Alisa robbed me of those little bitches I was going to ransom."

"I told you I won't promise anything about Chaos. He can't be ridden."

"You'd better change his mind. Because if you don't, I'll make it my life's work to hunt down Alisa Flynn and make certain that she suffers for what she did to me."

It was the one weapon she'd hoped to prevent him from gaining against her, she thought in despair. "That's an empty threat. You'd do it anyway."

"Probably, but you might be able to bargain if you give me what I want. You'll have to try, because I remember how very friendly the two of you appeared to be in that photo. I think you care very much for her. We'll have to see tomorrow, when you whisper to Chaos that he has to please me."

"Those people who told you there was no such thing as a horse whisperer were right." Why was she even trying? She knew it was no use protesting. He would only listen to what he wanted to hear. "I'm good with horses, not a miracle worker. I won't be able to help you."

"You will," he said. "I have faith in you. And I'm afraid I'd consider it a cardinal sin if you betrayed that faith. Don't do it." He paused and reached for his phone. "I thought you might need a little encouragement, so I took the precaution of getting Alisa Flynn's phone number so she can join our party. Would you like to hear her voice? I would." He was punching in a number with vicious force. "And I want her to hear mine and know what's in store for her. I want the entire world to know."

The phone was picked up, and Sasha heard Alisa's breathless voice. "Sasha?"

"No," Masenak said. "Sorry to disappoint you. Just a little technical trick I did with my phone to make sure you'd take my call, bitch. I believe you know who this is, don't you? I put a bullet in you. I assume you're still at the hospital recovering from it?"

"Masenak." Alisa's voice was shaking. "Sasha. Where is Sasha?"

"Why should I answer you? You and Korgan can burn in hell before I let you know anything about that little whore. You think you've beaten me? You'll never beat me. Everywhere you go, I'll be behind you. You'll never be sure when I'll reach out and take you down." His voice was suddenly heavy with malevolence. "But that won't be enough. Maybe I *should* tell you what happened to your Sasha so that you can realize I've already made the first installment in payback." He paused and then said softly, "Pretty little Sasha. Such a pity. The minute I heard all about who you were and what you'd cost me, I killed her."

Sasha stiffened in shock. She opened her lips to speak, but Masenak was glaring at her. This wasn't the time to aggravate him even more toward Alisa. Give him the victory.

"You're not saying anything, Alisa," Masenak said mockingly. "Did you think I wouldn't punish you? That I'd let anyone make a fool of me as you have?"

"No, I believe you want to punish me," Alisa whispered. Sasha could hear the agony in her voice. "And I believe you're capable of anything. How— did you kill her?"

"Are you asking if I was merciful? No, I wasn't about to use anything as quick as a bullet. We were going upriver at the time and I drowned the bitch. Slowly. Very slowly. Drowning is a very painful death if done correctly. I was thinking about you when I did it."

"You bastard." Her words were vibrating with agony.

"Ah, that hurt, didn't it? I thought it would. I've enjoyed talking to you, Alisa. I don't believe I can resist calling you again whenever I feel the need to reminisce about our mutual friend. Perhaps I'll give you more details next time." He cut the connection. Then he looked at Sasha. "And perhaps if you're a good, obedient girl I won't make that call. You could hear how she was suffering. She must love you very much. I almost felt sorry for her."

"Liar. You were incredibly cruel to her."

"Yes, but I did find that conversation almost addictive. That *is* the truth. And you'll have to do exactly as I tell you so I won't indulge that addiction." He turned toward the door. "I'll see you at six A.M., Sasha."

CHAPTER

10

A re you sure you couldn't trace that call?" Alisa asked. "All that technology you have. There should be some way, Korgan."

"Yes, there should," Korgan said. "Wherever he is, Masenak is in an area where he can't be hacked. Which probably means he's reached Jubaldar." He added quietly, "But he had to be lying to you, Alisa, Sasha's not dead. He was just saying that to hurt you."

"Or to hurt her." Alisa was struggling to keep her voice steady. She was still shivering, as she'd been doing since she'd taken Masenak's call thirty minutes ago. "Or to force her to do something she didn't want to do. Anything is possible." She drew a deep, shaky breath. "The only thing that I won't accept is that he's killed her. That would hurt too much. I couldn't take it."

"Because it's not true," Korgan said. "I was afraid you'd believe him."

She shook her head. "I told you, I can't do that. I *have* to believe Vogel's report. Masenak wanted to tear me apart, make me bleed. I could hear it from the moment he came on the line. That's why I asked how Sasha died. I hoped it would give me some confirmation one way or the other. And it did. He couldn't resist making sure it would hurt me and chose drowning while they were going up-river. He's right, it's not an easy death. But I'm glad he did, because Vogel reported Sasha being on that helicopter after they'd left the river. She was still alive."

"Yes, she was," Korgan said gently. "And that means that no matter how he feels about you, he still has a purpose for keeping her alive. It has to be a damn strong one if it could survive that big a blow to his ego."

"Chaos," she said curtly. "It has to be Chaos." She was trying to think, but all the ugliness and pain and shock Masenak hurled at her had stunned her. "But you're right, he does hate me, and I can't let it touch me. There should be some way I can turn all that hatred he's feeling toward me against him." She reached up to rub her temple. "But I can't

seem to think of that now. I can't think of anything
but getting out of this hospital and on that plane
to Morocco." She headed for the door. "Because
he lied. She's still alive, Korgan. I know she's still
alive..."

AKBAR VILLAGE
ATLAS MOUNTAINS
1:40 A.M.

"The village should be just below this ridge."
Korgan pulled the Land Rover over to the side of
the road. "Want to get out and stretch your legs?
We won't go into the village itself. It gets a lot of
tourist traffic since it's in the foothills, and that's not
why we're here." He was out of the car and around
to the passenger side the next minute. "Gilroy said
that he'd be here as soon as he could break free of
the elders he was talking to."

"Elders?" Alisa took his hand and let him help
her out of the car. This wasn't the time to be independent. She was stiff and aching from the drive
from Mohammed V Airport in Casablanca to the
mountains on these bumpy roads, and her shoulder
was throbbing. This was a very welcome break.
"What elders?"

"Elders, heads of the village, chiefs. You can't say the Berbers aren't individualists. Gilroy tells me almost every Berber village he's run across up here has its own particular council and titles. Akbar has its elders." He added mockingly, "As well as its own thriving criminal element that sometime interacts with the elders for the greater good." He helped her across the rough road to a large rock at the shoulder. "And interacts with almost anyone else for their own commercial good if the price is right. That's why Gilroy chose Akbar to begin his search."

"Information? Then why didn't Gilroy find out more about Jubaldar when you sent him here before?"

"He would have, if they'd known anything. Gilroy is very good, speaks the language, knows the customs. But he came up with zeros when he tried. He was almost sure that no one in the village knew anything about Masenak and Jubaldar." He smiled. "But that was months ago. Gilroy makes contacts wherever he goes, rather like you. He lays the groundwork and then finds ways to persuade people to bring him the answers he needs."

"If there's time to do it." She carefully sat down on the rock and kept her back very straight so he wouldn't realize the effort it took to remain upright. It hadn't been only pain that she'd been having to fight but also the tension induced by that

call from Masenak. "I'm beginning to think Jubaldar might not even exist. Screw the castle. Right
now I'd settle for just having proof Sasha's alive and
somewhere, anywhere, in these mountains."

"Baldwin thought it existed and described it in
detail under the influence of zantlatin."

"Except how to get to the damn place. I'd think
that Gilroy could have nudged him a little more
in that—"

"Complaints. Complaints." Gilroy was turning
on his flashlight as he came around the curve of
the road. "You're being completely unfair, Alisa. It
would have been like nudging a slug, with about
as much brain power." He shone the beam on her
face. "But I'll forgive you because you probably
have a right to be crabby. You still look a bit pale
and fragile. Though not as bad as you did when
Korgan whisked you off to Geneva."

"I'm not *fragile*."

"But definitely bad-tempered." He turned to Korgan. "It would probably be better if I talked to you.
You might be bad-tempered, but I don't have to
worry about damaging your ego by accusing you of
being fragile." He was walking toward them. "And
I really don't have time for all this at the moment.
I have to get back on the road." He was pulling a
piece of paper out of his pocket and unfolding it.
"And no, this isn't a map to Jubaldar. Even I'm not

that good." He pointed to two X's on the map that appeared to be some distance apart. "Samlir and Kabada. Two villages that looked most promising to the elders. They're both high in the mountains and cut off from the other Berber villages for most of the year. That's why they didn't know much about them." He paused. "Except my contact, Roj Cazvar, whom I dealt with when I was up here before searching for Masenak. He's a trader who travels through the mountains and brings supplies and goods to the tribes. At that time he said he didn't know anything about Masenak, but I paid him to be on the lookout for anything I might find interesting and let me know. He might have come through for me this time. Again, no word about Masenak, but Cazvar says that both those villages are clearly barely able to eke out a living. Yet lately they seem to have a decent enough income to purchase his goods with practically no bargaining. But they're very vague about where those funds come from. And nervous, very nervous. You'd think that they'd be bragging about any sudden influx of wealth."

"Unless they were told they'd get their throats cut if they talked too much," Korgan said. "You think it's worth exploring?"

"I thought I'd head for Samlir after I leave you tonight. Cazvar is going to take me to meet a few friends he made among those villagers thanks to your extreme generosity. One or two of them are on the village council. With a few more bribes, you can never tell where it will lead me."

Alisa was gazing at the map. "I'm going to go with you."

"Not possible," Gilroy said. "You'd blow it for me. If you want to help, go check out the other village, Kabada, and see if it pans out."

Samlir seemed a much better prospect, but there was no way she'd chance blowing his mission. "Okay, as soon as Margaret gets here, we'll head for this Kabada and see what we can find out."

"You'll have to leave the Land Rover and be on foot for the last fifteen miles of the trip."

"What a terrible fate for someone as fragile as I am," she said ironically. "Perhaps if I ask nicely, Korgan can help me make it through."

"I might," Korgan said. "But only if you stop baiting Gilroy. I realize you've gone through a lot today, but he did a good job getting that info and he can't help it if you're feeling weak and frustrated and want to strike out."

"You're defending me?" Gilroy murmured.

"Don't let it go to your head," Korgan said. "Everyone does a good job occasionally. And I'm really feeling like we're kindred spirits at the moment. I've been stepping back and watching her try to be Wonder Woman for the past three days and it's beginning to piss me off." He looked at her. "So admit that through no mistake you made, you're not physically perfect at the moment, and let me help you now and then."

"I don't need your help." She added jerkily, "And you're wrong. You screwed up with those calculations, but I did make mistakes. If I'd been more alert and not distracted, I'd have seen Masenak in that tent behind us. He should never have been able to put me down and take Sasha."

Korgan cursed beneath his breath. "I should have known you'd be going down that road as soon as you started thinking about it. But this time I can't let you do it. No one is responsible but me. I promised you a positive outcome and I didn't give it to you." He glanced back at Gilroy. "And you did give her as positive an outcome as she's going to get for the time being, and she knows it. She told me she thinks you've been terrific as far as Sasha is concerned. She might even be swallowing that bullshit you hand out to all and sundry."

"I don't need you to interpret for me, Korgan." Alisa turned toward Gilroy. "And if that's an apology, I'll make my own." She paused and then said stiffly, "Which I might be doing now. Sometimes I'm a little impatient." She hesitated. "And scared. It makes me say things that I . . ." She stopped. "Thank you for what you've done so far. I'll be grateful with my whole heart for anything else you can do for Sasha."

"It will be my pleasure, Alisa," he said gently. "Take care of yourself. It was bad enough we let you get shot before. Sasha can be pretty fierce defending you. I don't want her to go after me with daggers drawn if she believes I screwed up again."

"I'll put in a good word with her." She smiled at him and turned back to Korgan. "You see? I did it much better than you possibly could."

Gilroy nodded. "She's right. It made me want to go to battle. You only handed me a weapon and a signed check, Korgan." He added quickly, "Which I took with supreme gratitude, but there's something to say for inspiration." He turned away. "I'm out of here. When it comes time to ditch the Land Rover, you'll find there are a lot of caves in these mountains where you can shelter. But keep an eye out for scorpions and snakes. I'll be in touch."

She watched him walk away. Damn, she wanted to go with him and not wait here for Margaret. Gilroy was doing something constructive. He might be getting something done. She looked back down at the map Korgan was still holding. "What are we waiting for? Shouldn't we get back on the road?"

"If you like, until you admit that it would be better to wait until it gets lighter. Losing a few hours is better than driving off the mountain." He held out his hand and pulled her to her feet. "It's pitch dark and we're not going to run into any cozily lit villages anywhere along the way. As Gilroy said, these Berbers are principally nomads and live rough."

"We can try to get as far as we can," she said quietly. "If it gets too bad, I won't insist. It would be stupid of me to risk your life."

"Only your own? Because you think you made a mistake?"

"That might be part of it. But it's because I can't bear it if I don't do everything possible to keep her alive." She added, "You know that, Korgan."

"Yes, I know that." He was pulling her across the road toward the car. "Okay, I'll leave it up to you. We'll go as long and as far as you tell me go." He smiled recklessly. "I won't stop until you tell me to do it. I'm in this for the long haul."

She gazed at him uncertainly. "That's not like you. You always want control."

"But tonight I'm yielding it to you. That means I'm going to have to trust you, aren't I?" He opened her door. "I'll even let you determine how fast I should go." The next moment he was behind the wheel and turning on the headlights. "Because I do trust you. You're smart and you won't let me die out here because you're in too much of a hurry." He was pulling into what served as a center lane on the rocky road. "How fast, Alisa?"

She frowned. "Are you daring me?"

"No, I just want you to know that I'm totally at your disposal. That's what you've been telling me since you came into my life. Now the roles are reversed, and I want to make certain you're aware of it. I'm the one who put Sasha in danger. The sensible thing would be for us to work together to save her. But if that's not the way you want it, then I'll handle it however you do." The headlights were spearing the darkness ahead, and she could see both the crumbling edge of the road and the darkness of the valley five hundred feet below. "I'm not playing chicken. I just want you to understand."

She was tempted to tell him to speed up just to see if he'd do it. But that would have been incredibly stupid. She could tell this was no bluff. He meant every word he'd said. So make the decision how to handle it.

She only waited until he'd driven around the next bend in the road before she said, "Find us a place to park that won't mean this Land Rover might end up crunched like a tin can in that valley below. We'll crawl into our sleeping bags and nap in the back of the van until it gets light."

"If that's what you want."

She didn't say anything else until after they were settled in the back of the van fifteen minutes later. She was huddled in her sleeping bag on her side of the van, her gaze on the darkness outside the side window. "You're crazy, you know. They call you this renaissance man, but you're no da Vinci, you're just plain crazy. Why?"

"We have to trust each other. I won't have you thinking you're alone in this. You have to know there's nothing I won't do to make this right for you."

"You've said that before."

"But now I've taken one more step in making you believe me, haven't I?"

"Maybe." She suddenly chuckled. "Or maybe I was just afraid that markets would come crashing down all over the world if I was responsible for Gabe Korgan biting the dust."

"Well, then you've prevented economic Armageddon. Feel proud of yourself."

"Crazy," she repeated.

"Hey, look, I know you're impatient and what we're doing seems slow and ineffective right now. But it's not the only arrow to our bow. We have Reardon."

"What?"

"Vogel isn't only on standby to bring Margaret and her pooch here when she says the word. He's monitoring the team hacking Reardon's business and personal devices. Masenak might have been able to close us out at Jubaldar, but that doesn't mean Reardon can. He's smart and hired the best to maintain his cyber privacy, but he doesn't have a mountain to run interference with signals. It took us over two years to break through his firewalls, but we finally did it. We've had a tap on Reardon's phones for months, and if there are any calls between him and Masenak, we'll know about it. If Reardon goes to see him, there's a good chance we'll be able to locate Jubaldar through him. Since Masenak is in trouble now, I'll bet one of those leads will come through. Does that make you feel better?"

It did make her feel a little more relieved. Of course Korgan would have taken this step to tighten the noose around Reardon. It would have been his first move after he'd begun to suspect collusion between him and Masenak.

"I can see that being more promising than those Berber villagers." Her gaze was still on the night sky beyond the window. She felt strangely safe here next to him in this cocoon on the mountain. His scent that seemed more comforting than sexual in this moment. The light sound of his breathing...She knew he was watching her intently but felt no threat. It wasn't unusual for him to watch her. She had noticed he was always curious about people around him, and because of the circumstances she supposed he found her more interesting than most.

He was just familiar and *there*, and for the first time since she'd opened her eyes this morning, the panic and fear began to subside. "I'd swear the sky is getting lighter in the east. Do you suppose that's true?"

"No, I think you just want it to be true. It won't be light for another few hours. Close your eyes and try to sleep."

"You could be wrong."

"I wouldn't dare to disagree after I swore I'd let you have your way in everything. But it's only a little after two and it's not likely."

"What time is dawn here?"

"Around six A.M."

"Then I suppose you're right."

"It happens sometimes." He went still. "You're suddenly stiff. Okay?"

"No. Yes. I was just wondering what was happening to Sasha right now." She added unsteadily, "What's been happening for the last few days."

"Do you want to talk about it?"

"No, it wouldn't do any good. I've said what I have to say. I just have to trust that she's well and that we'll get to her soon." She swallowed. "You're right, I'll close my eyes and go to sleep. In a few hours we'll be able to start after her again." She shut her eyes. "You said six, didn't you?"

"Yes." His hand reached out and gently squeezed

her good shoulder. "It will be here before you know it. Six A.M."

———◆———

JUBALDAR
6:14 A.M.

"I didn't expect the stable to be this busy." Sasha's gaze wandered over the dozen or so stable boys working in the horses' stalls. They were all moving with almost frantic alacrity on the sharp orders of a tall, gray-haired man standing at the exterior stable doors at the end of the aisle. "Though I suppose I should have. You made it clear that the horses are the only thing important to you. Is it like this every morning?"

"If it's not, the stable help isn't allowed to repeat their mistakes. Davidow has his orders to keep his staff efficient and productive. I decided it would be easier and safer for me not to bring any labor up here other than guards. Any other help comes from the villages near here, and it's worked very well. Living is very hard for them here in the mountains, so I had my pick of men, boys, even a few women I thought might be trainable for entertainment. It didn't take them long to learn that as long as they obey and keep their mouths shut, money would regularly be sent to their families. If they turned out to be troublemakers, they had unfortunate accidents in the stables or on the track and their bodies were returned to the villages. Davidow knows his job is on the line if I'm not pleased."

"Some of those boys are only teenagers," she said bitterly. "What is it with you? Is dealing with adults too difficult for you? And if they grew up in the mountains, some of them probably know practically nothing about horses. Even if they wanted to please your trainer, they wouldn't be able to do it."

"Some work out, some don't." He shrugged. "I admit, since I sent up the horses from St. Eldon's, Davidow's been having problems with keeping and training quality staff. But now that you're here, I fully expect that might be resolved."

"And he's supposed to keep me efficient and productive, too?"

"He might try now and then, but he realizes you're in a special category. Though I don't deny he might be happy if you proved to be a failure. That would also make him look good in comparison." He called out to the trainer, "Are you ready for us, Davidow?"

"Of course, sir." Davidow's accent was British and his smile polite but forced. "We've been out here since three. As I told you, it's a problem dealing with that stallion. Chaos is on the track and waiting for—"

You're here. It is good. You should not have left us.

Zeus!

She whirled toward the white Arabian stallion in the stall they were passing as she caught the thought. Memories and affection suddenly flowed through her as she saw this old friend of her childhood. Zeus had been one of the first horses Zeppo had bought for her and her father when she'd joined his act.

I know I shouldn't have done it, Zeus. I couldn't help it. Stop staring at me like that. I know you don't like this place. I can feel it. But I'm here now and I'll take care of everything.

"Sasha!" Masenak said sharply.

"I'll be right there," she said over her shoulder as she moved toward Zeus. "I just ran across an old friend." She was standing before Zeus and rubbing his muzzle.

Zeus closed his eyes with pleasure, but he was still disapproving. *You're going to Chaos. You should stay here with me. He's angry and will probably break you as he did that boy yesterday.*

He won't break me.

He almost broke you before. He was angrier than the rest of us when you left us this time. He's young and doesn't understand that breaking you would make you leave him forever.

Then I'll have to make him understand. She gave him a final pat. *Stop worrying. We'll all be together soon.* She started back toward Masenak. *I'll see you later.*

Zeus was not convinced. *He'll break you.*

"You kept me waiting," Masenak said harshly as she reached them. "If I hadn't been curious, I have taken my quirt to both you and that horse."

"I don't doubt it. But you already figured out I've had these horses for a long time. You should have realized I'd feel a certain amount of affection for them. That was Zeus, one of the first horses I ever rode." She looked back at the stallion, who was still gazing at her worriedly. "Nothing for you to be curious about in that."

"I was just curious to see your interaction."

"And you saw nothing in the least mystic about it." She met his gaze. "Did you? Not a hint of a horse whisper. Just me and a horse I've cared about since I was a little girl." She turned to Davidow. "What about you? You're a trainer. You must know what you're doing, or he wouldn't have hired you. Do you believe all this bullshit Masenak is spinning?"

"I wouldn't disagree with him. Let's say, I believe in results, and I've never seen any results that would reflect any kind of psychic connection between man and beast. Certainly none between woman and beast." Davidow's mocking smile had a touch of malice. "But I'm willing to be convinced. Actually, eager. I lost another stable boy yesterday when he was trying to put a saddle on Chaos. He ended up with two broken legs. But Masenak wants this horse tamed, and I'll try anything to give him what he wants." He gestured for her to precede him. "It's entirely on his head...and yours. Chaos is waiting."

The racetrack itself was impressive, Sasha thought. It could have held its own with Churchill Downs, Santa Anita, Ascot, Meydan in Dubai, or any of the other racetracks she'd seen in the books Alisa had bought Sasha for her library. Everything pristine and clean and beautifully built. The grandstand didn't have the capacity of those other tracks, but the seats were far more luxuriously crafted.

"Admit it." Masenak's gaze was on her face. "It's bloody wonderful."

"Why ask me? My opinion shouldn't matter. I don't know much about racetracks." She was climbing to sit on the top rung of the fence dividing the track from the grandstand. "I've always been more interested in the horses." She took another look around. "I guess it's okay. The art-deco-style furnishings in the grandstand look a little ornate."

He stiffened. "You know nothing about—"

"There he is," Davidow interrupted to gesture down the track. "I left two stablemen to keep an eye on him and make sure he didn't go wild again and hurt himself trying to break down the barricades." He smiled crookedly. "I don't know why. If anything did happen, there's no way they could get near enough to help him unless they shot him with a sedative."

"Magnificent," Masenak murmured, his gaze on the black. "Not the usual thoroughbred. But look at his lines..."

She *was* looking at them. She had always thought he was the most beautiful horse she had ever seen. Tall, proud, splendid. The slightly bony knobs on that wonderful head, the graceful arch of his back, the shining black of his coat. The spirit...That fantastic spirit. Nisean. Pure Nisean. She tried to keep her expression noncommittal. She mustn't let Masenak see that she cared about him. Every emotion was a weapon in his hands.

But she was afraid she might have revealed something. He was gazing at her too intently. "Don't you want to go say hello to him as you did Zeus, Sasha?"

"Why should I? I didn't know Chaos as well as I did Zeus." Chaos would know soon enough that she was here. They'd always been able to sense each other. Right now she only wanted to examine the way he was standing, the tension in his muscles. There had been times when she could read his next moves, almost what he was thinking, by the energy stored in his shoulders. Today that tension was explosive.

He's going to break you.

Chaos suddenly lifted his head.

He'd recognized her scent. He knew she was there.

She found herself tensing, too.

"Go see him," Masenak said softly. "*Now*, Sasha."

"If you like." She slipped off the fence onto the track. Chaos was turning toward her. She could sense the tension growing in him. "You want another victim, Masenak?"

"No. I want a success. I've had nothing but failure lately, and it's got to stop. But if you can't give it to me, then I'll take the victims instead. Two victims. You're no good to me if you can't do your job. Chaos is no good to me if he can't be ridden. If you don't produce, you'll get a taste of the failure I've been suffering...right before I put a bullet in Chaos's head." His voice was low, almost a hiss as he added, "And then it will be your turn, Sasha. I told you everything was going to be different. I'm out of patience. Show me that either one of you is worth keeping."

If she'd had any hope that she might be able to persuade Masenak that she would be of no value working with Chaos, it was gone in that instant. His anger and humiliation had gone too deep. She would give him what he wanted, or he would kill both her and Chaos. "I'll try," she said quietly. "It might take longer than you'd like. Remember, if you lose that patience, you're only hurting yourself. Give us a chance." She didn't wait for an answer but focused her attention back on Chaos. She could sense his tension growing stronger. And the anger, so much anger. She was surprised that the stallion hadn't made a move yet.

Hello, Chaos, what are you waiting for? All that ugliness stored inside you wanting to burst free. Why don't you do it? Is it because you know you're wrong, and I'm your friend?

Not friend. Stupid word. I told you so before. Means nothing. I am alone. I have no need of you. And I am never wrong.

Not a stupid word. And I have need of you.

You left me. You didn't come back. The anger was rising out of control. *You said you'd come back.*

I'm here now.

Too late! He was streaking toward her.

She dodged to the left, but his hip caught

her shoulder and sent her spinning. Then before she could catch her balance he had whirled and rushed her again. This time he knocked her to the ground.

He was rearing above her!

She rolled to the side, but her ponytail was caught beneath that iron hoof.

He reared again!

But by that time she was scrambling away from him and crawling desperately for the fence. She'd barely reached it and started climbing when he rammed into her from behind.

Pain.

She clutched the rungs of the fence, bracing herself for another onslaught.

But he'd whirled away again and was running down the track.

Sasha quickly managed to climb to the top rung before he turned around.

But Chaos wasn't running toward her again, she realized. He was standing still, head lifted. *I could have crushed you like I did that young boy the other day. You used to be much quicker.*

You didn't kill the boy. You only broke him a little. And you didn't kill me. You know you could have savaged me instead of bruising me. You must think I'm a little worthwhile. Maybe "friend" isn't such a stupid word.

You left me. I didn't want you to leave me.

I was taken. By the same men who brought you here.

Then we should crush them for doing it. They are fools. I was going to stomp on all of them anyway.

Chaos was nothing if not direct and simplistic, Sasha thought wryly. *But not right now. Do you believe me?*

I might . . . if you don't go away again.

Only if I'm taken.

Then do not be taken. Stomp on them.

I'll keep that it in mind. Since I'm not as good at stomping as you, it would be easier if we find ways to do it that don't involve stomping. Right now we need to make these fools think we're beaten. Be careful and use courtesy and respect at this point. Chaos was only partially reconciled and accepting. *Will you permit me to ride you? I won't use a saddle this time.*

He hesitated and then slowly walked over to the fence toward her. *What next?*

She slipped off the fence and onto his back. *We run. Very hard. Very fast. He wants to see how wonderful you are, and we won't mind it as long as you're in control.* She bent her head, winding her hands in his mane. *Will we? Let the lightning strike. Let the wind blow. We'll be ahead of all of it, my dear, dear friend. Ready?* Her palm slapped his haunch. *Let's go!*

Chaos leaped forward!

Lightning.

Wind.

Dizzying speed.

Stretching out.

More speed.

Together.

More speed.

The wind was stinging her cheeks now.

How long had they been running?

Probably far beyond the race distance limit. She should try to slow him down. She didn't want Masenak to be aware of too much about Chaos's capabilities.

Slow. Enough.

But Chaos wouldn't go slower. He was fighting her. When they were together, he wasn't accustomed to having her try to rein him in. It was all joy and speed and what they were together.

Her grip on his mane tightened, pulled hard.

He didn't slow.

And she was beginning to become anxious. Chaos was very excited and if she tried to pull him over when he reached Masenak and Davidow, he might attack them. Stomping was very much on his mind right now.

Please. It's time to stop. Things aren't what they seem. Next time. I promise. She repeated over and over. *Stop. Stop. Stop. Stop.*

At first he ignored her, but then his stride broke. He was gradually slowing. But not happy about it, she thought ruefully. Very mean-tempered. Too bad. At least she might make it through this without getting either one of them shot.

Masenak and Davidow were right ahead of her on the track, but she knew she wasn't going to be able to stop Chaos. Just slow him down a little more and that should be enough...

She swung her legs so that she was riding sidesaddle for the last yards. Concentrate. It was only a simple circus trick she had performed thousands of times before. As she was passing Masenak she kept her grip on Chaos's mane, timed the flying dismount, and then made her jump to the ground, careful to keep her knees bent to absorb the shock.

Yes.

Chaos streaked past the two men without trying to savage either one. She had made the jump and not ended with her face in the dirt. Not a bad outcome. If she could get Chaos to stop running, it would be perfect.

Worry about it later.

She staggered a little but quickly regained her balance. She whirled to face Masenak. "Satisfied? Is that what you wanted?" She was barely aware of him or anything else around her. She was breathing hard. She could feel the heat in her cheeks. She was almost as excited as Chaos. All she wanted was to jump back on him and ride and ride and ride...

Masenak's face was strangely pale as he took a step toward her. "Shut up." He glanced at Davidow. "You got the time?"

"Of course I got the time," Davidow said hoarsely as he held up the stopwatch. "Two minutes nineteen seconds on the first time around the track. I stopped checking after that. I told you that he was a wonder. You didn't seem to believe me."

"I wanted it too much." His gaze returned to Sasha. "No, I'm not satisfied. If you can do that just hanging on that nag's mane, you can do a hell of a lot better if you spend time training him."

"No, I couldn't. What you saw was all Chaos. I had nothing to do with it. He can't be broken, and you try to put a jockey on him and he'll either refuse to run or find a way to kill his rider." She glanced at Davidow. "As he almost did with that stable boy."

"But he didn't kill you today," Davidow said. "Though I thought for a minute he might." He was gazing at the dirt on her riding pants, her shirt that was ripped halfway down her back, her hair that was completely out of the ponytail and hanging about her face. "I imagine you must have, too. However, Masenak seems to have solved that problem."

"Until I try to do something Chaos doesn't want me to do," Sasha said dryly. "You saw what he did to me. I was lucky today."

"I prefer to think that it's skill instead of luck," Masenak said. "Anyone could see that you were reaching that devil horse somehow." He smiled. "And that's what you'll continue to do." His eyes were suddenly glittering recklessly. "I can't wait to call Reardon and see if I can increase our bet. I believe I'll introduce you to him on Skype. Particularly since you look very much the worse for wear and the farthest thing from a skilled jockey. Reardon is usually overconfident, and it won't hurt to feed that fault if I can do it carefully." He took out his phone and was punching quickly. "Hello, Reardon." He reached out and yanked Sasha to him to appear on the screen. She was suddenly confronting a compact, fortyish man with wide-set hazel eyes whose salt-and-pepper hair was slightly receding. "You look surprised, Reardon. It's such a beautiful morning, and my new horse I told you about has had such a great workout that I thought I'd share it with you. I hope your Nightshade is in equally good shape?"

"Fantastic," Reardon said absently, his gaze on Sasha. "Who's the girl?"

"My new jockey. My horse, Chaos, is a bit unruly and gave Sasha a bad time. But he'll still beat your Nightshade. I was wondering if you'd want to double the bet we made last week." He paused. "Unless you're afraid you'll lose your shirt."

Reardon was silent, his gaze narrowed. "Nightshade is faster than she was last year. Why should I be afraid of racing her against a horse no one has ever heard about? You're sounding ridiculously cocky. I'm just wondering if your latest disaster has you in such financial straits that you're getting desperate to recoup." He paused. "You do know that if you lose this bet, I'll send my most efficient and lethal men to retrieve my money?"

"I'd expect nothing else of you. You agree to double it?"

"Oh, yes. I can afford it, even if you can't." He glanced at Sasha. "As long as you throw in the mystery horse and the jockey. Is she as young as she looks?"

"Fifteen. Not as young as you like them, but you'd find her entertaining. It's like you to try to screw me in all ways possible. But if you'll agree to give me Nightshade when I win, I'll agree. It's a deal?"

"It's a deal. I'll see you in a couple of weeks." Reardon cut the connection.

"I've *got* him." Masenak's eyes were almost shimmering with excitement in his pale face. "All these years he's been lording it over me and telling me what to do as if I wasn't his equal. I'm going to take the arrogant son of a bitch to the cleaners."

"Providing she can make Chaos do what you

need him to do," Davidow said. "You'll forgive me if I'm still skeptical."

"She'll do what I tell her. I know our Sasha. It will only take a few adjustments to make her come to heel."

Alisa. He threatened to call on Alisa to make those adjustments was Sasha's first thought. "You'd have to discuss those adjustments with Chaos. I keep telling you that it's not up to me."

"I don't have the time to argue with you at the moment," he said harshly. "Neither do you. I'll find a more permanent fix after the race, but in the meantime you're going to spend every waking moment for the next two weeks with Chaos. You'll train him, you'll gentle him; when you say run, he'll fly like Pegasus. If I don't see progress, I'll find ways to encourage you. You have other horses in my stables that I don't value as much as Chaos. You seemed fond of Zeus..." He was reading her expression. "That frightened you. Don't you want to rush and start working with Chaos right away? Yes, I can see you do."

No choice. Not now. She turned to Davidow. "If Masenak wants me to train him, I don't want you or any of the stable help to get near him. That obviously wasn't a success. I'll take care of him."

"I'm not going to object. I'm short of help now anyway and I don't want to lose any more."

Davidow's lips twisted sardonically. "I assume you're the one who's going to catch that devil and get him back to the stable?"

She nodded. "It will take me a little while to quiet him. Then I can start trying to persuade him that he doesn't want to stomp on everyone in sight." She glanced at Masenak. "It would help if you'd keep out of view. I believe he has a particular dislike for you. I wouldn't mind if he stomped on you, but he might like it too much and get overexcited." She started down the track to where the horse had finally come to a halt. "And we all want what's best for Chaos, don't we?"

CHAPTER

11

Korgan and Alisa had been on the road for more than four hours the next day when Korgan got a call. He glanced at the ID. "Vogel." He punched ACCEPT and put it on speaker. "Hold on. If it's important, I have to find a place to pull over so that I can talk to you. Some of these curves are hairpins. The higher we go, the rougher the roads."

"I'll wait. I believe Alisa would think it's important."

Alisa's fingers clenched. Sasha. It had to be about Sasha. "Important" could mean anything. Bad. Good. Death. Life. "Find a place, Korgan," she said through set teeth. "Right away."

"I'm looking," he said quietly. "Give me a minute."

But it seemed more like an hour to her before he

found a layby along that treacherous road where he could pull off and say, "Go ahead, Vogel."

"I'm sending you a photo. We intercepted a Skype communication between Reardon and Masenak at nine seventeen this morning. We managed to get the entire message, but I thought you'd want to see the photo first."

She heard the ping and saw Korgan accessing the photo. He glanced at it and then said, "Good judgment call." He handed Alisa his phone. "I think you'll agree."

Sasha. Dirty. Torn shirt. Hair loose about her face.

But Sasha *alive*, her eyes staring out at the camera with all the boldness and intensity with which Alisa was so familiar.

Korgan said softly, "Nine seventeen this morning, Alisa."

"Yes." Her eyes were stinging, and she had to swallow to ease the tightness of her throat. "I've been so afraid, Korgan. All those nice, encouraging reports Vogel gave you could have been bullshit. I didn't *know*. Masenak could have killed her anywhere along the way."

"Yes, he could. But he didn't, and at nine seventeen this morning she appeared to be healthy enough and presumably essential for Masenak to use in a plan that involves Reardon." He spoke into the phone. "Is that right, Vogel?"

"Oh, am I back with you again?" Vogel asked dryly. "My reports are never bullshit, Alisa. They always have substance, and there was every chance Sasha was still alive."

"'Chance,'" she repeated. "I have a problem with that word connected to Sasha. Is Korgan right? Does Masenak seem to have an agenda that could keep Sasha alive for the long haul?"

"Yes and no. I'll play the conversation between him and Reardon, and you can judge for yourself. It all seems to depend on this race and a horse named Chaos and another called Nightshade. The call was short, and I didn't understand a good deal of what they were talking about. I had an idea there was a lot going on that wasn't on the surface. I thought I'd throw the ball in Korgan's court and see if he could figure it out."

Alisa stiffened. "Chaos?"

"Did that strike a chord?" Korgan asked. "Something Sasha mentioned?"

"Oh, yes, that struck a chord. Chaos is one of Sasha's horses that was stolen with the others from St. Eldon's. She hasn't mentioned him to me lately. And I guarantee she would never have mentioned him to Masenak if she could help it." She shook her head in frustration. "But how can we tell what she was forced to tell him during those last days before the attack? She was so alone and might have been trying to handle everything on her own." She gestured impatiently. "Just play the video and I'll try to make sense of it."

"Right." He punched the button. "Here it is."

It *did* make sense to her, she thought after the Skype had finished. It was as brief as Vogel had said, but she could understand and predict every nuance of what was going on among the three people involved. Particularly Sasha, who had not spoken at all. Alisa could tell Sasha had been trying to remain expressionless, but Alisa could read every emotion.

And what she was seeing was terrifying her. Chaos... She felt physically ill. Waves of cold were bombarding her as she thought about what this development might mean to Sasha. Caught. She'd be caught and wouldn't be able to free herself.

"Alisa?" Korgan's gaze was on her face. "Bad?"

She nodded jerkily. "We've got to get to her right away. No matter who wins that race, she'll die."

"No, she won't. There's always something we can do. First, we decide which way we want the race to go. We should be able to—"

"She'll *die*," Alisa repeated. "You don't understand. Masenak thinks he knows what he has, but he doesn't really. Either it hasn't sunk in, or Sasha's managed to keep the details of how really special

Chaos is from him. I believe it has to be the latter or Masenak would have been bragging to Reardon on that call. But Sasha knows and she'll be getting ready. We've got to get her away before she does anything reckless."

Korgan took another look at her expression and stopped arguing. "Then we'll do it. It will be your way. No problem. After you tell me why. You're right, I don't understand. But I'm damn well going to." He started the car. "I'll call you later, Vogel. Any news of Margaret?"

"She said she'll be ready to leave Geneva by tomorrow morning. I've arranged for a helicopter to bring her from Casablanca to where you are in the mountains to meet you, if you can find somewhere to land up there in the stratosphere."

"We'll find it. I'll give you our location later." He ended the call. "Don't say anything right now, Alisa. No pressure. You're upset and not ready to deal with questions or anything else right now. I'm going to drive for a couple more hours and then find a place to stop for the night." He was backing out of the layby. "But then I expect you to be ready to tell me everything I need to know about Chaos..."

———◆———

Korgan had to drive another three hours before he found a place where they could stop for the night. He settled on an open cave that was set several yards back from the road and surrounded by scrawny pines, branches, and brush. "It appears dry enough and we can use those branches for fuel for a fire."

"Fire?" Alisa asked as she got out of the Land Rover. "We're not going to sleep in the Land Rover again?"

"Maybe. It depends on how low the temperature drops. We're high enough now that it could go below freezing. But we can start out with a warm fire and a hot meal this evening." He was pulling out their backpacks, water, and supplies and tossing them on the ground. "Or we might use the cave if it's habitable. I'll go check it out for scorpions, snakes, and other critters."

"I'll do it." She was scowling as she grabbed her flashlight from her backpack. "You'd be more efficient gathering wood and making a fire. I'm still using this damn sling, so searching for scorpions is about the only useful thing I can do." She headed for the cave opening. "I'm sorry about that. But I promise this is the last day I'm going to pamper myself. I've hated it, too."

"I know you have." He smiled faintly. "Nothing could be more obvious. But the only actual thing I hated was that I was getting impatient from having to restrain myself from helping you more. Which is a natural instinct and has nothing to do with your capabilities. But you're far from being a gracious receiver in that department." He waved his hand at the cave. "By all means do what you like. I won't offer to help. Personally, I wouldn't want to be the scorpion attacking you."

"Thank you." She paused before she went toward the cave. "I don't believe you. You would offer to help. You couldn't help yourself. And I'm sorry that I can't be gracious about stuff like that. I wouldn't know how." She turned on her flashlight. "But Masenak is worse than any scorpion, and I'm taking your help swatting him. Tell me how to be gracious about that and I'll do it."

———◆———

Alisa ducked her head and entered the darkness of the cave.

"No scorpions. No snakes," she announced when she came out forty-five minutes later. "Just some weird bugs that skittered all over the place when I came near them. They were probably first cousins to cockroaches. Margaret said they're going to inherit the earth. I told her I'd prefer dogs or horses." She glanced around the small clearing. "You've done a good job." A small fire was burning, and she could smell coffee from the pot Korgan had set on the stones beside it. "But regardless if that cave is safe and livable or not, I'm not going back in there tonight. I'll opt for my sleeping bag, either out here or in the Land Rover. I don't mind roughing it, but I have problems with cockroach wannabes."

"I thought that's what you'd choose." He passed her a handful of towelettes. "Get some of the dust off you while I pour you a cup of coffee. Do you want to eat now or later?"

"Later. I'm still inhaling that dank cave." She was wiping her face and neck, then hands and arms. At least she felt a little cleaner now. She took the coffee cup he handed her. "How very 'gracious' you're being," she said mockingly. "Are you trying to teach me by example?"

"No, I'm only making you comfortable. That's what all of this about. Even sending you to go brave the scorpions and cockroaches."

"Sending me? You didn't send me to—" She stopped. "Or did you? Manipulation, again?"

"I merely guessed which way you'd choose to go. I told you this was coming. But I could feel you becoming more tense all day. You needed a distraction to make it easier for you." He went back to the fire and poured himself a cup of coffee. "Sit down."

She slowly came over to the fire. "Only you would choose cockroaches as a distraction."

"I didn't know about the cockroaches. We were discussing scorpions and snakes. That would have been much more interesting for you." He lifted his cup to his lips. "But what we weren't discussing was a horse called Chaos. Talk to me. Why did finding out Chaos was going to be in that race put you in a tailspin?"

"I wasn't in a tailspin." She dropped to the ground beside him. "Or maybe I was." She made a face. "But you didn't need to hand me a distraction as if I was a kid who couldn't handle it."

"I don't think many people were handing out distractions to you when you were a kid. Maybe I thought that I'd like to be the first." He met her eyes. "Stop stalling. Chaos."

She moistened her lips. "Chaos belongs to Sasha."

"One of the horses you bought for her when she agreed to become your ward?"

"Not exactly. Chaos came later. He's only a three-year-old. Sasha had already started school at St. Eldon's when she heard about him from Antonio Rossi, the breeder who had sold the four horses she used in her act to Zeppo, the circus owner. She'd been writing to Rossi, asking questions about care for her horses ever since her father died and she'd taken over the act. They didn't become friends, but they were both crazy about horses and Rossi could see how his horses responded to her. Sometimes he'd find ways to bribe Zeppo to let her come out to his farm so that he could use her when he was trying to gentle a horse." She paused. "Or when a mare was birthing. Sasha was magic... Anyway, a year after Sasha left the circus and went to St. Eldon's, I received a letter from Rossi politely asking me to bring Sasha to his horse farm to help deliver a foal. And Sasha called me from school right afterward begging me to let her go. She was more excited than I'd ever seen her. She said she knew the mare's background and she was wonderful, and the foal was going to be very special. What could I do? We were on the next flight back to Italy."

"And that foal was Chaos?" Korgan asked. "Not an encouraging name for a supposedly special foal." He tilted his head as a thought struck him. "But maybe it is when you think about chaos theory."

"What?"

"The branch of mathematics that deals with complex systems whose behavior is highly sensitive to slight changes in conditions, so that small alterations can give rise to strikingly great consequences."

"You would make that connection," she said dryly. "Rossi named him. And I don't believe he was thinking about a mathematical theory when he did it. It's more likely that he thought Chaos might cause a total upset in everything around him."

"Isn't that what I just said? Was he as special as Sasha thought he'd be?"

She nodded. "He was gangly and awkward like all colts, but even at birth you could see how beautiful he was going to be. Sasha fell in love with him the minute she helped him come into the world."

"And you tried to buy him for her?"

"There wasn't any way I could. Antonio Rossi, the breeder, wasn't going to let him go. He'd been trying for decades to breed a stallion of his own with pure Nisean blood. Besides, not only was Chaos absolutely unique, Rossi was sure he was going to take the racing world by storm and make him millions, if not billions."

"So much for being crazy about his horses," Korgan said cynically. "In the end it all goes back to money."

"I believe Rossi did care about the foal, at least in the beginning; it was only later that he became dazzled by the potential he saw looming. Like I said, Chaos was unique. The chances of his bloodline being duplicated were almost nil. Niseans are considered extinct."

"What?" Korgan was suddenly alert. "I never heard of the breed, but then I'm not into horse breeding. But extinct automatically means cash in the bank in most categories. I imagine that's why you suddenly went into a panic. Let's go back and start over where you should have begun. Why is a Nisean horse so unique?"

"All kinds of reasons. I didn't know about them, either, but Antonio Rossi had almost brainwashed Sasha about them over the years. That was why she was so excited." She drew a deep breath. "Okay, I'll be as brief as I can. The Nisean horse breed was once native to the town of Nisaia, located at the foot of the southern region of the Zagros Mountains in Iran. The first written reference was in around 430 BC in Herodotus's *Histories* when the king was given ten sacred horses that were said to have been of unusual size. They didn't have the smaller Arabian head but a more robust one that was like that of a great warhorse. The Nisean horses were known to be the most valuable horses in the ancient world and the most beautiful alive. The Chinese called him the *Tien Ma*—heavenly horse—or *Soulon*, vegetarian dragon. Two gray stallions pulled the shah of Persia's royal chariot and four others pulled the chariot of Ahura Mazda, the supreme god of Medea and Persia. Cyrus the Great rode a Nisean when hunting lions. The Greeks imported them to the Iberian Peninsula, where they influenced the ancestry of the Barbs and Andalusians, among others. Marc Antony acquired the first Roman Nisean horses when he conquered Armenia." She took a sip of her coffee. "Sasha could go on and on about their history, but I don't remember it all. However, you can see that they were once the most desired horse on the planet, and there was good reason for it. Everyone wanted them. During the reign of Darius, Nisean horses were bred from Armenia to Sogdiana. The Greeks, mainly the Spartans, imported them and bred them with their native stock. Not to mention the nomadic tribes in and around the Persian Empire that imported, captured, or stole Nisean horses."

"If the bloodline was that prevalent, it's difficult believing it could become extinct."

"Yet records show it happened in 1204 at Constantinople. But who knows what really happened back then? Someone arbitrarily saying there were no longer any pure Niseans? Still, that announcement might automatically discourage a breeder from keeping the bloodline of his horses pure. Over the centuries, stating it was true could contribute to making it so. But Rossi regarded it as a challenge and spent decades trying to find any breeders who had kept those ancient bloodlines pure."

"One hell of a challenge."

"He did it, Korgan," she said quietly. "He started at the beginning in Iran and then traced those horses up to those nomadic tribes I told you about. He'd decided the only chance he had was to find one of those wandering tribes whose people and horses had the least opportunity of being touched by civilization. He searched, desert, mountains, wilderness... Then bingo, he came upon this tribe of traders who also bred horses who seemed to fill the bill. Rossi even found out they'd sold some horses through the years, but that they weren't of particularly good quality. It discouraged him, and he decided he wasn't going to pursue it. But then he heard that same tribe also kept another smaller herd in a nearby canyon in the desert that they'd refused to sell. They wouldn't even let a prospective purchaser go to look at them. They said that the horses were part of their heritage and tradition and must stay with the tribe."

"And naturally that would intrigue Rossi," Korgan murmured. "Yet he managed to get a few horses?"

"Just the mare and a stallion. But the stallion was only on loan and had to be returned to the tribe as soon as the mare was bred, and the foal reached full term. But they were as wonderful as Rossi hoped. Fantastically beautiful and the fastest horses he'd ever run across. He spent two years with the tribe before he managed to persuade the chief to let him buy the mare. He mortgaged everything he owned and sold off most of his own horses. He devoted that entire two-year time to studying the horses, verifying their pedigrees, and trying to learn the history and secrets of how they'd been raised and what would work with them."

"Work with them?"

"They might be wonderful but that didn't mean they weren't major problems. In that nomad camp, those horses were treated like the heavenly bodies the Chinese called them. They were totally wild, and over the decades it became ingrained. They couldn't be broken even if those nomads had wanted to bother. When Rossi got them home, he found that out, but he wasn't about to risk damaging them." She paused. "And then he remembered that little girl in the circus who had been able to do magic with those four horses he'd sold to Zeppo. Why not find a way to use her?"

Korgan smiled. "It was just as well that was pre-Alisa in Sasha's life, or he would have found a reason why not. You would have killed the son of a bitch."

"But I wasn't there, and Sasha only thought about having two more splendid horses in her life. She couldn't have been happier. She spent three or four days at Rossi's farm and settled the mare and stallion beautifully before she went back to the circus. Even those high-strung, wild Niseans loved her. That's why Rossi wanted her back when the mare was about to give birth." Her lips tightened. "That's when Chaos came into her life. I should never have taken her back to Rossi's horse farm. It was the worst thing I could have done. I should have found a way to keep her away from him."

"And you had a crystal ball that told you that? Not likely. Which brings us back to square one. You've practically given me the entire history of Chaos and his ancestors, which was interesting enough, but not really first on my agenda. Why is it so urgent that you get Sasha away from Masenak before the race with Chaos?"

"Because of what Chaos can do and what he is. Why else would I tell you all that stuff if it wasn't important? I could see that Masenak knew how good he is when he was talking to Reardon. He wasn't being cocky as Reardon might have thought. He was excited. He must have forced Sasha to show him just how fast Chaos is."

"And how fast is he?"

"Very. Remarkable. The last time I visited her at St. Eldon's, he was tearing up the roads at blinding speed—and that was in the hill country."

"Comparison?"

"No comparison. Rossi thought he was going to be better than any horse in history if he could find a jockey capable of riding him." She grimaced. "All of the horses in that herd the nomads raised were superfast. Remember the descriptions of those ancient Niseans being bigger and more powerful than other horses of their time? Well, it would have been perfectly natural they'd be a hell of a lot faster, too." Her hand was clenching on her cup. "The minute that race shines a spotlight on Chaos, it's like a gun being aimed at both Sasha and the horse. What do you think happens when a horse with that kind of speed erupts onto the racing scene? He becomes a phenomenon. He sets records and he captures the imagination of everyone around him. Everyone will want a piece of him. The way an owner makes the big money on a racehorse isn't from the purses he wins. It's the stud fees. And since he's a Nisean, and supposedly one of a kind, those stud fees will be enormous." She was speaking fast, gazing into the fire. "Once Masenak and Reardon realize what they'd have in him, neither is going to let him go. They'll end up by fighting each other, and whoever wins, Sasha loses. Because she's the pawn and they're both greedy. They'll try to force Chaos, speed up the process of making him king of the turf. There's a good chance that they'll end up killing him." Her voice was hoarse with pain. "But Sasha won't let that happen. She loves that damn horse. She'll fight them no matter if she has a chance of winning or not. And what kind of chance do you think she'll have by herself surrounded by all those scumbags at Jubaldar?"

"Perhaps better than you'd believe considering

how well she handled herself in the Szarnar Jungle,"
he said gently. "I've never even met your Sasha, but
I've become a fan."

"And so you should be. No one deserves it more.
I tried to tell you that from the beginning."

"Be fair. At the time you were throwing all that
psychic business about Margaret and her dog at me,
too. Somehow your horse whisperer, Sasha, got
caught up in the mix."

"Yet you used Margaret and her dog when you
went after Masenak." She stared him in the eye.
"And you've just told me that you respect Sasha.
Does that mean that you're leaning toward believing
that they're both exactly what I say they are?"

"No, it means that I still have no evidence, but
I'm willing to accept that there might be something
out there that I don't understand yet." He added
quietly, "And I do believe in everything *you* are,
Alisa. I've never believed in anyone more than I do
in you. Which means I might be almost there."

She suddenly couldn't breathe. She couldn't look
away from him. She was aware of everything about
him. His eyes, his lips, that intensity that was always
with him. "It's about time." She cleared her throat.
"You've been a little slow, Korgan."

"I'll catch up." His gaze never left her as he
reached over and covered her hand with his own.
"And when you decide you can forgive me for the

mistake that got you shot and Sasha in this mess, I'll
make a good friend to you, Alisa." He smiled. "I've
got excellent references."

"Have you? I don't. I've been too busy working to make many real friends." She could feel
the warmth of his hand and his thumb moving
back and forth on her wrist. She should probably
move her hand, but she remained still. It wasn't
like the touch on her shoulder last night that had
been so comforting. This one was gossamer light
and sensual and yet almost erotically electric. It
confused her, and so did all this talk about being
friends. But that didn't matter. Both times he had
been kind and caring and honest as few people had
been in her life. It wouldn't hurt to accept anything he offered as long as she was careful not to let
it mean anything to her. She added quickly, "But
I've got Margaret and Sasha and that's enough. And
you don't have to say you'll be a friend to me because you feel guilty you weren't perfect about that
drone. I told you that you almost got everything
else right."

"How generous of you." He sighed and shook
his head. "You're impossible." He gave her hand a
squeeze before he released it. "I do feel guilty but
that's not the reason I want to be a friend to you.
I'd much rather work on that down the road. But
I'm beginning to realize that there are only two

ways I can go. I'm trying to choose the one that
protects you."

"That's bullshit," she said bluntly. "I don't need
anyone to protect me for any reason. This entire
conversation is ridiculous. I don't know how we
got on the subject when I was only trying to figure
out a way to block whatever Masenak and Reardon
might try to do with Chaos."

"I know exactly how we got on the subject. My
mind is never very far from it. It just kind of slid
into it. Of course there's no way we'd leave Sasha
alone to deal with them. I'll work on it." He shook
his head. "Correction: *We'll* work on it. But we
can't do anything to stop them until we manage to
get to Jubaldar. However, the options for finding
it are multiplying. We have the hack on Reardon's
phone, and we know he intends to join Masenak
for the race in two weeks. Vogel might be able
to arrange to follow him. If that doesn't pan out,
we might still be able to do what we planned and
locate it by using one of the village workers. I'll
call Gilroy this evening and see what progress he's
making at Samlir. Margaret will join us tomorrow
and you said that the two of you should be able to
track down that other village." He smiled. "What
are you worried about? We're golden. All we have
to do is wait for one of those options to drop in
our laps."

"Yeah, we're golden. What was I thinking?" She forced a smile. "After all, this is nothing after I conquered the cockroaches." She finished her coffee. "I want to look at that map again and then I guess we should break out the rations."

"I'll do it." He turned away. "But first I need you to take off your shirt and bra."

"What?"

"You were a little too determined about losing that sling from now on. I won't be able to talk you out of it, so I have to examine that wound and make certain the bandage isn't going to give you any trouble. Any objection?"

She frowned and then started to carefully remove the sling. "No, I guess it's a sensible precaution."

"Glad you think so. But then I knew you would, since you're such a sensible woman. Always doing what's necessary…" He was reaching into his backpack for a bottle of water and the first-aid kit. "Sit down by the fire. Let's get it over with."

She'd already removed her shirt. "You'll have to help me with the bra. You should have told whoever bought these clothes for me to get a front opening."

"The discussion never came up." He unfastened the bra and slipped it carefully off her shoulders. "Just another mistake I made in my dealings with you. I'll remember next time."

"But then I might not need it. I could manage it if I didn't have this wound." She stepped back and took the bra from him. "You said you wanted me to sit by the fire?"

"Did I? I don't remember." He was staring at her breasts. "Beautiful..."

She inhaled sharply and stiffened. She'd known there was a possibility of this, but he'd been so noncommittal that she'd thought that she might be wrong. But there was nothing noncommittal about his expression now. Nor her own reaction to his gaze on her breasts.

They were swelling, the nipples becoming taut, so sensitive she felt as if they were burning. The muscles of her stomach were clenching. "You want this?" She moistened her lips with her tongue. "It's all right. I don't mind. It doesn't matter."

"Why did I know you'd say that?" he said hoarsely. "A reward for doing *almost* everything right? But it does matter, and that's why I'm going to go nuts until I finish checking out this wound." He pushed her down before the fire and then knelt before her. "And cursing my idiocy while I'm doing it."

She could feel the heat from the flames on her bare breasts. They felt heavy...waiting. But it was no hotter than the ripples of need jolting through her. As he started to work on the bandage, she could feel his warm breath on the hollow of her throat and breasts making her even more taut... "I think you're being foolish. It's all very simple." She added in a low voice, "And I'd probably... like it."

"I know I'm being an ass," he said jerkily. "And I'd make damn sure you liked it. But there's nothing about you or this that's not complicated. Now just be quiet until I can finish and get my hands off you."

She sat there quietly while he cleaned, washed, and rebandaged the wound. "Are you finished?"

He sat back on his heels and drew a deep breath. "Not nearly. Not in a thousand years. It almost killed me."

"Then you deserve it." She got to her feet. "You were being stupid. Besides, you made me feel... I'm not a child or a victim. Don't you ever treat me like one again." She went to her backpack and started looking through it for another bra. "Now go somewhere I don't have to look at you for a while. Call Gilroy or Vogel or make one of your super master plans while I find us something to eat."

"I have every intention of getting away from you ASAP. I've taken enough punishment for one day," he said roughly as he headed back toward the road. "I'm a little limited about where to go to remove myself on this mountain. But you can bet I'll try to oblige without jumping into the abyss."

She didn't answer, and when she looked up he

was gone. She drew a deep breath, stopped, and straightened. Now she could gain control again. She had shown him that she was mature and let him know that she wouldn't tolerate being considered any other way. She wasn't that fourteen-year-old girl he'd pitied and thought a victim.

Perhaps would always think a victim...

Screw him. He was the idiot he'd called himself. She'd done everything she could to change his mind. What else could she say after she'd told him she'd probably like it? He'd been close enough to her that he could see the changes in her body, which she hadn't been able to hide even after he'd rejected her.

And those changes were still present. Lord, she'd wanted his mouth on her breasts. She closed her eyes as she felt the heat clenching between her thighs. She knew sex, but she'd never known desire like those minutes kneeling before Korgan. She'd been having all kinds of fantasies when his hands had been on her. They wouldn't go away even now.

Korgan: It had to be because it was Korgan. Margaret had said that she'd always had an obsession with Korgan even before she had met him. She had denied it and told her it was only admiration for how clever he was and what he'd accomplished. But what she'd been feeling just now had nothing to do with admiration for his mind, and everything to do with sex. Nothing to do with payment for services rendered, and everything with bringing him into her body and making him want to stay there.

The acknowledgment that she'd lied to herself came as a shock. The depth of how much she'd wanted Korgan brought its own sense of panic. Only earlier she'd been telling herself it was going to be okay to accept anything he offered as long as she was careful not to let it mean anything to her. But this situation clearly had its own dangers.

Back up. Think about it. Don't make a mistake...

FOUR HOURS LATER

Where the *hell* was he?

Alisa strode to the edge of the road where Korgan had disappeared all those hours ago. Darkness. The sun had gone down over two hours ago, and it would have been stupid for Korgan to be strolling around on that curving road, which was dangerous even in a vehicle in broad daylight.

But Korgan was very sure-footed and climbed mountains for sport. Who knew what he might decide to do? She'd told him she didn't want to see him anytime soon, and she shouldn't worry if he'd taken her at her word.

But she *was* worried. Her palms were clammy with cold. Even the best climbers could lose their footing if the ground gave beneath their feet.

And then he'd plunge all that distance to the valley, and she might not even know she'd lost him. No, that couldn't happen. Maybe she'd better go and see what had—

"You should be painted with that fire framing you in the darkness. Very effective," Korgan called out to her from the bottom of the road. "I can't decide if you look welcoming or like a demon spirit casting a spell. I'm sure you'll let me know soon."

The relief was overwhelming, and she was glad for that darkness so that he wouldn't see it on her face as he walked toward her. "Why should I look welcoming? You did exactly what I told you to do. I was only wondering if you were going to stay out there all night."

"I was busy. I lost track of time." He went past her and got a bottle of water from the carton sitting beside the fire. "But I did get thirsty." His demeanor was as cool and brusque as if those moments by the fire had never happened as he opened the bottle and took a long drink. "And Gilroy and I were doing a lot of talking. It got fairly involved. But some good things might have come of it."

"What kind of things?" she asked warily.

"You ordered me to come up with a plan, didn't

you? I told you that to hear was to obey." He took another swallow of water and then went to stand before the fire. "Besides, you know very well that it would take me time to cool down. But when I called Gilroy, he'd come up with some information that distracted me enough to make me actually think about throwing together some kind of plan."

She stiffened. "What kind of plan?"

"Ah, that interested you. Gilroy found the answers he was looking for. We're not going to have to complete our trip to Kabada. Those Kabada villagers might have been dealing with Masenak, but it wasn't extensively. It seems that Samlir has been providing most of the labor for Jubaldar for the past few years. Principally in the stables and household, but occasionally they bring in women to provide fun and games for the guests." He paused. "At any rate, they know where Jubaldar is located."

"Sasha!" Her eyes widened with excitement. What he'd said meant they were going to find her. "Then they can tell us where it is."

"If they choose, but no one in the village is willing to do it. Jubaldar is an armed fortress, and what he demands of those workers comes close to slave labor. They're afraid not only of Masenak, but also of Simon Davidow, the trainer who runs the stable and oversees the household." He tilted his head as he thought about it. "There still might be a way around it. It appears that the stables have been losing personnel lately due to injuries. Yesterday one of the stable boys was sent back to the village with two broken legs, and there have been three other injuries in the past two weeks. When Davidow had the boy brought back to the village yesterday, it was with orders to the council to send immediate replacements if they want the present financial arrangements to continue."

"They seem to be chewing those boys up and spitting them out," she said bitterly. "The council might decide it's better to have healthy citizens than continue to feed Masenak's need for forced labor."

Korgan shook his head. "According to Gilroy, they've gotten used to having that additional money in the community till. The council gets its percentage for being cooperative. I'm willing to bet they'll scavenge and find some men to send to Jubaldar to make up the extra." He paused. "Which will probably be better for us."

"You mean we can follow them?"

"Yes, but we need to do more if you want Sasha to have someone there to protect her. We should have someone in the castle for her."

She didn't know if she liked where this was going. "Can you bribe one of the villagers who are already there?"

"Again, would you trust someone you didn't know to protect her? Of course you wouldn't." He paused. "I promised you I'd find Sasha and take care of her. So it's really my job."

"No!" The rejection she felt at the idea of Korgan going to Jubaldar, even to make contact with Sasha, was immediate and violent. "You believe no one on the planet would recognize you while you were skulking around that castle?" she asked sarcastically. "It's not as if you can go anywhere incognito. It would be suicide. And by now Masenak has to know you're responsible for what happened to destroy the Szarnar camp. He's going to want to draw and quarter you the minute he gets a chance."

"Not necessarily." He grimaced. "From the way he attacked you, I'd bet you'll be first on his list now that I managed to make sure Lakewood gave you credit with the CIA and media." He shrugged. "There are always ways and means. First, I'll have to think of a way to make it work with those villagers. Gilroy said he might need me to come and influence council members and anyone else who could be tempted to tattle to Masenak and save their necks. The bastard seems to have done a good job of terrorizing those villagers since he started bringing them to Jubaldar as servants. I think I might need to snag that helicopter that's bringing Margaret tomorrow to take me to Samlir."

Her fists clenched at her sides. "Because even primitive Berbers, who live on mountaintops at the back of beyond, can be influenced when the great Korgan pays them a visit?" Her panic was growing with every minute. She could see she wasn't going to convince him, and it was beginning to terrify her. "Why don't you admit you were just frustrated that you had to be practical and cerebral and didn't get to play war games like Gilroy and the rest of us? Gilroy has been saying that about you since he showed up at base camp. Well, it wasn't a game to me."

"Nor to me," he said quietly. "Not this time. But this could be a break, and I'm going to work with it. You should try to work with it, too." He paused. "Why are you so angry?"

She didn't know, but she was beginning to suspect. She couldn't let him see beyond that emotion that wasn't really anger. "Because you're an idiot and all you can see is that you have to be in control. Even if Masenak kills you." She added jerkily, "So much for you doing whatever I want. Well, you've done your part in finding Jubaldar. It's not as if I can't take it from here if I need to. By all means, go and have your talk with those Berbers."

"I will." He muttered a curse. "Because it's the intelligent thing to do, and I don't know why you won't admit it." He turned away. "All I've said is that I'm going to look the situation over and you're putting up all kinds of barbed-wire defenses and threatening to go ballistic."

"You're exaggerating."

"Not much. Look, we're closer to Sasha than we've ever been, and that might be why you're so emotional and—" He stopped and suddenly looked over his shoulder, his eyes narrowing. "But that's not like you, either."

And he was coming too close. Shy away and don't let him see how vulnerable she was right now. Of course she'd get over it, but he was too sharp not to pick up on every nuance if she didn't hide it carefully. "You're right." She had to wait a minute before she could meet his gaze and force herself to smile ruefully. "It's not like me. And I'm tempted to slug you for accusing me of being overemotional." She paused. "If it wasn't true. I'm still tempted, because you wouldn't accuse Gilroy of being too emotional under any circumstances. Is that reserved for women in your eyes? However, I might not have been thinking straight, and this is too important to me to let that happen. I have to take a step back and consider all angles." She turned away. "So I'm going to curl up in my sleeping bag and do just that. I'll talk to you in the morning." She dropped to her knees beside her sleeping bag.

"Your rations are over there beside your backpack. Good night, Korgan."

He didn't answer for a moment. "Good night."

She could still feel his gaze on her as she crawled into the bag and turned her back on him. She'd been a little abrupt, but he'd probably accept that she was pissed off because of the chauvinism she'd accused him of. She'd lie here and close him out and tomorrow she would have herself thoroughly under control.

And he would never know why she had been thrown into such shock and panic at the thought that it was not only Sasha who could be in danger when they made their move on Jubaldar.

She might lose Korgan, too...

———◆———

NEXT DAY
2:40 P.M.

Alisa could see Margaret waving to her as the helicopter cautiously descended. It was so good to see her. She lifted her hand and watched until the copter reached the ground. But the rotors had barely stopped whirring when Korgan stepped forward and opened the passenger door for Margaret. "Good to see you." He lifted her out of the cockpit and watched as Juno jumped to the ground beside her. "And you, too." He took out her duffel and set it on the ground before turning back to Alisa. "I don't know how long I'll be. I'll let you know later. You'll be all right?"

"Of course I will," she said impatiently.

He nodded. "Of course you will," he repeated. He jumped into the helicopter. "Let's go, Harris." He motioned to the pilot to take off. "Take care of her, Margaret."

"You're joking." Margaret laughed as she stepped back away from the chopper. Then her amusement faded when she caught his expression as the aircraft lifted off. "Or maybe you're not . . . " She turned to Alisa. "What's happening?"

"Nothing." She bent down to pet Juno. "Korgan is being Korgan. He's off trying to save the world all by himself and didn't want anyone to get in his way. I just let him know that wasn't necessarily how it was going to play out and there was always a step two. It made him a little uneasy." She straightened and turned toward the fire. "Coffee? And have you fed Juno yet?"

"Yes. And yes, Juno ate before we boarded the helicopter in Casablanca. Not much. She was a little sad at leaving Jeanne. But she knows Lili will take good care of her. Did I tell you that Jeanne talked to her mother on the phone last night?" She smiled. "It went well. They talked about Lili, the new puppy, and nothing else."

"Because you spoke to her and told her what to say."

"I gave a few suggestions. But her mother will know herself when she sees Jeanne with Lili together. There's such a thing as maternal instinct." She took the cup from Alisa, and her gaze lifted in the direction of where the copter had disappeared. "Korgan's uneasy? I thought there was something going on. Yet he wasn't uneasy enough to take you with him to Samlir. From what you told me on the phone this morning, that's where the action may be starting."

"Starting, not ending. It's where you end up that counts." She shrugged. "He probably would have taken me with him, if I'd pushed it. I didn't, because I knew I wouldn't be able to resist trying to mold the situation the way I wanted it to go. But this is Sasha, and I couldn't take the chance of a wrong move." She smiled wryly. "Especially not when I had Korgan in the wings, who's an expert at molding and persuading and making events happen on a planetary scale. Of course I had to use him to take the first step."

"First step," Margaret repeated, her gaze on Alisa's face. "And what's the second step going to be?

You said Korgan wasn't willing to give up saving the world."

"Whatever we choose it to be once we get to Jubaldar. We'll have to see what Korgan and Gilroy come up with at Samlir today." Alisa tried to make her voice sound casual. "Korgan seemed to have some idiotic idea about going in and contacting Sasha himself. Very impractical."

"Completely," Margaret said. "Unless he could find a way to—"

"Masenak would kill them both," Alisa interrupted harshly. "He's clever enough to have found out that it was Korgan who ruined everything for him in the Szarnar Jungle. He'll want to cut his throat. There's no 'unless' about it."

Margaret's brows rose. "You're right, of course." She tilted her head consideringly. "It's much more sensible for you to do it. Then Masenak would have a captive he could torture and use against Sasha. Wouldn't that be great? Just what we all want."

"Margaret."

"Just pointing out options. I know that would be your choice, and it's even worse than Korgan's idea. Which is probably why he's so 'uneasy.' Depending on location, I might be able to get Juno close enough to her to convey a message, but you wanted someone on-site if she needed help."

"I don't want her to be alone again," she said unsteadily.

"I know you don't," Margaret said gently as she met her gaze. "But now the problems have multiplied, haven't they?"

She should have known Margaret knew her too well not to see beyond any defense Alisa could raise. "Not really. I'll work it out. It's only temporary."

"Nothing is ever temporary for you. But you're right, you'll work it out." She lifted her cup to her lips. "And I'll be around to help if you need it."

"You always are." She grimaced. "But right now the only help I need is getting Sasha away from Jubaldar before that damn race."

"At any cost," Margaret said softly. "You forgot to add that. I'm sure Korgan could read it between the lines. It's no wonder he was being foolish enough to tell me to look out for you." She shook her head. "We won't go in that direction. We've been friends too long. We'll sit here and drink coffee and talk about old times while we wait for Korgan to go through his step one. Then we hope like hell he'll come back to us with a plan for step two that makes sense to us. Deal?"

Alisa nodded. "Deal." She poured herself a cup of coffee and then lifted it in a half toast to Margaret. "To my friend, to old times, and to step two."

CHAPTER

12

Y ou got it?" Gilroy sprang to his feet as Korgan came out of the council chamber. "It took you long enough. I thought a man who was once invited to help negotiate a U.N. trade accord wouldn't have a problem with a handful of Berber politicians. Have you lost your touch?"

"Those handful of Berber politicians knew they had me over a barrel," he said dryly. "And that they were the only game in town for what I wanted. I had to get guarantees and permission for their village to be used for anything I choose. As well as getting them to forbid any of the villagers to discuss what was going on to anyone." He added, "And then we had to go into the bargaining phase so that they'd be sure that they'd have enough to support their villagers for some years to come, to make up for the loss of revenue from Masenak."

Gilroy gave a low whistle. "They took you?"

"They took me," Korgan said. "But they agreed to send word to Davidow, that trainer at Jubaldar, that they were sending two laborers to replace the ones who had been damaged and would expect compensation. They gave me their guarantee the villager they'll send will give me full cooperation and see that any messages I need transmitted to Sasha will reach her immediately. That's the main thing I wanted, so I guess it was a draw."

"Not really. But I guess you did as good as you could considering. When do I leave?"

He stiffened. "I didn't say you did. You're not listening. This is a bit different than slipping into a tent in the middle of the night. I'll have to set up a camp in the cliffs near Jubaldar and bribe or intimidate my way into the castle when the time is right."

"And you think you're qualified? Really, Korgan. Will you stop trying to be a hero? It requires a certain dramatic dazzle and pizzazz you'll never possess. Leave it to me. I'm perfect for the role."

"So you keep telling me."

"And it pisses you off." His smile vanished. "Particularly now when you're feeling so rotten about Alisa and Sasha and wanting to set everything right.

But do you actually believe you're going to be able to keep Alisa away from Sasha if you're not there to monitor what she's doing? I got a little taste of what she's going through night before last, and I don't think you have a chance in hell. Besides, you know damn well that we're going to have to take down Masenak and Reardon, and that means bringing in the CIA and our own crew and staging everything down to the last shot fired. I can't do that, but you can." He added soberly, "So let me be the hero again. I speak the language and I can pass for Berber with a little theatrical makeup. You know I'm right. I promise I'll do my usual fantastic job."

He was silent. "*Damn* you."

Gilroy nodded, his eyes suddenly gleaming with mischief. "I thought you'd agree with me. I just had to appeal to that brilliant mind that always gets in your way even when you don't want it to." He pulled a notebook out of his jacket pocket and tore out a page scrawled with notes. "That's why I made a list of things you'll need to have the helicopter pilot bring to me after he drops you off with Margaret and Alisa. Everything from skin bronzer to dark contact lenses to make me look like one of those admirably tough Berber types who have been slaving at Jubaldar. Believe me, you couldn't have pulled it off."

"And evidently I'm not going to get the

opportunity to make the attempt," Korgan said through set teeth. "You know, someday I'm going to murder you."

"Someday, but not today. I called the helicopter the minute I saw the ceremonious way you were being escorted out of the meeting house, and Harris said he'll be here to pick you up in ten minutes. Be sure to tell him I want those supplies here before morning..."

3:32 A.M.

Korgan jumped out of the helicopter and waved the pilot to take off. "Get going," he said curtly. "You have your damn list, Harris. Get everything on it fast and make sure it's absolutely correct. He wants it right away."

Korgan was definitely in a foul humor, Alisa thought as she got out of her sleeping bag. It didn't bode well for whatever he'd accomplished at Samlir. She and Margaret had let the fire go out during the night, and she reached for her flashlight to see his expression. It was as impatient as she'd thought it would be. "Hello, Korgan. Since we didn't hear from you, I guess we can expect bad news?"

"Why would you think that?" Korgan growled. "I've been busy. It went as well as could be expected. According to Gilroy, it went even better than expected."

"Gilroy," Margaret repeated as she came toward them. "But he has a unique way of looking at things. I think you'd better elaborate. First, Jubaldar. Are we going to be able to use those villagers to find it?"

"Of course. What do you think I've been doing all these hours? And I don't have to follow any of the villagers to get there. I have a map and can show you the exact location." He muttered a curse. "If I had more light. You let the damn fire go out."

Very nasty mood, Alisa thought again. But his words had given her hope, and she wasn't about to let him ruin it for her. "Then light it again. You couldn't expect us to keep it burning like a lamp to light your way home. For all we knew, you'd forgotten about us."

He was silent. "You'd be hard to forget. You're too much trouble." He knelt down and started to rebuild the fire. "If it's not too much bother, shine your light down so I can see what I'm doing."

"I don't think it's too much bother. Not if you brought me what you say you did. I'll even forgive you for being such a disagreeable bastard." She fell to her knees beside him as the wood caught fire and flamed high. "I'd forgive you for anything. Just *show* it to me."

He unfolded the map and laid it on the ground near the fire. "Compliments of the Samlir village council. You'll find it very detailed and accurate. Evidently, they didn't want any of their villagers getting lost and falling off the mountain . . . or running into any other hazard. So over the years they've been compiling information from their workers past and present. Just another little expense they added onto my total bill." He pointed to the outline of a towering three-story structure sketched on the map. "The castle. It's a rose-stone building built into a cave wall. Windows only on the north and south sides. One huge stained-glass amber rectangle facing the front. The south wall overlooks the stables and leads directly to the racetrack and grandstand." He pointed to a canyon to the west of the castle. "Here are garages for utility vehicles as well as a helicopter pad."

"Masenak's eternal escape solution," Alisa murmured.

Korgan nodded. "You're right, that pad is reserved exclusively for his use in case of attack, but it's much larger and more substantial than the one he had at Szarnar. He has warehouses and caches for weapons, food storage lockers, even a field where he grows marijuana. And Reardon is permitted to have his own racehorse flown into the canyon area near race day." He pointed to another blocked section to the east. "This is another pad where Masenak and his guests usually land when he comes here. That's the one Baldwin mentioned. It's only a short walk from the castle and keeps Masenak's canyon emergency transportation vehicles private."

"You're right, very detailed," Margaret said. "But no access where Jubaldar could be watched?"

"Not as far as we know. But that doesn't mean we can't find one. The entire area is networked with canyons and cliffs." Korgan pointed to a curving indentation that disappeared into a rocky cliff that looked to be fifty or sixty feet above the castle. "That might be a possibility. None of the Berbers have made any overt attempt to spy on Jubaldar. The council wanted Masenak's money, and they're afraid of him. They only gathered the information they have to protect themselves and the workers."

"Then we might find a better place of our own to do it," Alisa said. She reached out and touched the north side of the rose-stone castle with her index finger. "That's where Sasha is..."

"Almost certainly," he said quietly. "The stable boys who were returned to the village hadn't seen her before they left, but they'd heard she was being kept in one of the harem suites in the main castle."

"She wouldn't be there now. She'd want to be close to Chaos. She'd find a way to get to him." Her hand went to the south wall and traveled down to the stable area. "I'll bet she's somewhere here."

"I'll be sure to let Gilroy know," he said caustically. "If he doesn't already. He probably wouldn't tell me if he did."

"Gilroy? Why would you want to do that?"

"It appears he's going to be our go-between with Sasha until we can get her out of there. He tells me he's my best choice whether I like it or not."

Hence the extremely bad mood, she thought. Gilroy always managed to strike home and get what he wanted from Korgan when no one else could. "I can't see you meekly agreeing to anything."

"I'm *not* meek." He scowled. "The son of a bitch made sense. I could have handled the situation in a different way, but it might not have turned out to be the right way. There were things that had to be done that only I could do." His lips thinned. "So I delegated again."

And it was irritating the hell out of him, Alisa realized even as the relief poured through her. He wasn't going into Jubaldar, which could be a deadly trap for him. "How did Gilroy talk you into it?"

He lifted his eyes from the map to her face. "He gave me his usual bullshit collection of reasons, but he was right on a couple of points. He's good at what he does, and I can trust him. *You* trust him to do what's best for Sasha, and that may keep you safer." His lips twisted. "So I guess I'll have to forgive him for telling me how lousy I'd be if I tried to handle it myself. Maybe he's right about me lacking the pizzazz and dazzle to pull it off."

"He went that far?" She sat there looking at him. He didn't even realize how absurd he was being. But then he couldn't see the man she saw. The power. The brilliance. The intricacy of the search for knowledge that never stopped. The honor that had made him keep his word to free those students no matter what got in the way. The splendor of the curiosity that made him dig deeper when others gave up. Genius. Artist. Engineer. Scientist. Renaissance man.

And human. Oh, my God, how human.

She tore her gaze away. "Even if it was true, it wasn't kind of Gilroy," she said lightly as she glanced at Margaret. "What do you think, Margaret?"

"I think that Korgan will manage to survive Gilroy. He seems to do just fine." She was still looking down at the map. "And I think we need to do some more exploration around the entire area. When can we leave here?"

"Later this afternoon," he said. "I have some calls to make, and I want to make sure that Gilroy has everything he needs and is on his way to Jubaldar. We can take the Land Rover for the first part of the journey, but we'll have to leave it here." He indicated a spot some distance from Jubaldar. "From there we're on foot, so we'd better travel by night and find a place to camp out that's close to the castle and yet safe."

"Calls?" Alisa repeated. "You said there were things you could do that Gilroy couldn't. Who are you calling?"

"Vogel." He added, "And maybe Lakewood." He saw her tense and said quickly, "We're going to need him. I have to prepare him. You know it."

"I know if you bring the CIA in too soon, you'll get Sasha killed," she said curtly. "Lakewood is going to be like a hungry lion when he goes after Masenak. He's had all those diplomats and power figures on his ass for a solid month. All he wants is Masenak's head on a platter."

"Then I won't let the lion have Masenak until we get Sasha out. I'll hold off Lakewood until we have her safe. Trust me." She didn't answer and he went on, "Look, these mountains are going to be hell to negotiate. We'll have to slip in troops and weapons and place them where we can before any attack. But I can do it. I'll handle it. I'll never let anything happen to either of you again." He paused and then asked, "Will you trust me?"

She was silent. "I might," she finally said. "Even though Gilroy says you have no dazzle or pizzazz, I've always found you to be an honest man. That has to count for something." She looked back down at the map, her finger once more reaching out to trace the south wall leading to the stable. *Soon, Sasha. We'll be there soon.* "But if you don't keep Lakewood under control, I'll go after him myself. Remember that, Korgan."

"I'll remember," he said wryly. "I'm just grateful you didn't say you'd go after me."

———◆———

1:40 P.M.

"Who the hell do you think you are?" Lakewood bit out. "You must have been reading your own press clippings, Korgan. You call me and tell me that you're taking down Masenak and Reardon and I'm just supposed to sit quietly on the sidelines until you give me permission to make a move? The CIA does *not* ask permission. Why did you ever believe I'd let you run a show like this? Give me the location where I can grab Masenak and I'll snatch him so fast his head will spin."

"You're not mentioning Reardon," Korgan pointed out. "I want both of them, Lakewood. I was afraid you'd back off dealing with Reardon if you had Masenak in your sights."

"Because Reardon will be a political nightmare to prosecute if we gather him up with Masenak. He's a respected businessman as far as anyone knows. He has contacts all over Africa. And he's smart enough not to leave any evidence. We pick him up and he'll walk anyway."

"Then the answer is for you not to pick him up. I understand that your organization is under intense scrutiny these days and it might be awkward. I'll do it for you, and I guarantee you'll have a confession from him that will please everyone. I even promise that there won't be any sign of abuse." He paused. "The only thing I won't guarantee is that I'll turn him over to you afterward. I won't have you sticking him in a cell and letting him lawyer up so that he might end up getting a medal instead of a death sentence."

"I might consider it, after I get Masenak. Now tell me where I can find him. You wouldn't have called me if you hadn't thought you might need us. You pulled off the rescue of those students, but you're not as golden as you think you are. No one cares about Reardon. Masenak is the monster knocking on the front door. Murderer, terrorist, kidnapper. He's the one everyone wants dead."

He was definitely the one Lakewood wanted dead, Korgan thought, and he was proving intractable. "I care about Reardon," he said quietly. "And I told you about my friend Karim Raschid, who would have cared very much. Besides, the job of freeing those students isn't finished yet. He still has Sasha Nalano captive in that castle. She's the ward of one of your operatives, and that should count for something."

"Of course it does. But I shouldn't let Company business influence my decisions. That's why I'll assign one my most effective operatives to head the assault. I've used Walt Edwards many times before. He has a sterling record, and he'll wrap up the operation in no time."

"I'm sure he's excellent, but there are more things to consider than speed. Sasha is in a very vulnerable position. I prefer to handle it myself."

"Too bad," Lakewood said. "It's my way or nothing. Give me the location where I can find Masenak or you won't get my help. I'll send out a team and we'll find Masenak on our own."

"I'll think about it. I believe we should both consider possible consequences. Suppose I call you tomorrow?" He hung up the phone and glanced at Alisa. "You heard him. The son of a bitch wants Masenak so bad, he's not even thinking straight."

She nodded. "Everyone at Langley knows that

Lakewood is more politician than CIA operative these days. Masenak made him look like an amateur to the entire world." She shivered. "And Sasha may pay for it."

"No, she won't. I'm just stalling him until I see how I can work around him."

"We don't have much time to stall. Do we have to have Lakewood's team for the assault? Couldn't we just use the same team we did at Szarnar?"

"We will. But we need more feet on the ground in these mountains. We'll have to strike Jubaldar from several different directions, with painstaking coordination from all team leaders."

"That's why you want to be in charge."

"Lakewood would say I always want to be in charge. I'm surprised you didn't."

"No, you always have a good reason," she said absently. "And Lakewood should have realized that, too. He was just in too much of a hurry to catch Masenak." Her lips tightened. "It was clear he was already considering Sasha collateral damage given in sacrifice to the greater good. It's like him to expect me to give up a family member so that he could have Masenak that much sooner. Not bloody likely. If we need those additional teams from him, we'll get them."

He gave a low whistle. "Just the response I thought you'd have. Now tell me what you know about this Walt Edwards. How good is he? And can we work with him?"

"He's very professional and skillful." She paused. "But he's also what Lakewood said. He's goal-oriented and ambitious and would want to wrap up the attack quickly and hand it to Lakewood any way he was ordered to do it." She added harshly, "And I'm not having him anywhere near Sasha."

"Then he won't be," Korgan said. "I had to ask. I'll think of something else."

"Or I will. You're not the only one who has experience," she said as she got to her feet. "Now that you've told me what we need, we'll just go and get it."

His brows rose. "Right this minute?"

"No, you gave Lakewood a reprieve until tomorrow. I want to get as far as we can on the way to Jubaldar before dark and be ready to explore those mountains surrounding it by tomorrow morning. Gilroy should definitely be there in the castle by that time, and I want him to have whatever support we can give him." She glanced at him over her shoulder. "I'll leave you to think about what an ass Lakewood is turning out to be and what we can do about it to keep Sasha alive, while I go tell Margaret it's time we got busy. Screw these maps. By tomorrow afternoon I want to be looking at Jubaldar. I want to *see* where that bastard is keeping her."

———◆———

They didn't make it to Jubaldar by afternoon the next day. By the time they did the initial exploration and discovered a place high in the cliffs above the castle that both Margaret and Korgan considered a safe observation site, the sun was going down.

"Satisfied?" Korgan asked Alisa curtly as he caught up with her at a stand of tall boulders overlooking the canyons below. "Too bad if you're not. We should have forced you to stop two hours ago to rest. This is where we set up camp."

"No, I'm *not* satisfied. It's not close enough. I can barely see the castle. We should get farther down. From here I can't see the stables, and I know that's where she'd be."

"If you could see the stables, you'd be right on top of the castle. You might be able to see them, but they'd also see us. From here we can see all activity around the exterior. See arrivals and departures. Be available to receive signals if Gilroy needs to send any. We have a cave and a stream a mile away, and these boulders block any vision from below. It's as good as we're going to get."

"It's not close enough." She couldn't take her gaze from the castle. "We could keep searching and we might—"

"No." His voice was no longer curt but gentle.

"This is what we need. You'll be safe here. I know that it must seem like a mirage to you that you could be this close and not reach out and touch Sasha. But the closer you get, the greater will be the temptation. And you're not thinking straight. You know we have to take it slow."

"Do we?" Her gaze was still focused on that mesmerizing streak of sunlight illuminating the tall windows of the castle. It seemed to be calling her. "You saw how good I am with locks and security systems. I'd have no problem getting in that damn place. All I need is a plan to get her out."

"And not get caught and make it worse for her. Gilroy is down there now, and he's good with locks and bypassing security, too. Not nearly as good as you, but he won't have to be. The report from the council says that the Jubaldar interior security is barely basic. He'll be able to reach Sasha without putting her life on the line." He paused. "Which you would be doing, Alisa. You know it."

She did know it. There was a plan in place, and it should be followed. But it was agony looking down at that castle and knowing Sasha was there, just out of reach. "She's alone down there, Korgan," she whispered. "Just as she was at the camp at Szarnar. I want to be with her."

"I hear you." His lips twisted wryly. "So do I. But I've been told I'm not good enough to be down there. So we're just going to have to suck it up and do what we know is best, aren't we? She'll know she's not alone soon."

"Typical silver-tongued Korgan. Putting us both in the same boat so that I'd see your point of view is the right point of view."

"And do you?"

"Yes," she said wearily. "It was just a moment of temporary insanity. But I don't promise not to have another one or two before this is over."

"Then I'll be there for you until it is," he said quietly. "Just reach out and I'll be there."

She felt the warmth flow through her as she looked at him. The sadness and desperation were still with her, but he had given her comfort with no hint of judgment in those moments. She turned back to the castle. "You mentioned surveillance? We can do that, of course, but it would be more efficient for us to make certain Samlir's maps and diagrams are as accurate as they thought. Tomorrow Margaret and I will start out early and go over the entire property. I'll send you and Vogel emails and photos that will give you a hell of a lot more information than that council did."

"Good idea." His lips were twitching. "Not to mention letting you get closer to that castle. Just don't get too close."

"I wouldn't be unprofessional. But accuracy is

important." She turned away from Jubaldar. "Now I think we'd both better go up to the cave and be there for Margaret in case she needs help setting up camp. She probably would have called us if she hadn't decided your persuasive efforts would be better used in making me productive." She started up the incline. "She approves of division of labor..."

———————◆———————

JUBALDAR

TWO DAYS LATER

"I was watching you this afternoon." Masenak was waiting for Sasha at the stable as she walked Chaos down the aisle toward his stall. "I wasn't pleased. You had your instructions and you didn't obey them. I won't permit that."

"If you were watching me, then you know that I was working with Chaos all day," she said coldly. "It takes time and patience when you're dealing with a horse like him. He made progress."

"You're making excuses," he said impatiently. "You didn't ride him."

"But Chaos let four other horses with riders on the same track with him without attacking them. How can you expect to have a race if Chaos won't

allow Reardon's horse on the track? And he let me
put a saddle on him this afternoon. Ask Davidow if
that isn't progress."

"I want you to *ride* him. Reardon will be here in
another few days and you'll make me look like a
fool to him if he doesn't see you on his back."

"I have a little time," she said flippantly. "I might
get there yet."

"Bitch!" Masenak took a stride toward her and
his hand reached out, his nails digging into her
shoulder. "You'll get there tomorrow, do you hear?
Or I'll have you—" He broke off and jerked back
away from her. Chaos was suddenly rearing behind
Sasha and lunging toward Masenak!

"I heard you." She turned and tried to quiet
the stallion. "So does Chaos. He doesn't like you.
You'd better get away from here or he might hurt
himself trying to bash your head in. He's very fond
of doing that. Then you wouldn't have any fine
horse to show off to Reardon."

Masenak was breathing hard but backing away.
"Tomorrow you ride him," he hissed. "You understand?" He turned on his heel and strode toward
the stable door.

He's gone. She opened Chaos's stall door. *Now stop
that nonsense. He's not worth your effort.*

Nor yours. Chaos went into his stall. *You should not
have let him touch you. But since you're so pitifully weak*

and weaponless, I will do you the favor of stomping the fool for you.

No. All she needed was to have to defend Chaos from a vengeful Masenak. *Well, not right away. Not until I tell you that you can. There might be problems. And I'm not all that weak.* She changed the subject. *But I thank you for allowing those other horses to share your space on the track today. It was very helpful to me.*

I don't know why you would want them there, since I am clearly all anyone could need. He was becoming interested in his oats, but he was taking his time. *But I didn't mind them being there. They stayed out of my way, and I could tell how much they were admiring me. It was good that they realized how superior I was to them.*

Yes, it's always nice to have fans. I thought you might feel that way. No one can say you're overly modest.

I am king. Everyone knows that but you. Sometimes I want to kick you for being so blind.

But you don't, because I'm your friend, and I would care for you even if you weren't king.

"Friend." That word again. Wrong. When will you learn? King.

Friend. Much better than king. When will you learn? She turned away. *I have to go and shower in that other place. I'll come back later and check to see if you need anything.*

And stay with me again? He lifted his head. *I*

don't like having you go to that other place. I did not mind it too much having you here with me. You should do it again.

We'll see. A shower doesn't do me a great deal of good if I come back and curl up on the hay for the night. I only did it last night to show Masenak how meek and obedient I was about working with you day and night.

Foolish. You should do it because I wish it, not because he does. Tomorrow you must not get in my way when I stomp him. You understand?

She understood that they had come full circle. *Maybe I'll stay with you if you agree not to get in my way when you believe I'm handling Masenak foolishly. King or not, this is important to me.*

He went back to eating. *I might allow you to be foolish for a little while longer.*

And she was probably going to spend another night in the stable, she thought as she turned away and headed down the aisle toward the stable door. Oh well, it didn't matter. Cleanliness aside, she'd far rather stay here with the horses than in that luxurious harem where she could sense all the pain and subjugation that must have taken place within its walls. It was the difference between natural and the—

"Sasha!"

She jerked to a stop in the middle of the aisle.

"Don't speak. Don't look at me." The voice was a

sudden, low whisper in the dimness. "I don't know how closely this stable is being watched by the guards. Maybe pretend you're having trouble with the door latch?"

She froze. Her heart nearly jumped out of her chest.

She *knew* that voice.

Gilroy?

Her hands automatically went to the latch on the door as she said, "Don't look at you? How could I? Where the hell are you, Gilroy?"

"One stall back on your left."

She turned to face the stall, but he was only another dark shadow in the dimness of the entire area. "No guards here in this stable. Only two in the courtyard outside that leads to the main house." She was whispering like him until she realized what she was doing. "No audio or cameras," she said in a normal tone. "The main stable has all those bells and whistles, but this is a special add-on facility used by Reardon when he brings his horses here for the races. Davidow took it over for Chaos when he realized how antisocial he could be."

"And not only with other horses." He was coming forward and paused at the door of the stall. "I was afraid I was going to have to step in if he ran you down getting to Masenak."

"That would have been a mistake. Chaos is very

quick. He could have taken down both of you. I've seen him—" She inhaled sharply as she got a good look at him. "You look terrible."

"I do not," he said with mock indignation. "I look authentic Berber. Everyone at the village gave me their seal of approval. I think I even look more Berber than Naleek, the man they sent along with me to run interference with any other Berbers from the same village." He smiled, revealing teeth that were a little stained with a broken incisor in the front. His skin was a dark bronze; his hair was mussed and ended just above his shoulders. The blue eyes were now covered by dark-brown contacts, in a face that was weather-roughened and made him appear older. He was dressed in loose black cotton trousers, black leather boots, and a beige shirt like most of the other stable hands she'd seen since she'd arrived here.

"And beggars can't be choosers, Sasha. The only other people standing in line for this job were Korgan and Alisa."

"Alisa." She was jarred out of her shock and reached out to grab his arm. "How is she? Masenak said she was in some hospital in Switzerland, but that's all he'd tell me."

"She's alive and well," he said gently. "She had a rough time for a couple of days but she's on the mend and not far from here."

"She has to stay away. He's so angry with her, and that will only make the punishment worse if thinks he can use her against me...and Chaos."

"Korgan isn't going to let her get close to you if he can help it. That's double trouble as far as he's concerned. That's why I'm here."

"You've told me why. Now tell me how you got into this stable. I've seen how Davidow treats the stable help and I can't see him letting you sneak in and out as you did my tent at the camp at Szarnar. When did you get here?"

"Naleek and I arrived yesterday afternoon. We were put to work immediately and shown how humility and hard labor was going to be our lot in life by Davidow's foreman. I'm very good at being humble and was duly intimidated and kept my head down but my ears open. Which let me start picking up everything I could from the other workers. I learned that you and Chaos were scheduled to be on the track with three other horses today, and that he isn't being held in the main stable. But I needed more, so I had to put off approaching you until today." He grimaced. "However, they worked us so hard from the time we got up that I didn't get a chance to find out anything about the stable where Chaos is being kept. I had no idea what kind of security I could expect to run into. I had to rely on learning it from you."

"How did you get in here?"

"You said it yourself: It adjoins the main stable. The workers' quarters are a big room on the other side of that stable. There are fifty—no, closer to sixty—of us curled up in our blankets on the floor. Some of the laborers work in the house, but most of them are in the stable, track, grandstand, or outdoor gardens. Our day ends at sundown. They feed us and then let us go to bed so that we're up at dawn the next day. Believe me, it's no problem slipping out of that room at night. Those laborers are exhausted by the end of their day, and the food they're given is sparse and not particularly healthy. I'd say most of them are fighting malnutrition.

"It doesn't surprise me."

"Anyway, tonight I waited for an hour after everyone bedded down and then started exploring."

"And you ended up in this stall when I brought Chaos back from the track?" She made a face. "It was probably good he was distracted. He's usually aware of everything around him."

He looked back down the aisle at Chaos. "He's having his dinner? My presence doesn't seem to bother him."

"You're being ignored. Evidently, he feels you're not enough of a threat to cause a problem even to a person as weak as he considers me. That's no compliment. He regards me as very stompable."

"Stompable?" He frowned. "I don't know what the hell you're talking about."

"I know. You'd have to have been there." She raised a shaking hand to push back the hair from her forehead. "And I think I'm a little dizzy because you're here and I wasn't expecting it. I could only hope, and sometimes hopes don't come true."

"But sometimes they do," he said quietly. "If it makes a difference, I wanted to come. And I'm sorry I'm not the person you want to be here for you at a time like this, but I'll do my best to—"

"Shut up." She suddenly launched herself into his arms and held him tight for the briefest instant. Then she backed away. "You talk too much and most of the time it doesn't make sense, but you're *here*. You wanted to be here for me. Do you think I don't know and appreciate what that means? Other than that you're not very smart? There's no one I'd want with me more than you right now. You might even turn out to be like that stupid movie hero you call yourself." She frowned. "But you could also get yourself killed. I can't let that happen."

Gilroy smiled. "You don't seem to be making a lot of sense yourself right now."

"I'll be better soon. I told you I'm a little..." She took another step back. She was already feeling awkward about that impulsive moment. Touching was reserved for special people...friends.

She seldom reached out to anyone but Alisa and Margaret, but that heady gratitude had taken her by surprise. Yet wasn't Gilroy perhaps also a friend now? "How long do you think it will be safe for you to stay here? Because there are things I should know, and I'm not thinking straight right now."

"I told you, no one is going to be looking for me right away."

"But you can't be sure about that. You've only spent one night here. I've seen how many chances you take."

"And you want to make certain that I do the right thing? You've got to accept that I know what I'm doing, Sasha."

"Maybe," she said doubtfully.

He chuckled and shook his head. "You have no choice. Alisa would want me to remain close to keep an eye on you, but it seems that's going to be limited to between dusk and dawn. Maybe less, depending on what happens here when Reardon and Masenak's other guests start showing up. If I'm not here for you to order about, you'll have to trust that I'll do the right thing for both of us."

She drew a deep breath. "Then I suppose I'll do it."

His smile faded and he said crisply, "And everything you do from now on must appear absolutely normal and not arouse any suspicion for both our sakes. A little restraint might be welcome, too.

Where were you going when I stopped you from leaving tonight?"

"Back to my room in the castle to shower and eat something. Then I was going to come back here to be with Chaos."

"Masenak allows you to come and go as you please?"

She shook her head. "He kept me locked up at first. But since he put me in charge of Chaos, he gives me freedom to go between here and my quarters at the castle. But it's not the way it was at the Szarnar camp. There are guards trailing me wherever I go." She added bitterly, "And he's not really worried about me trying to escape since he told me he'd kill every one of my horses except Chaos if I did."

"Bastard."

She nodded. "He learned how to stop me cold in that first couple of weeks at Szarnar. Any person or animal that will hurt me to lose is a target. That's why I mustn't ever have Alisa near me."

"That will be difficult, but we'll make the adjustment. Will you see Masenak while you're at the castle? Does he dine with you?"

"No, if he sees me at all it would be unusual. He was upset with me today and he might try to reinforce the orders he gave me, but I doubt it. He's fairly lost about how to handle Chaos. I'm hoping if I show him occasional minimal improvement, it'll keep him from exploding while we figure out how to get Chaos away before that race."

"What if we can't do that?"

She was silent. "It wouldn't be good. Let's not consider it."

"We'll try not to do it." He paused. "What about your relationship with Masenak? Has it changed since you came here?"

"Do you mean does he rape me?" she asked bluntly. "He threatens sometimes when he's angry, but I think he's as confused about how to treat me as he is about Chaos. Yet he's much more vicious now and nothing is a game to him any longer. He doesn't even want to be around me unless it has to do with Chaos." She remembered something else. "I saw the guards taking a woman into his quarters when I was leaving to go back to the stable last night. She was young, pretty, scared. Maybe one of the women Masenak had sent from the village?"

"And maybe a way to get to Masenak," he murmured. "Name?"

She shook her head. "She was just another poor girl who reminded me of those students at the prison camp. Maybe he even wanted me to see her to remind me that I couldn't change anything he did."

"But we *can* change what's happening. I'll ask

Naleek about that woman and see if she's from Samlir. We'll just have to work on the rest. Korgan and Alisa know I'm here and talking to you. Korgan was starting to have discussions with Lakewood at the CIA even before I left the village. It was too risky to bring a phone or weapon into the castle, but once I had a description of the setup here, I asked Korgan to drop off phones and weapons where I could retrieve them. He chose the toolshed at the back of the garden area. Tomorrow morning I'll locate them, and tomorrow night you'll have a phone and can talk to Alisa."

A phone. It was strange and wonderful how those words raised her spirits. She'd be able to actually speak to Alisa for the first time since that chilling night when she'd seen her shot and all hope had turned into a disaster. They'd be able to talk and plan and find a way to fight all this ugliness around them. Suddenly everything seemed brighter and more manageable.

"That will be great. I've been so worried about her." She was thinking, going over everything he'd said. Much of it she'd already been doing anyway. The only thing different was that she'd have to try to be less argumentative. She'd been telling herself that since that first day at the racetrack, but she hadn't been doing a very good job of controlling her temper. "I'll keep on being as normal as I can be. You should probably leave now. I'll go back to the suite now and take a shower; if I run into Masenak, I'll try to convince him he's going to get everything he wants." She turned to go. "But we should both think about where to hide those phones. If it was too risky for you to bring them here, we have to make sure they're going to be safe." She reached for the latch to open the stable door. "Wait here in this stall. Don't go near Chaos while I'm gone. Believe me, even Indiana Jones wouldn't have a chance with him."

"Don't worry. I've heard of Chaos's reputation and I'm properly terrified."

"That's good. It will save a lot of trouble." She stopped abruptly as she was opening the door. "Perhaps more than a little," she murmured as a thought struck her. "We could put the phones and weapons under the straw in Chaos's stall. No one would think of going in there if they had a choice. These days I'm the only one who works with him."

"Providing he doesn't smash them underfoot. You mentioned stomping."

"There are ways to keep him from doing that." She was frowning thoughtfully. "But you should really be able to go into his stall yourself to have access to them when we need them." She shrugged. "I'll work on it. We won't get them until tomorrow anyway. I'm certain by that time I'll figure out a way to make you and Chaos more compatible." She opened the door and slipped out into the courtyard. "Good night. Be safe." The door swung shut behind her.

Gilroy stared after her for an instant; then his gaze shifted to Chaos, who had raised his large head and was now staring balefully at him. He gave a low curse. More *compatible*?

Joking, right?

CHAPTER

13

NEXT DAY

6:05 P.M.

A re you hurt?" Masenak was glaring down at
Sasha on the ground as she slowly and painfully raised herself on her elbow before sitting up.
"You'd better not be hurt. You let that horse toss
you into the dirt, bitch. Where's all that skill I heard
about before I raided that damn school?"

"You said you wanted to see me on Chaos's back
today." She got to her feet and swayed a moment
to get her balance. "I obeyed you. I just didn't stay
on him for very long. I tried to tell you that was
the way it was going to be. I'm no magician, I'm
just good with horses. That was the second time he
bucked me off today. Maybe tomorrow I'll be able
to stay on him a little longer."

"There's no time for that bullshit. Reardon is

going to be here in another two days, and I won't be humiliated by having him watch my jockey dumped in the dirt." He turned on his heel. "You're running out of maybes, Sasha. Tomorrow I'm going to Skype Reardon and he's going to see you on Chaos, and you're going to look professional, not like a schoolgirl who has no idea what she's doing. If you please me, I might not start shooting your horses."

She watched him walk away before she turned and started to limp toward Chaos.

"He didn't really hurt you, did he?" Davidow asked from where he was leaning against the fence. "I didn't think Masenak had anything to worry about. You know how to fall, and Chaos didn't try to savage you either time he tossed you today. It surprised me. You did a hell of a lot better than that Berber kid who couldn't get near him."

"I'm okay," she said curtly as she took Chaos's reins and started to lead him back toward the stable. "Masenak just doesn't understand Chaos and what's possible and not possible with him. You might tell him that Chaos is doing very well... considering."

"I don't tell Masenak anything. I find that's the safest and most profitable way to get whatever I want from him." He smiled. "But I'll tell you that you're doing exceptionally well... considering."

She stiffened. "What do you mean?"

"I know horses. I know jockeys. In these last days, I've watched you with Chaos and I've found it interesting. You're careful, but there's still something..." He shrugged. "As I said, interesting, and as long as it doesn't affect me, I'll ignore it. Masenak isn't blaming me for anything you do. You're probably just trying to survive Masenak like the rest of us." He turned and strolled away.

Not good. Davidow was sharp and knowledgeable. She might be able to deceive Masenak into believing that Chaos was too much for her, but there were signs to the contrary that only an expert like Davidow would pick up on. Though having her seem a failure might even be to his advantage, evidently, he wasn't going to act on anything he'd seen as yet.

Yet.

But she didn't want Davidow watching her at all. As long as Masenak thought she had little or no control over Chaos, anything the stallion did that was wild or out of the ordinary might catch him off guard. She might need that slight edge at some point. Though who knew when or where.

The sun was going down.

Her pace unconsciously quickened to eagerness as she reached the stable. It had been a rough day but now it was over. She would be able to talk to Gilroy soon if he'd managed not to get himself killed. The idiot took so many chances... *Don't think of that. He'll be fine.*

And he had promised she would be able to talk to Alisa tonight. That was something to which she could look forward. Gilroy had never broken a promise to her yet...

———◆———

10:40 P.M.

"What took you so long?" Sasha jumped to her feet as she saw Gilroy open the door connecting the stables. "I thought that you'd been caught and thrown off the damn mountain."

"Please." He looked pained. "You insult me. I would have thought you'd appreciate my skills more by now." He shut the door behind him. "Do I have to remind you my time isn't my own at the moment? I didn't have an opportunity to retrieve that phone I promised you until this evening because unfortunately my slave labor services were required elsewhere. It seems that Masenak wanted the castle spruced up for his guests' arrival." He was coming toward her. "I've decided I won't make slave labor one of my chosen sidelines in the future. I'm sure I did it far better than anyone else, but it doesn't appeal—" He broke off as he looked down at the hand she'd extended palm up to him. He grinned as he reached into his tunic pocket, pulled out a small phone, and placed it in her palm. "You're welcome."

"I'll thank you later." Her hand was trembling as she punched in Alisa's number. "Though I'm glad they didn't throw you off the mountain. I didn't—"

"Are you all right?" Alisa asked the instant she picked up the phone.

"That's just like you," Sasha said shakily. "You're the one who got shot, Alisa. That should be my question. But I know you won't answer me until I tell you that I'm as fine as I can be with Masenak threatening to kill you, my horses, and anyone else he thinks will give him an edge. Gilroy didn't lie when he told me you weren't hovering at death's door?"

"I walked twelve miles through these mountains today and I could have gone a hell of a lot longer if Korgan hadn't been such an ass about it."

"I'm beginning to like the sound of him." Sasha had to stop to clear her throat. That last remark had been pure Alisa, and nothing could have convinced Sasha more that she was on her way back to normalcy. "Maybe you should keep him around."

"Only until we get you out of there. He has many more profitable and intriguing projects to keep him amused. But since he has a vested interest in ridding the world of Masenak and Reardon, I believe we'll be able to maintain his involvement while he works at doing that." She paused. "Which we're doing nonstop. We know that we can't get you out of there while they're still alive. It's only a matter of time, because you know that's going to happen."

"Of course I do." She added lightly, "You sent me Gilroy, didn't you? I guess you could consider that a beginning."

"Ouch," Gilroy murmured. "I'm never a beginning. Find another description. Perhaps the grand climax."

She ignored him. "Masenak *and* Reardon. What do you need from me?"

"I need you to stay away from them. Don't do anything to antagonize them."

"What do you need from me," she repeated.

Alisa sighed. "Anything you can tell us about them that might be used as a weapon. We know only the bare bones about their relationship."

"I don't know much more than that right now." She thought about it, trying to remember bits of conversation. "Masenak is jealous of Reardon. He said Reardon had always treated him like an underling. Maybe he feels a little inferior to him? One of the reasons he loves Jubaldar is that he knows Reardon wants to own it. He also wants to win this race and is willing to do anything." She stopped. "I can't think of anything else, but I'll be on the lookout. Masenak is used to me probing and digging at him."

"I can imagine," Alisa said dryly. "Just listen, don't dig. Okay?"

"If you'll do some probing of your own." She'd remembered something Alisa had said. "I'm caught in this place and Gilroy can't help me because he can't leave, either. But you said you walked twelve miles today. You can find out for me."

"Find out what?"

"The horses," she said simply. "Ever since Masenak started threatening them, I realized that he'd use the horses as hostages just as he used those students. At any sign that I was resisting, the first thing he'd do would be to start killing my horses. He already threatened Zeus because I mentioned he was the first horse I ever rode. Chaos might be safer than the others, but there's no telling what he'd do if he was angry enough. I have to find a place to send them away from Jubaldar if I need to. I can't do it myself so it will have to be you." She paused. "If you'll do it, Alisa."

"You know I will. I'd already figured out that Chaos would be on the list of refugees. What's four more? I can assign Juno and Margaret to finding a safety net for them. I'll get back to you when I can tell you how we'll work it out." She hesitated. "Korgan needs to talk to Gilroy now about the setup and scheduling at the castle. I won't call you unless it's an extreme emergency. It's safer if you call me."

"It will be tomorrow evening. Masenak said he wanted to Skype Reardon tomorrow and show me to him on Chaos. Maybe I'll have more to tell you."

"No probing."

"No, I'd have to be more careful with Reardon. In a way, I think he could be worse than Masenak. There's something about him...It's good that Chaos is fast enough to leave Nightshade at the gate. No probing, but I'll definitely listen." She paused. "I love you. Take care. Pay attention to Korgan and don't overdo it."

"You can hardly keep from paying attention to Korgan—as you'll find out when you meet him. I love you, too. I'll talk to you tomorrow."

Sasha handed the phone to Gilroy. "Korgan wants to talk to you."

He took the phone. "Probably more an interrogation."

And he was listening more than speaking, Sasha noticed, which was probably unusual for him, and indicated an impressive amount of respect for Korgan. It was just as well. She wanted a few moments to catch her breath and get over the emotional trauma she'd experienced while talking to Alisa. She sank down on the floor and leaned back against the door of Chaos's stall. She'd known Alisa would come to her rescue where the horses were concerned. Not only did she care for them, but she would realize they'd be an automatic stumbling block to anything positive Sasha could do. But she'd hated having to throw another burden on Alisa in this situation, which was already difficult. No choice. Sasha would do what she could to make up for it. But innocents must always be protected from evil. And no one was more evil than Masenak...except perhaps Reardon. She would have to see.

She felt something moist and familiar nuzzling at the back of her neck.

Chaos. Reaching out in an unusual gesture of affection.

She lifted her arm, and her fingers rubbed his muzzle. *I'm not at all sure you're one of these innocents I was thinking about, but I'll protect you anyway.*

Nonsense. You're the weak one. I need no protection. Innocent? What is that?

I didn't think you'd understand that concept. But understand or not, I think you have to be included.

You're doing very strange things lately. Why did I have to buck you off today?

Perhaps to prove that you're not innocent to the evil ones. You did it very well and didn't hurt me.

He liked that answer. *To make them fear me.*

Or make them not fear me.

He didn't like that one at all. *Very strange things.* He was nuzzling her neck again. *I don't know why I put up with such stupidity.*

Neither do I. You're very patient. As a king should be.

Yes, I am.

"Both of you look like you're half asleep." Gilroy was chuckling as he hung up the phone and came toward her. "That's the first time I've seen Chaos this mellow."

"He has his moments." She gave Chaos a final pat and got to her feet. "Not many. And he always wants them appreciated."

"Nothing wrong with that."

"Typical male response. But I agree with you. I always let Chaos know that any signs of softness please me."

"Will it help to break him?"

"I told you that he can't be broken. It would mean a crushing of spirit and telling him that he has to serve me. That's been the role of horses all through the centuries. I'd never ask it of him." She took Chaos's empty water bucket and strode toward the pump at the end of the aisle. "But a polite suggestion, friend-to-friend, might make him forget all the ugliness and rage now and then. It's what I've been trying to do ever since Alisa bought him from Rossi for me." She was pumping the water. "I was making progress during the month I had him at St. Eldon's, but then Masenak took him and he forgot everything he'd learned. All the hate came back, and I had to start over."

"'Hate' is a strong word."

"Rossi shot Chaos's mother. It wasn't malicious. She and the colt were in the field and she tried to jump the fence. It was too high for her and she broke her leg. But Chaos saw Rossi shoot her and he's never forgotten."

"Or forgiven?"

She nodded. "It was his mother. Rossi knew how intelligent Chaos was, and he should have realized that he'd associate her death with him and any other person who came near him. Rossi was in too much of a hurry to start training him, and he paid the price. He ended up with a broken back. That's when he gave up and agreed to sell him to Alisa."

"But Chaos didn't blame you?"

"I was there with his mother when he was born, and that evidently put me in a special category. But it still took weeks for him to start getting close to me again." The bucket was full, and she stopped pumping and lifted it to take back to the stall. Gilroy stepped forward to take it from her, and she gazed at him incredulously. "Really? I've been toting these buckets almost from the time I was a toddler."

"Forgive me." He held up his hands. "I'm sure it was very good exercise. I forgot myself."

She suddenly smiled brilliantly. "I do forgive you. You kept your word and brought me that phone."

"Two phones, two revolvers, and ammunition. Korgan's going to slip a Remington rifle into that shed later that I might need for distance shots." He grimaced. "And you used the phone to try to set up an escape for your horses. That wasn't what I had in mind when I gave it to you."

"Well, someone had to do it, and neither of us could go hunting for a place where they'd be safe." She added, "What did Korgan want from you?"

"A complete schedule and estimate of personnel in Masenak's little army here. When and where the guards were stationed. I told him there might be changes once Reardon got here. He wants those changes as well." He frowned. "He mentioned that Director Lakewood might be a problem that we'll have to deal with sooner rather than later. I didn't like the sound of that."

"Then you should go take care of it yourself. I'm sure you don't have enough to do here at Jubaldar."

"Sarcasm, again."

"A little. I actually think Alisa will be able to handle her boss if there's need. Surely he'll help if he sees any threat."

"He might not know how extreme the threat could be. Or feel a little too eager to squash the threat and ignore any victims." He shrugged. "But Korgan will take care of him."

"I'm not concerned with Korgan at the moment." She set down the bucket at Chaos's stall. "Give me the phones and the guns. We've got to hide them."

He took the phones out of his jacket pocket and handed them to her. "With Chaos as guard?" He was scowling as he also pulled out the two guns from his jacket and gave them to her. "I still don't like the idea."

"You will. You know it's the safest place." She put the phones and guns in a burlap feed bag and opened the door of the stall. "Once you become accustomed to each other."

"Dogs like me. I'm not sure about horses. The most I can say is that none of the horses has kicked me when I was cleaning out the stalls since I've been here." He was gazing warily at Chaos. "That's not exactly conclusive. Rather than chance it, I'm willing to let you be sole custodian."

She shook her head. "Just give me fifteen or twenty minutes alone with Chaos to explain what we're doing and then I'll let the two of you get to know each other."

"I can hardly wait," he said dryly.

"It will be fine. Would I let anything happen to you? I need you. I even like you." She drew a deep breath as she entered the stall. As Gilroy had noticed, Chaos seemed mellow tonight. If she was persuasive and played on what she knew of the stallion, this might work out. But she'd still better stay very, very close in case it didn't.

Chaos, my friend, I have something I want you to guard for me. I wouldn't trust it to anyone but the king you are because those fools wish to take it and hurt me. She paused and then went on quickly. *However, there's one other thing you should know that you might not entirely like . . .*

She had to stay with Chaos over an hour instead of the twenty minutes she'd told Gilroy would be necessary. "I think it will be okay," she said as she left the stall. "But it's up to you if you want to risk it. These days Chaos doesn't trust anyone but me, and he's very protective. He doesn't have a hell of a lot of respect for my ability to do it myself. I've told him that I've chosen you to take care of me whenever he's not around, because you're brave and will stomp on anyone who tries to harm me."

"Stomp?"

"He respects stomping."

"I see."

"In the end, what it will come down to is if Chaos believes I'm smart enough to be a good judge of your qualifications in that arena."

"Is there an audition for this stomping?"

"Lord, I hope not." She shook her head. "Stop joking. It could work out fine, or you could end up dead if I don't get to you in time."

"Well, we'd better see which it's going to be." He reached out and slowly opened the stall door. "Where did you put the burlap bag?"

"Underneath the straw between his front two hooves. I thought it would be better if he could see you at all times. He'd feel more secure."

"By all means, let's not make him nervous." He looked the stallion directly in the eyes as he edged past him into the stall. "One of us is enough."

"You don't have to do this."

"But you were right, it's the best way." He was suddenly smiling recklessly. "Now hush, I've got to concentrate on being friendly yet absolutely unstompable. I wouldn't want to destroy your reputation with him." He was at the far side of the stall now and slowly slid down to sit on the straw. "Okay, we're in this together, Chaos," he murmured. "I don't mind being a stand-in for you." He reached out and slowly placed his hand protectively on top of the straw-covered bag. Chaos had turned his head and was glaring at him. "I'm not taking my hand away. While I'm in here, it's my job to protect it, too. I'll just sit here for a while and let you get used to it." He leaned his head back against the wall. "See? No threat." His gaze shifted to Sasha. "It's late and I have to get out of here. I can't give it more than forty-five minutes. I'm hoping that may be enough. I'd appreciate it if you'd stick around to warn me if you think that I'm going to end up decorating this stall with my life's blood before that time."

"I don't think you will," she whispered. "But I can't read him right now. I believe he's confused. And he can be...impulsive."

"I'll take that into consideration." He gazed back at Chaos. "And as you know, I can't read him at all, so I'm in your hands. But then so is Chaos, and that means we have common ground. Maybe he'll sense that and let me get out of here with bones and head intact."

"Maybe." She moistened her lips. "But it's going to be a long forty-five minutes."

"Nah, it will pass in a heartbeat. I'm sure you persuaded him what a fantastic addition I'll be. Relax. He only has to get used to the idea."

She gazed at him skeptically. Pass in a heartbeat?

It seemed more like hours watching him sitting there, Chaos towering over him, before she saw him pat the feed bag and re-cover it with straw. Then slowly, very slowly, he stood up.

Chaos's muscles were tensing.

"Gilroy!"

"Leave me alone. I've gotten this far. Let me do it myself." Gilroy was edging around Chaos again until he stood with his back to the door, facing him. "We've done it, Chaos. Not so bad, was it? I'll see you tomorrow. Take care of her." Then he was out of the stall and shutting the door. He quickly walked a few yards away before looking back at Sasha. "How close was it?"

"I have no idea." She shrugged. "Pretty close right before you left him." She smiled wryly. "But maybe he decided he liked you and didn't want you to go."

"Yeah, and pigs can fly."

"Maybe they can, I'll have to ask Margaret the next time I see her." She added, "But I'm cautiously optimistic about everything at the moment. That's not how the day started out, so I'll take it."

"You were worried about that Skype with Reardon tomorrow."

She nodded curtly. "I don't believe I can find a way to stall Masenak. I'll have to see." She drew a deep breath and lifted her chin. "But I have to look on the bright side. I talked to Alisa today, and she's well and going to help save the horses.

That's all good. And Chaos might even begin to like you and not try to kill you. I'd say that's very good, too."

"I agree." He was smiling over his shoulder as he moved toward the door. "I particularly like the bit about him not killing me. So tomorrow can't be all that bad, either. Good night, Sasha." The next moment, the door shut behind him.

She turned away and went back to Chaos's stall. She was exhausted. She'd try to get to sleep and then wake early and go shower. She wanted to be alert for whatever she was going to have to face with Masenak and Reardon.

Because she was almost sure there wasn't going to be any bright side to be found tomorrow no matter how much she searched.

"She wants you to save the horses?" Korgan asked Alisa after he'd cut the connection after talking to Gilroy. "You can't say your Sasha isn't consistent."

"Of course she is," Alisa said jerkily. "That's been her mantra since the day I met her. *Don't think about me, I'll be fine, save the innocents.* That's why I knew I had to find a way to get those four horses away from Zeppo or she'd never leave that damn circus." Her lips twisted. "And then when I thought I had her safe, she found some other innocents to save at St. Eldon's."

"Deplorable," he said lightly. "Why on earth didn't she follow your example and be completely selfish?"

"I *was* selfish," she said impatiently. "I wanted Zeppo to lose his meal ticket, and I wanted to see her happy. I did what I had to do to get what I wanted."

"There's something slightly askew in your logic." He waved his hand. "But I'll let it go for now. You made a promise. I have to fulfill it. Do you have any idea how I can do that?"

She shook her head. "It was my promise."

"I told you that I was in this all the way. This is what you want." He was frowning thoughtfully. "You said you were going to ask Margaret to help find a place to stash the horses and keep them safe. That might prove a kind of a massive operation if you're thinking of kidnapping Chaos along with them. It's a better idea to concentrate only on the four horses she thinks are threatened, and then not move them until the last minute so that it's unlikely there will be a search for them. She believes Chaos is too valuable for Masenak to hurt?"

She nodded. "It wouldn't make sense for him to kill him. He'd have to be crazy."

"There's evidence of that possibility, too," he said

grimly. "But I think there's too much self-interest involved to let it come to the forefront. So we just have to remove the other four horses so that Sasha is free to take care of Chaos."

"Which is like moving a small herd," she said sarcastically. "No problem."

"A beautifully well-trained herd," he reminded her. "Not like Chaos. Which also means that they'd presumably be obedient to anyone who knew what they were doing around horses."

"Gilroy?"

"Not on his résumé. That's one of the reasons why we had to send Naleek with him—to make sure he didn't screw up when he was working in the stable." He was frowning. "And we'll need more than Naleek if we have to move those horses quickly and silently out of the stables. It would have to go absolutely smoothly."

"I can do it." She leaned forward. "And I'm pretty good. No one could live with Sasha and not know how to ride."

"We might have to use you." He added grimly, "But I'd rather not be put in a position where I'd have to ransom you instead of one of those horses. I think I'll pay a visit to Samlir tomorrow and get the council to give me a few volunteers. It should only cost an arm and a leg."

"How will you get back there?"

"I'll hike down to the area where we parked the Land Rover and drive it to where it will be safe for the helicopter to pick me up. I should be back by tomorrow night."

"Can't you phone someone in the council?"

"Not if I want it done. Those are tough negotiators. I know about bargainers."

"I'm sure you do." And it was obvious he was already in full action mode. No use arguing with him. "Thank you," she said awkwardly. "I'm sorry about this. Horses weren't in our agreement."

"Neither was you getting shot." He shrugged. "If I can find a way of rescuing the horses, I figure I'll be on my way toward making recompense. The only thing I ask is that you let me set up the timing so that I don't get those horses killed. I don't believe either one of you would ever forgive me."

"Don't be ridiculous. You're always superb with that damn timing. You've been torturing yourself about that stupid wound since it happened. It's boring, I wish you'd forget about it."

"Difficult to do."

"You've done difficult things before. As far as I'm concerned, the slates are clean and your help with the horses deserves my gratitude. I don't like admitting that any more than you do. So shut up about it." She got to her feet. "I'm going to talk to Margaret and go over the maps again. If we have to move those horses at the last minute, we'll have to take them somewhere very close to Jubaldar. I think I remember a canyon that we ran across this morning if we can find an access..."

———◆———

JUBALDAR RACETRACK

"Davidow tells me Chaos hasn't thrown you today," Masenak said as he strolled across the track toward Sasha. "Very good." His gaze ran over her. "And you look very professional. Are you turning over a new leaf?"

"I managed to stay on his back so far today. That doesn't mean I'll be lucky in the next hour or two. And I look clean and what you call professional because I haven't been in the dirt yet." She paused and then said urgently, "Cancel this race. Give me another two or three weeks to work on Chaos and I'll have him ready to race...and win. I can't guarantee what he'll do right now."

"You'll guarantee what I want. And what I want is that you'll get on Chaos and show Reardon the fastest horse he's ever seen." He indicated the computer he was carrying. "Five minutes and I'll make the call. I've promised him a preview of what's going to happen when he's on this track for the race."

"That's not very smart. If I get Chaos around the track, Reardon might back out of his bet when he sees his speed. Just put off the race and I'll—"

"Don't tell me what to do," he said coldly. "I know exactly what Reardon's reaction is going to be, and I'm prepared for it. In fact, I'm counting on it. I've thought it over and I may be changing strategy. So get out there and do what I ordered you to do." He nodded behind her at the horse one of the stable boys was leading out of the stables. "Or you'll lose your faithful buddy from times past."

Zeus. Beautiful, graceful, prancing as gracefully toward her as he had the first time she'd seen him when she was a little girl.

And the threat was as clear as if Masenak was pointing a gun at Zeus's head.

"You understand?" Masenak asked softly.

"I understand," she said jerkily as she turned away and started down the track toward Chaos. "Make the call."

She heard him laughing as she stopped in front of Chaos.

You're angry . . . and sad.

Yes, but you'll be happy. You're going to get to run.

Then why are you sad? It will be joy.

No choice. He would hurt Zeus. She gathered the

reins and jumped on his back. *So let's give him what he wants and worry about everything else later.* She gave him a gentle kick. *Take the joy and save an old friend. Now!*

Chaos bolted forward!

No breath.

Stinging wind!

Blurred colors.

Thunder of his hooves.

Silken movement.

Faster.

Faster.

Faster.

And then it came.

Joy.

Joy.

Joy.

She could see Masenak ahead.

Stop, Chaos.

He was paying no attention.

She tried again. *Enough.*

Never enough. But he was slowing. *You aren't sad now.*

No, I'm not. Thank you. But I have to leave you now. Stop, Chaos.

He didn't come to a stop until he'd passed Masenak. *It was wrong that he wanted to hurt Zeus. Even if it meant joy for us. When can I stomp on him?*

Soon, I hope. She jumped to the ground. *Though stomping isn't always the answer.*

You only say that because you're weak and don't have the power to do it yourself.

She didn't answer because Masenak was impatiently motioning for her to come to him. His eyes were gleaming, his face pale with excitement. "Very good." He jerked her in front of the computer screen. "Reardon wants to congratulate you. He was impressed. Though I told him you could do better."

"When I can stay on him," she said. "Did you mention that was a problem."

"No, I didn't." His grip on her arm tightened painfully. "Because the problem is only temporary, as you just proved. Both Reardon and I are great problem solvers." He looked at the screen. "When we believe in a project. Isn't that right, Reardon?"

"What do you want me to say?" Reardon asked curtly. "Yes, that was a spectacular run. Yes, Nightshade will have difficulty coming close to that speed. But that doesn't mean I'm giving up. Anything can happen in a horse race." His eyes were narrowed on Masenak. "And is that why you staged this little preview? To remind me there might be other options available?"

"It could be. I'll discuss it with you later." He reached out and touched Sasha's hair. "But you said you wanted to talk to my jockey. You see, she can be presentable."

"More than presentable. She was exciting on the back of that monster of a horse." He was gazing at Sasha. "How did it feel?"

There was something almost sensual in his tone that made her uncomfortable. "He's very smooth."

"But rough, too," he said softly. "I bet you'd like it rough."

"No." She suddenly wanted to get away. It was ironic she was glancing at Masenak, seeking escape. "I should get back to Chaos. Do you need me for anything else?"

He shook his head. "I think Reardon is finished with you for right now." He looked at Reardon. "Yes?"

"For the moment." He spoke directly to Sasha. "Run along, I'll see you soon."

She broke away from Masenak and strode back toward Chaos. She didn't like anything that had gone on in the past few moments. Masenak's attitude toward Reardon had been a combination of smug satisfaction and a kind of eager subservience. She didn't like this change. She preferred the arrogance and half-bitter excitement of the first call, when there had been conflict on the horizon. There had been an element of kowtowing in Masenak's attitude today.

And she hated the way he'd deferred to Reardon in his attitude toward her just now. After Szarnar, she knew all the signs of lust, and she'd seen it in Reardon. Whatever new deal Masenak might be offering Reardon, she couldn't be certain she wouldn't be offered as part of it.

But Reardon wasn't due here at Jubaldar for another three days. Perhaps Alisa could get her out of here before she had to face the looming problem.

Perhaps.

———◆———

ATLAS MOUNTAINS
10:35 A.M.

"Wait for me!"

Korgan looked behind him to see Alisa striding from the road toward the bank of pines where they'd parked the Land Rover. "Something wrong? Why didn't you call me?"

"Because there was nothing wrong. I was just on the phone and got a late start. I knew I'd catch up with you." She got into the passenger seat. "And I did."

"But you didn't mention that you intended to come with me. I would have waited." He made a face. "Though I don't know why you're coming.

It should be a boring trip. Negotiating with those council members will cause your eyes to glaze over."

"Not if they manage to get the best of you. I'm sure it will be a learning experience."

"There were reasons why I—"

"Excuses?"

"Reasons," he repeated as he started the car. "And the last I heard, you were talking about going down and exploring that canyon passage near Jubaldar with Margaret. Why are you here now?"

"I'm waiting on a return of the call I placed last night, and I changed my plans. I decided I'd rather go with you. Samlir will be more convenient for me." She smiled. "I promise I won't be bored, and I won't get in the way of your negotiations with the Berbers."

He was silent. "What call?"

"Just a little negotiation of my own. I'll tell you about it if I manage to pull it off."

"Alisa."

"That's all you'll get from me." She looked away from him. "How long will it take for us to rendezvous with that helicopter?"

"Almost an hour, and then another forty-five minutes to get to Samlir."

"Not exactly a convenient distance if we need them to help launch an attack on Jubaldar."

"That's the second time you've used the word 'convenient.'" He shook his head. "Forget convenience. Nothing is convenient in these mountains. That's why Masenak built his castle here. He's as safe as it's possible for him to be considering what a murdering asshole he is. There are ways to get around it, but it's damn hard." He scowled. "And your director isn't making it any easier. But all I can do right now is make sure that Samlir is on our side and cooperative."

"From what you told me about the council, that isn't going to be simple, either."

He shrugged. "We'll see. The council members are basically politicians, and it's been my experience that you can stop them in their tracks by appealing directly to the people they represent. I've been working on it. I'll know when I get there and talk to Cazvar."

"Cazvar?" Then she recognized the name. "The trader whom Gilroy first got to bring him to Samlir? What's he got to do with anything?"

"It had better be plenty. When I knew Gilroy was going to be going to Jubaldar, I drafted Cazvar to act for me at Samlir. So far, he seems to be working out. He's the quintessential wheeler-dealer, very money hungry, but he knows these people and how to reach them."

"That sounds as if you're planning an uprising."

He smiled. "Only a minor one. And I promise everyone will be happy with it except the council members."

———◆———

Alisa began to understand what he meant when their helicopter started its descent on the edge of Samlir Village. There was a crowd of people looking up and smiling and pointing. "A welcoming committee?" she asked Cal Harris, their pilot. "Are they always this enthusiastic?"

"Hell yes, it's my third trip here this morning," he said dryly. "And now they know what to expect when I unload the cargo bin."

"And what do they expect?"

"You'd have to ask Cazvar. He makes the lists. I just fill them and deliver."

"What do you mean?"

"It's been Christmas since the night I delivered Korgan here that first day." Harris grinned. "Instead of a sleigh I use a helicopter, but the presents are impressive enough that nobody gives a damn."

She glanced at Korgan. "Bribery?"

He shook his head. "This village is poverty-stricken, and its people are now my allies. Why wouldn't I share with them? I couldn't be sure the council would be equally generous. So I told

Cazvar to make lists of what people needed that would make their lives better and start shipping it." His eyes were twinkling. "It's purely coincidental that it would make me more popular and make anyone on the council who won't give me what I need very unpopular."

"You're joking, but I believe you would have done it anyway."

"Would I?" He nodded. "Maybe. I've always liked the Santa Claus fable. And these days I can indulge exploring it. The process of making money is a hell of a lot of fun, but giving it away can be even more satisfying." The helicopter was now on the ground and two villagers were struggling to keep the crowds back while a bearded third man was striding toward the cockpit. "There's Cazvar doing his duty. He doesn't look too happy, does he? I don't think he agrees with me. He's been a trader most of his life, and it offends him to just give things away. Plus, distribution can be a hassle." He glanced at her. "But I don't believe you'd mind doing it. Would you like to help Harris and Cazvar unload the cargo and play Santa while I go deal with the council? I don't think it would bore you."

She gazed at the eager, excited faces of the men, women, and children in the crowd and slowly nodded. "No, it wouldn't bore me." She was opening the cockpit door. "Introduce me to Cazvar."

CHAPTER

14

Alisa was definitely not bored during the next four hours. She found that Cazvar was as organized and charismatic as Korgan had said. Once Korgan turned her over to him, he took full advantage of having another pair of willing hands and eyes at his disposal. Most of this shipment consisted of small farm equipment and carpentry tools, but there were also toys and board games and special teas and spices. After the helicopter was unloaded and the goods designated for various households on Cazvar's list, they put them on a small truck, delivered them, and checked them off the list. Those homes were just as poverty-stricken as Korgan had told her, but most of the people were polite and contained their bubbling excitement at receiving the gifts. Except for the children. They were like children everywhere. A basketball or a Hula-Hoop or a doll was magical, and magic could never be contained.

Korgan caught up with them when they were almost through with the deliveries. Alisa was outside in the street with a young boy and didn't notice him until she heard his voice behind her. "I send you to work and find you out here playing with the kids?" he asked, amused. "Cazvar must be too easy on you."

"Hush." She unfurled the *Star Wars* yo-yo with a flourish again. "I'm teaching him Walk the Dog and he's almost got it." She watched the child copy her movement. "Yes." She beamed. "Wonderful." He gave her a toothy grin and ran across the street to join two other boys. She turned back to Korgan. "I'd almost forgotten how much fun yo-yos could be. Very simple, but you can amuse yourself anywhere."

"Did you teach Sasha?"

"No, she taught me. I told you that I never knew who was the kid sister. We taught each other so many things. We both had to catch up on things we'd missed."

"I can see how you would." He turned to Cazvar, who had just come out of the house. "What's her progress? Evidently you've put her in charge of the yo-yo and sundry toy division."

"She's doing well enough for not knowing the language. She speaks fluent Arabic, but not the Amazigh Berber dialects," Cazvar said. "She makes herself understood combining Arabic with sign language." He frowned. "But she gives too many orders. I turn my back for one moment and she told Harris to go back to the helicopter and take off for Casablanca and bring back another shipment."

"We didn't need him once we had the cargo unloaded," Alisa said. "It seemed the reasonable thing to do."

"I would have told him myself when I got around to it," Cazvar said. "You should not have done it."

Alisa nodded. "You're in charge. I'll remember."

Korgan chuckled. "Which is more than I've been able to make her do."

Cazvar shrugged. "She works hard. I have no real complaint." He turned and went back into the house.

"Why are you here?" Alisa asked Korgan. "I don't believe it was because you wanted to check up on me. Are you finished with the council?"

"Not quite. But I got a phone call from Vogel and I thought I'd take a break and come and tell you about it. I didn't want you complaining to me later that I didn't keep you informed."

She stiffened. "Something's wrong?"

"Maybe. I'm not sure. Something's different, and with Reardon and Masenak that could signal a change either way. Reardon wasn't scheduled to arrive at Jubaldar for another few days, but he altered his plans and Vogel said he ordered that Nightshade be ready to be picked up and flown out early this morning. Evidently Reardon is either anxious or excited about what's happening with Masenak and wants to be on the spot. He should be arriving late today."

She frowned. "I don't like it."

"I didn't think you would," he said. "But it's only one day. It could mean nothing."

"But you've studied Reardon and you know him. You don't like it, either."

"I think it's worth noting. Reardon rarely does anything on impulse," he said. "It's a repositioning at an earlier time. I want to know why. But Sasha might be able to tell us that if she contacts you tonight. We're not going to know before that." His gaze was focused on her face. "Though I know you hate the idea of being this far away from Jubaldar when there seems to be any action going on. If you hadn't sent Harris to Morocco to pick up that other shipment, you could have him take you back."

"And hover?" she asked grimly. "Yes, I want to be as close as I can to her, but I couldn't do anything there but wring my hands and wait for answers. She has Margaret and Gilroy nearby to do that. But I might be able to get some answers of my own if I stay here."

"Because Samlir is more 'convenient'?" he asked softly. "What are you up to? Isn't it about time you told me?"

"No. Not until I know I have a chance. I'll let you know when I do, Korgan." She turned to follow Cazvar back into the house. "In the meantime, I'll keep busy. Go back to the council and get me the four riders we need to move those horses."

"It's almost finished. The members have mellowed considerably since the first negotiations. I'm the hero of the village since those shipments started to arrive. They might erect a statue to me." He lifted his hand. "If I tie up the loose ends before you do, I'll be back to help you finish the distribution. If there are many more yo-yos or games in those boxes, I imagine you'll still be on the job."

"You're just jealous," she called after him. "It's much more fun playing with kids than it is with those politicians."

"Too true." He chuckled. "I can see why you had to have a Sasha in your life." He disappeared around a turn in the street.

Yes, he understood, she thought. He understood so many things about her. He had been
able to read her from the beginning even though
she'd put up a virtual smokescreen between them
at first.

And now she was beginning to know him, too.

But it wasn't enough.

Stop thinking about Korgan. Close out everything but what she was doing this minute and what
she would say when she got that phone call.

It was late afternoon and she should have gotten
that call already. Was he ignoring her? No, he
wouldn't do that. Maybe he was analyzing the
situation before he got back to her.

Just *call* me, dammit.

Fifteen minutes later her phone did ring, and she
jumped to answer it. But it wasn't a call but a text.
She read it quickly.

"Shit!"

———◆———

Korgan was smiling when he caught up with her
three hours later. "We have our riders," he said.
"And I heard from Harris. He's on his way back
from Casablanca. We can have the shipment unloaded and be back on our way to Jubaldar in four
or five hours."

"No, we can't," she said curtly. "We have to stay here."

His brows rose. "I beg your pardon?"

"You heard me." She was on edge and a little defensive. "I'm not finished here. Things didn't work out as I hoped. But that doesn't mean they still can't. There's just been a delay. We'll have to adjust." She started walking down the street. "But we won't have to be uncomfortable while we're waiting. Cazvar is giving us his place for the time being. I'm taking you there now. He even has a neighbor woman cooking us some kind of stew or something for dinner. He says it's clean and it will be fine until—"

"Until?" His hand grasped her arm. "Until what, Alisa? Answers. I want answers. What are you up to? What are we waiting for?"

"Not what. Who." She scowled. "Jed Novak. We're waiting for Novak. I wanted to have all the explanations out of the way and a commitment from Novak before I got the two of you together, but then I couldn't get in touch with him and had to leave messages. That never happens. I can usually reach him."

"A commitment? What kind of commitment?"

"If we're not going to allow Lakewood's fair-haired boy Walt Edwards to take over the attack on Jubaldar, we have to have someone else we can trust and who has the clout with the director to get him to be accepted as a substitute. The only person I know who has both those qualities is Jed Novak. He had more influence than anyone in the CIA, but he's busy as hell in Maldara. He's not going to like the idea of taking on both the political bullshit as well as the attack itself connected with the job. That's one hell of a commitment."

He nodded. "You said he owed you a favor. But you wouldn't ask him to go after Masenak in that jungle. This is different?"

"What I was doing at Szarnar could have been a career breaker. I couldn't ask that of anyone. This will be difficult as hell, but Novak could turn it into a stellar career move if he does it right."

"And you have faith he'll do it right."

"I worked with him. He's the best. If he agrees to do it, we'll be lucky to have him."

He smiled. "Then it appears you've found a solution to one of our bigger problems. Now let's go get him."

"I've been trying. I emailed him I needed a favor and asked him to come here today so that I could explain. I couldn't reach him until a few hours ago." She added in frustration, "Then I got a text that he'd been in Brussels giving confidential testimony at a war crimes tribunal about the civil war in Maldara. He's on his way back, but he won't arrive before this evening or tomorrow morning."

"So we'll wait," he said quietly. "Why are you upset? It was a great idea; you did something very smart but weren't able to complete it yet. No big deal."

"I *know* it was a good idea. It could work for us. But I didn't want any mistakes. It was something only I could do, and I wanted everything to go smoothly. I wanted to be able to do it for Sasha. I wanted to do it for *you*."

"You're giving me Jed Novak as a gift?" He smiled. "I'm touched. But from what I've heard about him, he might be a surprise package on several levels."

"You're joking, but why shouldn't I step up to the plate and help? Everyone expects you to do everything, even me. It's been like that since the moment I burgled my way into your study. I bet it's like that with everyone in your life."

"I'm not joking." His smile vanished. "Well, maybe a little. But I am touched. Is that why you wouldn't tell me why you wanted to come here?"

"I didn't want to offer you something and then not be able to give it to you. I needed to nail it down." She added, "Novak couldn't safely meet us at Jubaldar, and I knew I couldn't get him to commit until he met you. Neither of you is a trusting person. You had to meet and come to an agreement. I just had to be the conduit to bring you together."

"And you've done it." His grasp tightened on her arm. "So stop worrying. I know how persuasive you can be. You'll be able to coax Novak into doing anything when you get him here. You've already proved what putty I can be in your hands. Everything is in place. All we have to do is wait until Novak shows up."

"Bullshit." She shook his hand away. "He's not easy. But I think I can make it happen. We were always on the same wavelength." She stopped before the pine door of a small house near the end of the block. "This is Cazvar's house. He said the door would be unlocked and the fireplace lit." She pushed open the door to reveal a small room with a table and four chairs tucked in one corner, a narrow cot-bed pushed against the right wall, and a bubbling black pot hanging over a blazing fire in the fireplace at the far end. She sniffed. "Whatever it is, it smells good. Spicy...but maybe lamb." She went toward the fire to warm her hands. "I'm glad of the fire. The winds whip around these mountains and chill to the bone..." She looked over her shoulder at him. "There's supposed to be a tiny bathroom with a shower, but there's no chance of hot water so it will have to be very quick. But I haven't had a bath since Margaret and I found a stream running through that canyon yesterday morning, so I don't give a damn. I just hope there are plenty of clean towels."

"No problem. I'll go scavenging through the village and get them for you. After all, I'm the man they're going to build a statue to honor." He turned to leave. "Just explore the nest, relax, and I'll be back to cover you with warm towels, blankets, and anything else I can find."

"There you go again. Trying to take care of everything. All I asked was for towels." She was looking into the pot. "Definitely promising."

"Yes, it is." She looked back to see him still standing in the doorway. "And not only the stew," he said gently. "We made progress today. *You* made progress. So stop worrying about mistakes you didn't make. You couldn't drag Novak out of a war crimes hearing because he was screwing up your plans. You did good, Alisa. I'm proud of you."

Then he was gone.

Warmth was flowing through her as she stared after him.

I'm proud of you.

A few words that meant so much. Too much.

Respect, understanding, companionship were all

encompassed in that single sentence. It was what she had told herself she wanted from him, and it was there now.

And it wasn't enough.

She turned away, picked up her backpack, and headed across the room toward the narrow door of what must be the bathroom. Go take that shower. Do something distracting. Forget it. Block it out. That first glowing warmth had been...nice. For now, take what was there and don't dwell on anything else.

—◆—

Two hours later when Korgan walked into the house, she was standing huddled close to the fire, wrapped in the blanket she'd taken from the bed. "You couldn't wait?" he asked, his gaze running from her damp hair flowing past bare shoulders to her equally bare feet. "So much for relaxing. You'd have done better to wait and trust me. I'm not sure that blanket is sanitary. I promise you everything I brought you is pristine."

"The blanket looked okay. Better than either of the towels. I didn't want to wait." Her eyes were narrowed on him. "You've changed your clothes." She noticed something else. "And you're kind of...gleaming. Why?"

"You're not going to like it." He shrugged. "I went to the council house and asked them to send some of their people to gather what you needed. It was going to take a little while, so I had time to kill."

"Why are you gleaming?" she asked, every word precise.

"The council has a steam room for the members to use in the back of the building. They offered to let me use it while I waited."

"Steam." She could imagine the wafts of moist heat, the feel of it on her skin. "Do you know how cold that water in the shower is?"

He nodded. "I can see the goose bumps."

"You should have seen me before I stood before this fire for the last twenty minutes. Did you know about this steam room before you went to ask help from those members?"

"No. The offer came out of the blue. Though I should have guessed they might have tucked away a few luxuries for their personal use."

"And you didn't ask if I might be able to use that damn steam room?"

"I did. It was my first thought. But traditionally no women are permitted in the steam rooms, and it took me a little while to persuade them to make you an exception."

"No women? Son of a bitch!" She stared at him

in fury. "They loll in comfort and yet forbid it to their wives and daughters? The unfair *bastards.*"

"I felt the same way. And I knew damn well what your reaction would be. But I decided that I wanted to get you into that steam room, and I'd hold off on a general equal rights campaign until later. I could have pushed it, but they've given us everything we want so far, and I wanted them to keep on doing it. I didn't believe you'd want me to blow diplomacy to make a statement when I can do it more subtly later. Was I wrong?"

"No, you're not wrong," she said between set teeth. "You handled everything with your usual skill. I just hate it."

"And it didn't work out anyway." He made a face. "I didn't realize you'd get impatient and jump into that icy shower. No steam bath for you."

"No steam bath for anyone but you and those male chauvinists. Just diplomacy."

"I'll make it up to you."

"Yes, you will. I'm already considering ways and means."

"That sounds dangerous. I'd better have the booty I had the council gather for you brought in to distract you." He called out to the street. "Cazvar, have them bring in the baskets."

Cazvar and two other men streamed into the small room carrying large baskets overflowing with towels and blankets, and pots and pans that they placed on the floor. As he turned to leave, Cazvar glanced at Alisa by the fire and then said to Korgan, "You told her about the steam room?"

He nodded.

"Foolish." He smiled maliciously. "You should have kept quiet. She's not a woman who would accept such a slight for herself or others." He left the room.

Korgan stepped toward one of the baskets and rifled through it, then pulled out a pale-green-and-rust-striped cotton blanket. "This should do it. Pristine, as advertised." He offered it to her. "Trade you."

She took the striped blanket and let the other one drop to her feet. She wrapped the fresh blanket around her and tucked it over her breasts. "Find me a clean towel to dry my hair while I see if there are any bowls in that cabinet. I'm hungry."

"Yes, ma'am." He was rummaging through the baskets again. "Steam room discussion over?"

"Over, but not forgotten," she said as she pulled out two wooden bowls. "I guarantee we'll both remember it."

"I don't have the slightest doubt," he said ruefully.

The stew wasn't bad, but the spice-mint tea that Alisa had found in the cabinet and brewed was even better. She was in a considerably better mood after the meal as she leaned back and smiled at Korgan. "I'm tempted to forgive you, but then I look at you and see that gleam from the steam bath." She waved her hand. "And poof, temptation's gone."

"I'm glad you enjoyed your meal. I had trouble concentrating on it." His gaze went to the striped blanket that was covering her breasts. "My appetite might have improved if you'd gotten dressed first."

"Too bad. I wasn't in the mood to pamper you. I was damp and cold and pissed off. I'll get dressed later." She lifted her tea to her lips. "Or not. It depends on if Novak is going to be—" Her phone rang. She glanced at it on the table beside her. "Novak!" She punched ACCEPT and then the SPEAKER button. "Where are you? Are you coming?"

"Just arrived in Morocco. Give me a break. I've got a press conference and then I have to talk to my staff. I'll be on my way right afterward and should be up there early tomorrow morning." He paused. "I've been going over the notes you sent me. It's a tough proposition. Very tough."

"Yes."

"You never make things easy, do you?"

"You can say no."

"Can I? You didn't say no to me when I needed you. You almost got killed."

"It was worth doing."

"Yes." He paused. "Lakewood has his nose out of joint about Korgan being involved in the rescue of those students. You can see how he doesn't want a repeat performance. He wants to be the one to shine."

"Let him shine somewhere else. If Korgan hadn't been involved, those girls would still be in that camp being brutalized."

"So I've heard, and it's something of an open secret that Lakewood would like to squash. If he was directly responsible for capturing Masenak, it would go a long way in doing that."

"We don't care about the damn credit for the kill. We just need to take him out in a way that will be certain and avoid collateral damage. If Lakewood brings Walt Edwards into the mix, we can't trust that will happen. He'll be marching to Lakewood's drummer. You know that, Novak."

"Yes, I know that." He paused. "And you've been saying 'we,' which means that you're solidly in Korgan's camp. I'd have to accept him if I agree to help you?"

"That's right." She met Korgan's gaze across the table. There was none of her own tension in his expression. He was leaning back, smiling slightly, perfectly at ease. "I couldn't be more solidly in his camp."

"Then he's probably listening to this call," Novak said wearily. "It's just as well. All cards on the table. By the time I get to Samlir, I'll have done the research and have a basic knowledge of what to expect from Korgan. I can make my own judgments. You might trust him, but I've heard he can be persuasive as hell."

"Absolutely. I didn't expect anything else from you. Let me know when you're about to arrive." She added haltingly, "I didn't want to ask this of you. Thanks for considering it, Novak."

"I couldn't do anything else. You're important to me. I owe you. The only thing left to decide is whether what you're asking is as worthwhile as what you did for me. I'll see you in the morning, Alisa." He cut the connection.

"Novak might do it." She put her phone down on the table. "It probably depends on whether he believes he can work with you. I knew it would come down to that when I asked him."

"Because you know him so well." He tilted his head. "And you're important to him. It was interesting listening to the two of you. There was an intimacy..." His gaze never left her face as he asked softly, "How intimate were you, Alisa? Did you sleep with him?"

Shock. She went still. "That's none of your business."

"Do you think I don't realize that?" His voice was no longer soft, but rough. "It's not my business, and it shouldn't matter anyway. But it does, and so I asked. I was having a purely barbaric, male moment and you should feel free to ignore it."

"I will."

"After you answer me," he added recklessly. "Novak said all cards on the table. You want our meeting to be civilized and friendly in the morning. I'll be much more civilized if you satisfy my curiosity."

"Curiosity is seldom barbaric. So I don't believe you can call it that." She shrugged impatiently. "You're being weird, but this isn't worth arguing about. I never slept with Novak. I like and respect him, and I think he's the best CIA operative in the agency. And even if it had occurred to me that I might like to do it, I knew how many trips he took to get together with a journalist named Jill Cassidy." She added, "Any other questions? Are we done?"

"We're done." He rose to his feet. "And now I'm going for a walk to give you some time to forget how weird I can be. It was that cerebral versus physical conflict again. But it might not have manifested itself tonight if you'd had something on besides that blanket." He headed for the door. "You'll be waiting for Sasha's call?"

She nodded. "*If* she calls. I hope she does."

She watched the door close behind him before she got to her feet and went to stand before the fireplace. She didn't really need the heat, she thought ruefully. It was purely emotion that caused her to shake a little. Though the conversation with Novak had gone as she'd thought it would. Nothing could be certain, but she was hopeful.

It was those few short sentences with Korgan afterward that had disturbed her. She'd been so involved with convincing Novak that she hadn't been ready when Korgan had asked that question. He was usually so cool and totally collected where Masenak was concerned, she'd thought that beneath his almost casual facade he was as focused as she was. Then she'd looked at him and seen that intensity that had nothing cool about it. It was good that he'd walked out the door, because she hadn't known what to do after she'd instinctively tried to ignore, to pretend, to protect herself. She must have done it well, because he'd left her.

But she wouldn't be able to keep on doing it. It wasn't her nature to hide away and be something she was not, even to protect herself.

So she had to sit here and think, to come to

terms with who she was, while she waited for Sasha to call.

———◆———

Sasha phoned an hour later, and Alisa jumped on the call. "Is everything all right? Vogel told Korgan that Reardon was on his way to Jubaldar early this morning. Why?"

"I have no idea. And he's not on his way, he's *here*. He arrived an hour or so ago. Though I haven't seen him. He's probably with Masenak." Her voice was edgy. "All I know is that he's already causing problems. When I got back to the stable after working out with Chaos today, I found Davidow there with Reardon's jockey putting Nightshade in one of the stalls in the same stable annex where Chaos is quartered. I should have expected it, I suppose. I was told the annex was always given to Reardon for the horse he brought to the race. The only reason Chaos was put here was that he was such a hell raiser."

"Are they going to move Chaos back to the primary stable?"

"I think I kept that from happening. I got Chaos to display his less-than-charming side. He did minor damage to his stall and terrified Lee Chan, Nightshade's jockey, but it reminded Davidow why he'd isolated Chaos. Then I made a show of getting Chaos under control and calmed down and told Davidow that if he wanted me to keep him that way, he couldn't have Reardon's people moving around those stalls disturbing him. Any care given to Nightshade had to be done by me."

"And Davidow agreed?"

"Sure. Davidow doesn't like to report problems to Masenak. He said he had no objection to making me work harder if Masenak and Reardon gave their okay."

"How much harder will you have to work? You don't need the care of another horse on your plate right now."

"I don't have any choice. I want Gilroy to have as much access to this stable as I can give him, and it won't be safe unless I can keep everyone else away. Besides, Nightshade won't be any trouble. She's no Chaos. She's a beautiful, splendid thoroughbred, but well trained and almost too well behaved." She added wearily, "Though perhaps I'm just telling myself that. Anything I do to give Gilroy access might not matter now that Reardon and his people are here. Things are changing so quickly that it's hard to keep up."

"Not for you." She had to clear her tight throat. "You're riding high and knocking everyone out of your way. Can't you see that? Just what you've told me today should let you know that no one is ever going to take you down."

Sasha didn't speak for a moment; then suddenly she chuckled. "Yeah, I did pretty good handling Davidow. I don't believe anyone could have done it better." She added thoughtfully, "But it still might be better if Gilroy doesn't come unless I really need him. It's a risk for him. Maybe I just wanted him here because I felt so alone. You can't feel alone if Gilroy is around."

"No, you can't, but Gilroy wouldn't be there just to hold your hand so stop pushing him away. It's what you've done ever since I saw you riding Zeus in that circus ring."

"And then you stuck around and wouldn't go away until you taught me not to do it," she said softly. "Though I still forget and fall back some-times. But then I remember you're somewhere out there, and maybe if I let the world in now and then, it won't be all that bad."

But Sasha had seen so much that was bad in these last months, Alisa thought with aching pity. Yet she had faced it with incredible strength and endurance. "No, there are so many beautiful things in this world. You showed me a lot of them. The birth of that magnificent foal, how to ride through the hills and feel as I was part of everything around me, all the explorations, all the silences, all the words... We found them together. We'll keep on finding them when this is over. We just have to hold on and not let all this ugliness surrounding us make us forget to reach out and take the joy that's there." Her voice was unsteady. "Okay? Is it a deal?"

"Don't be silly. Of course it's a deal."

She drew a deep breath. So much emotion, and she had to move away from it for both their sakes. "Good. Then I can stop lecturing you on things you know already and tell you that Korgan and I have been working hard today. Things aren't going quite as badly on our end as they were for you. We're close to solving the problem with Director Lakewood, and Korgan turned his attention to Zeus and your other horses..."

Alisa was still leaning back against the stones bordering the fireplace an hour later, drinking another cup of tea, when Korgan came back into the room. "You were a long time."

"I went back to the council house to negotiate that damn steam room for the women of the village."

She blinked. "What? Tonight?"

He dropped down in a chair. "It was bothering you. I asked them to get the members back in session because I had an offer. They could smell the profit and came running back."

"To give the women access to their steam room?"

"Well, not the council's steam room. There was that tradition thing I'd have had to battle. So I donated the money and labor to have a steam house of their own built for the women of the village." He grinned. "So that they'd be able to form traditions of their own that might include the right not to allow any male chauvinists to come near their steam house, which will have all the bells and whistles."

She started to laugh. "Outrageous."

"I thought that bit would please you."

"It does. But what about diplomacy?"

"The road to diplomacy is often paved in gold. I persuaded them that it would keep their women happy *and* add value and prestige to their village." He paused. "Isn't that what you wanted to happen?"

She nodded slowly. "I hadn't thought it out, but that's what I wanted."

"Good. Then we're finished with it. They're happy, you're happy. You won't make any more comments about how I'm gleaming."

"I don't promise that." She took a sip of her tea. "But you went to extravagant lengths to make sure everyone was happy. Thank you."

"Not so extravagant. A steam house is not the Taj Mahal."

"But it will be to those village women. It would have been to me when I was a kid."

"Then you should be the one to design it to get the proper bells-and-whistles element."

"I might do that. I'll ask Sasha to help. She'd think it was fun." She grimaced. "But that's down the road. She called tonight: Reardon is at Jubaldar, but that's all she knows. Except that it's going to be more difficult for Gilroy to contact her."

"She's upset?"

"Of course, but she's handling it. She always does. I got more emotional than she did. I was telling her all the positive things that we had to hold on to, and one thing struck home." She met his eyes across the room. "I said that we shouldn't give up who we are and stop reaching out for joy and beauty because of all the ugly things around us. Wise words, but I wasn't paying attention to them myself." She moistened her lips. "Because I was nervous and afraid, and I didn't quite know how to go about it. I might have even been a little intimidated."

"Intimidated?" He shook his head and smiled faintly. "Not you, Alisa."

"I'd agree with you, but not when it comes to you."

"Me?" He was no longer smiling. "How did this get to be about me?"

"I don't know. It just happened. We're talking about being honest, and I have trouble being honest with you. You've always been my Achilles' heel. Even Margaret realized that was true. I've been sitting here, thinking about it, and there's every chance that intimidation was a big part of it."

"You're not making sense," he said quietly. "What are you trying to say?"

"You'd know if you stopped putting up barriers. You can read me so well. It used to annoy and frighten me until I realized that it was just an integral part of who you are. Then it became comforting because it shut out all the loneliness." She shrugged. "But you don't want to read me now because what you feel for me is all confused, and you don't want to hurt me. I'm not going to let you get away with that, Korgan. Because you're cheating me of the joy I told Sasha we had to hold on to. But there's only one way I can think to do it." She put her cup down on the floor and got to her feet. "And that's to not let you say no." She came toward him. "And be honest and try to say the words that won't make you push me away."

"What the hell are you doing, Alisa," he asked warily.

"I'm seducing you," she said unsteadily. "At least,

I hope I am. Because I want you inside me and I'm tired of you pushing me away. This has nothing to do with payment, or gratitude, or your memory of that fourteen-year-old girl who seems to bother you so much. You've made it too complicated when anyone can see you want me. I'm not a victim or a cross to bear. It's simply sex and the fact that I've probably wanted you since that first night in your study. Maybe before." She took his hand and pulled him to his feet. "It's me, going after you. No commitment. You can walk away any-time." She reached up, opened the striped blanket, and let it drop to the floor. "But I don't think you will."

"I'd be crazy if I did," he said hoarsely, his hands moving to her breasts and cupping them, his fingers on her nipples. "I'm not crazy." His hands left her breasts and reached up to frame her face in his hands. "This isn't a good idea. I'm about to go up in flames," he whispered. "I don't want this for you. I don't want to be just another taker."

"You're an idiot." She was quickly unbuttoning his shirt and then pushing her naked breasts against his chest and rubbing them back and forth. "If you can't see I'm the taker." She pressed her teeth against his nipple and bit down. "Now will you get inside me?"

"Oh, yes." He was suddenly pulling her down

to the floor, tearing off his shirt, pushing her legs apart. "Any way, any place I can. I've waited too long for this."

"Your fault." His fingers were suddenly inside her and she gasped as they started to move. "You were thinking too much. You should have been doing this..."

"Be quiet. I'm too hot." His fingers were going deeper, twisting, plunging. "You've said all I want you to say for the time being. You did too good a job seducing me and now it's all in my court. And thinking isn't all that bad if it keeps me from hurting you." His mouth was on her breast, sucking, biting. "Are you ready for me?"

"I couldn't... be... more ready."

She was vaguely aware his mouth and fingers had left her as he tore off his clothes. Then he was over her, in her, plunging deep!

She cried out and lunged upward, trying to take more of him.

He gave her more.

Full. She was so full. Yet he was reaching around and cupping her buttocks, lifting her to every thrust, giving her still more. "Korgan..."

"I want you to feel me in every part of you," he whispered. "Here." He bent his head and licked first one nipple, then the other. Then his mouth moved up to the hollow of her throat and he sucked slowly, sensually as his strokes became deeper and deeper. "Here. Do you feel it here, Alisa?"

"You know...I do."

His hand moved down to her belly, stroking her in rhythm. "And here?"

"Everywhere." She was on fire, every muscle tense, ready. "Finish...it, damn you."

"You had only to ask. I've been holding on by a thread." He was gathering her closer. "Come to me. I want every bit of you..."

Wildness.

Depth.

Fullness.

Her nails bit into his shoulders.

Fire.

Frantic merging until there was nothing left to merge.

Yet it seemed to go on forever.

Until there was no more forever.

The tears were running down her cheeks as she clutched desperately at him.

She could feel him shudder against her, and then he lifted up to look down at her. "Shit." He reached out and touched the tears on her cheeks. "I hurt you?"

"I should have known." She shook her head. "You're impossible. Are you looking for something to feel guilty about? Tears don't only come from pain, you know. Sometimes emotion can have a hell of a lot to do with it." She closed her eyes. "Now let me have a moment to catch my breath. I don't know what I was expecting, but this was...different."

"Definitely." Then he was gone. A moment later she felt him beside her again, gathering her up in the curve of his arm. "Be still," he murmured. "I just want you to be more comfortable." She felt the cool damp cloth running over her body, and then he took a longer time massaging between her legs. "Not too cold? You felt burning hot when I was in you and I thought this would be okay."

"Not too cold." She opened her eyes. "But you're spending entirely too much time rubbing me down there if you want to be soothing."

"I got distracted." He smiled down at her as he gave her a final lingering pat. "You're absolutely ravishing here. I wanted to play."

"You want me again? Go ahead. I only needed a minute."

"I can wait. Barely." He pushed her away and reached for the striped blanket she'd shed when she'd come to him. "You were very generous, and I hope that generosity will continue, but I won't take you for granted. Right now I just want to take care of you. I find I like the idea of doing that very much." He draped the blanket around her and fastened it over her breasts. "You didn't finish your tea before. I'll get you a fresh cup." He got to his feet and walked over to the fireplace. "Just stay there. I'll be with you in a minute."

She watched him move naked around the room, remembering how every one of those sleek muscles had felt against her body. Graceful, tough, totally sensual. Lord, he was beautiful.

"Come on. Over to the fire again." He was standing in front of her, lifting her to her feet. "Your tea is ready, madam." He settled her on a large, cushy pillow before handing her the tea. Then he stretched out beside her with his own cup cradled in his hands. "Comfortable?"

"How could I help?" She frowned as she saw a large pot of water set to one side of the hearth. "What's that? I didn't notice you going to fetch it."

"I think we might both be a little blurred right now. I thought after you had your tea, I'd heat water in case you wanted a bath. I'm still feeling guilty about depriving you of that steam bath."

"Well, it had a good result down the line."

"But not for you."

"That's not true." She smiled as she raised her cup to her lips. "The result down the line was that I got exactly what I wanted, even though it wasn't the steam bath."

His eyes narrowed on her face. "It was a result I wasn't expecting. What triggered it?"

"Is it bothering you that I was aggressive?" She met his gaze. "Is that why you set me up for a heart-to-heart discussion here by the fire?" She nodded. "Yes, that's it. You're always probing, trying to get to the truth of any puzzle. Did I make you uneasy?"

"You almost blew my mind," he said flatly. Then he added, "And you'll remember I didn't allow you to be aggressive for more than a heartbeat or so before I was dragging you down on the floor and inside you. You could hardly call that being overaggressive." He paused. "But you mentioned something about being intimidated by me, and I just wanted to make certain that it wasn't something that I'd done that had forced you into a corner that—"

"Forced?" She was looking at him in bewilderment. "How could you force me?"

"How the hell do I know? Force doesn't have to be obvious; it can be subtle. Like I did with those council members tonight." He added wryly, "Like I do all the time."

And he had wanted to make sure he'd not been unfair to her. "No force," she said gently. "Obvious or subtle. If I was intimidated, it's because you're not like anyone else and very smart, and I admire you and even want to be like you in some ways. But only some ways. It would probably impede what I want to do myself. Your star burns very bright, and it could be distracting."

"Distraction..." He raised his brows. "So I'm only a temporary fling?"

"In the end, we both know that's what you'll want it to be. After this is over at Jubaldar, you'll become interested in something else and go off to create something intriguing and wonderful. It's what you should do." She concentrated on keeping her voice steady. "But as I told you, I wanted to have sex with you. I didn't see why I shouldn't, and I appreciate you accommodating me. It was everything I thought it would be. I promised you that there wouldn't be even a hint of a commitment. I'll keep my word."

"What a courteous and completely reasonable little speech." His expression was totally enigmatic. "There were a few things I liked very much about it. But there were others that showed a basic lack of understanding of who I am. It's that cerebral-physical thing again, merged with the fact that I'm very possessive and tend to keep anything that really pleases me for an inordinately long time." He added softly, "And you've pleased me since the first moment you walked into my study and disabled the XV-10, so I'm going to have trouble not getting obsessive." He leaned closer and flipped the edge of the blanket open to reveal the nakedness of her lower body. "Do you suppose you could stave off tossing me out until I become accustomed to the idea? Since I was so 'accommodating'?"

"It's possible." It was starting again. Her heart was beating hard; she was readying. It didn't matter that Korgan's attitude was a little inscrutable. Maybe that was natural. She'd worry about it later. "You were certainly that and more. I told you I wasn't playing coy. You can probably have me whenever you want me. I only wanted everything to be clear and honest between us."

"And it is." She could feel his breath on her belly, then faint prickly stubble as he moved lower, rubbing his cheek back and forth against her. "Honest and clear and everything that I want..."

CHAPTER

15

6:40 A.M.

Her phone was ringing...
Novak!

Alisa jerked up in bed, wide awake, as she picked it up. "How close are you, Novak?"

"I'll be there in another forty-five minutes. I just received a message from Korgan sending me coordinates for the helicopter landing pad and telling me that he'll meet me and then we'll join you later. Is that the way you want it?"

Typical Korgan. Taking charge and confronting Novak on his own without even consulting her. But wasn't that the best way to handle it? For her to step out of the way and let them size each other up and talk and see if they could work together. They were both brilliant and experienced, and she trusted both of them to get the job done. If there was a stumbling block, she could try to step in later to repair any damage. "That's the way I want it. Tell Korgan to bring you back to Cazvar's house and I'll give you a cup of tea. I'll see you soon, Novak." She cut the connection.

She drew a deep breath and swung her legs to the floor. Nothing like being tossed headlong into dealing with real life and all its problems before she was fully awake.

Where was Korgan?

She must have been sound asleep not to wake when he'd gotten out of bed and left the house. More likely unconscious, she thought ruefully. She didn't know how many times they had come together, but it had been wild and more erotic than anything she had ever experienced. Even now her breasts felt heavy, ripe, her skin...glowing. And just thinking about it was making her tingle, ready...

So she mustn't think about it. She got to her feet and slipped out of bed. Go wash, find something to wear, and get ready to meet with Novak. She had seized that brief moment and she would not be sorry for it. But it was time to put it aside and get to work.

Not so easy, she found immediately.

Before he'd left, Korgan had put that pot of water for her bath on the fire to warm.

And he'd washed the teapot and set it on the cabinet with her cup and the canister of tea beside it.

Right now I just want to take care of you. I find I like the idea of that very much.

Small things to make her feel so treasured, but impossible to ignore . . .

———◆———

She heard nothing from either Novak or Korgan for another four hours, and she had to stifle her impatience and the impulse to call them. *Look on the delay as a good sign*, she told herself. *Let them work it out.*

But she was still outside the house impatiently waiting when she saw them come down the cobbled street toward her. Neither of them was smiling, but they were talking very fast and intently. Her gaze went from one to the other. "You took long enough. Is it yes or no, Novak?"

Novak grinned. "You're more patient than I remember you being, Alisa. The woman I knew would have been hunting me down and firing arguments at me." He glanced slyly at Korgan. "Instead of sending an underling like him to do your dirty work. You're lucky I have a tolerant nature where arrogant billionaires are concerned."

"I'm sure your tolerance grows in leaps and bounds

with the amount of cash I'm willing to invest in the project," Korgan said dryly. "And whether you can talk me into relinquishing command. Stop trying, Novak. It won't happen."

"Answer me," Alisa said. That interaction between them had almost convinced her, but she had to be sure. "Yes or no."

Novak shrugged. "It was a tentative yes even before I got off the helicopter this morning. Getting rid of Masenak and Reardon is a project definitely worth doing. The only question mark was Korgan. I had an in-depth report on the rescue of those girls at Szarnar sent to me while I was on the helicopter last night." His lips turned up at the corners as he glanced at Korgan. "It's no wonder Lakewood's nose was out of joint. You were quite..." He seemed to be searching for a word. "Acceptable."

"Enough of that puckish humor. I know you're enjoying it, but he got them out, didn't he?" Alisa asked. "Why tentative?"

"I had to meet him and see if that rescue was a lucky fluke. And if it wasn't, if he had a plan in mind to make this attack come together fast. From what you told me, there's an urgency."

"Yes, there is," she said. "You were satisfied?"

"About Korgan?" He nodded solemnly. "I believe he'll do in a pinch." He added quickly when Alisa frowned, "And I like the idea of using this village as a secondary base to launch troops and drones. From the map it appears to be the right distance from Masenak, and safe until the actual attack. Plus Korgan appears to have the council tucked into his pocket. That's why we were running so late. I had Korgan take me to that council house and introduce me to the members."

"Drones?" She had caught that word and whirled on Korgan. "You didn't mention using drones again?"

"I wasn't sure I would. But they can be precise and deadly weapons if used correctly. Precision is even more important for an attack on Jubaldar than it was on Masenak's camp. Sasha, Gilroy, all those innocent workers..."

"Will you be using the same experimental drones you used at the camp?"

He shook his head. "Not necessary. That jungle was a nightmare. I can set up the usual overhead drone to navigate these mountains and program it to zero in and go down at exactly the right moment."

"You'll be here doing it yourself?"

"No *way*." His voice was adamant. "Not again. I'm going to be at Jubaldar. I was trapped by my own technology at that base camp. No one else could do it." He nodded at Novak. "But Novak's experienced with drones and these aren't anything innovative. He'll be able to set them up and launch after I give him the figures."

"Lucky me," Novak said wryly. "So, I'm to make an armed camp of Samlir, maintain a crew on standby ready to launch, and be your techno specialist. Not exactly what I'm accustomed to be doing."

"I imagine we'll be able to add to those duties ... if you prove acceptable."

"Bastard." But Novak was grinning. "You're damn right we will. I'm going to be putting my career on the line manipulating Lakewood, and I'd better come out of this looking like no one else would have been able to do it."

"You will," Alisa said.

"And how much time do I have to do it?"

"Not long," Korgan said. "I want to target the attack on Jubaldar for three days from today." He counted it off on his fingers. "Today and tomorrow the guests will be flooding into the castle, the next day is the race, and the following day Reardon is scheduled to go home. If we want Reardon, the last possible day I can launch an attack is right before he gets on that helicopter and waves goodbye to Jubaldar."

"Three days is going to be damn close. Reardon is absolutely necessary?"

"Absolutely," Korgan said flatly. "He could be more of a war criminal than Masenak."

Novak shrugged. "Then we'll get it done. I'll manage somehow."

"You always do," Alisa said. "Now do you want to come in for that cup of tea I promised you and relax?"

He shook his head. "Too tame for me right now. I'm charged. I want to take a look around the village and see what I need to do with it. Then I want Korgan to introduce me to Cazvar and let him know he's under my orders from now on. After that, I should be back on my helicopter and heading back to Maldara to gather personnel and equipment to bring back here."

"Is that all?" Alisa asked ironically.

"It has to be. Because all my time on the helicopter is going to be spent talking to Lakewood. It's going to take that long to persuade him that this is all his own idea, that I'm not trying to upstage him, and there's no way he would even consider using Walt Edwards." He lifted his hand. "I'll be in touch."

"Thanks, Novak," she called after him.

"Like I said, it's worth doing." He was striding quickly away. "I'll meet you back at the council house, Korgan."

"Right." He turned back to Alisa. "Good man. Extraordinary. But he could be difficult."

"So can you," she said. "But it will be good for you having to deal with someone who won't kowtow to you." She smiled. "Just being around him makes me remember just how good he is, and why his team thinks he can move mountains."

"Well, there are mountains to move here."

"He'll do it." She suddenly straightened as the energy flowed through her. "*We'll* do it. I'm charged, too."

"I can see you are." His gaze went to the door of the hut. "Charges are not to be wasted. Do you want to go inside and have...tea?"

She quickly shook her head. If she thought about it, she was afraid she'd give him another answer. "I don't want to do anything but get Sasha away from Jubaldar. When I called Margaret yesterday afternoon, she said that she'd found a cliff passage from Jubaldar to that pine forest where we park the Land Rover that we might be able to use to move the horses. I need to get back there right away to help her check it out. I can feel how close we're getting. Can't you?"

"Yeah." He pushed the hair away from her face, his fingers lingering in the strands at her temple. "I just tend to become distracted and confused these days about what's important and what's not at any given time. But I know Sasha is number one on that list." He brushed his lips across the tip of her nose. "I'll call Harris and tell him we're going to want him to pick us up in the helicopter and leave for Jubaldar right after Novak takes off. Is that soon enough?"

She nodded. "Things didn't seem to be going that bad for Sasha, but you can never tell what's happening from one minute to the next."

"No, you can never tell. So we'll get you there so that you can feel closer to her." He was striding up the street. "I've got to meet Novak. I'll see you at the helicopter pad."

She lingered, wanting to call him back. She didn't do it. She turned and went into the house to get her backpack.

———◆———

JUBALDAR
3 P.M.
50 HOURS TO RACE TIME

Margaret was waiting when Korgan pulled into the forest and parked the Land Rover.

Alisa's tense gaze flew to Margaret's face. Then she relaxed as Margaret smiled at her and started toward the car. Nothing must be wrong.

She jumped out of the car. "I tried to hurry back. But then Novak showed up and he and Korgan had to—"

"Stop apologizing, Alisa," Margaret interrupted. "You told me all that when you called to tell me you were on your way." She gave her a quick hug. "Nothing happened here that I couldn't handle myself, and you accomplished a hell of a lot more by bringing Novak to the table." She turned to Korgan. "But you'd better make sure those riders you're appropriating from Samlir are damn good. That cliff passage I found is narrow and dangerous. It's not much more than a ledge. The horses could end up going off it in at least two places if they get nervous or don't trust their rider."

"They're good. The council guaranteed them," Korgan said. "And I hope we won't have to use that passage if I can figure out what else I could do to nullify the threat."

"Sasha didn't think that would be possible," Alisa said sharply. "She asked me to do this."

"And we will. Don't be defensive. I realize you gave Sasha your word. But I've told you before sometimes there's more than one way. Go check out that cliff passage with Margaret and see what you think."

"I will." She turned away. Then she whirled back to him. "What are you going to do?"

He smiled. "Not anything that's going to alter your promise to Sasha. Stop being so suspicious. I believe you've found that everything I do for you is only aimed at giving you pleasure. Isn't that true?"

His body moving above her, his hands . . .

"Isn't it?" he repeated softly.

"There have been times you've made your own choices about what you think would make me happy," she said dryly. "What are you going to do?"

"I'm going to go make a few phone calls and arrangements. With Novak on board, we'll be moving forward at top speed. He said he was going to pick up personnel and equipment from his base in Maldara. I have to have Vogel mobilize our team and get them here." He added, "And the equipment I'll be bringing will be those drones I have to deliver to Samlir and also any other explosives that we left at the base camp. I'll probably only have today to get it done because I'd bet Novak will be at Samlir tomorrow and he'll want me there to help solidify his position with the council and citizens." He paused. "Make sense? Satisfied?"

She nodded. "Yes, I'm satisfied."

"Excellent." His smile had a hint of recklessness. "I'm not at all satisfied at the moment, but I'll get there eventually. It's clear I'll just have to be patient." He started moving down the path. "I'll see you both later."

Margaret stared after him and murmured, "He doesn't appear to be as pleased with the progress as you are. Did he do something wrong at Samlir?"

"What are you talking about? It's Korgan. He seldom makes mistakes. And he did everything right while we were there."

"Oh, did he?" Her speculative glance shifted back to Alisa. Then she smiled. "That's nice to know."

Oh, shit.

Ignore it.

She looked away from Margaret and grabbed her backpack from the car. "Just get me to that canyon. You've got me worried about that passage."

"Don't worry." Margaret was smiling. "I think I might have the problem solved even if those Berber riders aren't absolutely perfect."

"How?"

"Juno. Juno was with me whenever I visited you at St. Eldon's, and all the horses are familiar with her. She was even with us when we were riding in the hills. It was a game to all of them. If I tell her to lead them down that ledge, they'll follow her with absolutely no hesitation."

Alisa should have known Margaret would come up with something. She chuckled. "By George, I believe you've got it."

"Not yet," Margaret said as she motioned to Juno to follow her. "First, we have to take Juno up to that ledge and let her run it a few times so that she's letter-perfect when it comes time for her to lead the charge. She's got to realize that it's duty this time and not just fun..."

———

JUBALDAR RACETRACK
4 P.M.
49 HOURS TO RACE TIME

"Sasha, get over here," Masenak called. "Come and meet our guest! And bring that fiend from Hades so Reardon can see what a beauty he is."

She whirled and saw Masenak and Reardon strolling toward her from the stables. They were both smiling and appeared very satisfied with themselves. She braced herself, her hand tightening on Chaos's lead. "Did you warn him that Chaos might decide to smash his head open if he gets too close?"

Masenak's smile disappeared. "I told him that you were having a few problems with him that you'll resolve given time and effort. We discussed solutions in depth last night at dinner. Now get over here."

She walked slowly toward them.

Chaos was holding back. *You're shaking. I don't like it. Can I do something to them?*

No, don't hurt them. That would make it worse for me. I'll take care of it. I'll be all right in a few minutes.

Stupid. It would be so easy. Wouldn't make it worse. We could each take one of them and then they would be the ones shaking.

No, Chaos. Just wait.

Because you're too weak to help me? I don't really need help. I only offered because I didn't want to insult you again. I've decided that since I am king, I should show mercy.

She tried to make the thought more forceful. *No, Chaos!*

She'd almost reached the two men and she was staring directly into Reardon's face. So cold... She'd only seen him on Skype before, and it didn't compare to the full impact of the man. He wasn't like Masenak. Those features were sharp and intelligent, his intensity cruel rather than brutal. But his pale-hazel eyes were dead and without feeling.

"Ah, there you are." Reardon was smiling at her, but it didn't reach those pale eyes. "I was telling Masenak I couldn't wait to meet you. I could see all that strength and spirit and thought how unusual it was that such a young girl would possess it. I told him it was a shame to waste it on those horses."

"He wouldn't agree with you. He believes that's

exactly where I should be. He's told me that any number of times." She glanced at Masenak. "Isn't that right?"

"I'd hate to argue with such an old friend," Masenak said. "There might be room for two sets of thinking on the subject. We've been talking about combining our efforts on Chaos once you've got him under control. Reardon has some interesting ideas that might benefit both of us."

"But you don't have to do that," she said swiftly. "Once Chaos has won the race, you can do whatever you wish with him."

"You seem to be certain Nightshade won't win," Reardon said. "Chaos is obviously a phenomenal horse, but you've been telling Masenak that he's too unstable to trust on the track. Have you been lying to him?"

"He's wild. Ask anyone if they can ride him."

"I don't have to ask anyone. I have my jockey in you. If you can ride him once, you can ride him again." He took a step closer, and then closer. "And again and again."

She forced herself not to take a step back. That's what he wanted her to do. "It can't happen that way. I'd rely on Nightshade, if I were you. She won't embarrass you in front of your friends."

"I have no friends. Just people who admire me and wish they could be like me." He added cynically,

"Like my partner Masenak here. It appears his finances are in shambles. Even if Chaos wins and my money is in his pocket, he'll still have problems making Chaos the asset he could be. He's a criminal on the run, and he wouldn't be able to handle either the racing or the breeding possibilities. But if he lets the world believe Chaos is mine, then all that hassle goes away. I'm a respectable businessman and no one knows any different. Masenak will split any future profits with me in return for me providing him with a front he couldn't get anywhere else. So Nightshade will run in our race, but I'll hedge my bet with Chaos. No matter what the outcome at the end of the race, the next day you and that horse will be coming home with me. Now get on that stallion and show me what he can do."

She glanced at Masenak.

He nodded. "Not unreasonable considering our new arrangement. And Reardon wants you to come to dinner tonight in my suite. Seven, Sasha."

She instantly shook her head. "I have to take care of Chaos and Nightshade."

"Seven," Reardon repeated. "Go to your suite first and change to the more suitable clothing I'll have sent to you. I've designated myself to set up scheduling. I believe I'll be better at it than Masenak. He appears to be a trifle overindulgent with you. His idea about holding your other horses hostage wasn't bad, and I might sanction it, but I prefer more personal ways to break both of you." His tone hardened. "Now mount Chaos and go twice around the track. I want speed and obedience. If I get less, you'll both regret it. After that you may go back to the stable until it's time for you to put in an appearance later."

She hesitated. Defiance or temporary compliance? She was having trouble thinking through the frustration and panic. It was an entirely new ball game, and it was clear Reardon was in charge of every move. If she disobeyed, it would force him to punish immediately to establish his dominance. She had no choice.

She turned and jumped on Chaos's back.

Run! Let's get this over with.

Chaos sprang forward!

She bent low over his neck. No joy. No lightning. Just the glory of speed and the togetherness that even Reardon couldn't smother.

Once around the track.

And Chaos was sensing something wrong. She could feel his muscles tightening. *Why?*

Just run.

Twice around the track.

Enough. She pulled him in, signaling him to stop.

He didn't stop. *Wrong. It should not have been like that for you. Should I go back and make them hurt?*

No, we're going back to the stable. He'd slowed down and she managed to jump off him. *It wasn't wrong. Sometimes you have to give up a little to win.* She glanced back at Reardon and Masenak and she wished she hadn't. Masenak was smiling, but Reardon's exultant expression was triumphant. She shivered. Evil. Pure evil. She'd thought Masenak was terrible, but she had an idea Reardon was a devil incarnate. As well as having power over Masenak to shape his treatment of her and what happened at Jubaldar during the next days. She had never felt this helpless when dealing with Masenak.

It was not little. You're shaking again. But Chaos was letting her lead him from the track. *I don't think I can let it happen again.*

———◆———

Sasha had to stop a moment to get her breath after she'd finished feeding and watering Chaos and Nightshade. *Slow down,* she told herself. She'd done all she could for the time being. She'd been working hurriedly, trying not to think, because she was dreading going to the suite for another encounter with Masenak and Reardon. But she had to face it.

Alone.

Gilroy hadn't come last night. She really hadn't

expected him; had even told Alisa she shouldn't let him come. He must have heard about Reardon's arrival and known Nightshade was here and she might be having to make adjustments. But she had still found herself waiting.

Just as she had this evening.

But this evening if he came, he might find her gone. He'd never been able to get here before almost nine. It was almost six thirty and she had no intention of being late and giving Reardon a reason to go on the attack.

She left the stable and hurried across the court-yard and up to her suite. The outfit Reardon considered "suitable" was draped on the bed, and it wasn't as bad as she'd thought. A simple white pleated tunic, tan trousers, sandals instead of boots. She ducked into the shower, was out and dressed in fifteen minutes, and then was running toward Masenak's quarters.

"Right on time." It was Reardon who opened the door. He said over his shoulder to Masenak, "I told you she'd be prompt. She's very smart and wouldn't want any immediate confrontation." He pulled her into the suite. "Now let's see how she looks before we sit down to dinner." He tilted his head as he gazed at her from head to toe. "Not bad. That loose white shirt makes you look a couple of years younger, which I prefer. But the hair is all wrong." He grasped her wrist and dragged her in front of a mirror over the sideboard. "But I can take care of that, pretty Sasha," he whispered as he quickly began to unfasten her ponytail.

———◆———

9 P.M.
44 HOURS TO RACE TIME

Sasha barely let the door of Masenak's suite slam behind her before she was running down the stairs, and then across the courtyard to the stable.

Then she was inside. Safety.

She was breathing hard and leaning back against the door, panting.

"Sasha?"

Gilroy. Her gaze flew down the aisle of stalls to see him coming toward her. "Should you be here? Is it safe for you?" She was running toward him. "Reardon is here. Everything is different. Maybe you should—"

"Hush." He took her shoulders in his hands and gave her a gentle shake. "I was careful. There's so much fuss and confusion about Reardon's arrival that it's safer than it was before. I just had to be certain before I screwed up." He was gazing at her. "But if I was reading body language right when you came through that door, you're not finding it safer. Where were you?"

"Masenak's suite, having dinner with him and Reardon."

He gave a low whistle. "Not good."

"No." She was recovering now. "But it was stupid of me to panic. It was what Reardon wanted me to do. I couldn't let him see that I—but I hardly made it out that door after dinner before I broke. He kept staring at me all through dinner with those pale eyes like a cat who wants to—" She broke off. "I hated it. Will you wait just a minute? I kept thinking of what he was seeing, and I have to get rid of it." She pulled her hair back from her face and fastened it into the ponytail she usually wore. "That's all I can do right now. But I can still feel his fingers in my hair while he was combing it out. It was...creepy."

"I can imagine," he said quietly. "Did he do anything else that was 'creepy'?"

She shook her head. "Just threats." She moistened her lips. "He likes young girls. When I was sitting across from him at the table, he made me feel...like Jeanne. I could see him treating me like those men treated Jeanne Palsan."

He swore beneath his breath.

"But he didn't touch me...except for my hair." She tried desperately to put together anything else that might be of importance. "Masenak and he have some kind of deal about Chaos, and I think Reardon is in control. Or at least heading that way. Masenak's given him permission to take Chaos and me home with him on the day after the race. But I believe Masenak would fight him if he tried to snatch Chaos away." Yet she remembered how Reardon had almost ignored Masenak this evening, attempting to control the conversation and intimidate her. "I could see how much Reardon likes control. One of the reasons he might have wanted me to be afraid is that I can handle Chaos. He might think that to control me will be to control Chaos."

"Don't count on it. Korgan thinks that Reardon is a son of a bitch on every level, and no one knows him better."

"He might be right." She shivered. "It's just easier for me not to think of myself as another Jeanne Palsan. But I should let Alisa know that there might be a way to drive a wedge between Masenak and Reardon. I'll call her soon." She moistened her lips. "But I don't want to have her asking me questions right now."

"Because you don't know if you can fend them off at the moment." He shrugged. "I'll do it, if you'll fetch the phone from Chaos's stall. I'd offer to do it myself after I proved myself so splendidly the other night, but he's been very restless while I was waiting for you. I don't want to damage my new image by having him pound me into the dirt. Maybe having to share his stable with Nightshade is causing him to be a little on edge?"

She shook her head. "No. He has no trouble at all with Nightshade. He's been practically ignoring her all the time she's been here. Even when I had them both on the track together for a while this morning, he was being his usual kingly self and showing off how much better he was than her. More likely it's Reardon and Masenak who are making him edgy. He didn't like what was happening on the track today." Her lips tightened. "Neither did I."

"And neither do I. So get me the phone so I can express my outrage to Alisa and Korgan and save you from doing it."

She wasn't going to argue with him, she thought wearily. She wasn't able to be calm yet about what had happened tonight, and she didn't want it to upset Alisa when there was nothing to be done about it. Better to let Gilroy handle it. "No outrage. Just give them the facts." She turned and headed toward Chaos's stall. "I'll be right back."

She heard Chaos moving before she reached him. Definitely restless. *I'm coming in to get one of the things you're guarding for me. Are you okay with it?*

It's good you ask permission. At least you realize my importance.

And definitely bad-tempered. *I'll be in and out in seconds. And then I'll go and get you and Nightshade fresh water before I return the phone to you.*

You need not get anything for her. She does not deserve it.

Don't be selfish. She was in his stall and reaching for the phone. *She hasn't done anything to you. Of course I'll get her water.*

Then she was out of the stall and handing the phone to Gilroy, who was coming toward her. "It's just as well you left it to me. He's in a rotten humor."

"I've always wondered how you could tell the difference." He ducked into a stall four down from Chaos and started to make the call.

Sasha shrugged and shook her head. There was no way she could explain all the beauty and spirit that was Chaos, so she wouldn't try. He had to be experienced. She turned, grabbed the buckets, and headed for the pump.

———◆———

Gilroy didn't try to reach Alisa. He called Korgan directly. "I'm giving you a report for Alisa. Sasha had a rough time today, but she said to tone down the outrage, so you do it for me. I'm in no mood."

"How bad? Masenak?"

"For once he wasn't the main perpetrator. Reardon showed up and stepped up to the plate. What you'll be most interested in is that the situation is getting tighter. If you were planning on taking Reardon out on the day after the race, you might have a problem. When Reardon leaves Jubaldar, he's taking Chaos and Sasha home with him."

"What! Why?"

"Some deal Masenak and Reardon have concocted between them. But like I said, if you were counting on having another couple of days to stage the attack, or just to get her out of Jubaldar, you'd better consider that she might be joined at the hip to Reardon."

Korgan was cursing. "Of course I was planning on staging the attack by the day after the race. And we can do it, dammit. I just heard from Novak that he's on his way back to Samlir with his team. But this means there can't be anything last minute about it. It's almost the same as losing a day." He paused. "And I don't like this for a number of reasons. What kind of deal? What does it involve?"

"Chaos, of course." He added bitterly, "And it might have something to do with Sasha. It seems he likes young girls and decided to groom Sasha to be his next choice."

"Shit! My reports on Reardon indicated that might be a problem, but I was hoping it could be avoided if he showed up just before the race as usual."

"Hoping?" Gilroy cursed low and vehemently. "Bullshit. You should have been prepared for it. He's here, and Sasha is having to take care of it herself. I can't do a damn thing about it."

"Except you're already planning on how you can," Korgan said grimly. "And you could blow everything to hell and get her killed if you're that reckless. How is she handling it?"

"How do you think? Like she always does. Like she did when she was facing Masenak in that prison encampment. Pure guts and endurance. But it's different this time. I could see it when she ran into the stable tonight. She was scared and shaking and trying not to show it. But she was talking too fast and she mentioned Jeanne Palsan. She saw too much in Masenak's camp, and she was always in danger herself." He suddenly burst out, "Dammit, how much does she have to take?"

"More than she should. We all know that. The question is, How long do we have before Reardon's threat becomes reality." He paused. "Or has it already reached that point?"

"No. Masenak and Reardon are involved with Chaos and they may be using Sasha as a chess piece. But there's no telling when one of them might declare checkmate before that. You can't expect me to sit here and let that happen. I won't do it, Korgan."

"I'm not asking, I'm just telling you that you have to cool down and let me see what I can do to change the scenario. Reardon screwed us by showing up early. He had time to assess the situation and start negotiating. Now he's ready to fold his tents and leave with the spoils." He was silent, thinking. "All Masenak's guests have arrived at the castle now, is that right? How many?"

"Fifty or sixty. Davidow and the housekeepers are going crazy."

"Why?"

"Why do you think? When they come, it's nonstop turmoil in the castle and stables. Masenak's choice of party friends are generally petty criminals and whores who are here to curry favor and provide an enthusiastic audience. In return they're allowed to have the run of the place."

"Good to know." He was quiet again. "Very disruptive on the day before the race. Anything could happen."

"What?"

"I'll let you know," he said. "But the situation isn't

that bad. With Jed Novak on board with handling the attack from Samlir, and Vogel delivering those drones to him sometime tomorrow, it will cinch the preparations."

"I don't want promises. I want you to come through for her."

"And I will. Do you think I could face Alisa if I didn't? Do you think I could look in the mirror?"

"No," he said harshly, "I just feel so damn helpless."

"Well, that's a first. All I can suggest is that you be sure you're as ready as you can be. We'll do the same." He cut the connection.

Gilroy sat for a moment, looking down at the phone. He was still pissed off and frustrated and scared for Sasha, but talking to Korgan had helped a little to make him remember that he didn't have to shoulder the nightmare alone. That was Korgan's job, wasn't it, he thought sourly. Why become a damn icon if you didn't want to accept the bullshit that went along with it?

He got to his feet and strode out of the stall to see Sasha standing a few feet away in front of Chaos's stall. "I didn't talk to Alisa, but I gave your message to Korgan not to alarm her."

"That's good," she said absently, not looking away from Chaos. "I could have done it, but it gave me time to get over being such a wuss." She held out her hand to take the phone. "Thanks."

"You're welcome." He ignored her outstretched hand. "I think I'll keep my phone for the time being." As she started to protest, he shook his head. "If you hadn't been so determined to make Chaos guardian of our stash, I would have found a place before this. Using him was a good idea, but Korgan said that from now on we should be as ready as we could be for anything that comes our way. I can't do that unless I can get to my gun and that phone quickly. I'll take over the job of finding a safe place for mine."

"'Anything that comes our way...'" She shook her head. "I don't think you were successful in not alarming him."

"He won't let Alisa see it." He shrugged. "I'm not too proud to call in reinforcements." He turned to open Chaos's stall. "To prove it, I'll have you stand there on guard while I go in and get my gun from Chaos's less-than-tender care."

"No!" She jerked him back. "I'll do it. I told you something wasn't right with him." She slipped inside, got his gun, and then was back. "Change 'bad-humored' to 'savage.' Don't go near him."

"Sick?"

"I don't think so. I hope not. Masenak isn't going to believe me if I tell him he's too ill to run." She squeezed his arm. "Get out of here and find a place to hide that gun and phone."

He still hesitated.

"Nothing's going to happen to me. I couldn't be safer than I am here." She made a face. "If I get nervous, I'll take a blanket and sleep in Chaos's stall. He might not be liking me right now, but he'd really hate anyone who tried to bother him tonight. And I'll be just as safe once I'm on the track tomorrow with all of Masenak's guests gawking at us. Masenak won't want my concentration disturbed any more than necessary."

"You have it all thought out. You've been planning strategy." He smiled. "I told Korgan, all guts and endurance." He turned and added lightly as he headed out the door, "But do me a favor and take good care of yourself? I can't be bothered to be worried about you when I have to find somewhere to stash this gun."

———————

MIDNIGHT
41 HOURS TO RACE TIME

"Wake up." Alisa was vaguely aware Korgan was standing there, framed in the lighter darkness of the cave opening. "I know you're tired, but I need to talk to you." He glanced at Margaret curled up in her sleeping bag and held out his hand. "Outside."

She scrambled to her knees and let him pull her to her feet. "I'm not that tired." It wasn't true. After she and Margaret had worked with Juno on negotiating that ledge, they'd taken photos of the guards' barracks before tackling the canyon where Masenak's helicopters and warehouses and vehicles were kept.

Then they'd taken Juno down the ledge run leading to the pine forest again one more time before inching down it themselves, checking for any possible weakness. She and Margaret had gotten back to the cave just before dark, emailed the photos to Novak, Vogel, and Korgan, cleaned up, and climbed immediately into their sleeping bags. "You're the one who should be tired. You were still working on those drone calculations when I went to sleep hours ago. Is there a problem with them?"

"No." He had stopped as they reached the boulders overlooking Jubaldar Castle. "But there may be a problem about when we can deploy them. I got a call from Gilroy and the situation has changed."

She stiffened. "What's wrong?"

"Masenak has made a deal with Reardon. Regardless of which horse wins, Reardon will be taking Chaos and Sasha home with him the day after the race."

"What? Why? That could make any attack twice as difficult," she said, panicked. "We might not be ready."

"Then we'd better get ready," he said grimly. "Because it seems we don't have a choice. I've called Novak and told him that the deadline has been upped and that I'll be joining him at Samlir right away to help set up. I ordered Harris to pick me up in the helicopter as soon as he could make it." He was frowning. "Dammit, I wanted to stay here and let Novak handle Samlir by himself."

"I know you did." She dazedly shook her head. "It's all right. Margaret and I will be okay here. We've almost finished taking the photos we needed of Jubaldar. It's only surveillance now. We don't need you. It's not as if we can't take care of ourselves."

"Heaven forbid that I even hint at that," he said ironically. "But I'm still calling Vogel. He's landed on the north cliffs, and his team is starting to work their way down into position to deliver the drones to Novak. He can pull someone and send him here ASAP."

"He might just be in the way. It's not as if anyone knows we're here. We'll be able to keep an eye on Jubaldar and follow any instructions you find you need to give us." She was still puzzled. "But I can't fathom why Reardon would suddenly strike this deal with Masenak and take Sasha and Chaos so quickly."

He didn't speak for a moment. "I was half expecting it. Reardon has always been into power. It's the reason he destroyed Karim and his homeland. It's one of the reasons why he felt he had to dominate Masenak. Then Chaos appears on the scene with Masenak in control, and the bastard probably rubbed in his victory with a heavy hand. Reardon wouldn't have been able to stand it without retaliating, so he set himself to making sure that he took everything connected to that victory away from Masenak as quickly as possible. First the deal itself, then the prompt removal of assets."

"Everything connected . . . " she repeated. "Sasha."

He nodded. "She would have been an important part of his victory. A rider for Chaos."

She was remembering something else from that first Skype hacked by Vogel. "That wasn't all. Masenak told Reardon that Sasha was fifteen and he usually preferred them younger."

"Yes. Forget it. We won't let that make a difference."

But she couldn't forget it. "What else did Gilroy say?"

"He said Sasha is okay, but a little shaken. But you know she'll handle it. We're just going to have to make certain she doesn't have to stand it for too long. I don't like the way this is playing out. If Reardon is taking charge, then there's no telling what else he might do." His lips tightened. "But I'm not going to be caught off guard like this again. I'm going to push *hard*, and I won't be back here until it won't make a damn bit of difference what he pulls. We'll be ready."

"Shit," she said hoarsely, her hands knotting into fists at her sides. "You're damn right we will." She suddenly launched herself into his arms and buried her face in his chest. Comfort. Safety. Warmth. "Hold me," she whispered. "Just for a minute. I'll be okay in a minute."

"Shut up." His arms were around her, crushing her close. "My pleasure. Just let me be here for you, *help* you. It's not often that I get the chance to break through that wall you keep so firmly in place."

"That's not true," she said unsteadily. "I had sex with you all last night and if I had any walls left to break, they'd be shattered by now."

"Would they? Sex doesn't always do the trick. You won't let me close enough to get beyond that first barrier." He pushed her back and looked down at her. "It's a wonderful, deceptive barrier that welcomes me even as it keeps me from going too deep. It has all kinds of barbs of protective-ness and generosity that can be confusing but are erotic enough to let me accept anything you want to tell me or give me." He reached out and traced her lower lip with his index finger. "Whether or not I entirely believe you. That's why I appreciate it when you invite me inside."

She tried to laugh. "You can't say I haven't done that extensively in the past twenty-four hours." Her lip was tingling beneath his touch. It was strange how quickly heat had emerged from that instant of fear and emotion. She stepped back. "But you're getting too complicated and analytical. That's not what I wanted from you." She paused. "And that's not what I wanted to give you."

"No, what you wanted to give me was freedom and really great sex. You made that clear. It's what you want from me that I'm still bewildered about. My instinct is to ignore what you're saying and work it out for myself. I can't afford to make a mistake, and what you're going through with Sasha might be confusing you. I say that with extreme trepidation." He smiled crookedly. "But I'll give you more time, and perhaps it will all come together. In the meantime, I'll try to tamp down that analytical bullshit and give you the basics you've demonstrated you do enjoy. Does that sound agreeable?"

"What would you do if I said no?" she asked unsteadily.

"I'm such a civilized man that I'd try another way, of course."

"Now, that's true bullshit. You'd just up the ante."

"Which I'm doing right now." He took a step closer. "And the ante just became making you put aside how much you're worrying about Sasha and fretting about what we can do to bring those bastards down." He unbuttoned her shirt. "That's very high, but you can meet it. I have faith in you. Because you know we can do it together. I'll never let you lose." His lips were on her breast, licking delicately. "So should we take this little bit of time to demonstrate that Reardon and Masenak can go to hell as far as we're concerned? We'll get back to them with all the graphic details later."

Later. But he'd said he was leaving soon, and she didn't know when he'd be returning or what he'd be facing when she wasn't with him. "That sounds reasonable enough." She was swiftly tearing off the rest of her clothes.

"I told you I was a civilized man." He was lifting her legs over his hips, searching.

Then sinking deep . . .

She cried out and arched against him. She started moving.

"Easy," he murmured, his fingers digging into her buttocks. "Maybe not so civilized as I thought."

"Don't tell me that," she said unevenly. "Not

when you just told me you're leaving. I don't give a damn about being civilized. Now *move*."

"As you command." He was chuckling as he lifted her. "As the very civilized Oscar Wilde once said, 'I can resist anything...'" He started to move. "'...except temptation.'"

CHAPTER
16

He was gone.

Alisa stared after Korgan as he disappeared around the bend to make his way down to the forest where the Land Rover was hidden. She was still trying to catch her breath. Her fingers were clumsy as she finished getting dressed. Those moments of passion had gone by so quickly and crazily that she was still dizzy with emotion. That was probably what Korgan had intended. He'd wanted to take her mind off any threat to Sasha and the fact that their plans had to go into hyper speed. And he was so damn good that he'd been able to distract her until he'd just walked away from her.

But now reality was striking home again.

Who knew what else could happen when horror

seemed to be all around them? She moved out of the boulders and looked down at Jubaldar. It was dark except for the glow of the garden lanterns and the lamps shining from an occasional window.

She's handling it.

That was what they always said about Sasha. It was as if they took it for granted.

But how long could Sasha handle all the ugliness and horror that was constantly attacking?

"Are you going to stay out here all night?" Margaret asked as she came to stand beside her. "If you are, we'd better go get our sleeping bags. Because I'm not leaving you alone."

"I'll come back to the cave soon. I was just looking at the castle."

"You're always looking at the castle," she said. "I don't know how many times I've seen you come down here and stare at the place." She shrugged. "Who could blame you? Particularly now."

She glanced at Margaret's face. "Now? Korgan talked to you when he went back to the cave to get his backpack?"

She nodded. "He told me to take care of you. As if we didn't do that all the time anyway. He's getting repetitive. Though I'm glad he did this time. You might have gotten all quiet and made me dig." She added, "Korgan will see that nothing gets dropped between the cracks. It just means we'll have to move faster."

"I know that. I know everything you probably want to say to me." She smiled shakily. "I guess I'm in worry mode. Ignore me."

"I will. The minute you tell me if I should go get our sleeping bags."

She shook her head, then took Margaret's arm and started back toward the cave. "I'll be fine, and Juno will be upset and come looking for you if he wakes and finds you gone. Korgan will let me know soon enough if I have to worry." She grimaced. "Or maybe he'll let you know and let you break it to me gently. That appears to be the way he's handling things these days."

"The way you're letting him handle things," Margaret corrected. "We both know that it will only last as long as you permit it." She glanced back at Jubaldar. "Or as long as those bastards keep making mistake after mistake that irritate the hell out of you."

———◆———

JUBALDAR RACETRACK
9 A.M.
32 HOURS TO RACE TIME

"He's looking in good shape." Davidow's gaze was narrowed on Chaos as Sasha led him onto the track. "Maybe a little too good. The last time I saw him that sleek and menacing was right before he went after that stable boy and broke his legs."

"Who you should never have forced to get near Chaos," Sasha said. "That was entirely your fault."

He shrugged. "You're avoiding the subject. I haven't seen Chaos this on edge since the first day that you started handling him. Are you losing your touch? Am I going to have to pick up your battered remains and scramble to get someone else to ride him tomorrow? I won't be pleased if I have to give Masenak that news."

"At that point, I don't believe I'd be worried about how you're feeling, Davidow."

"Answer me," Davidow bit out.

There was no use antagonizing the trainer, she thought wearily. He was so wary of Masenak firing him that he'd go on the attack at the least encouragement. Her best bet would be to keep him as neutral as possible. "He's not in the best mood. I might have a few problems with him today." Davidow started to curse, and she held up her hand. "I'll work through it. It can't be that bad. He let me put a saddle on him, and he wasn't too impatient while I was saddling Nightshade." She glanced back at the chestnut thoroughbred being led out of the stable by Nightshade's stable boy. "But you might have to move her to the main stable if he keeps on being temperamental. I don't want her hurt."

"And have Reardon on my ass? No way. Handle it some other way. I've got enough trouble keeping those damn guests from overrunning my stable. Six of them showed up this morning wanting to go for a ride before breakfast. Most of them don't even know how to mount a horse. I had to send some of my help with them so they wouldn't break their necks." He turned on his heel. "And then I come here and find you having trouble with Chaos. Fix it!"

Sasha turned back to Chaos. *You heard him. I'm supposed to fix you. I don't want you to stretch out and wear yourself out today. A gentle run? Or are you going to toss me?*

I might let you ride me. Pause. *But she will go with us.*
What? Who?

That female who is so stupid she doesn't even appreciate who I am or how honored she should be that I let her stay. She will go with us.

Nightshade? I'm surprised. But you could hardly blame her for not being honored. You were ready to let her die of thirst last night.

I would have let her drink. I just had to be the one to permit her to have it. You got in my way.

As she stared at him, she was beginning to believe

that she had done just that. The restlessness. The volatility. The disturbance and impatience. Blind. She must have been blind. *And now you don't mind Nightshade being with us?*

She is stupid. Those foolish men have ruined her. How else will she learn?

How have they ruined her?

Maybe not ruined her . . . yet. I have decided to save her. But they have made her so tame that she doesn't know what it is to be free. She's even confused why I would want to talk to you. And she doesn't realize that I am king. I have to show her.

I see. She was having trouble keeping him from sensing her amusement. *But you said she was stupid. Is it worth your effort?*

Perhaps not that stupid. I can feel she realizes I'm amazingly beautiful and wise. How could she not? She just doesn't understand the rest. I have to teach her.

That's very generous of you. She glanced at Nightshade standing quietly waiting. Nightshade was also amazingly beautiful, and her wisdom might be entirely different from Chaos's. The chestnut thoroughbred had a serenity and control the Nisean would never possess, but it didn't indicate a lack of strength. It was probably that strength that was attracting Chaos now, along with the inevitable draw of sexual mating. He was the lightning and she was the slow-rolling thunder that moved the storm.

What a team they would be. This might bring her endless trouble, but it was also a miracle and Sasha refused to be sorry about it. *Though you'll have to be patient.* She pulled herself into the saddle. *Because Nightshade might believe she deserves respect herself since she's so foolish she doesn't know you're king. Suppose we take it very slowly?*

———◆———

5 P.M.
24 HOURS TO RACE TIME

Davidow was waiting when Sasha brought Chaos and Nightshade back to the stable. She stiffened warily, her gaze flying to his face. It was totally noncommittal. "I hope you had a better day than you expected. You'll be glad to know that I had no problem with Chaos. I was able to run both him and Nightshade for most of the day. He must have worked out his bad temper on the track."

"I know. I had a glimpse of him a couple of times today when Reardon called me back here to watch you."

"Reardon?" Her eyes widened. "I didn't notice either of you."

"You were busy." He was scowling. "When you got Chaos to run, he took off like a lightning bolt with Nightshade right behind him. He might have broken a record today."

"No, he didn't." She frowned, puzzled, as she got off Chaos. "He's always fast, but I deliberately kept his pace slower than usual today. I wanted to keep both him and Nightshade rested and fresh for the race tomorrow."

"That's not how it looked to me," he said shortly. "And it's sure as hell not how it looked to Reardon. It would have been better if you'd tried harder to make him look a little less enthusiastic today." When she opened her lips to answer, he waved his hand impatiently. "I don't want to hear it. It's done now. Just get Chaos into the stable and get him settled like you usually do."

She didn't have to be told twice. She was already leading Chaos into the stable. She didn't like anything about Davidow's attitude or Reardon showing up today. "I'll be back in a few minutes to put Nightshade into her stall."

"Don't bother. Reardon has a few questions for Nightshade's jockey." He turned to Lee Chan, the jockey who had been riding Nightshade all day. "Get down. I'll call him and tell him you've brought her back."

Sasha glanced back in bewilderment. Lee Chan was hurriedly getting off the thoroughbred, his expression uneasy. She hoped the jockey hadn't done anything to displease Reardon. It was difficult to have any real feeling for him, because he'd been so stoic and without personality any time she'd had him ride Nightshade when Sasha had her on the same track with Chaos. But he'd obeyed everything she'd told him to do and didn't deserve a confrontation with Reardon.

No one deserved that. She could feel her own heart beating hard, her palms cold with sweat as she took off Chaos's saddle and put him in his stall. But she would probably have to face a confrontation herself, and she had to brace herself. She bent down to pick up Chaos's water bucket. She had escaped it all day but after last night she didn't think that she'd be lucky enough to—

A scream!

High. Shrill. Agony.

A whip.

She heard it lash against flesh. Again and again.

Another scream.

The jockey?

She dropped the bucket and ran toward the door.

She stopped in shock.

That was not the jockey screaming.

It was the horse. It was Nightshade!

She threw open the stable door and stared in disbelief. The jockey was standing holding the horse's reins to keep her still.

And Reardon was beating Nightshade with a quirt. The lash came down again and then again before Sasha's shock vanished and she launched herself at Reardon. "No!"

She was reaching desperately for the quirt, kicking at his shins. Her boot made contact, and she heard him swear. Her fist struck his mouth.

"Get the bitch off me!"

And then Davidow was pulling her away from Reardon. She was fighting him, too, struggling to get back to Reardon. "Let me go. You saw him, Davidow. He was hurting her. That whip...He has to be crazy. Who would whip Nightshade? She's the gentlest horse I've ever known."

"I was afraid you'd cause him trouble," Davidow said. "Don't be stupid. He can do what he wants with her."

"But it doesn't make any sense." But cruelty never made sense. Reardon's expression as he'd lifted that whip had been a devil's face. He was turning toward her now, those pale-hazel eyes flickering with rage. He took a step toward her. "Yes, I can do what I want with her. Because she belongs to me. Just as I can do anything with you." The quirt came down hard across her chest. "Like this."

Pain.

"At least that makes some sense," she said fiercely.

"Because I *want* to hurt you. She didn't do anything. There's no reason."

"She's a racehorse." The lash came down again across her hips. "She's supposed to race. She acted as if she wasn't even trying when she was out there today with Chaos. No horse I own will perform like that."

"She was trying. She was doing exactly what I wanted. They both were."

The lash came down again. "Then you're the one to be punished. You're teaching my horse not to do as I wish. Take her into the stable, Davidow. She doesn't want me to beat Nightshade? Then I'm going to let her take her place."

"What a fool you are," Davidow muttered as he dragged Sasha into the first stall they came to and threw her on her stomach on the straw. "You should have just let him do it. She's only a horse. Reardon beats all his horses whenever he has an excuse. I think it gives him a rush. But Masenak isn't going to like any of this. I'll call him and see if he can do anything with Reardon to stop it. Until then just take it and don't fight Reardon. If you just let him get his kicks and do a little damage, you might live through this."

Then he was gone.

But Reardon had come into the stall.

"Such a small, lovely body. Such a pretty back."

His hand ran down her spine. "I wonder how long it will take to heal..."

And the quirt came down with full force on her back.

———◆———

9 P.M.
20 HOURS TO RACE TIME

"Alisa, dammit, I don't know what the hell to do," Gilroy said the instant she picked up the phone. "He *hurt* her. I don't care what Korgan says. I think I'm going to kill him."

"Sasha?" Her hand tightened on the phone. "What happened? Reardon? What did the son of a bitch do to her?" She jumped at the first thought she'd had. "Rape?"

She saw Margaret raise herself on her elbow in her sleeping bag across the cave.

"No," Gilroy said. "That's what I thought, too, when I saw her lying in the straw when I came into the stable an hour ago. Her clothes were ripped, and she was curled up in a ball in front of Nightshade's stall. That's what I asked her and all she'd say was that Reardon had beaten her because of Nightshade. Beaten her? She's bruised and she has whip marks all over her back. Hell, she's almost in shock. I did what I could. I examined her, and she doesn't have any broken bones or pulled muscles. But she wouldn't say anything more and just kept telling me to go away. She said she'd make sure Nightshade would be okay."

"Nightshade?" That was as bewildering as everything else in what Gilroy had told her. "Nightshade, instead of Chaos? What happened there tonight? Is there any way you can find out?"

"How would I do that?" he asked sarcastically. "Go knock on Reardon's door and ask? I guarantee if I did, he wouldn't be alive for more than two minutes."

"Do you think I don't feel the same way," she said fiercely. "I'm just confused and trying to see my way clear to how to help her. You absolutely can't get answers from her?"

"I told you, I've never seen her like this. It's not unusual for her to push me away. I doubt if she lets anyone close to her. But this is different. I don't even know if she's going to bounce back." He was silent an instant. "I wasn't exaggerating when I used the word 'shock,' Alisa. I need help. Tell me what to do."

She closed her eyes. Gilroy's worry was profound and dead honest, and it was terrifying her. Tell him what to do? She was lost in ignorance, darkness, and hate right now. She had no idea what to do.

Yes, she did.

Her eyes flicked open. "Don't be an idiot, Gilroy. Of course she'll bounce back. Do you think she'd let that asshole get the best of her? She just needs help, and we'll give it to her." Her mind was racing, trying to make decisions. "And what you'll do is stay with Sasha and talk to her and maybe hold her hand...if she'll let you. It will take me at least forty-five minutes to hike to Jubaldar. While I'm on my way, you're going to go over with me the placement of any guards that might give me trouble once I get inside. Plus any hints that will make it easier for me to get to that connecting access door to Chaos's stable." She got to her feet. "And you'll stay out of Masenak's and Reardon's way. I don't want Sasha to suffer any more trauma than she has already."

Silence. "You're coming here? Korgan's not going to like that."

"No, but I think that you knew it would come down to this when you phoned." She was stuffing her .38 revolver into her backpack. "You're very clever, and you realized I wasn't going to be able to handle this long distance. You probably didn't like the idea, but you liked Sasha's condition even less. So you made a choice."

"You're tough, and you're the only one she really cares about. She's just a kid."

"I didn't say it was the wrong choice. I've got

to hang up now. I'll call you back after I'm on my way." She ended the call and turned to Margaret. "That bastard Reardon hurt her. She needs me."

"So I heard," she said. "Will you let me go with you?"

"No, it's my job." She smiled shakily. "If she's not hurt badly, I'll be back in a few hours." She drew a deep breath. "And from what Gilroy says, it's not horrible. I think maybe she just reached the point of maximum intake and couldn't handle any more." She paused. "I'm not calling Korgan. I'll let him know what happened when I get back."

"Which is not going to please him," Margaret said dryly. "I'll probably get the blame. He told me to take care of you."

"Which everyone knew was bullshit."

"It was probably his way of knocking on wood. I knew it was only a matter of time before you were going to go after her. Korgan's too smart not to realize it, too." She was suddenly beside Alisa, giving her a hug. "Keep safe," she said quietly. "Don't make me come after you."

"I wouldn't think of it." She grabbed her backpack and strode out of the cave. She could see the lights of Jubaldar in the distance. Five minutes later she was reaching for her phone and calling Gilroy.

"Hey, what do you think you're doing, Sasha? You scared our Indiana Jones wannabe into shouting for help. You've spoiled his entire shtick."

It was Alisa's soft voice, Sasha thought. No, it couldn't be. She was just dreaming. Alisa couldn't be here.

"Open your eyes. I didn't walk all that distance to have you ignore me."

It *was* Alisa. Sasha opened her eyes and saw her face. Wonderful face. Full of character and love. "Hi." Her voice sounded a little woozy, and she cleared her throat. "I was hoping it was you." No, that wasn't right. It would have been bad to wish Alisa here when she'd been trying to keep her away. "I mean, I've missed you, and I'm glad to see you."

"I know what you mean." Alisa carefully put her arm around Sasha's shoulders, lay down next to her, and then cuddled close. "I'm glad to see you, too. Though I would have preferred it not to be like this. How bad are you hurting?"

"That's what Gilroy kept asking. He wouldn't stop talking about it. So I told him to go away."

"Very rude. But he can be persistent, and it must have annoyed you. You wouldn't answer any of his other questions, either?"

She cuddled closer. "I just wanted to close my eyes and forget for a while. So that's what I did."

"That's what I thought you were doing, what you've always done. Fight as hard as you could and then go away for a while and rest and heal. But Gilroy didn't understand, and it scared him."

"I don't care. I wasn't ready to come back yet."

"And you're still not coming back, because this time it hurt too much." She was gently stroking Sasha's temple. "But it's time, Sasha. You know it. And I do understand, so you have no excuse. Talk to me and we'll get through it."

She tried to fight it, but Alisa was right. She could come back now. Alisa was here and she'd help to absorb some of the pain as she always did. Yet she couldn't say the words. It was a few minutes before she said stiltedly, "I couldn't stop it. I tried, but I couldn't. I didn't know how."

"Nightshade? It was something about Nightshade?"

"Reardon was beating her because he thought she wasn't trying hard enough. It was crazy. But Davidow said he always does it when he gets it into his head that he's not getting his money's worth from a horse." She shook her head, her voice breaking. "But Nightshade was a champion when he bought her two years ago. He had to know she was giving everything she had in every race." The tears were running down her cheeks. "Evidently he didn't want to believe it. She's so gentle...It's no wonder she's so quiet and well behaved. She wouldn't have dared be anything else. I couldn't *stand* it, Alisa."

"I know you couldn't." Alisa's voice was low. "So you fought Reardon and he savaged you. You must have put up a good fight."

"Not good enough. If I had, I would have been able to take a whip to *him*. I wanted him to hurt."

"And he will."

"And I'll never let him hurt Nightshade or Chaos or any other horse."

"I believe you."

She laughed shakily. "Are you just saying what I want to hear?"

"No." Alisa's tone was suddenly passionate with feeling. "We'll make everything you want come true. After what you've gone through, I just wish I could give it to you right now." She kissed her forehead. "But I admit I was hoping you would answer a few of those same boring questions Gilroy was asking. Are you in much pain?"

She tried to decide. She was feeling less numb now, and Alisa wanted to know. "My back throbs but I don't think the lash broke the skin."

Alisa flinched. "How kind of Reardon. I must remember that. Gilroy said you don't have any broken bones, either."

She nodded. "That's what Masenak said. He was yelling at Reardon when he came and made him stop. He was accusing him of trying to ruin his chances of winning the race if I couldn't sit a horse."

"So he helped you?"

"He looked at my back and checked for broken bones. He wouldn't let Reardon beat me any longer. I guess that was a help."

Alisa said bitterly, "And then tossed you on the floor of that stable and left you."

She frowned. "That didn't matter. It's where I wanted to be. After they left, I knew I'd have to check Nightshade and make sure she was okay. And Chaos was upset and trying to get out of his stall. I had to stop him."

"Which you did, and then just curled up by Nightshade's stall where Gilroy found you."

She made a face. "And wouldn't let me rest."

"He wouldn't let me rest, either, but I might give him a medal for it."

Sasha suddenly jerked upright, fully awake. "He called and told you to come here? He shouldn't have done that. This is my fault." She was glancing wildly around the stable. "What if Masenak comes back? What if they catch you? You have to leave right away."

"No, I don't. I have time. Gilroy is keeping an eye out for Masenak or Reardon, but I doubt if either one of them is going to be checking up on you. From what you said, they treated you like a piece of trash."

"You should still go. How did you get in here?"

"You forgot how good I am with locks. Jubaldar's security system looks like it was created by Neanderthals compared with Korgan's XV series. All I had to worry about was dodging the guards, and Gilroy helped with that." She paused. "I could get you out of here tonight, Sasha. Let me do it."

She shook her head. "And have Masenak and Reardon hunting you down along with me? Have them go through the stables with shotguns and shoot all the horses and Gilroy and any of the stable boys who got in their way? I won't do that, Alisa. You're the one who has to go."

"I didn't think I had a chance. I'll go." She reached for her backpack. "After I put some salve on those bruises, and I brought some painkiller sedatives to make sure you'll have a decent night. Sit up."

Sasha sat up while Alisa gave her the pill and then carefully removed the torn shirt and started working on her back. "Hurry."

"As quickly as I can." Alisa's voice was suddenly thick. "These bruises... Shit, he was a monster."

"Yes, he hurt Nightshade and she didn't even know why. I told him he should be angry with me because I was the one who wanted to hurt him." She was barely feeling the pain of what Alisa was doing because she was so intent on making her understand. "And I do, Alisa. The one thing I was so angry about was that I didn't know how to kill him. Remember when I asked you to show me how to do karate and you said that wasn't the time? It's the time now, Alisa. I have to make all the pain stop because I can't go on like this. I can't watch it any longer."

"But we're so close, Sasha. Just a little longer. We'll make this happen."

Sasha wasn't getting through to her. "I know you will. But I can't wait for you or Korgan or Margaret to stop them. It might not be in time. They might do something else horrible like what they did to Nightshade. I'm here. I have to do it." She paused. "I have to do it now."

"The hell you do." Alisa turned her around to face her. Her face was pale. "You're not thinking straight. You have to rest and then you'll realize that you should leave this to us, leave it to *me*." She was trying to smile. "After all, I didn't get the chance to teach you karate yet."

"I have a gun."

Alisa looked as if she'd been struck. "Yes, you do. But we didn't give it to you to help you go on the hunt. It was to protect you."

"Killing them would protect me. And it would protect you and all the other innocents they'd hurt and kill." She stared her in the eye. "Because this is going to happen again, and it will be soon. They can't help themselves. There's so much evil that it overflows. I have to be ready for it when I see it coming." She added quietly, "Or when I see I have to bring it to them."

"Don't *do* this."

"Don't worry, I won't be stupid about it." She leaned forward and went into Alisa's arms and held her tight. "You have to go now. I'm not going to let them hurt you, too."

"Listen to me." Alisa's voice was hoarse. "I know I can't talk you out of this, but just don't do anything right now. Let me see if I can get with Korgan and manage to come up with something that will satisfy all of us."

"Pull something magical out of your hat? Buy me four horses and change my life?" She smiled sadly. "You've done it before. But it might not work this time."

"And it might. Just rest and take care of Chaos and Nightshade tonight. Don't decide anything. Let me work on it and get back to you."

"If you'll promise to leave right now. I'm not in any shape to argue with you." She shook her head to clear it. "I think that sedative you gave me is beginning to take effect."

"I'm gone." Alisa released her and jumped to her

feet. "It's going to be okay. I promise you." She was heading for the connecting door. "We'll work it out." Then she was out the door, silent, confident, moving like a shadow.

And Alisa would do her best to work it out, Sasha knew. She was wonderful and clever, and she loved Sasha as much as Sasha loved her. But she didn't realize that it was too late for her to step in and try to make everything perfect this time. She had to do this herself. She had to end it, or it might never end.

And she had to keep it from ever happening again . . .

———◆———

Alisa called Korgan when she was twenty minutes away from Jubaldar. The instant he picked up the call she asked, "How close are we to taking out Jubaldar?"

He was silent. "Soon. We're now looking at early on the morning after the race, just before Reardon leaves. The drones were delivered and ready to go. We're sending the four riders we need to move Sasha's horses tomorrow. Vogel and his team are on the north side of Jubaldar, and by the time of the race they should be in position to take out the main castle guards on command. Novak's designating a team from his forces to send with me when I come back to take over—" He broke off. "Something's wrong. Why the sudden interrogation?"

"Because it's probably not soon enough. If anything else happens, she won't wait." Her voice was shaking. "And she's right, the odds are that they'll do something terrible, because that's who they are. I can't take a chance. *We* can't take a chance, Korgan."

"What are you talking about, Alisa?"

"I'm talking about Sasha, whom I just left at Jubaldar after listening to her coolly tell me she was probably going to hunt down Reardon and Masenak and kill them. No, not coolly, she was sad and resigned but determined." She was trying to keep her voice steady, but it kept breaking. "So damn determined. She said that she couldn't wait any longer, and she wouldn't let them keep hurting and killing. She meant it, Korgan. She's fifteen, just fifteen, and she was talking about her gun and it might not matter if I hadn't taught her any other way to—"

"Start at the beginning," he said harshly. "What the hell were you doing with Sasha at Jubaldar?"

"Gilroy called me. It seems Reardon decided to beat Nightshade in front of Sasha and then when she went after him, he took his temper out on her. If you could have seen her back..."

"Why didn't Gilroy call me?"

"Because he didn't know what to do with Sasha afterward, and he didn't think you would, either. He was right to call me."

"The hell he was. Listen to you. Sasha tore you apart."

"Yes, she did. Because she was brave and in agony and she was right. It's gone on too long for her, and this was the crowning blow. She wasn't even talking about what Reardon did to her. It was all about Nightshade and all the other innocents he could hurt if she didn't do something."

"You couldn't talk her into waiting for us to take him down?"

"She's waited too long already. That's what this is all about. Reardon is so angry with her, he's going to leave right after the race and take Sasha and the horses with him. She knows that would make her even more helpless than she is now. She told me she wasn't going to be stupid, and she won't be. But she said she could see it coming and she won't dodge it." She swallowed to ease the tightness of her throat. "So I ran out of there and came to you in a panic. Just as I did when I hopped the wall at that palace in Morocco. You'd think that I'd learn that you can't fix everything even if you want to. Because the only way I can see to stave off what may happen is to keep her away from

Masenak and Reardon. That's why I asked how close you are. We can't let him take her. We even have to cut down the risk time of her contact with them. But maybe it would help if we bring her into any planning. She might feel more willing to wait if she felt she was doing her part in taking them down."

"For someone in a panic, you're already thinking of ways to solve it." He was silent a moment. She could almost sense the wheels turning. "This is what I was worried about. He's making his move to take total control of Chaos from Masenak. I'd bet that's the reason he changed the departure again. He might have been angry tonight, but he's also using it as an excuse. I've been working my ass off to keep him in check, but it's not going to be easy to block him."

"We've got to *do* something."

"I didn't say we couldn't. We'll have to switch our thinking and scheduling and maybe go at it from an entirely different direction."

"I'm afraid to do anything else. You didn't see her face."

"No, I didn't. So I'll have to take your word for it." He was silent again. "What the hell. Changing any plan is always a challenge. We escalated at Szarnar Jungle, but this sounds like more than any escalation is needed. Where are you?"

"Starting the climb up the cliff. About thirty minutes from the cave."

"Then keep on going. Once you're there, stay put. If Gilroy calls you again, don't pay any attention. Do you hear me? I don't want you going back there."

"If Sasha needs me, I have to—"

"From what you've said, she appeared not to want any interference from you. If she does contact you, tell Gilroy to handle it. He sure didn't do it the last time. I'm the one who needs you now. I'm getting Harris to bring me back there right away. We're going to go over every bit of planning and see how we can adjust. I'll want to be able to talk to you while I'm on the helicopter."

"I don't have any ideas how we can—"

"You'll get them. Stop arguing. You have one of the brightest minds I've ever run across. I need to tap it. We don't have that much time. So start thinking and be ready for me when I call you from the helicopter." He cut the connection.

He *needed* her.

She'd called Korgan because she had needed him, but the fact that he'd said those words made her almost forget her own need. She knew it was rare that he would ever make that admission to anyone.

She couldn't fail him when he needed her.

Her pace quickened as she climbed the cliff.

When Korgan walked into the cave an hour later, Alisa had the maps and photographs of Jubaldar spread on the stone floor and was going over them. She looked up, her eyes glittering, her expression intense. She pointed to the rocky canyon where Masenak's emergency helicopters and vehicles were housed. "On that second day, I sent you photos of this entire area. What kind of security does Masenak have down there?"

"Two sentries who guard the north exit leading from the main area. Three to five guards who rotate around the helicopter pad, the different warehouses, and the marijuana plantings. Maybe a few more than your photos showed since he's allowing Reardon to airlift Chaos and Nightshade from there." His eyes narrowed. "What do you have in mind?"

"I was sitting here racking my brains trying to think of a way to bring Jubaldar crashing down before they killed Sasha." She shook her head. "That was what it was all about. Protecting Sasha. Our hands were tied because everywhere we looked, there was a threat to Sasha. So we brought in Novak and Vogel and drones and all the rest of it." She smiled bitterly. "But Sasha eliminated all of that tonight. She won't let us protect her. So to hell with bringing Jubaldar crashing down. She was right: The only ones who have to be destroyed are Masenak and Reardon. We can work around the rest. That would cause enough confusion that Davidow and the other guards should be stopped cold. The way to kill a snake is to cut off its head. But to do it, first you have to trap it." She tapped the map. "And this canyon looks like a good place to stage a trap to catch those cobras. That shale road down to the canyon floor is only a mile or so from the castle and connects with one that runs parallel to the racetrack. We know that Reardon's probably already arranged to fly Sasha, Chaos, and Nightshade out of there after the race. After tonight I'll bet he can hardly wait. I wouldn't want to disappoint him. I think we should find a way to be down there to greet Masenak and him."

He gave a low whistle. "I don't mean to discourage you, but there's bound to be a chain reaction when you try to stage a move as bold as that. Don't underestimate it. Jubaldar is still an armed camp."

"I can't think about that now. You said you were almost ready to move. You and Novak and Vogel do anything you have to do about Jubaldar. But this has to come first."

"A trap?" His sober gaze lifted from the map to her face. "Have you thought this through?" he asked quietly. "You'd have to have something pretty irresistible to bait that trap."

"Do you think I don't realize that?" she said hoarsely. "I haven't been able to think of anything else. It's scaring me to death. When I tell Sasha, she's not going to have it any other way. Because it will do exactly what she told me has to be done. We've just got to make sure that they can't strike out and hurt her."

"There isn't anything sure about what she could face." His voice was gentle. "Why do you think I'm trying to make you think twice about it? I'll do everything possible, but there's always a random factor in a situation like this. I disappointed you before and almost got you both killed. I can't do that again."

"You can do anything you have to do," she said fiercely. "Just as I can. If you're still blaming yourself for that damn miscalculation, go ahead. It will just give you more reason to make certain that Sasha comes out of this alive. I might call to your attention the fact that I'm the one who's painting a bull's-eye on Sasha's back this time. Now sit down and help me stage this so that all the pieces will fall just the way we want them. Judging from what's happened between Sasha and Reardon lately, I'd guess that Reardon will be the major stumbling block we'd have to target. You're the only one who knows how he thinks, what the trigger would be to drive him to react. Get to work."

He stared at her for a moment. Then he smiled slightly and nodded. "You're right, we can do whatever we have to do." He fell to his knees and leaned closer to the map. "Reardon has always been stronger than Masenak, and we'll have to deal with that. But there's a possibility of striking a balance to use their antagonism against them. I'll deal with that later. Right now I want to see how difficult it would be to spring your trap." His gaze was narrowed intently on the winding road leading from the helicopter pad and utility garages to the cliffs on the north side of the canyon. "I think you might have chosen very well..."

"Of course I did," she said. "As you said, there are only two guards that patrol that north escape road. We'd have no trouble getting rid of them. And if Masenak hasn't altered the numbers and locations of the other guards, then taking them out would be completely manageable."

"I can see that. But you don't only want manageable," he said absently as his finger traced the road from the castle down to the canyon floor. "It has to be fast, distracting, with maybe a little surprise...Let's see what we can do to polish this a little..."

CHAPTER

17

T he horses." Sasha had listened carefully to everything Alisa said, but that was the first thing she'd asked her when she'd finished. "What about Zeus and my other horses?"

"As soon as the race starts at five this afternoon, Margaret and those Berber boys from Samlir will have them out of the main stable and on their way. I promise. Margaret and Juno will get them the rest of the way down to the pine forest. The race itself will be a massive diversion, but we'll also stage another one if necessary." She paused before adding, "But if all goes well, you won't have to worry about them being shot anyway."

"Because no one but Masenak and Reardon would want to kill them," Sasha whispered. "Because we can save them. They won't be able to hurt anyone anymore."

"It's a big chance. I'm letting you run such a risk. Please say no. I don't want you to do this."

"I know you don't. But this is what I want, and you gave it to me. I can't let you take it away. If you hadn't found this way, then I might have been on that helicopter tonight and I couldn't bear it. And I'm not the only one running risks." Alisa didn't answer, and Sasha said softly, "Stop worrying. You're smart, and you're not going to let anything bad happen. You've told me exactly what to do, and I'll do it. If anything changes, I know you'll find a way to let me know." But she didn't want to talk about things going wrong when Alisa was this upset and added quickly, "I have to hang up now. It's almost dawn and someone might come in to check on me."

"Because they want to reassure themselves that they haven't damaged you?" she asked sarcastically. "I want to know, too. How are you, Sasha?"

"Sore. But otherwise I'm fine. Bye, Alisa." She cut the connection.

She sat back on her heels and took an instant to try to pull herself together. She had not expected that call from Alisa, which had sent her spiraling from depression to hope in the space of a few minutes. But the hope had come, and now she had to do everything possible to make all Alisa and Korgan's plans a reality.

She got to her feet and moved over toward Chaos. She turned the phone off and ducked into his stall. One last time to hide this phone away. She only hoped she would never need it again.

She stopped as she was leaving and leaned her head against Chaos. Nightshade had recovered quickly, but Chaos had been terribly upset. He had been quiet all night, but now he pressed against her as if trying to comfort. She slipped her arms around his neck. *Very bad night, my friend.* She could feel the tears sting her eyes. *But I promise today will be better.*

———◆———

"It's set," Alisa said as she turned to Korgan. "She's going to do it. Though who knows why. Make your plans."

"She's doing it because she trusts you," Korgan said quietly. "And she should. Because there's a good chance we can pull this off."

"Not a good chance the way it stands." Her hands clenched at her sides. "So many things can go wrong and she'd be lost. We need a backup plan."

"I'm listening."

"I don't *know*. You can't just pull something out of

the blue at the last minute and expect it to work." She ran a hand through her hair. "You have to have plans and contacts. And there's not much time."

"But you might be able to do it?"

"How the hell do I know? But I won't be able to do anything if I don't try. I have to—" She stopped. "But maybe..." She turned and strode out of the cave. "I hope your plans don't call for Cal Harris," she called back to him. "I might be needing him..."

———◆———

4:40 P.M.
20 MINUTES TO RACE TIME

"A little stiff?" Masenak asked as he watched Sasha pull herself into the saddle. "You're doing much better than when I dropped into the stable to check on you this morning. I was afraid that Reardon might have ruined my chances of winning by being so overenthusiastic."

"I'm fine." Sasha looked down at him. "A little stiff, as you said. I just needed to rest a little more. But I knew you wouldn't allow me not to ride Chaos in this race. You and Reardon made it clear that I wouldn't be the only one to suffer if I pampered myself." She gazed out at the grandstand several yards past the starting gates in the distance. It was now filled with people running back and forth to talk to guests in other boxes, loud music, and waiters popping champagne corks and handing out goblets. "And think how sad I'd be to miss your party. Your friends have such class. Like to like."

"Shut up. I'm not going to listen to that sarcastic tongue. I would have thought Reardon had taught you something." He was scowling at those same starting gates. "Chaos isn't going to balk at them, is he? You should have practiced bringing him into the gates. Why didn't you think of that?"

"Because I knew he's never nervous about anything you'd think he'd be nervous about. He'd just believe he could knock the gates down if they got in his way." She looked beyond the gates to the now roaring crowd in the grandstand. "Those idiots shouting will annoy him more than the gates. If you want to worry about something, you should go make sure no one throws any of those wine bottles out on the track."

He gestured to several uniformed guards standing beside the steps leading up to the grandstand. "I have men to make certain nothing like that will happen."

"If they're not afraid to do it. You've told them to be extra polite to your guests." She shrugged. "But if you have that much confidence in them, why should I care?"

He frowned, looking over his shoulder, and then wheeled toward the stands. Then he abruptly swung back to face her. "You seem to be very calm. After all those hysterics you put us through yesterday, I thought you might be more upset. It seems Reardon was right about you. All you needed was a little discipline."

"But in the end, you always believe Reardon is right, don't you?" she asked coldly. "As far as both of you are concerned, might is right, even when it comes to punishing a defenseless animal." She looked at Reardon, who was talking to Lee Chan, the Chinese jockey now mounting Nightshade outside the stable. He was frowning, obviously giving him instructions. "Will that bastard beat her again when she loses to Chaos? Even though he knows that there's no way she could win against him?"

He shrugged. "Probably. It always releases his frustrations. Reardon doesn't like to lose. He made the best deal he could with me about Chaos, but we both know I'm the one who came out on top." His smile was more of a smirk. "And that top is going to be stratosphere high, Sasha. Is it any wonder I'm willing to let him have a few pleasures to soothe his ego?"

"Pleasure that comes from punishing innocent

animals." She was staring at him with sick horror. "No, it's no wonder. It's just hideous and horrible and not to be borne. What a coward you are, Masenak."

His face flushed; his satisfaction turned to rage. "But you *will* bear it, bitch," he hissed. "Because Reardon will make sure you do. What he did to you yesterday is nothing. If I hadn't stopped him, you wouldn't have been able to get on that horse today. But we won't need you to ride Chaos for a while after this race and you'll have plenty of time to recover. I'm just sorry that he's whisking you away so soon and I won't be able to join in the fun."

"I'm sure you are. Now that you've decided that I'm no longer of any use to you." Her gaze left him to go to Reardon again. His hand was on Nightshade's neck, and though it appeared to be casual she wanted to rush over and protect the horse. She forced herself to look away. "But I'll be able to survive him, just as I did you."

"I let you survive. He won't." His lips curled. "I'll give you some advice. Don't even think about holding Chaos back and letting Nightshade win. I'm going to win my bet with Reardon."

"You've seen us on the track. Did it look like I could hold him back? He's only a little less wild than that first day when he dumped me in the dirt. Put him against competition and it would be twice as hard for me." She stared him in the eye. "I promise Chaos will win this race."

Masenak nodded slowly. "I believe you." His anger was fading, and he was smiling again. "Then I'll give you another bit of advice. Make certain it's a close race. I'd love you to humiliate Reardon, but I want you to be alive to win future races for our partnership. I'm not sure he'll let that happen if you make him look foolish in front of this crowd."

"I'll do what I can. But again, I'm not in control with Chaos. Nightshade is a champion and should be able to perform like one. But I guess we'll have to leave it up to the horses, won't we?" She looked out at the crowd. "Your guests are getting impatient. Are we ever going to start this race?"

"By all means, now that I know whatever happens I'm going to be the big winner." He signaled to Reardon to send Nightshade to the gates. "And now that you're finally going to get all the punishment you've deserved since I found you that day at St. Eldon's." He strode toward the gates. "It's going to be a great race."

"Masenak seems to be in great spirits," Reardon said sarcastically as he came to stand beside Chaos. "He's already counting the money he's going to win from me." He was silent. "I hate losing. I might be easier on you if you didn't put me through that humiliation. I just heard from the helicopter pilot who is going to pick up those horses that he's about to land and will be waiting for me after the race. I could tell him to be sure not to let the stable help and guards on duty hurt them."

"I wouldn't trust you."

"Of course you wouldn't. But you might make the attempt. The offer naturally doesn't extend to you. I'll be taking you in my own copter, and I've been anticipating having you to myself since Masenak stopped me last night. But you sacrificed yourself for Nightshade once, why not again?" He turned and strolled toward where Masenak was standing. "Think about it."

Clever. He'd attempted to freeze her with fear and intimidate her on any level he could before the race. She gave Chaos a nudge forward.

Chaos didn't go four steps before he made his feelings known. *I was angry, but as I promised I did nothing. You should not have asked that of me. They hurt you. Since you're too weak, I have to protect you.*

No, you don't. You just have to do exactly as I tell you for this little time. You have to be my friend and trust me. I've explained that to you. She was guiding him into the gate. *Will you do it?*

I'm king. I should choose what I do. What if I believe you're being foolish, and I don't like it?

You'll like it. She looked at Reardon, who had joined Masenak after the jockey had positioned

Nightshade in her gate. They were smiling at each other as they waited for the bell and the gates to spring open. Enjoying themselves, yet responsible for so much evil and cruelty committed against all the innocents of the world. *I know you will.*

How?

She leaned forward, tensing, getting ready.

Because I'm going to stomp them . . .

HELICOPTER CANYON
10 MINUTES TO RACE TIME

"Could you have cut it any closer?" Korgan murmured as he checked his watch. "I told you to move fast, Gilroy."

"Always complaining." Gilroy slid down behind the ammunition crate beside Korgan. "You sent me to take down both of those sentries guarding that north canyon. And I had to use a knife, not a gun. If you'd wanted speed, you should have gone with me. I could only give you perfection."

"I was a little occupied myself," Korgan said dryly. "I managed to take out these two guards in the ammunition warehouse. Plus I had a few last things on the checklist I had to go over with the rest of the team here before I called Vogel. I had to discuss his agenda, which I'm sure you wouldn't have regarded as important."

"Vogel is a good guy but seldom interesting. And if he'd been here, he would have spoiled your fun. I have to admit you did very well. It was like old times." He loaded his gun but then replaced it in his holster. "Only three more of Masenak's scumbags to send to hell. Want to flip for them? Tell me you're not enjoying it."

"I'm not enjoying it," he said flatly. "Because I heard from Vogel that Reardon's transport helicopter is only minutes away and it should be here anytime now. And it's almost five and you know what that means."

"Hell, yes." His smile faded. "It means you're worried and scared, that I'm an ass, and I should have been quicker."

Korgan nodded as he turned and crawled toward the door. "Exactly. Now let's clean up the rest of this mess."

———◆———

JUBALDAR RACETRACK
ONE MINUTE TO RACE TIME

The starting gates were going to open any second.

Sasha took a last look around. *Memorize everything.*

The grandstand, the guards. The gates leading from the track to the outside road. Imprint it. Absorb it. She might not be able to remember it during what was to follow.

The bell sounded!

The gates opened!

The crowd roared!

Chaos leaped forward!

Wind.

Lightning.

Speed. Speed. Speed.

No breath.

First time around the track.

A mile and a half like the Belmont distance. But Reardon and Masenak had agreed the distance be extended another full mile and a half to complete the race.

Chaos started the next lap!

She took a glance behind her. Nightshade was making a valiant effort, but she was already falling behind.

Almost there.

Over the finish line.

Second time around the track!

There was no doubt that Chaos had won the race. Nothing could be clearer. Lee Chan, Nightshade's jockey, was already pulling her to a walk as she reached the grandstand.

But Sasha didn't stop.

She could sense Chaos's question as he realized he was running alone. *Joy?*

Yes, this is just for us. Bring it on. Let the lightning flash. She leaned forward. *Joy!*

Speed!

Together!

Let them see what you can do!

Show them what a king you are!

Joy.

Joy.

Joy.

The grandstand again.

Already?

Stop. I know it's hard. But just for a little while. I'll let you go again soon.

Chaos was fighting her, but he finally allowed her to pull him to a stop.

She was breathing hard with excitement herself as she turned to face Masenak and Reardon. She suddenly realized the crowd in the grandstand was silent. She had not expected that reaction. She had wanted to humiliate Reardon, to throw him into a complete rage; Alisa had said it was important. But even this crowd of idiots had recognized that the defeat was overpowering. And that last lap she had taken to rub salt in the wound had been a slap in the face of a man they knew was deadly. When she saw Reardon's expression, it was frightening, almost demonic. Even Masenak was silent, his expression wary.

Ignore it. Don't waste the effect. Take advantage of what she'd done. Alisa said she'd not only have to win the race but do it in such a way that Reardon wouldn't be able to think of anything but following her to the canyon. That's what she'd said, but Sasha knew what she'd meant was that the anger had to be so strong, he'd follow her to the gates of hell to punish her for that humiliation. Well, she'd done it. Now she only had to finish what she'd started. "I couldn't resist letting him loose." She lifted her chin. "You're a complete loser, Reardon. He not only won, he wiped the floor with you. I don't know how you'd dare come back and face any of these people."

"You fucking bitch." He could barely get the words out. "I'm going to cut your throat."

"Nightshade ran a great race, but she was outclassed." She was edging Chaos closer to the fence gate. Alisa had told her that Gilroy would make sure it was left slightly ajar so that a push would send it flying open. "She didn't mind. She enjoys running with Chaos. Only people like you are vicious enough to punish for excellence."

He was taking a step toward her. The anger was

almost out of bounds. But he had to lose it completely. Time to take him the rest of the way.

"Neither of you deserves having fine horses." She was almost at the fence gate. "So I believe I'll have to take them away from you." She nudged Chaos, and his shoulder pushed the gate open wide. "Burn in hell, you asshole!"

Then they were through the gate and on the road outside! She heard Reardon shout behind her as she kicked Chaos into a run.

Follow me, bastards. If she could get them down that canyon road and trap them, it could well be the gates of hell for them.

Nightshade?

She'll be here. Chaos was impatient. *She didn't like the idea of bucking him off, but she must be taught.*

She glanced over her shoulder and saw Nightshade ramming over the people trying to get through the gate and then streaking after them down the road. *She learns faster than you'd think.* Then she saw Masenak and Reardon tear through the gate and run toward the BMW 3 parked beside the front entrance of Jubaldar and forgot everything but urging every bit of speed she could get from Chaos. A mile to the turnoff, Alisa had said. A mile and they might be safer. A mile was nothing to Chaos or Nightshade.

You wanted the joy, Chaos. Now is the time to take it.

But Masenak's BMW was very fast, too. And Sasha heard a screech as he tore out of the drive and raced after them.

"She's got to be crazy," Reardon said. "Why would the stupid bitch think she could get away? I'll *kill* her. This is your fault, Masenak. I told you that you were too soft on her."

"Stop raving," Masenak said between his teeth. "This wouldn't have happened if you hadn't taken that quirt to her last night. If she's crazy, then it's because you scared her shitless. I told you to leave her alone until after the race. And now she's riding *my* Chaos and I'll be lucky if she doesn't break his leg on these son-of-a-bitch roads."

"Then catch her, dammit. Step on it." He took his gun out of his jacket. "Or I'll put a bullet in both of you."

The turnoff should be right ahead, Sasha thought. But it might not be in time. Not only were they being chased by Masenak and Reardon, but there was another vehicle behind them. Davidow? She couldn't tell. It was a blur. Then it wasn't a blur, it was a truck filled with Masenak's soldiers!

There was the turnoff!

Only seconds later Chaos was making the turn, closely followed by Nightshade. They were both running full speed down the rocky shale road toward the complex of warehouses, garages, and helicopter pad below when Sasha saw the huge orange transport chopper hovering in the center of the canyon over the pad. It was about to land.

Not good.

There was no doubt the pilot and any other of Reardon's men on board would be armed and lethal. And that meant there might be no safety for her or any of the other people down there that Alisa had sent to help them. Reardon and Masenak were so close, and they must have seen the helicopter, too. All Reardon would have to do was make a call to order that firepower turned loose on them.

A bullet whistled by her head, burying itself into the shale rocks of the road ahead!

And it came not from the helicopter but from Masenak's car, which had just made the turn onto the canyon road.

"What are you doing?" Masenak reached out to grab Reardon's gun. "She's valuable. We've got to catch her, not kill her."

"She made a fool of me." Reardon knocked his hand aside. "Do you think I'll tolerate that? I've watched you indulge her and let her treat you as if you were nothing. Well, she won't treat me like that. It's the horse that's important, not the girl. I'll get another jockey. That was a warning shot. Then next one won't be."

"She's valuable," Masenak repeated. "And she'd be much more entertaining if you kept her alive. You have that helicopter sitting down there on the pad. Call the pilot and order him to send out the crew, grab the other sentries on duty, and go after her. We'll trap her between us."

Reardon swore savagely. But the next instant he reached for his phone.

———◆———

The shot hadn't been that close, Sasha thought desperately. Maybe they'd only wanted to frighten her into stopping. But though the bullet had obviously been aimed at her, the horses were also in danger. She had to get them all off this access road and then take them to somewhere down below where she could find cover or protection. Alisa had said they might only have to hide for a short time before she could get to them. The road exit wasn't far now. Only a short distance...

———

"I'm going to take the shot," Gilroy said as he sighted his Remington carefully. "They're getting too close to her."

"Don't do it," Korgan said sharply. "We need them closer. From up here on these cliffs, that's a trick shot even for you. There was only the one bullet, and it was probably a warning. Either they're arguing about what to do or they've made a decision not to take her out yet. I told you that might happen. But there's a truckload of Masenak's soldiers on their heels. If we start firing, they're liable to let loose a barrage of bullets that will hit Sasha."

Gilroy was cursing. "That's a hell of a judgment call. You could get her killed. Alisa would never do this."

"No, she wouldn't." His lips tightened. "Neither would you. So you can both heap the blame on me if I'm wrong. I'm used to it. But the percentages say I'm right. So just don't take that shot." He suddenly tensed as he noticed the activity in the back of that truck. "Son of a bitch!" He took out his phone. "I believe it's time we called in a little help."

She was off the road! Sasha glanced up to see the other two vehicles still barreling down the canyon road. Not even minutes away—more like seconds. And that orange transport helicopter was on the ground now. Uncertainty and threats all around her.

All she could do was make certain that Chaos and Nightshade were safe and rely on Alisa. She'd promised to get to Sasha as soon as she could after reaching the heliport area. Until then Sasha's job was to hide and protect.

But where to hide? She took out the gun she'd hidden in Chaos's saddle and turned him quickly toward the maze of buildings she could see a short distance away.

We can go after them now?

Not yet, Chaos. Just take care of Nightshade.

It wasn't the answer he'd wanted to hear. *She has to learn that lesson, too. Soon?*

Very soon. She put the gun it into her jacket pocket and urged him to go faster.

Make it be the truth, she prayed. Please make it be the truth.

Because Masenak was pulling off the access road behind her right now.

"She's headed toward that warehouse area," Reardon said. "We've got the bitch." He jumped out of the car and signaled to the pilot of the helicopter, pointing to the warehouse. "I'll hunt her down like the vicious little whore she is. I'll make her scream when I—" He stopped. "Where the hell are your security guards. Masenak?" He was suddenly looking around warily. "I don't like—"

The helicopter door was opening! A woman jumped out and dropped to her knees, lifting a portable missile launcher and aiming it.

"Down!" Masenak shouted and hit the ground. Reardon had already dived clear of the car to one side of the road.

An explosion shook the ground!
Blam!
Fire.
Screams.
Heavy smoke.

The missile had not been aimed at them but at the truck behind them carrying the soldiers!

Masenak didn't have to give the vehicle more than a glance to realize it was almost entirely destroyed.

And now the other doors of the transport helicopter were opening, and armed fatigue-clad soldiers were pouring out. "Trap," Reardon said in disbelief, jumping to his feet. "It has to be a trap. She hijacked my helicopter!" He was cursing as he ran toward the warehouse where he'd last glimpsed Sasha. "We have to get hold of that bitch. We can use her to get out of here."

There was nothing else to do. They were lucky the smoke from the explosion was so heavy that it would be hard to see them. Masenak was following him at a dead run as he pulled out his phone and tried to call Davidow to send help. He couldn't get through. "Dead. No power."

"All carefully thought out," Reardon said. "They've blocked the signal from the canyon. Technology at its best. And damn familiar. Do I have to guess who the woman was who fired that missile?"

"Alisa Flynn." Masenak could feel the same hatred sear through him that he'd known when he'd recognized her with that missile in her hands. How could this happen to him? "But you're right, get Sasha and we'll stop Alisa Flynn and Korgan and anyone else we need to." He pulled out his gun. "If we don't, I'll fight you to be the one putting a bullet in her heart."

CHAPTER
18

W here is she?" Alisa demanded when Korgan ran up to her a few minutes later. "Masenak and Reardon have disappeared in all this smoke and now I can't find Sasha. You said she was okay when you called me to take out that truck."

"And she was. She was off the access road a few minutes after I called you and heading east. Gilroy and I have been searching for her, too. Look, one of your instructions to her was to hide once she managed to get off the access road. That must be what she's doing. She couldn't get too far with Chaos and Nightshade in tow."

"You don't know her. She's here, isn't she? But I won't know if she's in trouble with Masenak and Reardon still out there."

She was straining desperately to see through the smoke. The entire canyon complex was now swarming with people. She got a brief glimpse of Gilroy giving orders to his team, which had taken over the heliport.

Then when the smoke cleared again, she saw Cal Harris securing the hijacked helicopter. No Sasha. "She went east from the road?" She was already heading in that direction. "We have to find her, Korgan."

"I know," he said quietly as he took her arm. "I told Gilroy to keep on searching. I just came to get you so you wouldn't be alone. You were a target, too, the minute they knew you were the one who set off that missile. That was necessary, but very showy, Alisa."

"And it caused all this damn smoke!"

"We had to get rid of that truck and soldiers. They were setting up a Browning .50-caliber machine gun in the back of that truck, but even without that firepower they were too close. Once they joined with Masenak and Reardon, they would have been like a wolf pack hunting down a doe. We might not have had time to reach Sasha from the heliport before they caught up with her." He grimaced. "Look on the bright side. At least the smoke is hiding her, too."

"That doesn't make me feel better. It wasn't

supposed to be this way. I thought I'd be able to track Sasha from the minute she got off the access road and go after her." Alisa realized how futile that sounded now, but it was true. The plans they had made had been simple and streamlined, and Korgan's absolutely lethal team should have had no trouble accomplishing every detail. They were to take out Masenak's guards at the heliport, electronically isolate the entire area from the castle, and then wait for Sasha to come down that hill. When she was off the hill and safely out of Masenak and Reardon's range, they'd move in to take them out.

Alisa's own part had been to hijack Reardon's livestock helicopter right before his men could depart for his horse farm in Marrakech. She'd provided backup, additional firepower, and the "surprise" Korgan had thought might be a necessity.

It was a plan that should have worked, but when did any plan work perfectly? They hadn't counted on the truck full of soldiers with all that firepower trailing so closely behind Masenak. "The only way I'll feel better is to piss off Masenak and Reardon by finding Sasha before they do."

"Which we're on our way to doing." He checked his watch. "And they're soon going to have an even better reason to want to send us both to hell. You told me Novak is very efficient, and that means three drones will explode in the racetrack, military, and guard barracks in exactly four minutes. They'll do enough damage that when Novak's and Vogel's teams go in afterward to do clean up, I doubt if Davidow or any of Masenak's men will still be around."

"Four minutes," she repeated. She'd been so absorbed with just getting here to Sasha that she'd barely been paying attention to anything else.

"Just following your orders. You told me to handle it. So I had Novak send an initial commando team on-site to Jubaldar ready to strike the minute he sent off the drones. He'll follow with a second team himself when he's free. By that time Vogel's forces should be getting there. I know you like to be consulted, but I figured you were a little too busy with hijacking the helicopter Reardon was expecting and getting it here in time to be backup if we needed it."

"And we did need it." She was shaking her head in frustration. "But none of it is going to do any good unless we make sure Masenak and Reardon won't get away. They're like Houdinis. Close your eyes and they're gone." She could feel the panic rising. "And they're not stupid. They'll know that Sasha is still a card they can play." They'd reached the access road, and she jerked her arm away from him. "We've got to find her before they do. We'll have to split up. If one of us locates her, fire two shots." She was running toward a maze of warehouses and garages. "She might have just tried to get lost in all those buildings over there. You check out the west area."

"Alisa, dammit..."

She glanced over her shoulder and saw that he was coming after her. "Forget about me. You know I'll be okay," she said fiercely. "Find her!"

She ran into the first warehouse. It was huge and stuffed with Masenak's treasures and furniture. You could hide a herd of elephants in here, not to mention one small girl and two racehorses.

Kaboom!

Kaboom!

Kaboom!

She had to grab on to the wall as the floor shook and dust came down from the high ceiling.

Novak's drones. Right on time. Just as efficient as she'd told Korgan. And powerful. This area was more than a mile away from where the bombs had hit, but the explosions had been very strong.

She hoped Masenak had heard and realized it was his wonderful Jubaldar that had taken the hit.

But it would also make him as furious as Korgan had said, and she had to find Sasha and make sure she wouldn't be exposed to that rage.

She took a cursory glance around the rest of the

warehouse. She was almost finished when she saw the wide-open door at the end of the corridor. It looked as if someone had run out of the building and just left it flung open.

She stopped and moved toward it. As she came closer, she could see glimpses of forests that ran from the access road toward the distant cliffs.

And whoever had flung open that door had been excited to see what she was seeing now. Why not? With two horses Sasha would gravitate to any area where she could fade away into the natural camouflage of forests or boulders.

And they would figure that out, too. Someone had opened that door. Careful. She mustn't make any—

Pain.

Darkness.

———

"Wake up." Alisa was being roughly shaken. "You're not hurt. I was careful not to hit you too hard. I don't want to have to drag you if we have to get on the move."

She opened her eyes.

Reardon. A savagely angry Reardon. She tensed, reaching for her gun. It was gone. Of course it was gone. What else could she expect?

She put her hand to her temple. She was bleeding... "Where is Sasha?"

"We'll talk about the bitch later." He was pulling her to her feet. "I have to get you to Masenak and see how we can arrange to get out of this hell-hole." He took out his gun and jammed it into the center of her back. "No noise. Do you understand? I don't know how many men you brought in on that helicopter, but I'll kill anyone you try to warn."

"I won't warn anyone." Her head was clearing now. How to get out of this? She didn't have a weapon, but she had strength and skill and that could be enough. The bastard was nervous, and all it would take would be a moment of distraction and she might be able to bring him down. "I might be a little slow. I'm dizzy..."

"If you're slow, you're dead. You've caused me too much trouble, and I won't let you con me." He jammed the gun in her back again. "Very quickly, Alisa."

"Hello, Reardon," Korgan said softly from behind him. "It's been a long road and I can't tell you how happy I am to see you. Just drop that gun and step away from her."

Reardon whirled to face him. "Korgan." His hand tightened on his gun, still pressed against Alisa's spine. "Why should I drop it? You seem to have made the mistake of coming after her alone. You evidently want her alive, and that puts me way ahead of the game. If you shoot me, I'll still press the trigger and she'll die anyway."

Korgan was here. Alisa felt a rush of relief. Together they could handle Reardon. Just concentrate on finding the right moment.

Korgan was smiling at Reardon. "Or I can stand here covering you until my old friend Gilroy appears with a team that will make your death absolutely inevitable. Stalemate."

"But with the same end result," Reardon said. "You don't like failure. That's why you've been so annoyingly persistent about that Noura matter. I never understood why you interfered with my handling of Karim Raschid. Sometimes examples must be set. It was just business."

"Business?" Alisa repeated. "Like the way you treated Sasha. Was she an example, too?"

"No, she was going to be pure pleasure. I got a taste of it last night. I guarantee I'll have my fill if you're not accommodating." His gaze shifted back to Korgan. "We're a good deal alike. We're both successful businessmen, and I admit that you might have a slight advantage at the moment. But I can overcome that with a single bullet in this woman's back. If she doesn't die, she'd probably be crippled for life. So let's get down to the deal. I want passage out of here. You put me on that helicopter, and I'll let her go when I reach Morocco."

"What about your friend Masenak?"

"I don't care about Masenak. If you can find him, take him. Just get me out of here. He's never understood the art of the deal, which is why he's such a failure."

"Where is he?" Alisa asked. "Did he find Sasha?"

"He thought he caught sight of her and told me to stay here on watch. It was fine with me. Sasha might be the prize, but I knew you'd be on the hunt. If I could gather in either one of you, I'd still get what I wanted." He gestured with the gun. "And I'm very close now. You're an optimist, Korgan. If you let me go, you're going to think you can track me down again. Take the chance, and she might live."

"Why do you think she's important enough to me that I'd take that chance?" Korgan asked coldly. "You know you've always been my prime target. The only reason I've been helping her is that I knew she'd eventually lead me to you and Masenak. She's done that now."

A faint flicker of unease crossed his face. "I don't believe you. You're soft, Korgan. Everyone thinks you're this great humanitarian. You wouldn't let me kill her, even if you care nothing for her."

But Korgan's words had managed to shake him, Alisa realized. Distract him. Push a little harder.

And Korgan was doing it. "Really? But you know how obsessed I've been about bringing you down. Wouldn't you do anything you had to do? As you said, we're both businessmen, and we've learned that minor considerations have to be eliminated when we go after the big score." His glance shifted to Alisa's face, and he held her eyes. "I'm sorry, but I'm afraid that I can't go along with his offer. It might be time for you to fade out of the picture." Then his gaze focused again on Reardon. "*Look* at me. Unless you can offer me a better deal than that, you can shoot her and then I'll—"

Alisa tensed. Reardon had involuntarily looked at Korgan at those first words, and his attention was distracted. Move!

She whirled away from him and erupted into a barrage of strategic punches and kicks aiming at the six weak points: eyes, throat, nose, groin, knees, solar plexus. She struck Reardon's right forearm repeatedly, but the bastard somehow managed to keep a firm grip on his gun. She ducked to avoid his gun barrel as he squeezed off two shots.

Blam! Blam!

She hit him with a roll kick behind his right knee and he faltered. Now close in and take him down. Get that gun.

Blam!

But this time the shot didn't come from Reardon. He *screamed* as Korgan's bullet smashed into his hand, sending the gun flying.

And now Korgan was walking toward him as he tried to struggle to his knees. "No deal, Reardon. We're not at all alike, and in spite of what you might have heard, I have my moments when there's absolutely nothing soft about me. You can't imagine how much hardening took place while I was sitting at Karim's funeral in Noura."

Reardon took one glance at his face and then he was scrambling. "No! Let's talk. I'll give you anything you want!" He was trying desperately to get to his gun on the floor across the room.

Korgan shot him in the skull. Then he took two more steps and shot him twice more.

He stood there, looking down at the bloody corpse. "That was extremely satisfying." He glanced at Alisa. "I regret having to interrupt you when you were doing so well, but I thought you'd want to get to Sasha." He glanced back down at Reardon. "You said we had to cut off the heads of the snakes, and we've only done this one. Shouldn't we go looking for Masenak?"

Another darker, more savage side of Korgan that she'd never seen before. How many more would she see before this was over?

"Yes." She turned away from Reardon's body. "He was trying to force me to go out that door that leads to the cliffs and forests when you showed up on the scene. He mentioned Masenak. Let's go."

———◆———

Stay here! Sasha slipped from Chaos's back as soon as she reached the forest trail that led up to the cliffs. *Don't follow me. Take care of Nightshade.*

She didn't wait for him to complain but started up the shale slope of the trail along the cliffs. The horses should be safe in that forest area below, but she needed to get higher so that she could see what was going on. Though that might not do any good. There was smoke everywhere. She'd heard the explosion and the screams right after she'd left the access road, but she hadn't stopped to find what had happened. Masenak and Reardon had been too close, and she doubted those screams had come from them. Alisa had said to run and hide and not emerge until they came for her. That's what she would do, but she had to know if they were safe here or if she should go deeper into the forest.

"Stop right there or I'll blow your head off, Sasha." Masenak.

She froze.

"Or I might decide to do it anyway. I'd like

nothing better." He was climbing the rocks behind her, his gun pointed at her. "You've ruined me. I wish I'd killed you that first day in that stable at St. Eldon's."

"You were a ruin to begin with. Ugly and greedy and evil. What you did to those girls was—" Her head snapped back as his hand whipped across her face. *Pain. Dizziness.* Then she was able to speak again. "And Jeanne Palsan. You should burn in hell. I think you probably will." He struck her again and she staggered back. She wasn't thinking straight. Verbally attacking him wasn't going to do any good. The gun. He didn't know she had a weapon in her jacket pocket, and he wasn't used to thinking of her as a threat, only a victim. So figure how she could get that gun out without him shooting her. "I thought Reardon might even be worse than you, but he isn't. You're just the same. Where is he?"

"He'll be here as soon as he knows I've caught you. And he's probably even angrier than I am about the humiliation you handed him." He motioned with his gun toward the cliffs she'd just climbed. "But he's always bragging how great he is with negotiations, and you might stay alive if they go well enough to please us. You're our ticket out of here. Let's go down and get started."

There were boulders to the right of the trail. She'd have to pass Masenak, and this might be her only chance to make a move before they joined Reardon. "It's not going to work, you know," she said as she moved toward him. "It's all over for you. Why don't you—" As she passed him, she pushed him with all her strength! He staggered back, half losing his balance.

She ducked behind the nearest boulder, struggling to get the gun out of her pocket.

A bullet plowed into the boulder next to her!

She ran!

That shot might have only been a threat, but Masenak had been clear about how much he hated her. Find another boulder or tree to hide behind before she tried to use her gun to protect herself. She didn't know enough about guns to have a battle while she was running down this damn trail.

Another shot!

It hit the pine tree only a foot from her head.

She could hear him cursing, and he was getting closer. Her hand tightened on the gun. There was another pine several yards ahead. She would dive behind it and try to get off a shot at Masenak before he was on top of her . . .

"Down!"

Alisa's voice. Alisa tackling her, bringing her to the ground, covering her with her own body.

"No!" Sasha desperately pushed at her. "Get away. He's right behind me."

But he was no longer behind her. Masenak was struggling with someone. A dark-haired man who had his hands on Masenak's throat, strangling him. Even as she watched, Masenak broke free and was running away, streaking toward the forest. But he still had his gun, she realized. He was still a threat. He could come back and hurt Alisa.

And he could hurt the horses, she realized suddenly. He was running right toward Chaos and Nightshade. She started struggling again. "No, I have to stop him!"

"Lie still." Alisa's arms tightened around her. "You don't have to do anything. Korgan is going after him."

It had been Korgan who had been struggling with Masenak and almost put him down, Sasha realized. But that only meant the threat was to him, too. She pushed Alisa aside and sat up to see Korgan running toward the trees after Masenak. "Masenak still has his gun."

"Not for long."

"No, not for long." She grabbed Alisa's arm as Alisa opened her lips to speak. "Hush for a minute. I have to do something." She closed her eyes and concentrated.

He's coming toward you, Chaos. He has a weapon, and he'll try to hurt you and everyone else. We can't let him do that.

He's trying to hurt you?

Yes, me, too. He's a little crazy right now and he's striking out to hurt everyone. Be careful, but make sure he can't do that.

I see him running toward me. She could sense Chaos's eagerness, but he was making sure he knew what she meant since she'd refused him before. *You're giving him to me? I can stomp him?*

She didn't hesitate. She said the words.

You can stomp him!

Then Sasha drew away from him and waited.

She didn't have to wait long before she heard the first scream.

It was long and terrified and full of agony.

Alisa heard it, too, and whirled to face her. "Sasha?"

She didn't answer.

More screams, and then silence.

Done.

Sasha jumped to her feet. "I've got to go make sure Chaos and Nightshade are safe," she said quietly. "You can tell Korgan that he won't have to worry about Masenak's gun any longer. I didn't hear a shot."

"Neither did I. But then I remembered Chaos is very, very fast. Masenak wouldn't have stood a chance." Alisa added grimly, "I'll go with you. I want you to have someone with you if you're going to face what I think happened to Masenak just now."

Sasha smiled wryly. "Always trying to spare my feelings. But I'm the one who caused that. I did it deliberately, and I won't feel guilty. My only regret is that I had to use Chaos, and that means I might have to go back to square one in gentling him."

"Good. But I still don't want you to have to face it alone." She took her hand. "So shut up and just let me do this. I've been scared to death all this time and all I want is to surround you with all the comfort and love I can. Is that too much to ask?"

"That's not too much," she said huskily. Warmth. Love. Togetherness. Her hand tightened affectionately on Alisa's. "As long as you don't get sappy about it."

———◆———

Alisa shook her head as she watched Sasha going over Chaos and Nightshade with fastidious care. She hadn't even looked at Masenak's battered body after she'd entered the woods. She'd just gone directly to Chaos and stroked him and murmured to him before she'd started to examine him.

"She seems to be in good enough shape." Korgan had come to stand beside Alisa, his gaze on Sasha. He grimaced. "Much better than Masenak. Chaos was very thorough. Not a hell of a lot left of him that's not broken or shredded."

"Sasha used the word 'stomp.'"

"Very good description. Chaos didn't cut the head off that particular snake, but he came very close. Gilroy will be disappointed that he didn't get his chance at him. He hated the son of a bitch." He paused. "And Gilroy just called, and he's heard from Vogel. Jubaldar is a madhouse with no one in charge. He and Novak are going to take advantage by hitting the castle in the next thirty minutes. I'm going to take half the men we have here and join them."

She straightened. "Great. I'll be with you as soon as I get Sasha settled."

"No, you will not. We don't need you. I've put Gilroy in command of the rest of the team we're leaving here and told him to keep you and Sasha with him until we wrap it up." He touched the cut on her head. "You've both seen enough action today."

"Bullshit. I'm okay. You don't know what you'll find over there. You might need—"

He interrupted. "From the damage report after the drone attacks, you might just be standing around." His glance shifted to Sasha. "And do you think she'd let you leave without her? She's gone through hell today."

Yes, she had. And Korgan was right, Sasha wouldn't

be left behind. But Alisa didn't like the idea that she wasn't needed. The knowledge made her feel flat and purposeless after all that had gone before.

Then the realization hit her. Of course she wasn't needed. Not thirty minutes from now at Jubaldar. Not tomorrow or the next day. Not next month. It was over. Sasha was safe. Masenak and Reardon were dead. Everything that Korgan had promised, all the revenge and justice he'd been working toward all these years, had now been accomplished. Everything they'd done together, been together, was at an end. He would be leaving and going on to some other project just as she'd known he would.

He was looking at her inquiringly. "Alisa?"

"You're right. You don't need me." She forced a smile. "It was foolish to think you would. Besides, I need to be with Sasha for a while after this. She seems tough, but sometimes the nightmares attack when you least expect them. They did with me."

"Did they?" He reached out and gently touched her cheek. "Then it's good she has you standing by her." His hand dropped away and he muttered a curse. "I should get out of here, but I have a feeling that I've done something that's going to cause me trouble down the line."

"You haven't done anything, and you *should* get out of here." The smile never left her face. "So I'll make the first move." She was walking toward where Sasha was now examining Nightshade. "See you later, Korgan. Be safe."

She thought he muttered another curse, but when she glanced over her shoulder he was gone.

Don't look back again. Look forward toward Sasha, look forward to all that was new in life. Look forward to the next exciting thing she'd learn. It was right around the next corner.

"Okay?" Sasha had stopped to look at her. "Is something wrong?"

"No, Korgan says everything is going very well. If you hadn't been so focused on Chaos, I would have introduced you. Maybe another time. How is Nightshade?"

"Fine. She's not as strong as Chaos, but that run didn't even faze her. I think she would have flown like Pegasus if Chaos had asked her." She paused. "I have to have her for Chaos, Alisa. But she's a champion and belonged to Reardon and that's going to be all kinds of trouble, isn't it? What can I do?"

It didn't come as a surprise. Naturally, Sasha would want to protect Nightshade and keep her safe from all harm. "Yes, it will be a problem. So I think we'll tap Korgan before he heads down the road and let him handle it. He likes to have all the loose ends tied up anyway."

"He won't mind?"

"He'll think of it as a challenge." She added,

"And he's an extraordinary man who'd like the idea of making something Reardon touched with his ugliness turn out with a happy ending."

"I like that," Sasha said softly. "I knew you'd think of something."

"All I thought about was Korgan." That was who everyone thought about first. And what she had told Sasha was the truth. He would solve Sasha's problem with skill, ingenuity, and generosity, and Alisa would let him do this last thing for her. She would owe him, but she would watch and monitor him over the years and someday she'd find a way to pay the debt. "Well, now I'm thinking that we have to go find Gilroy and try to find something to eat for ourselves and these fine horses." She took Nightshade's reins and pulled herself into the saddle. "And then we'll call Margaret and check on Zeus and the other horses and see if we can get details about what happened at Jubaldar."

———◆———

Korgan didn't allow Gilroy to bring Alisa and Sasha back to the castle until the following morning. And then it was only to the safety area in the lower forest where Margaret had taken the horses.

Margaret shot a wary glance at Alisa as they watched Sasha getting Nightshade and Chaos settled. "You don't need to be here. I have plenty of help. I told Korgan that you weren't going to like being kept out of the action going on at the castle. But you don't even seem impatient."

"Because he's just being Korgan, taking control, protecting, doing his thing. He knows you'd let me know what's happening. You said he'd turned over complete command to Novak?"

"As soon as they'd received all surrenders from Masenak's forces last night. He wanted to make sure Novak was identified as the man who took down Jubaldar when he called Lakewood. A CIA victory Lakewood could release to the press."

"Very diplomatic. Just what he should have done."

"But he didn't tell you?"

"Why should he? We've always been on the same page where Novak was concerned. He was just following through. He's quite wonderful at tying up loose ends. I have one more thing I'm going to ask him to do for Sasha, but I'll call him later today when he's not so busy."

"That never bothered you before." Margaret's eyes were narrowed on her face. "Why now?"

"It wouldn't bother me now if it was urgent, but everything has changed. Korgan has other priorities. I can wait to fit into his schedule when I'm asking a favor." She smiled. "Doesn't everyone?"

"Not you."

"It's a different world, I have to adjust. We both knew it would be like this once the emergency was over. You adjust and move on and you don't look back." She met her gaze. "And you never hold on."

"Bullshit. I've watched you hold on to Sasha since the minute you saw her."

"And you, but that's different. You're my world. I'm allowed." She shrugged. "Anything else gets complicated. It's better to stick to the rules."

"I don't believe Korgan recognizes any rules. It's one of the things you admire about him."

"But we're not talking about him, we're talking about me. And I recognize my own rules." Though she had gotten perilously close to ignoring them this time, and Margaret knew it. But she wasn't calling her on it. She was only listening and staring at her with those wise eyes that always saw too much. "It's a good deal safer and more practical."

"Is it? But when have you ever cared about that when anything meant something to you?" She smiled. "And there are all kind of worlds out there and they're all different. All the better to explore. But if you want to bury your head for the moment and catch your breath, I'll go along. You deserve the rest." She turned and headed for Sasha and the horses. "Though I don't promise not to say *I told you so* later..."

EPILOGUE

Why are you in the main stable? Gilroy told me that Chaos always demanded solitary splendor."

Sasha looked up and saw Korgan entering the open stable door and coming toward her. She instinctively stiffened warily. It was the first time she'd seen him since the canyon, though his appearance was not unexpected. "I haven't seen Gilroy for a couple of days. Things change." She put aside the bridle she'd been working on, laying it on the bale of hay on which she was sitting. "No one knows that better than you. Because you change them, don't you?"

"Not if the status quo is satisfactory. I just have a problem with being bored and wanting to tweak it a bit." He held out his hand. "We've never officially met, have we, Sasha? I'm Gabe Korgan, and I hope we'll become good friends. Though I feel as if I know you very well right now. Alisa has been singing your praises since the first day we met."

She slowly reached out and shook his hand. She hesitated only an instant before she said bluntly, "Well, I don't feel as if I know you. I guess I'm supposed to be grateful you're going to help me get Nightshade, but you don't have to. I'll find a way to do it myself. All you have to do is say no."

He raised his brows. "Anyone would tell you I'm very good at saying no if I want to. When Alisa mentioned Nightshade, I liked the idea for a number of reasons." He was studying her expression. "But I believe I'm seeing a hint of belligerence that reminds me of Alisa. Why would you think I'd want to back out?"

"Alisa doesn't talk about you any longer," she said curtly. "Not since the canyon. Even before all that nightmare happened at St. Eldon's, she'd sometimes mention something you'd invented or what you'd said at some scientific meeting. I could tell she agreed with you most of the time. And afterward, whenever I'd talk to her on the phone at the stable, I'd hear about Korgan doing this and Korgan doing that, but once I was safe and Jubaldar secure, there was nothing. She just changes the subject. Did you do something bad to hurt her?"

He sighed. "You're on the attack. I might have waited too long for this meeting. No, I've tried never to do anything bad to Alisa, but she's a difficult woman. She doesn't accept good intentions unless they come with a written schematic in nine languages. You and Margaret are the only ones she trusts unconditionally."

She stared him in the eye. "And should she trust you?"

He smiled. "Oh, yes. To hell and back. I'll always be there for her."

"Then why is she angry with you now? Alisa is smart and an excellent judge of character. She doesn't make mistakes."

"No, she doesn't. But she sometimes tries so hard to avoid mistakes that she overcomplicates when she should just accept the simple explanation. Have you noticed that about her?"

She frowned but nodded. "Sometimes."

"Good. Then we're on the same page?"

She shook her head. "She doesn't talk about you."

He made a face. "I thought that was going to be hard to get around. My fault. I was so busy making other plans and arrangements after I turned Jubaldar over to Novak that I let Alisa have time to think."

"She's always thinking," she said coldly. "Now you're insulting her?"

He sighed. "No, just getting into more trouble. I expected to walk a tightrope with the two of you. What I meant is that I thought it would be a good thing if I left you alone together for a while after what you've both been going through. I didn't realize it would be a signal for her to draw inside herself and close me out. Though I should have, if I'd thought about it."

"Then it seems you're not as intelligent as Alisa. As I said, she's *always* thinking."

"Ouch." Then he grinned. "You don't have to defend her. I'm on your side. I'm not usually this clumsy. I'm screwing up because I want to impress you. But I should have known that you wouldn't be swayed."

That smile was incredibly appealing, and she felt her resistance fading. "I suppose a lot of people would be swayed by you. Why did you come here today?"

"I told you, to impress you." He was looking around the stable again. "And I'm curious. You didn't answer me. Why did you move Chaos and Nightshade into the main stable?"

She shrugged. "It was more sociable. Chaos needs to be around other horses so that all that kingly arrogance will be tempered a bit. So I suggested that Nightshade would be happier and learn more quickly if they both came here. Chaos is tolerating it."

"Suggested?" he repeated softly.

She met his gaze challengingly. "Suggested. Do you have any questions?"

"Not one. But I do have a suggestion myself. I'd try to make an effort to get all the horses in this stable as familiar and comfortable with each other as soon as possible in the next two weeks before you start to move them."

She stiffened. "Move them? I haven't been thinking about moving my horses yet."

"No, that's why I wanted you and Alisa to spend these few days together before you got down to work. You won't have much time once you reach Colorado."

"Colorado," she repeated. "What are you talking about?"

"You'll love Colorado. It's fantastically beautiful. Though sometimes it can be colder than your horses are accustomed to. But you'll get used to it because you're going to find the space and freedom worth it."

She frowned. "Why should I go to Colorado?"

"Why not? You can't stay here. After it's repaired, I've been thinking about arranging to give Jubaldar to the citizens of Samlir in payment for their cooperation. You could go back to St. Eldon's, but that would have sad memories and there wouldn't be enough room for what I've planned."

"*You've* planned?" She was beginning to feel indignant. "What do you have to do with me or my horses?"

"Nothing. If you want to turn me down. But you should really hear me out before you do. I think I might be offering you a deal you can't refuse."

"How can I turn you down when all you're doing is talking nonsense?" she asked in frustration. "You're not really saying anything. You remind me of Gilroy."

He chuckled. "Then I'd better clarify immediately. That comparison frightens me more than you can dream. We're not only taking your horses to Colorado, but bringing along every horse in this stable. That will be a total of thirty-two—which isn't overwhelming for a horse farm, since I'll be giving you plenty of help. I thought we'd ask Margaret and Gilroy to go with you for a while until you finish setting it up. It will give you time to become accustomed to running the business as well as the humanitarian side before you expand. You'll have to work hard because Alisa is going to want you to have a tutor to finish your education, and you'll have to spend a lot of time getting ready for the Niseans."

Her eyes widened and she lost her breath. "Niseans?"

"Didn't I mention I own an obscene amount of acreage in Colorado and Wyoming? It's a shame to let it go to waste. I thought you might want to go back to those nomads who sold Chaos's mother to Rossi and see if we can persuade them to sell us as many horses as they'll let go. Perhaps we can strike a deal for the entire herd if I can talk the chief into sending some of his people to care for them and ensure their traditions will be preserved. I've been told that when I'm motivated, I can be very persuasive."

"I believe it," she said weakly. "Are you motivated?"

He smiled and said softly, "I couldn't be more motivated."

"Why?" She moistened her lips. "Why would you do this for me. Alisa? It won't matter to her. I wouldn't let it matter to her."

"Neither would I. Some of it is Alisa, because if you're happy, she'll be happy. Some of it is me, because I can do it, and I like the idea of telling those authorities who say those beautiful horses are extinct that they haven't seen anything yet." He glanced at Nightshade in the stall in front of him. "And some of it is that from listening to what Alisa told me about you, I'm betting that once you're settled, it's going to be just the tip of the iceberg for you. What you saw happening to Nightshade that night changed you, defined you. You're not going to be satisfied, are you?"

How had he known? She shook her head, stunned. "No," she whispered. "How can I be?"

"'Destroy the monsters. Protect the innocents,'" he quoted, his glance shifting back to her. "That's what you told Alisa. Now you can't do anything else."

"No," she said unsteadily. "The cruelty has to stop."

He got to his feet. "We have a zillion humane protective organizations for animals around the world. But I think they could do a better job." He grinned down at her. "I think *we* could do a hell of a lot better. We've just got to figure out how to go the whole distance. So many so-called do-gooders stop before they get there." He headed for the door. "Keep that in the mind while you're setting up the horse farm in Colorado. Something might occur to you."

She stared dazedly after him, trying to catch her breath.

Niseans.

Horse farms.

Protecting the innocents.

Go the whole distance.

What was the whole distance for Korgan?

She had an idea it had never been measured.

He upset you.

She glanced at Chaos. His muscles were tight, and he was clearly on guard. He'd been overprotective about her and Nightshade since that hideous encounter with Reardon in the stable. She hurried to soothe him. *Not in a bad way. You might like him. He's not a king, but he acts like one. No, on second thought, you'd never understand him. Or maybe you might if we could get you hobnobbing with some of your Nisean brothers out in Colorado.*

He snorted. *You're talking foolish. I'm the only king of importance. All I wanted to know is if he might hurt you. And what is Colorado?*

She couldn't take her gaze off the stable door. *A place far, far away. That I believe we're all going to see very soon...*

———◆———

RISSANI MARKET, MOROCCO
SAHARA DESERT
TWO DAYS LATER

"Thank you," Alisa said in Arabic as she smiled at the young boy and tipped him generously. "You've been very helpful." She put the case of water and supplies into the back of the jeep before she jumped into the driver's seat. She had everything she needed, including information, and if she could get on the road quickly enough, she might be at that oasis by sunset.

She started the car.

But the boy was standing directly in front of the jeep, smiling at her. Maybe he thought the tip hadn't been big enough. Then she realized he wasn't smiling at her; his gaze was on the man opening her passenger door.

Korgan dropped down in the seat next to her and reached out and turned off the engine. "You just can't get reliable help these days. They've always got their hands out for a bigger score. But in this case, I called ahead and outbid you before you got here so you can't really blame the kid. Maybe you should have offered him a yo-yo?"

Don't let him see the shock. If she handled it right, this would be over soon. "I don't blame anyone but you. I should have known that you wouldn't consider this finished until you tied up the final details. Did Margaret tell you that I was heading for this market?"

"No, I was already checking it out. You're right, final details are important to me. I promised to rescue all those girls from St. Eldon's, and I didn't do it. I remembered that Sasha had told you there were several girls who were no longer in Masenak's camp because they'd been sold to desert tribes in the Sahara."

"You did what I asked," she said curtly. "I couldn't expect anything more of you. That's why I'm here, doing it myself. I called Lakewood and gave him the names of the tribes Sasha had been able to find in Masenak's records. He thought he'd have no trouble ransoming those girls back. But I'll have to track down the other tribes myself. I got a tip from this kid's father about one of the girls being seen with a tribe from Sudan heading toward an oasis near here." She asked, "Lakewood told you I'd be here?"

He nodded. "If I'd remembered, I knew you would. You'd want to find them quickly so that Sasha wouldn't try to go after them herself. I'm a little surprised she's not with you."

"Margaret told her that she should trust me to handle it. It took a little persuading, but she gave in eventually." Her lips twisted. "Though Sasha was probably torn because you'd tossed all the magnificent possibilities of Chaos, Nightshade, and the Niseans at her and she was scrambling to prepare them for transport."

"Was there a hint of bitterness there? I was trying to make her happy."

"And you did. No one but you could have

identified her dreams with such precision and then made them come true. No bitterness. I love her and I want whatever will make her happy." She glanced away from him. "It's not as if I won't see her. But I'm CIA and my missions are almost always out of the country. It just won't be as often."

"The hell it won't," he said softly. "Did you think I'd screw this up when it's going to affect my entire life? It's got to be just right. If you don't like some of the pieces, then we'll throw them out and start somewhere else. But there aren't going to be any mistakes for either of us." He reached out and touched her cheek. "Don't turn your head. I love those cheekbones and I want to touch you. It's been too long." He moved his fingers, exploring the hollow. "I've thought it all out, and here's how it's going to work."

That touch was gentle and warm, yet she was already tingling. "Lord, you're arrogant. I'm supposed to sit here and have you dictate to me when it's my life and career on the line?"

"You're supposed to listen. First, I'll go into that nonsense about you not being able to see Sasha as much as you want. The only reason I chose Colorado was that my headquarters are there, and I'll be better able to control and take care of Sasha there. If it turns out that's an inconvenience for you, then I'll move her wherever it's not. But if your job is the problem then we'll find a way to get Langley to adjust—or if you choose, you might change careers. You're brilliant, and I can open any number of doors where you can learn and experiment and grow in any direction you wish. We both know that you'd make a success of anything you touched."

She looked at him incredulously. "I don't want you to make a job for me or take me to Colorado because you have headquarters there. I already have a career."

"Just giving you options. Would you like me to close my Colorado offices and follow you? It would be complicated, but I'd do it."

"Complicated? You're joking. It would be a nightmare."

"Not if it was handled correctly." He tilted his head. "But you're making excuses, so I'd better skip practicalities and get to what's important." He went on quietly, "I'm positively insane about you. Call it love, obsession, sex, admiration, devotion. Anything you want. I don't know where it came from, but I'm glad it's here. You suit me in all the ways there are and some I believe we've invented for ourselves. You're special for me in all those ways, and I find it totally bizarre that you'd think I'd change or become bored and want to walk away for another project. It's not going to happen. If I walk away, you'll be with me." He stopped and then shook his head. "There. How is that for a confessional? I've left myself wide open. Now I'd appreciate it if you'd stop being so wary and be honest enough to admit that you're close to feeling the same way."

She could only stare at him for a moment. His words had been so overwhelming, so generous, that she was having trouble answering him. And when she did speak, it came out wrong, "Don't be ridiculous," she said huskily. "You know how I feel. You've always been able to read me. And I've tried to be as honest as I could without making you feel you owed me anything." She lifted her chin. "And you *should* think I'm special. I am. If I worked at it, I know I could make you so dizzy that you'd want to stay with me, and you'd enjoy every minute. But I'm a realist, and I can't see it lasting. Wonderful things happen and you think they'll be there forever and then all of a sudden, they're gone. And the worst thing I can imagine is to cling so desperately that you end up destroying that wonderful thing. It's better to let it go and not to risk—"

"Stop." He bent closer and kissed her, slowly, sensuously. "You don't trust me. That's okay. Hell, I know how you grew up. I knew it was going to take time. Why do you think I followed you into this damn desert? By the time we locate those girls and I manage to negotiate them away from the chiefs, you'll feel differently."

She found she was holding him and forced herself to let him go. "You're still thinking of me as that kid Zabron picked up out of the gutter, and I won't have it. I've fought and slain all my dragons."

"Yes, you have. Except this last one. We'll get rid of him together."

"You're not listening to me. You're not going with me. It's my job. I can take care of any negotiations." He was shaking his head and she said in exasperation, "Don't be an idiot. You'd only be a burden. If one of those chiefs recognized you, he'd probably kidnap you and hold *you* for ransom."

"Then you'd have to rescue me. I'm good with that. I trust you to protect me." He leaned back on the seat. "But until you have to do it, I've brought a tent where we can watch the stars and talk and tell each other all the intimate details about ourselves, and you can learn to trust me."

"I do trust you."

"No, you don't. You've only scratched the surface." He smiled. "But you will, and we'll both enjoy the learning process."

She knew that was true. And it meant she would be drawn even deeper, closer to him. What would that be like? she wondered. She'd always had a passion for learning, and learning Korgan could be the ultimate lesson. It would be difficult and challenging, but suddenly the thought was no longer intimidating. She made a last effort. "You shouldn't go with me. You won't change your mind?"

He shook his head. "No way."

She drew a deep breath. *Okay, roll the dice. Make the best of it.* And it could be a very good best—if she could shrug off all the fear and accept that there was a chance, she might have been given a gift that could last forever. Forever? Totally unrealistic. What was forever? Yet that could be another lesson to analyze and probe to see what was out there.

What she did know was that all gifts and lessons must be nurtured and explored and cared for, and she had learned how to do that. "Well, I won't argue with you." She leaned forward and turned the key to start the jeep. "But I wasn't kidding about you not causing me trouble if anyone in those tribes recognizes you. I'm in charge, and I'll take care of you and the entire situation from now on. Understand?"

His eyes were twinkling, but his voice was soft and very tender. "Perfectly," he said. "I understand absolutely perfectly, Alisa."

ABOUT THE AUTHOR

Iris Johansen is the #1 *New York Times* bestselling author of more than 30 consecutive bestsellers. Her series featuring forensic sculptor Eve Duncan has sold over 20 million copies and counting and was the subject of the acclaimed Lifetime movie *The Killing Game*. Along with her son, Roy, Iris has also co-authored the *New York Times* bestselling series featuring investigator Kendra Michaels. Johansen lives near Atlanta, Georgia. Learn more at:
irisjohansen.com
Twitter @Iris_Johansen
Facebook.com/OfficialIrisJohansen